Dead
Ex

Also by Harley Jane Kozak

Dating Dead Men

Dating Is Murder

Doubleday • New York   London   Toronto   Sydney   Auckland

Dead Ex

A NOVEL

Harley Jane Kozak

For Daniel Cory Reinehr,

who left us wanting more

No one wants to be the muse;

In the end, everyone wants to be Orpheus.

—LOUISE GLÜCK, "LUTE SONG"

Dead
Ex

One

Men, in my experience, do not like being interrupted during sex by a ringing telephone. I suppose it's true for women too. It's true for me, anyhow, which is why I never have a telephone in my bedroom.

In late December, however, I had no bedroom. I was sharing one with a guy named Simon Alexander, along with two cell phones, two answering machines, a landline, computer, TV, radio, surround-sound system, beeper, clock, printer-fax-copier, and smoke alarm, all of which had interfered with romantic moments, although some only when one of us rolled over onto a remote.

There was also a gun, occupying the bedside table. The gun hadn't interrupted anything yet, but I'd been living there only a couple of weeks.

Simon was an FBI agent.

We were in the thick of things that late Friday afternoon, in a sweaty, muscle-clenching, heart-pounding clinch, when a click from across the room reminded me I'd turned off the ringer on the phone. Simon's arm tightened around me.

"Wollie," the answering machine said. "Pick up. Wollie."

Simon's grip loosened. It wasn't a national emergency. Despite his technical sophistication, he preferred an answering machine to voice mail for its screening ability. "Simon, if you're listening," the voice said, "I gotta talk to Wollie. Wollie, please be there."

It was my friend Joey. Despite a masculine name, like mine, Joey, like me, is female. Knowing her as I do, I assumed that under the circumstances she'd want me to ignore her.

"Okay, you're not there," she said, her gravelly voice cracking. "I hate to say it to the machine, but you'll hear it on the news. David's dead. David Zetrakis. Our David."

"David?" I extricated myself from Simon's grasp and crawled to the machine. "Our David?" I said. Too late. The beep indicated that Joey had hung up.

Simon's hand found my thigh and gave it a squeeze. "You okay?"

"Yeah, I . . . yes." But I didn't move. After a moment I felt a comforter placed over me.

Simon stood. He was six foot five, as tall as anyone need reasonably be who's not in the NBA, and in great shape, too, which is not unusual in L.A., where gym memberships are as common as car insurance, but still, impressive in a guy approaching fifty. Our relationship, affair, hookup, whatever it was, was new enough that the sight of him naked could still distract me from anything. Even the death of an old boyfriend.

"Someone close to you?" He was checking one of his cell phones for messages.

"Very close. Once upon a time." I picked up my own cell phone to call Joey.

Simon bent down, grabbed a handful of hair, and kissed my shoulder. "Later, beautiful girl," he said. Then he retreated to the bathroom. Still naked.

"Joey," I said to her answering machine. "That's . . . so sad. Are you okay?"

David had been an old boyfriend of mine, but he'd been Joey's too, longer and more seriously. When she picked up the phone halfway through my message, she didn't bother talking. She cried. Joey Rafferty Horowitz was a fairly tough cookie, so hearing her cry, while not a complete novelty, was alarming. Eventually I asked what had happened to David.

"He had cancer," she said. "Pancreatic. Horrible. Untreatable."

I searched for something to say that wasn't a cliché, but gave up. "God, that's awful. I didn't even know he was sick." I design greeting cards, so you'd expect better from me, but when it comes to death, I'm an amateur like everyone else. "And so young," I added.

"Fifty-one," Joey said, blowing her nose. "It's a measure of how old we're getting that fifty-one seems young."

"Did he die in the hospital?"

"At home," she said. "Toluca Lake."

I wrapped the comforter around myself, cold suddenly, and walked to the window. Simon lived in a penthouse on Wilshire Boulevard, a stark, masculine, tall-ceilinged condo with oversized windows washed by a cleaning lady on the inside and a professional crew on the outside. The view went all the way to the ocean. Toluca Lake was to the northeast, over mountains, so it wasn't like I could see David's house, but maybe his spirit hovered above the Pacific.

"When did you last see David?" I asked, but Joey had put me on hold.

I watched the sun set. It was that week between Christmas and New Year's, a time to calculate end-of-year quarterly taxes and polish off gingerbread men and eggnog while making resolutions about sugar, carbs, and alcohol. The L.A. sky faded until the smog was indistinguishable from the sea. I heard the shower in the bathroom and considered joining Simon; he showered unarmed, so it was one place I could safely ambush him.

A click indicated that Joey was back on the line, but she didn't speak. "Joey?" I said.

"I'm just . . . scared. Wollie, would you still be my friend if . . ."

"Yes. If what?"

"If . . . never mind. Are you going to Rex and Tricia's cocktail thing tonight?"

"I have to. You'll be there, right?" I waited, then said, "Joey, what is it?"

"God, I'm making such a mess of my life." She sounded drunk.

"Honey," I said, "David died of cancer. It's not your fault."

"I didn't say he died of cancer," she said. "He was sick with cancer. What he died of was a gunshot wound to the head."

Two

Gunshot wound to the head.

Cop jargon came naturally to Joey, as half her family was in law enforcement and she herself had saved up for college by working in a morgue, but wouldn't "He committed suicide" have done the job as well? Now I'd picture David's face blown away when I thought of him. That it was anything but suicide—murder, for example—entered my mind and exited just as quickly. Who'd kill a terminally ill soap opera producer?

Suicide, though. What a sorrowful end. And why was Joey acting so strangely? Sad I understood, but . . . scared? Joey didn't scare easily; nor was she prone to despair. I was about to call her back when Simon emerged from his walk-in closet.

Simon clothed was nearly as compelling as Simon naked. He didn't dress like the FBI agents on TV; he dressed like he was off to the Polo Lounge. Tonight it was bark-colored pants and a burgundy shirt, suitable for the cocktail party I was going to, only he wasn't going to the cocktail party. I had no idea where he was going. "Work," he'd said, which could mean anything from a stakeout to a Lakers game. It was the second time that day he'd gone to "work."

I lay on the bed and watched him buckle his belt. "Is suicide a crime?" I asked.

"Is that what your friend did?"

"Apparently. Could you find out the details?"

He glanced at me. His eyes were glacier blue, an arresting color. "Why?"

"I don't know. I just . . . Joey's taking it really hard, and—"

"No."

"What do you mean, no?"

"I mean that if it's not FBI business, there's no reason for the cops to let me in on it, and if it is FBI business, I can't discuss it with you." He began to knot his tie.

I reached over to him, snagging my finger through a belt loop, pulling him close. He didn't resist. "What's the point of sleeping with Feds," I said, "if I can't get inside information?"

"How many Feds are you sleeping with?"

"Within your division or nationwide?"

He took my face in his hands and covered my mouth with his, cutting off my air supply. I didn't resist. When he straightened up, letting go of me, I reached forward, grabbed him around the waist, and fell backward, pulling him onto the bed with me. I'm not an athletic person, so I must've had the element of surprise on my side.

What we did next is the sort of thing you might not expect of a girl who's just been given the worst sort of news about someone, but as my Uncle Theo says, we grieve in mysterious ways. When we were done doing the thing we did, Simon had to do the other things all over, the shower, the fresh clothes . . . the game face. Work.

Simon was at the point in his career where field agents turn into supervising agents, but he liked being a field agent, on the street, with a new operation every few months. Unlike me, who dreamed of a desk job. Not that I was in the FBI, although I had worked for them, for five minutes. I'd worked for nearly everyone for five minutes. In between designing greeting cards.

Life occurs to me in line drawings. Some people hear voices—my brother, P.B., for instance, when not taking his meds—and I do too, sporadically, but mostly I see things. Stuck in freeway traffic, the car in front of me becomes a picture with a caption: *Volkswagens on Valium.* It's not something I work at. The work is giving the image a context and getting it on paper, but that's more fun than drudgery. I had a line of alternative greeting cards called Good Golly, Miss Wollie, and while this paid the rent, I also needed food, gas, and the occasional pair of shoes. Thus, I augmented my income in a variety of ways, some stranger than others. At the moment I was on the hunt for a new odd job and had no prospects. On the plus side, Christmas shopping was over with for another year.

Simon left for work, and I dressed for my party. Or tried; mostly, I just stood in the closet, clutching the comforter. I'm not a party person—groups of strangers bring out my Inner Wallflower—and now thoughts of death overrode fashion. David, my boyfriend very briefly, had been my friend ever since, ten years, even though I hadn't seen him in months. He was such a dynamic personality, it was hard to conceive of him gone from the earth; it was nearly impossible to believe he'd put a bullet through his head.

And what was going on with Joey? Why would his suicide scare her?

My comforter slipped from my shoulders, and I shivered. Time to get dressed.

I was living out of suitcases. Simon's closets—I had one all to myself—were big enough to park cars in, but I was hesitant to spread out, since there'd been no talk of moving in, but a vague "stay here as long as you need" invitation. I didn't need to, strictly speaking, but my West Hollywood sublet had been reclaimed by its rightful owner a few weeks earlier, and I was too busy being romantic to get any apartment hunting done. In any case, Simon showed neatnik tendencies, so I felt a need to sequester my stuff. I'd taken to drying my toothbrush, post-brushing, and returning it to the suitcase. I pocketed used dental floss so that it wouldn't clutter the Lucite bathroom wastebasket. I Windexed the shower stall daily, purloining supplies from the stash kept by Ilse, the three-times-weekly cleaning lady—were they still called cleaning ladies?—and maybe this was excessive, but I was a woman in love and I didn't want to mess up.

My address book lay in one suitcase, atop my makeup kit, and on impulse I looked up the number for Pete Cziemanski, a man I'd almost dated, at the West Valley Police Department.

I called Pete. While on hold, I tried on clothes, seeking that combination of holiday festive, Hollywood sexy, and my-friend-is-dead conservative, before going with a black velvet skirt and white silk blouse. It complemented the string of pearls Simon had given me on Christmas Eve, forty-eight hours earlier. The good news was, I would've felt beau-

tiful in a hospital gown, a happy side effect of having sex every day, multiple times a day. It was a feeling and a state of affairs that wouldn't last,
because it never lasts, but I was enjoying it nevertheless.

"Wollie," Cziemanski said. "Liked your Christmas card. What's up?"

So much for small talk. "Pete," I said, "is suicide a crime?"

"Uh . . . a sin, maybe. A crime? No. Why?"

I started to tell him about my friend David, but he interrupted.

"Zetrakis? Producer guy? That was no suicide."

"Are you sure?"

"I know the black-and-white that answered the 911 from the housekeeper."

"What's that mean? He could tell from the body position it wasn't
suicide?"

"He could tell by the gun. There wasn't one. Guys that blow their
brains out don't generally hide the weapon afterward. Should be on the
news if it isn't already."

"So it was . . ."

"Yeah. The 'M' word. Murder."

Murder. I hung up and walked through the masculine, state-of-the-
art, black-and-taupe penthouse, my heels loud in the empty rooms.
David was murdered, David was murdered, they tapped out, until I was
out in the hallway, triple-locking the door behind me.

Three

Rex and Tricia were newlyweds living in Sherman Oaks, twenty minutes north of Westwood, traffic permitting, although traffic rarely permitted. I wondered how it would be to live in a place where "traffic permitting" didn't qualify every description of time and space, where knowing shortcuts and alternate routes was not a survival skill. In L.A., people made small talk about traffic instead of weather. David, for instance, had considered it a matter of honor to make it from his home to the TV studio where he worked in under six minutes. I was born and raised here, but I'd never liked driving. In my dreams, I lived in a city of sidewalks.

Traffic was moderate, which is to say the 405 North was moving, albeit at the pace of a middle-aged jogger, and eventually I pulled up to the mansion Rex and Tricia had built to begin their lives together. A valet parking attendant opened my door and watched as I made the slow trip out of the car: my heels were high, my legs long, and my old Integra low to the ground. Valet parking is a regular feature of any gathering over twelve in certain neighborhoods, signaling that this would not be a cheese ball–and–Wheat Thins affair, and that what you drive may factor into any assessment of you.

"Wollie! Is your cell phone off? I've been calling you for an hour." It was Fredreeq, my other best friend, hailing me from across the driveway.

"Wow," I said. "Look at you. You look . . ."

Fredreeq was swathed in layers of transparent red fabric and a turban. "African," she said. "But why have you come as a nun?"

"You were with me when I bought this blouse. You talked me into it."

"Oh. Well, then." She fussed with my hair as though I were one of her children, then unbuttoned my blouse to show some cleavage. As I'm well endowed, there was a lot of cleavage to work with. "There, that's better. It's not meant to be a turtleneck. Where's Simon?"

"Working."

"That shouldn't interfere with partying. You two are in the Dopamine Phase. New love, your bodies flooded with chemicals—you should be spending every possible moment together."

"We are. We do." I lowered my voice. "Did you hear about David Zetrakis?"

"You mean that he's dead?" Fredreeq said, at full volume. "You mean that he had lung cancer, so he shot himself because he didn't want chemo?"

"I heard it was pancreatic cancer," I said. "And not suicide. Murder."

"Where'd you hear that? Lung cancer. He was smoking medical marijuana like a maniac. But I heard he smoked it before the cancer, when it was plain pot. Was he a pothead when you dated him? Joey says he was. She and Elliot aren't here yet. Fashionably late."

We approached the enormous double doors of the mansion, open to show the foyer drenched in candlelight, and I was momentarily distracted from thoughts of David.

I had a proprietary interest in Rex and Tricia's house, having seen it through the last stages of the building process, and wasn't prepared for how different it looked, overrun with people other than the paint crew. There was little furniture, as Rex and Tricia had recently returned from their Hawaiian honeymoon, but a grand piano dominated the living room, its black finish so polished you could check your lipstick in it. A tuxedoed pianist was playing the theme from *The Godfather*. A tuxedoed catering staff moved among the guests, serving hors d'oeuvres. Fredreeq and I followed a tray of bacon-wrapped cherry tomatoes into the kitchen.

"Everyone here's talking about David," Fredreeq said. "Big soap crowd."

David had produced *At the End of the Day*, a soap opera I'd tried to watch when I dated him, especially since Joey was acting in it. But I'd never acquired the taste for soaps, so eventually I gave up, after Joey admitted she never watched either. David had begun as an actor on the show, then directed a few episodes, then stopped acting altogether to produce. It wasn't a normal career trajectory, but it wasn't unheard of either, actor-director-producer: David had been, in Hollywood terms, a "hyphenate."

We found Rex, our host, and I was swept into a bear hug. He was a big guy, nearly as tall as Simon, an extroverted, transplanted Texan. He went on to hug Fredreeq, dislodging her turban, so he didn't see me staring at the walls.

I'd spent weeks in this kitchen painting a mural of frogs. Now, in their place, were white walls. Someone had painted over my work.

I felt ill. I grabbed a black granite counter for support, wondering if I might throw up onto the tray of potato pancakes with caviar being assembled in front of me.

Rex and Tricia had paid me in full for the frogs, and then they'd whited them out. I would give back the money. I would leave now and send them a nice note in the morning, with a check enclosed. I was about to grab Fredreeq and explain why I had to go—explain it before she could look up and say, "Where are those damn frogs?"—when a guy in a baseball cap placed a glass mug in my hand.

"Grugg."

"I beg your pardon?" I said.

"Grugg. Watch out, it's hot."

"You mean glögg?"

"Yeah, maybe. Tricia said everyone's gotta try it." He indicated an enormous punch bowl. "Want any of the floaty stuff?"

"What is the floaty stuff?" I asked.

He shrugged. "Prunes and stuff. Tricia made it. Well, that's what she said. She probably means some servant did." I caught a glimpse of the face underneath the baseball cap. He was young—late teens, maybe—and extravagantly good-looking, making me think he must be in soaps. Tricia herself was in soaps, I remembered. Maybe everyone here but Fredreeq and me was connected to soaps.

Before I could taste my glögg, I was hit by a wave of Opium. Two thin arms wrapped themselves around me, jingling with bangle bracelets, and I was in the embrace of a total stranger. A small, thin, heavily scented, jeweled stranger.

"Wollie!" a melodious voice said. "Tell me you're Wollie."

"I'm Wollie," I said.

"Wollie, my frog woman. It's me. Tricia. Your patron." She held on to me, but extended her arms in a "let me look at you" manner. She said, "My, you're tall." She glanced at my feet. "Oh, you're in heels, but still. You must be six feet. Are you six feet? Is she six feet, Trey?"

The handsome kid eyed me.

"I'm six feet," I said. Give or take a centimeter.

"Well, I wish you'd give me some of that height. I'm five-two. I look like a third grader next to Rex. Rex!" she called. "Here's Wollie!"

"I know, darlin'. I've already hugged her neck."

"God, isn't he a stitch?" She turned back to me. "I love it when he talks Texan. Now let me get you a big-girl drink and you tell me all about yourself. Did you see the honeymoon shots? They're being projected in the screening room. And you must try the beef satay—Rex calls it skewer of cow—and the unveiling's at seven-thirty, and oh—did you hear about poor David Zetrakis? Did you know him?"

"I slept with him." I had no idea what made me reveal that.

She nodded. "I did too. Long before the cancer, of course. He was supposed to come tonight. No one knows if it was suicide or murder, but we have the news anchor here, Angel Ramirez, so as soon as the press knows, we'll know. She's been on the phone all night. She's out by the pool, getting better reception. So anyway, Wollie, I want to hear all about you."

"Well—" I began, but just then Tricia flew from my side shrieking, "Tony! Genie!" arms outstretched and bangles jangling, to greet others.

Was murder less horrible if the victim was terminally ill? I wanted to discuss it with Fredreeq and wandered out to the pool in search of her. A dozen or so people huddled around patio heaters, eight of them on cell phones.

"You're Wollie Shelley, aren't you?" a woman asked, perched at a cocktail table. She was smoking, a pastime that many L.A. parties, along with restaurants, banish to the great outdoors. "I'm Jen Kim, I produce *At the End of the Day* and *SoapDirt*."

"I'm sorry . . . what?"

"*SoapDirt.* The show Tricia hosts."

"I thought Tricia was *on* a soap. As an actress."

Jen Kim nodded, exhaling smoke through her nose. She was pretty and Asian and looked too young to be producing anything. Or smoking. "Tricia stars in *At the End of the Day* Monday through Thursday. Friday she tapes *SoapDirt.* You should watch it because—"

"Ladies. Gentlemen." A big guy in a red turtleneck stood in the doorway with a bullhorn. "This is a five-minute warning. Please make your way to the kitchen for the unveiling." He reentered the house, limping.

"—because I'm looking for someone." Jen Kim pulled a business card from her Kate Spade purse and handed it to me. "I think you're it. Got a card?"

I always have business cards on me. Jen took the one I offered, stubbed out her cigarette, and said good-bye, following the man in the red turtleneck.

This whole party was a mistake, I decided, making my way into the house with the other poolside guests. I was only here out of respect for Rex, who'd hired me when I needed a job. I knew no one else but Fredreeq, who I could see anytime, I was being mistaken for whoever it was Jen Kim thought I was, I was depressed about David, upset about my frogs, and I needed some quality sleep, as Simon and I had been burning the candle at both ends for weeks. I'd sneak out and call Fredreeq from my car to explain my disappearance.

I went out the front door and gave my parking stub to the valet guy. While waiting, I called Simon, and I was leaving him a sexually suggestive message when the man with the bullhorn came and stood beside me. "Wollie?" he said. "You're not leaving, are you?"

How did everyone know my name? Was there a sign taped to my back?

"Do I know you?" I asked.

"Max Freund." He shook my hand with a hearty grip. "I work with Tricia. I'm a stage manager, so I've been sent to round up the cast and crew. For the unveiling."

"I *was* leaving. I'm not feeling well, so I thought I'd make a quiet exit, but I guess I—"

"—could endure another ten minutes? Thank you. I'm sorry you're not well."

"It's nothing physical. It has to do with . . . a friend of mine died today."

"David Zetrakis?" At my nod, he put an arm around me. "I knew him twenty-seven years. We grew up in the business. He acted, I stage-managed. He directed, I stage-managed. He produced, I stage-managed. Most everyone here knew David. Think of it as a wake."

I didn't see Tricia approving that description. "We better go in for the unveiling. You gave a five-minute warning seven minutes ago. What's being unveiled, anyway?"

Max smiled, a warm grin on a craggy face. "You don't know? Then I won't spoil it. But they won't start without us. I'm the stage manager. And you, my dear, are the star."

.   .   .

Passing the living room, Max gestured to the pianist with his bullhorn. The music went from Pachelbel's Canon to "Joy to the World"—the Three Dog Night version, with the opening lyrics "Jeremiah was a bull-frog," which the pianist belted out in an operatic voice.

We entered the kitchen to a smattering of applause. The kitchen area opened into the dining room, so it held the entire party. Rex was center stage, standing on a step stool.

"Wollie, I was just saying how you're the girl who gave me the nick-name Rex Stetson, which I adopted when I moved here. Tricia never would've dated me if I'd stayed Maurice."

"You got that right!" Tricia said. With Rex on the step stool, she was half his height. She acknowledged the laughter, basking in its glow, re-minding me for some reason of a poodle. A greeting card began to form in my mind, a dog and its trainer at the Westminster Kennel Club dog show, but Rex was talking again and gesturing toward the wall be-hind him.

I saw that this section of wall, unlike the others, was covered with a drape.

"Now, y'all have known Tricia," Rex said, "lots longer than me, every-one in her soap family. So y'all know how she feels about frogs. Her dressing room at the studio, it's straight out of *National Geographic,* and I wanted her to feel as much at home here as she does there. You can meet her live frogs in the sunroom, but these two here are my favorites. Ladies and gentlemen . . . portrait of Rex and Tricia."

The white drape lifted to reveal *Conraua (Gigantorana) goliath* and *Dendrobates azureus.* The former was a frog I'd painted in gargantuan proportions, due to a math error, and the latter a small, cuddly thing, bright blue with black spots. Together they were a pair so bizarre I'd nearly painted over them. But here they were, the only survivors of my mural, and someone had added the words *Rex and Tricia* beneath them, in ornate gold letters.

The crowd responded with oohs and aahs and laughter and I was congratulated. I'd had no clue that Rex and Tricia were of such disparate sizes as to resemble the West African goliath and the blue poison-arrow and hadn't meant to satirize them, but that's the thing about art. You do what you do, and people read into it what they read into it. Of course, captions are everything; no one knows that better than a greeting card artist. I wasn't used to being captioned by someone else, but being mistaken for a genius isn't the worst fate in the world.

"A masterpiece," declared a man next to me. "The only thing of value in this dreadful house. Edifice Rex. Who is the artist?"

A masterpiece? Had I wandered into my own infomercial? "I'm the artist," I said, introducing myself. The man introduced himself in turn, as Sheffo Corminiak.

Sheffo was in his seventies at least, a fragile little fellow with a sloppiness that suggested poverty. But the suit jacket over his arm, its tag exposed, was Armani. "What was your frog background prior to this opus?" he asked.

"I didn't know squat about frogs when I began."

He studied me. "And tell me, what do you know about Greek mythology?"

"Nothing, except in a high school world history sort of way."

Sheffo was now staring with an intensity uncommon in cocktail party acquaintances. "Yes," he whispered. "It is you. This shall work out very well indeed." Then, in a brisk tone: "I should like to hire you, Willie."

"Wollie," I said, correcting him. "In what capacity?"

"As an artist, of course. Have you an opening in your schedule?"

I had nothing but openings, I had a schedule full of holes, but why disclose that to—Sluggo? Sheffo. I opened my purse. "Here's my card. Is it frogs you're interested in?"

"It is gods, woman. Gods, demigods, kings. And common mortals of the heroic variety. All things Greek, in or around the period of twelve hundred B.C. I live on Mount Olympus."

"Hmm." He was drunk, I realized. And possibly delusional. I've spent a lot of time around mental illness, so delusions don't distress me.

"Electra Drive, before Hercules. Do you know it? I have a retaining wall."

"Oh!" I did a quick mental revision. Mount Olympus was a neighborhood in the hills above Hollywood Boulevard. I'd seen the sign whenever I was stuck in traffic on Laurel Canyon and always wondered about it. Was it all Greek themed, right down to the retaining walls? "It's okay with you that I know next to nothing about the Greeks?"

"Ignorance!" he cried. "Yes! From the Latin *ignorare*. You have heretofore *ignored* the Greeks, but now you shall open yourself to them and call forth oracular vision. The gods speak to the simple and ignorant as well as to the mighty. Your frogs are marvelously primitive."

"Oh. Okay."

He patted my hand. "A lovely lack of hubris. Come to the house. We'll discuss terms."

We agreed on the next afternoon. "Pay attention," Sheffo whispered. "You'll now begin to see Greeks everywhere. It is the gods, speaking to you. They surround us. Watch. Listen." Sheffo shuffled off to freshen his drink, passing Fredreeq on her way into the kitchen.

"Have you seen the swamproom?" she asked. "Oh, excuse me. Sunroom. I heard Tricia sunk twenty grand into it. Flew in frogs first-class from other countries. Makes you think twice about shaking hands with her. Hey, heard any gossip about David's suicide?"

I straightened her turban. "It wasn't suicide. It was murder. I happen to know that—"

"Did Sheffo Corminiak tell you that?"

"Who is Sheffo Corminiak, by the way?" I said.

"August Wrenside. On *At the End of the Day,* the family patriarch. He also did *Search, GL, GH, Days,* and *AMC,* in the olden days. He's two hundred years old."

I didn't know the significance of all those initials, but I was glad Sheffo was gainfully employed. That's an issue for an independent contractor, whether the client can actually cough up money. Not that I charged much, but I'd hate to be taking his Social Security check. I told Fredreeq about the proposed mural.

"Hmm," she said. "Yes, it's good for you to keep working. You can stop once you marry Simon. That man's clearly got family money, so you won't need a job."

"I'm not marrying Simon. We've only been dating three weeks."

"Shacking up three weeks. And the way he looks at you, if you can't get him to pop the question, you're no protégée of mine. The sooner the better. Because like sands through the hourglass, so are your childbearing days. You're not thirty anymore."

Thank God Simon wasn't hearing this. "Fredreeq, I appreciate the—"

"Go to hell, Horowitz!" The gravelly voice carried into the sunroom, stopping conversation.

Joey.

Fredreeq and I stared at each other. Then I grabbed her arm and headed down the hall.

In the living room was Joey, dressed in ripped jeans, T-shirt, leather jacket, and cowboy boots, the kind of cocktail party attire affected only by the very beautiful and/or very confident. Joey was both, but at the moment she was also tear-streaked, red-faced, and angry.

Her husband was near the piano, hands raised in a placating gesture. Elliot Horowitz was dressed more appropriately than his wife, in a suit, but minus a tie. He looked every inch the Harvard MBA he was—not the pocket-protector kind, the kind who made his first million two years after graduating. He also looked unhappy. "Joey," he said, "control yourself."

"Control myself? Control *your*self, you priapic, philandering prick."

"That's redundant," he said.

"*You're* redundant, sleeping with everyone on the Westside, you—" Joey's wiry body was twitching with rage. Rex put a calming hand on her shoulder and she whirled around like she was going to hit him, then stopped. "Sorry, Rex. Bad day. I shouldn't've—"

Rex hugged her and gestured to the pianist. The song "People" started, then stopped, as if the pianist had had second thoughts. He began again, with "Here Comes Santa Claus."

"She's drunk," Elliot said in the pause between songs, and his words carried.

Joey disengaged from Rex, grabbed a pitcher of glögg from a passing waiter, turned, and hurled it at her husband. She had good aim, but Elliot had good reflexes. He dodged to the right, getting hit with only a spray of airborne glögg and a couple of blanched almonds.

The pitcher and remaining glögg, along with soaked prunes, raisins, cinnamon sticks, and cardamom pods, hit the top of the raised grand piano and crashed into the exposed strings.

The music stopped.

Four

Bloodcurdling screams rose from the throat of Tricia, attesting to a long career on the soap opera set. "My Bösendorfer!" she cried.

"Her what?" Fredreeq asked, but I was already on my way to Joey. Rex brushed past me to help Tricia, who was shoveling fruit and nuts out of the concert grand.

"Towels!" Tricia shrieked. "Hot, soapy water!"

"Damn." Joey leaned against the doorjamb. "Call the piano paramedics."

"Come on," I said, tugging on her arm. "Let's get out of here."

"No, I gotta apologize to Rex."

"Later," I said. "After Tricia's sedated. Come on."

"Bathroom first."

An advantage of having worked in the mansion was that I knew the location of at least eleven bathrooms. I led Joey upstairs. As we entered a bedroom, a couple emerged from a walk-in closet, looked at us, and disappeared back into it. "Hey, Clay. What's up? Pharmaceuticals?" Joey called out, then said to me, "Prop guy. Always has good drugs."

I escorted Joey to another room with an adjoining bathroom. She walked unsteadily but spoke without slurring. "I didn't mean to kill her Bösendorfer," she said, pausing in the doorway. "It's not murder. Manslaughter or negligent homicide, but not murder one."

"Nobody thought you meant to murder the piano."

"They're gonna think I murdered him, though," she said, and shut the door.

Him? Whom? She couldn't mean David, could she? My cell phone rang. I looked at it. A restricted number.

"Simon?" I asked, answering it.

"Are you naked?"

"It's really not that kind of party."

"Go home," he said. "And I'll show you that kind of party."

I took this to mean he was not yet home himself, but before I could get into it, he got another call and hung up. I got another call too. Fredreeq.

"Where the hell are you?" she asked.

"Upstairs. You?"

"TV room. Joey?"

"Bathroom. Want me to conference her in?"

Someone yelled from downstairs. "It's on the news! David's death! Channel Nine!"

"Wollie," my phone squawked, "forget Joey and come down. You gotta watch."

"No, I don't want Joey wandering off, trying to drive—"

"You'll see her from here. Hold on. I'm on the move . . . approaching the living room . . . okay, I'm looking up at you."

There she was. Fredreeq appeared in the doorway of the TV room, which connected to the huge living room. Phone to ear, she gave me the peace sign. I waved back and hung up.

I knocked on the bathroom door to tell Joey I was going downstairs and asked if she was okay. She called back *Vaya con Dios,* which I took as a yes.

I made my way to a family room featuring a mammoth television hung from the ceiling. It was nearly the room's only furnishing, and partygoers were packed in, standing, tight as cigarettes. I stayed in the doorway to keep an eye on the upstairs bedroom, in case Joey emerged, but soon people pressed in behind me, blocking the view, so I turned to watch TV.

David Zetrakis filled the screen, larger than life and younger than I'd known him. He smiled, holding up a bottle of something orange while a voice enumerated his mid-career commercials. I remembered now that he'd been an actor since childhood.

The image changed. A reporter stood outside the gates of David's Toluca Lake estate, microphone in hand, her bulletproof hairdo unmoving, despite the wind that rustled the palm trees behind her. She was doing the stand-up, filling in the blanks of his life, turning it to legend. "The adorable child we fell in love with," she said, "grew up in front of the camera."

"Ten years before you were born, you maudlin idiot!" a man yelled. I recognized him as Clay, from the upstairs closet. Someone shushed him.

". . . went on to study directing at NYU," the reporter said. "He moved to Hollywood in the 1980s and guest-starred in popular TV series. A turning point came when he played serial killer–turned–town hero Zeke Fabian in *At the End of the Day,* which brought him his first Daytime Emmy, and countless fans." The camera pulled back to show others outside the gates with the reporter, holding a candlelight vigil. A soap opera clip filled the screen, featuring David slitting the throat of a nubile blonde in a swimsuit. There was laughter in the back of the room, and more shushing.

It's strange enough to see the face of someone you know on the news, although less strange in Hollywood, where everyone seems connected to television. More startling, somehow, was to see David's estate, sparkling with Christmas lights, surrounded by news crews. I'd eaten breakfast behind those gates, attended dinner parties, had intimate conversations, slept there. Now it was a backdrop to tragedy, the real estate equivalent of a car wreck.

". . . began directing episodes, then moved into the role of producer," the reporter continued. "At the time of his death, he owned a share of the successful daytime drama, had acquired seven more Emmys, and was considered one of the most accomplished men in the industry. Although he'd faded from the sight of the viewing audience, he never faded from our hearts." The photomontage moved backward in time and ended on a shot of David as a three-year-old moppet. A woman to my right sobbed. Jen Kim, behind me, announced that the photomontage had been put together for David's fiftieth-birthday party, a year earlier.

"The fatal shooting," the newswoman continued, in a tone that managed to be serious yet salacious, "contrary to earlier reports, was not suicide. According to a police department spokesperson, a homicide investigation is under way. No word yet whether robbery was a motive, but David Zetrakis numbered among his possessions a Kentucky Derby–winning racehorse, a rare-stamp collection, and a painting by Gustav Klimt valued at two million dollars. The police have not revealed the names of suspects at this time."

There was instant silence, except for the distant sound of croaking frogs.

"My God!" yelled a woman near the television, shattering the silence. "Let me through. I've gotta get to the newsroom for the eleven o'clock. This story's mine."

Angel Ramirez pushed through the crowd like a quarterback, judging by the "Hey, watch out!" comments. Near the doorway there was a short shriek, followed by a thud. I muscled my way through to see her facedown on the living room floor.

"Goddamnit!" she yelled. "This nose is brand-new. If I've broken anything, someone's going to pay for it—" A man helped her up and out to the foyer, where we could hear her screaming for valet parking.

I turned to see Joey, shaky but smiling, leaning on a wall for support. I reached her as she began to sink to the floor.

"I tripped her," she said. "I couldn't resist. David hated reporters."

With that, she passed out.

Five

sat on my knees, holding her head, not knowing what to do. I looked around for Fredreeq, but there was only a sea of legs, none of them encased in red chiffon. A man, Asian and handsome, squatted next to me. "Is she—out?" he said.

"Yes," I said. "Can you help me get her to my car? Before Tricia sees her."

"It's the kind of thing I excel at." He took off his sports coat and handed it to me, then scooped up Joey like a prince rescuing Sleeping Beauty. Joey was skinny enough and he, while short, was muscular enough to make this look easy. He carried her to the foyer. I followed. People stared.

"What are you, a fireman?" I said, opening the front door for him. Fredreeq appeared in the distance, her turban bouncing in the crowd, her hand waving.

"No, I'm an actor," he said. "Rupert Ling."

"I'm Wollie Shelley." I searched through my purse for the valet parking stub as we hurried toward the driveway. "That's my friend Joey you're carrying."

Rupert smiled. "I've carried her before. I used to be her half brother, with whom she was having an affair, on *At the End of the Day*."

"You were her stepfather too, don't forget," Fredreeq said, catching up to us, breathless from the exertion, "before Rosamund was struck by lightning and got amnesia. Hello, I'm Fredreeq Munson, and I'm very glad to meet you. I'm a fan of the show and you are nearly the only thing worth watching these days, if I may be blunt. What's going on with Joey?"

"Passed out," I said. "Let's put her in my car."

"Good idea," Rupert said. "Since I saw her husband drive off in theirs ten minutes ago. Where will you take her, home?"

"I don't think her home's a good idea," I said. "Under the circumstances. And I'm between homes. Fredreeq? Your home?"

Fredreeq shook her head. "Cats. She's allergic."

"I'd take her myself," Rupert said, "but I have a jealous, uh . . . tenant."

"Then I guess it'll have to be me after all," I said. How Simon would respond to an unconscious houseguest gave me pause. "Or maybe my Uncle Theo. I'll give him a call."

My Integra appeared and the valet guys helped get Joey inside. I was thinking that I should've gone to the car wash instead of having sex all week when a police cruiser pulled into the driveway.

"Go," Rupert said. "Get her out of here."

"Fast," Fredreeq added. "I'll be right behind you."

I didn't argue. I got in the driver's seat and rolled out of the driveway at a decorous pace, so as not to attract undue attention from the men or women in blue.

It was only when I hit the freeway that I wondered why exactly the three of us were so certain that Joey should not meet the police.

Six

Fredreeq and I stayed in cellular conversation all the way to West-wood.

"Uncle Theo's not answering his phone," I said, "and I don't have keys to his place on me. It'll have to be Simon's."

"Great," she said. "It's a good safe house. Joey's gonna be like raw meat to a pack of hyenas when it comes to reporters; we can't leave her lying around Glendale at Uncle Theo's."

"What are you talking about?" I looked in the rearview mirror at Joey, snoring softly.

"Joey and David," Fredreeq said, "were a hot item once."

"So? That was a hundred years ago." But images sprang into my head, of Joey and David attending every movie premier and charity fund-raiser in Hollywood. "Well, anyway, they were soap stars, not Oscar winners. There's a hierarchy."

On the phone, Fredreeq snorted. "I'll tell you something, missy. If you're just a little bit famous and you get yourself gunned down, or your arm eaten off by a mountain lion, it's jackpot time. Joey's a marked woman. While you two were upstairs, Angel Ramirez was sniffing around, asking about Joey and David, Joey and Elliot, was Joey having an affair *now* with David, was she divorcing Elliot over David, blah-*blah*, blah-*blah*—

and now that David's a murder victim, the press will be heat-seeking missiles, looking for a photogenic suspect."

"As long as it's the press, not the police," I said.

"Oh, like the cops don't watch *News at Eleven*? Drive faster. I want to catch it."

"The news? We just watched it."

" 'Channel Nine Extra Special Report'? Please. I mean hard news."

We pulled off the 405 South at 10:32 P.M. and made our way east on Wilshire. I parked under the building, went up through the lobby, said a cheery hello to Ali, the night doorman, then headed outside to meet Fredreeq, parked on Thayer. I used my keycard to get into the parking garage again, and we hurried down two levels, our heels echoing on the cement.

Removing Joey from the Integra was no picnic. It wasn't that she was weighty, but we didn't want to bruise her. Also, we weren't dressed for heavy lifting. We were, however, dressed for Simon's high-rise, including its spacious and gracious elevators. Fredreeq, as she pointed out, was also dressed for Kwanzaa.

"Now *this* is apartment living," Fredreeq said, reaching the top floor. We arranged Joey on a love seat next to the elevator so I could see if Simon was home—he wasn't—and then deal with the multiple locks and disarm his security system. "I've always been a home owner—gotta have my backyard barbecue—but I'd reconsider if I snagged a man like this."

We propped open Simon's door, then went to reclaim Joey. I was congratulating myself on not encountering any neighbors when a woman emerged from the elevator, leading a dog by a jeweled leash. She and the dog wore matching jackets, in white leather.

She blinked.

"Hi, there," I said, going backward, holding Joey's shoulders. Fredreeq had her feet.

"Cute dog," Fredreeq said to the woman. "What is that, a Labradoodle?"

"Schnoodle," the woman replied, and hurried down the hall.

We got Joey into the apartment, arranged her on the sofa, then went into the kitchen to explore Simon's cupboards. It was four minutes till news time.

"Protein. Protein powder. Protein bars. Protein drinks. Vitamins.

Vodka. Gin. Olives. And a twelve-pack of paper towels. This is a cry for help," Fredreeq said, arms akimbo. "This is a man begging to be domesticated."

"What do we do about Joey?" I said. "Not just tonight, but in the long run?"

"I vote we castrate Elliot. That'll perk her up. How long's he been cheating?"

"It's news to me, so it must be recent. Ever seen her this drunk before?"

"Well, lately she's been—. Listen, if my old flame got himself whacked and my husband was playing with his zipper, I'd get liquored up too. Come on." She headed back to the living room. "We need to get this TV operational."

But Simon's television, like all his electronic equipment, was as user-friendly as a space shuttle. Even his furniture intimidated me. After three weeks I was no closer to feeling at home in the penthouse than I'd been my first night. I felt like my Integra in the parking garage, a preowned bargain amid the Porsches, Rolls-Royces, and Beemers. Simon himself drove a Bentley.

Fredreeq frantically worked the remotes. "Eureka!" she yelled, achieving sound and picture simultaneously. "Okay, let's just see—" She changed channels at the speed of light. "Did you know Angel Ramirez was Allie Rumsfelt before she turned Latina?"

I looked with new interest at Angel's dyed-black hair as she introduced her segment, "Bloodbath in Toluca Lake." Only now, in addition to footage on David's career, there were old photos of David and various actresses on various red carpets, highlighting his prolific romantic history. Finally, they zeroed in on a photo of David and Joey. Red hair upswept in a professional do, Joey was described as a model-turned-actress, which wasn't quite accurate, but close enough. I glanced at the real Joey snoring on the couch, hair sticking out, face freckled and flushed with alcohol. Something stirred in me, a protectiveness I'd never felt about her.

"The acknowledged love of his life, Joey Rafferty, played out her on-again, off-again romance with David in front of the camera and behind closed doors for a decade. And in the last weeks of his life, it was she who remained by his bedside."

The picture changed to an interview with a woman described as David's housekeeper. "Miss Joey, she was here all the time, every day. All the time at night too, many, many nights. Until Christmas Eve. They have a big fight. Lot of screaming, like the old days. Then she leave."

"So many unanswered questions," Angel Ramirez said. "Among them: What part did David Zetrakis play in Joey Rafferty's publicly disintegrating marriage to millionaire entrepreneur Elliot Horowitz? And more disturbingly, what part did Joey Rafferty play in her former lover's murder? This is Angel Ramirez, reporting live from Toluca Lake."

Seven

B itch," Fredreeq and I said simultaneously to the TV. Joey snored on.
We watched David's body being loaded into a van. We assumed
it was David's body. It was a lump on a stretcher, certainly. My mind
turned the image into a greeting card and added a caption: *Congratulations on your fifteen minutes of fame.*

"That's it?" I stood, agitated. "That's the segment? It was all about
Joey! How can a reporter say those things, like it's journalism? It's gossip, only people are going to assume there's some truth in it since—"

"Thank you." Fredreeq nodded. "I have been trying to tell you all night."

"And what reason would Joey have for killing David?"

"Exactly. It's not like she was married to him. Like she was sick of the
way he flossed his teeth for the last ten years. Like he had a habit of saying 'uh-huh, uh-huh, uh-huh' while reading the paper and never listening to a goddamn word she said. Like he pretended never to know which
bin is for trash and which one's recycling so that she'd stop asking him
to take out the garbage after the first year of marriage."

"Fredreeq," I said. "You're scaring me."

"I'm just saying. Marriage is means, motive, and opportunity, one-stop shopping. But David never got married. Why?"

I aimed remotes at the TV, trying to turn it off. "Joey was the love of his life. He told me that once. I don't know what went wrong between them."

"Who inherits that house?"

"I think he had siblings."

"Wait. It's coming to me." Fredreeq swept into the kitchen and returned with a protein bar. "A guy, fifty, good-looking, rich, never marries—what's that say to you?"

I shrugged. "Commitophobe?"

"Homosexual." She ripped open the protein bar wrapper. "He was passing as straight, but one of his boyfriends threatened blackmail and David got a gun and the boyfriend came over and grabbed it and shot him. Case closed. God, I'm good at this."

"Fredreeq, this is L.A., not West Point. Being gay isn't a career ender anymore."

"I can name you twenty-seven actors trying to pass themselves off as straight."

"David hasn't acted for years. Anyhow, I slept with him. I should know."

Fredreeq's eyes narrowed. "Well? How was it?"

"Fine." I hesitated. "It was a long time ago. The details are fuzzy."

"Aha!"

"Not because he wasn't. . . . He didn't seem conflicted."

"But you're tall. There's something masculine about a six-foot woman. If you remove the breasts. Did you make love in the dark?"

"I don't remember."

"And Joey's flat-chested. She's like a boy. And no hips at all." Fredreeq snapped her fingers. "I see a pattern. He likes women he can pretend are men." She saw me staring. "Then ask yourself how come you two didn't live happily ever after."

"He didn't want kids, for one thing. Ever. He was very clear about that, and I knew I did, so we decided to quit before it got complicated."

Fredreeq frowned and set down the protein bar. She settled back into her leather armchair, meticulously arranging her layers of chiffon, and said, "Perhaps you should have discussed those issues before indulging in recreational sex?" Despite a taste for provocative couture, Fredreeq had a strict moral code.

"Perhaps," I said. "But we were young. I was, anyway. He broke it off.

I think he found me naive and didn't want to corrupt me. I've been thinking about this all day."

"What do you mean, corrupt you?"

"He had an experimental streak."

"In bed? And you knew this how?"

"Just the way he'd ask casual questions, like did I ever dress up or act out fantasies or do group activities. Use props."

"Those are casual questions?"

Hearing Simon's key in the door, I had a moment of paranoia, wondering if the room was bugged and Simon could hear us. It was the sort of thing my mother would warn me about, the downside of living with an FBI agent. Of course, my mother would say there was no upside to living with anyone employed by the federal government.

"Hi, Simon," I said, jumping up to kiss him. On the cheek, because Fredreeq's presence made me shy. He returned my kiss on the cheek with amusement.

If my boyfriend was surprised to come home and find his apartment taken over by three women, one of them comatose, he didn't show it. But Simon was professionally nonreactive. I assumed they taught that at Quantico. It's not that he wasn't emotional—I'd seen a wide range from him in the six weeks I'd known him—but he was in charge of what got expressed and when and in front of whom.

"Fredreeq, a pleasure," he said, reaching down to give her a kiss on the cheek too. He looked toward Joey. "Good party?"

"Not for her," Fredreeq said. "But you should've been there. Wollie was the star. They unveiled her frogs."

"Sorry I missed that," he said, loosening his tie.

"I understand you were working," she said. "Surveillance?"

"Fredreeq," I said, "if he won't tell me, he's not going to tell you."

"If it were *my* husband," she said, "coming in at midnight dressed to kill, I'd ask questions. You can't use that tired old 'national security' excuse forever, Simon."

"Fredreeq, stop," I said. "Stop, stop, stop."

"Speaking of security issues," he said, "please tell me that Joey walked up here of her own volition."

"As opposed to—?" I asked.

"As opposed to being hauled around by the two of you all through the parking garage and elevators, which was picked up by various surveillance cameras. Providing Ali with some interesting viewing."

"Who's Ali?" Fredreeq asked.

"Night doorman," I said.

"Well, I'm prepared to tell whichever scenario you want to hear," Fredreeq said. "Unlike Wollie, who's never told a lie in her life. That's the kind of trait a guy in your line of work looks for, by the way."

I tried to speak but choked, and went into a coughing fit.

"Just look at her, standing there," she continued. "Built like a lingerie model, a natural blonde, never has to worry about getting her roots done. Too tall for most guys, but a man like you, I don't see you with a woman much under six feet. And the best part about her? No police record."

"Yet." Simon nodded. "If you'll excuse me, I'm going to change. And then I may need a drink."

"He's not the only one," I said, watching him retreat to the bedroom. "Fredreeq, you have to lay off the—"

"Honey, every girl needs a Jewish mother. Go on in there with him. He may want help with his shoes or something. His pants."

"I thought you were against recreational sex."

"There's nothing recreational about this. This is purposeful sex, and I think you know what purpose I'm talking about."

I was telling her what I thought of her retro advice on snaring a husband when a cell phone rang. The sound came from Joey.

"Let's answer it," Fredreeq said, helping me roll her over. "If it's Elliot, I want to yell at him."

I unearthed the phone from the pocket of Joey's blue jeans. "Hello?"

"Hello. Joey Rafferty?"

"Who's this?" I said.

"Glen Gill, Associated Press. Miss Rafferty, I'm sorry for your loss. I wonder if you'd mind giving us your reaction upon hearing of the death of your boyfriend. Where were you when you got the news?"

"My what? Boyfriend?" I said, slow to understand the question.

"David Zetrakis. Hey, is it true that your marriage to Elliot Horowitz is breaking up and—"

"Oh, my God," I said, putting the pieces together. "Don't you have something real to report, like global warming? Get lost."

Fredreeq took the phone from me. "This is Miss Rafferty's mother,

Mrs. Rafferty. How may I help you?" She listened, then said, "Do you realize all the media in this country is owned by Reverend Sun Myung
Moon? You go get yourself a nice job. Working in a slaughterhouse, for
instance. Leave this poor girl alone." She hung up.

"How could they get her cell phone number?" I asked.

"The whole town's got her number. She's Miss Friendly. She used to
be careful about that sort of thing, but once she stopped working, she got
sloppy." Fredreeq shook her head. "This has officially turned ugly. And
it's gonna get worse before David's corpse is cold. Joey's rich, she's a red-
head, and she's been on the cover of *Vogue*. Unless they can implicate
Michael Jackson in this, they're gonna go with her."

We studied her. Normally, she had a skinny, tomboy look, but cover
her freckles, calm down her hair, and throw her into a Valentino, and
Joey was a runway model. "You're right," I said. "I thought you were exaggerating, but you can now say 'I told you so.' "

"I'm too classy." Fredreeq wrapped her layers of red firmly about herself. "Prepare for the onslaught. We could pop up in *People* too. Do not
leave the house in sweatpants. In fact, burn all fleece. That man in that
bedroom is not going to be seduced by fleece." She kissed me, then called
good-bye to Simon, who called good-bye in return.

That man in the bedroom was sitting on the king-sized bed reading
reports, his briefcase nearby. He himself was in sweatpants and a T-shirt,
both items looking either brand-new or ironed. All his clothes looked
new. No ratty socks. No faded jeans. No T-shirts from early Grateful Dead
tours.

I sat next to him, and he moved aside his papers, flipping them facedown.

"It's all right, I'm not going to peek at affairs of state," I said. "Sorry
about bringing Joey here. I didn't know what else to do with her."

"Does she pass out often?"

"Never, since I've known her."

"Well, with some people it doesn't take much. Two drinks and they're
gone."

"Not Joey," I said. "She can drink like a fish and half the time I can't
see any effect." I stopped. Simon was looking at me with a raised eyebrow, and I felt another protective surge toward my friend. "She had a
bad day," I said.

"She has bad coping skills."

"She has a philandering husband. She just found out."

"Getting wasted isn't going to help."

I wanted to defend her, but everything I could think of sounded . . . defensive. Her snores could be heard even here, in the bedroom, cutting into my thoughts.

"You don't know her," I said, after a moment.

"Do you?"

"Yes. What do you mean?"

He looked me in the eye. "She has a drinking problem. You're either unaware, which means you don't know her as well as you think, or you're in denial. Which is it?"

I stared at him. "Those are my choices? Can't someone pass out once in a while? She probably didn't eat today. She forgets to, and she's skin and bones. Plus, David died. And she's Irish. If you're Irish and someone dies, you drink. It's a cultural imperative."

"And the Irish have a cultural propensity for alcoholism," he said. His calmness annoyed me. "Have you ever passed out from drinking?"

"Yes. Our first date."

"You didn't pass out, you fell asleep. At three A.M. In your own home. I've never passed out either, and I've had some very bad days."

I considered a number of responses but opted for a dignified silence. I went into the living room to cover Joey with a blanket, then walked back through the bedroom into the master bath, where I spent forty minutes with a tubful of bubbles and the *Economist*, the only magazine Simon had lying around.

I put on pajamas for the first time in three weeks. I did not iron them. Simon was still working. I crawled into bed, turned my back to him, and mumbled, "Good night."

"Not yet," he said, pushing his papers off the bed. He threw back the covers I'd pulled over myself and settled his body along the length of mine, his front to my back. He breathed into my ear. "I'll let you know when it's a good night."

"You think so?" I said. "All right. Give it your best shot."

And he did.

When I woke in the morning, Joey was gone.

Eight

David Zetrakis didn't make the front page of the *Los Angeles Times,* but he was above the fold in the California section. The article focused on facts I already knew, with a sidebar listing film, theater, and television credits. Emmy nominations got an asterisk, and Emmy wins got a double asterisk.

There's something singularly disturbing about death the morning after. Night can sweep away memory so perfectly that you have to live through it all over again, turning off your alarm or shuffling into the bathroom, the tile cold on your feet as you realize something bad happened, something that will take you by sad surprise every morning for a long time. Now I read the *Los Angeles Times* as if memorizing it, as though to imprint it on my brain so that the news could never again come as news.

I put in time on paperwork, doing greeting card invoices, wondering how to squeeze more income from my business, but my mind kept straying to a note from Joey on Simon's coffee table.

W—thanks. I'm okay. I'll call you. J.
p.s. Can you believe he's dead?

No. And I couldn't believe she was okay. I called her and got voice mail. I hung up and my phone rang. It was the assistant for Jen Kim. It took me a moment to recall Jen Kim, the woman from the party smoking by the pool, but by then I'd already agreed to meet with her, on the studio lot where they shot *At the End of the Day*. The words *job interview* temporarily displaced thoughts of David and Joey.

I showered, dressed for success, and straightened the apartment to the standards of a four-star hotel. Simon was already gone, off to the gym at daybreak, sleep deprivation being another thing he seemed to thrive on, probably learned at Quantico.

News of David's death accompanied me north. The radio spoke of his battle with cancer, leading to early conjecture that his death was suicide. Now that people knew the wound wasn't self-inflicted, rumors of assisted suicide were surfacing. It was not reported who was doing all this conjecturing and rumormongering. I suspected the reporters themselves, desperate to create a story during a slow news week.

I headed over the hill to Burbank, a town thick with film and television production facilities. People lived there too, those willing to endure the heat of the Valley in exchange for relatively affordable housing. Burbank had little cachet and meant a crummy commute for those working in L.A., but it had a killer view, the San Gabriel Mountains in the distance like a painted backdrop, when not obscured by smog.

Maybe I could live in Burbank. Or Toluca Lake, right next door. I'd check the apartment listings. I couldn't stay at Simon's forever; even if things kept going the way they were going, it wasn't my place. My art supplies needed to stretch out. My drafting table would never feel at home in a Wilshire Boulevard penthouse.

At the studio entrance, a security guard disappeared into his wooden hut with my driver's license, perhaps checking it against a list of terrorists. Then he searched my trunk. Then he gave me a map and directions to a parking structure and Building 47.

Even on a Saturday, there was a buzz of activity. Golf carts rumbled down mini streets, with their own mini street signs, as if the studio were a town. It was much like the lot I'd visited when Joey had filmed her TV series *Gun Girl*, years earlier. Who were these worker bees, dressed in overalls, business suits, and, in one case, a full body cast? Crew, executives, actors. And where did I fit in?

Building 47 was a boxlike structure that had seen better days. Jen's assistant, a comely child, introduced herself as Sophie and escorted me into

Jen's inner office, offering coffee. Jen, she said, was held up on the set. I looked at a wall full of publicity photos from *At the End of the Day*, many of them autographed. There was unbusinesslike paraphernalia as well: stuffed animals, a cocktail dress hanging on a closet door, a lighted makeup mirror, three gift baskets still in their cellophane, a bottle of Moët & Chandon, fresh flowers, a gumball machine, and a miniature basketball hoop. On an end table, a heavy glass bowl filled with M&M's invited me to go ahead and pig out.

A photo of Jen with David Zetrakis dominated the desk. They stood in front of a pyramid and bright lights spelling out *Luxor,* and David had both arms around Jen's shoulders, like a proud father. Or a lover.

"Wollie," Jen said, striding in and shaking my hand. "Thanks for coming by. Did you get a chance to watch the show?"

"Uh—"

"*SoapDirt*. No problem. It runs six times a day. I'll send DVDs home with you. Sophie!" she yelled to the open door. "Get some *SoapDirts* for Wollie and last week's episodes of *At the End of the Day*." She talked fast, as if conversation cost money. "I line-produce *End* but my real baby's *SoapDirt*. With David sick these last months, I've been on overload. Sophie!" she yelled. "Coffee!"

She seated herself, removed a shoe, a sexy, strappy sandal in orange suede, and set it on the desk. She turned on a high-intensity lamp to study it. "They're building sets over on *End* and I got a glob of glue on it."

Jen, I suspected, wore the highest possible heels she could function in, being both diminutive and round-faced, not the best physical attributes for one in a position of authority. "Okay," she said, making the shoe disappear behind the desk. "What do I want from you?"

"Are you asking me?" I said.

"No. You're asking you. What does this Korean chick want from me? Here's the scoop. *Soap Journal* magazine is running a yearlong competition to see which show has the hottest guys in daytime. All categories. Juveniles, rapists, geezers. We're going to piggyback on that and do a segment on *SoapDirt* with a dating correspondent. You."

"Excuse me?"

"You date, right?"

"Well, yes. But not . . . professionally."

"But you have in the past. It's nothing to be ashamed of." Jen rummaged around on her overloaded desk, then yelled, "Sophie! Where's the Wollie Shelley memo?"

"On your desk!"

"Oh. Here it is." Jen read aloud. "Research subject for best seller *How to Avoid Getting Dumped All the Time,* which did a quarter million units in hardcover—"

"I was the Bad Example, though. The What Not to Do."

"No one cares. You won *Biological Clock.*"

"The show was canceled before the final vote," I said.

"You might've won. Anyway, the perception is, you're a celebrity, you're an expert, you're the Date Girl."

How to explain to Jen Kim that I had no desire to be known for anything but alternative greeting cards? My brushes with fame, failed romances, dismal dates—all this I hoped had faded from the public consciousness, of whatever public was conscious of me in the first place. But could a TV producer understand a desire for anonymity? "I think you're overstating it," I said. "And anyway—"

"No. You have a Q rating that's remarkable for a civilian. And it's not like we're going to get Paris Hilton, on our budget. The best we can do is a thousand."

"Dollars?" I said.

"Per episode. We tape five episodes every Friday, because Tricia works on the soap Monday through Thursday. I can get you a small per diem for the actual dates, and we'll throw in a car service. You want hair and makeup too?"

"No. Oh! Can I bring my own?" I asked, thinking I could get Fredreeq a job. She'd done facials for years but had recently begun branching out.

"No, I don't have the budget. But you can come to the set and use whoever's working on the show that day."

Sophie brought in mugs of coffee and set down packets of artificial sweetener in three colors—pink, blue, and yellow—along with artificial creamer. Apparently the only sugar on hand was what was in the M&M's.

"And what exactly will I be doing?" I asked. "Sorry to be slow, but . . ."

"Dinner with an actor, which means fawning and listening to how much they want to leave daytime and make it in film. Then you come on *SoapDirt* and dish. Only it won't really be dishing, because you want them to come off as sexy, but it's going to look like dishing, because that's our bread and butter. Think puff pieces disguised as investigative journalism."

This was not a good day for me to enter the field of journalism, feeling as I did about reporters. "You know, Jen, in real life I'm a greeting card designer. My area of expertise is pretty much . . . doodling."

"Don't worry, we'll help you with talking points. Tricia's a pro—she could get a good interview out of my grandmother, and my grandmother doesn't speak English. You just show up, you'll be fine."

I sighed. Who was I to turn down work, I, unemployed and living out of a suitcase? I needed an apartment, which meant first and last month's rent, plus security deposit. I'd saved some money from the canceled TV show that Jen set such store by, but most of it had gone to P.B.

My younger brother, P.B., was about to move from a state mental facility to a halfway house in Santa Barbara. A chunk of that was paid for by grants and governmental programs, but a chunk of it wasn't. And there was nothing I wouldn't do to ensure P.B.'s future with Haven Lane. They practically guaranteed a high quality of life, something my brother, as a schizophrenic, had not always experienced. I'd rob banks to make it happen. Robbing banks, however, did not seem to be my destiny. Appearing on cheesy TV shows did.

I shook hands with Jen Kim, who yelled to Sophie to dig out a standard contract. I walked to the reception desk alongside my new boss, who was off to a production meeting for *At the End of the Day.*

"Get her numbers on file, Sophie." Jen pulled a cigarette from her purse and hurried out the door. "Including fax and e-mail. We need to know where she is twenty-four/seven."

As Sophie typed Simon's fax number, I had my first second thought. Simon. Before I could follow that thread, a man appeared from the other end of a hallway, demanding to see Jen Kim. Hearing that she was unavailable, he turned his wrath on Sophie.

"Who's gonna reimburse me for damage to my truck?" he yelled.

"What damage is that?" Sophie, I saw, was fixated on the man's tattooed arms.

"It's got dings in places there never used to be dings, and it's down an eighth of a tank. Someone went joyriding in it while it was on the lot."

"Did you leave your keys in it?"

"Did I have a choice? Transpo makes you, in case they gotta move it."

Sophie pulled a form from a drawer and handed it to him. "Well, take it up with Transportation, then. You can fill out an incident report, but you can't expect Miss Kim to care about your car problems."

"Does she care that the prop master is drunk half the time?" he yelled, waving the form in the air as he walked back down the hall. "That the crew's furnishing their houses from the prop room?"

"Loser," Sophie muttered. "He's got a tattoo on one arm that says 'Hot Guy' and one on the other that says 'Stud.' How attractive is that?"

"Not very," I said. "Sophie, I have a problem too."

A wary look came over her. "Okay, what?"

"You know about this dating correspondent job? I just remembered that I have a boyfriend."

"Yeah?"

"I mean, we're pretty new. But I'm wondering—"

"—if he'll mind? That you're the *SoapDirt* dating correspondent? Oh, my God, guys think it's such a turn-on to have a girlfriend on TV. Don't even worry."

"Actually, I'm thinking that—"

"He'll be jealous?" Sophie shook her head, sending her long blond hair swinging through space. "Tell him they're gay. Guys always think soap actors are gay."

"But is it misrepresenting myself, to be dating these guys when I'm not emotionally available, when I'm going home at night to a boyfriend? Is it ethical?"

"Ethical?" She had a little button nose, which wrinkled now in confusion. I thought she was giving the question some deep thought until she said, "I sort of don't get what you're asking. Hold on—" She adjusted an earpiece I hadn't noticed before. "Jen Kim's office . . . Uh-huh. Uh-huh. Okay." She looked up at me and smiled. "They want you on the set. Do you know how to get there?"

. . .

At the End of the Day occupied Sound Stage D, a barn of a building on the other end of the lot. It took me twenty minutes to walk there, and if Jen did this multiple times a day, it was easy to see why she was so trim.

Especially if she smoked en route. Sophie had offered to call for a golf cart, but I'd turned her down. She'd added that Jen would soon have an office in the new administration building, to be built in the space now occupied by Building 12. "Much closer. It's so important for the kind of work she does, to be in there with her people," she added, as though describing Mother Teresa among the orphans.

I turned on my cell phone to call Joey. I'd lost the car adapter in my last move, so I was always conserving battery power, which meant turning off the phone and forgetting it. Now it hummed to life, alerting me to three missed calls. One was from Fredreeq, asking if I'd seen the morning news. The next was from P.B., a cryptic message having to do with comic books, and the last was Simon, saying he'd be home by late afternoon, should I have any interest in picking up where we'd left off the night before. As befits a federal agent using an unsecured phone, he was discreet about details. I called his voice mail and said simply, "Yes."

While dialing Fredreeq, I caught sight of the guy with the tattooed arms having a smoke alongside a battered white truck parked near a loading dock. If this was the truck that had survived a joyride, it looked to me like it could use a little joy in its life. I nodded to him, and he saluted me with his cigarette.

Fredreeq answered her phone. "Heard from Joey?" I asked.

"No, I expect she's avoiding everyone, but guess what was on the news? David had a humongous life insurance policy. Merry Christmas to whoever collects on that."

"That was on the news? Hold on." I paused at Sound Stage D to read a sign above the black steel door: DO NOT ENTER WHEN RED LIGHT IS FLASHING. I looked up at a red bulb. It didn't flash. I entered.

"Okay, I'm back," I said, my eyes adjusting to the dark. "What kind of insurance agency would give out information like that?"

"The kind that has a temp or a janitor willing to sell it to the tabloids," Fredreeq said. "The point is, I smell motive."

"Me too," I said, but a woman walking past told me there was no cell phone use on the set, so I signed off.

In the distance were bright lights. I moved toward them. People milled, loitered, or hurried by, no one paying attention to me. I paused at a folding table displaying a tray of picked-over bagels, flanked by a plate of brown-edged lettuce and a jar of mustard.

"Where'd you lose it?" a guy asked, helping himself at a watercooler.

"Excuse me?" I said, then realized he wasn't talking to me.

"If I knew that, it wouldn't be lost," another man said, opening an industrial-sized jar of aspirin. I recognized him as Clay, the prop man who'd been doing drugs in Tricia's upstairs closet the night before.

"One of the Berettas from last week?"

"Not even. Colt 1911 we haven't used in a month." Clay swallowed the aspirin without water.

I continued on my way, passing a baby crib decked out with gingham sheets and bumper and a clown mobile. I peeked inside. A doll lay there, dressed in a T-shirt and diaper. It smiled up at me with pink lips and blue glass eyes. I smiled back, then jumped when a voice behind me said, "Wollie Shelley. How are you this morning?"

I turned to see Max Freund, the stage manager. He approached, clipboard in hand, headphones on ears. Still limping. He removed his headphones and indicated a woman at his side in pigtails. "Carmel Graves, known as C.G. My co–stage manager."

C.G. gave me a smile and a bone-crushing handshake, then moved off.

"Jen wants me to introduce you to your three actors. You may have met Rupert last night. And Sheffo—wait, hold on—"

A woman's voice could be heard coming over Max's headset, as though a fairy were stuck inside. "Max, that detective needs a list of everyone at yesterday's production meeting—" Max reattached the headphones to his ears and unclipped a radio from his belt to respond.

When he finished talking to his appliances, I said, "Homicide detective?"

"Beg your pardon?"

"Sorry, I was just eavesdropping. Was that to do with David?"

Max nodded. "They're checking people's whereabouts at the time he died. Routine. Or so they say, but I guess they always say that. Where was I?"

"Sheffo," I said. "You want to introduce me. But I met him last night too."

"Yes? Good. He's gone home anyway. He had heartburn, so we bumped up his scenes in the shooting order. He'll be recovered by tonight, though. Don't worry."

I wondered why I should worry about Sheffo Corminiak's heartburn, but Max was on the move, limping off with me following. "How's Joey Rafferty doing?" he asked. "She seemed a little rocky last night." Before I could answer, a voice raised in protest caused Max to veer sharply to the left.

Tricia, in a ball gown and full makeup, was facing C.G. "I will not," Tricia said, "be sent outside like an errant child when I'm conducting legitimate business that impacts this show and, by the way, your paycheck."

"Tricia, it's not personal, it's policy," C.G. said, pigtails belying her authoritative tone. "No cell phones, no exceptions. I've asked Jen herself to step off the set, and Max always goes outside to take calls. They're doing legitimate business too."

"If you'd stuck to the shooting order, instead of catering to Sheffo, I'd be home already. I have furniture deliveries that cannot be rescheduled, and now I'm forced to pay my own staff overtime so that Sheffo Corminiak can leave early. That's fair?"

"Tricia," Max said. "Magnificent party last night. Come. Let's shoot your scenes and get you out of here, shall we?"

Tricia, however, had noticed me. "What's she doing here?"

It was clear from her tone that my stock had fallen precipitously since the cocktail party. "I'm here to meet guys," I said, which didn't come out quite right.

"Rupert and Trey," Max said. "Wollie's the *SoapDirt* dating correspondent."

Tricia looked stunned. "What? When was this decided? I'm calling Jen."

"Call her outside," C.G. said, steering Tricia toward the door. Tricia pulled her arm away and I flinched, expecting her to swat C.G.

"Okay, Wollie, let's hurry," Max said. "Before the storm breaks." He stepped up the pace, leading me to a well-lit spot in the cavernous space, a lighted makeup mirror attached to a table. A beauty salon chair sat nearby, occupied by a sleeping beauty of the male persuasion, the kid who'd offered me glögg at Tricia's party. Next to him was Rupert Ling, reading *Daily Variety*. Rupert was dressed like a gymnast, in workout clothes too tight to work on anyone but an Olympic athlete. Happily, Rupert looked like an Olympic athlete.

"Wollie," Max said, "you remember Rupert."

"Hey. How's Joey?" Rupert asked.

"She's—I don't know, actually."

"And that's Trey Mangialotti," Max said. "Rupert, when Trey wakes up, tell him he's at lunch. You too. Back for touch-ups in an hour. Wollie, I'll walk you out. I'm trying to reach wardrobe, but they're out shopping, so we'll bring you back early next week. Meanwhile, I'll call to schedule tonight."

"Max," I said, "I've got to tell you, I have no idea what I'm doing here—"

He frowned. "I thought Jen explained. These are men you're dating this week."

"Trey and Rupert? Both of them?"

"Three of them. Starting tonight, with our patriarch. Sheffo Corminiak. We work fast around here."

I don't know what my face was doing, but Max put an arm around my shoulder. "Don't worry. *Was mich nicht umbringt, macht mich stärker.* 'That which does not kill me makes me stronger.' Friedrich Nietzsche." He smiled down at me. "Welcome to daytime."

Nine

I was driving south on Beverly Glen, the winding canyon road, when I found Joey via cell phone. Reception, however, was iffy.

"How are you?" I said.

"Troubled," she said. "Any chance we could meet?"

"Yes. Your house?" I spoke quickly, fearing imminent disconnection.

"No," she said, her voice going in and out. "I'm—Topanga and Ventura—god-awful—ice-cream pita—"

"I'm on my way!" I yelled, not knowing if she heard me or where I was going. God-awful indeed. What kind of culinary mind would fill pita bread with ice cream? I saw a turnout on the road ahead and slowed. Only for my best friend would I attempt a U-turn on Beverly Glen.

Twenty minutes later I found a strip mall on the corner of Topanga Canyon and Ventura boulevards, centered around two grocery stores, Ralphs and Vons. Since Ralphs and Vons were nearly interchangeable as far as size, price, and selection, putting them next to each other, separated only by a tiny Indian food restaurant, defied reason. I drove the perimeter of the mall and found California Pita Grill/Polar Bear Ice Cream.

"Thanks for coming," Joey said, giving me a full-body hug. She seemed thinner already. There are people who stop eating during times of stress. Joey is one. I am not.

I sat. There were a lot of tables, and few customers. "How are you feeling?"

"Like I've been sautéed in something and left on the counter overnight. Do I smell?"

"Not from here," I said. She was still in the clothes she'd worn to the party, but in spite of that, and the rings under her eyes, and the scar running down the side of her face, she looked beautiful. I told her so. "What are you doing here?"

She looked around. "I was at a—a thing in Toluca Lake, but a reporter spotted me, so I jumped on the freeway to lose him, but I was low on gas, so I pulled in here."

I looked around too. None of our fellow customers were paying us any attention, which was reassuring. "How'd you get your car?" I asked.

"Took a cab home from Westwood. I saw Elliot's BMW in the driveway, so I didn't go into the house, I just grabbed my own car and the hide-a-key from the carport and took off. Except I thought my purse would be in the car and it wasn't. He must've taken it into the house last night. Or maybe I left it at the party."

By my calculations, Joey had put in over fifty miles already, and it wasn't much past noon. "So," I said. "I guess things are not so good with Elliot?"

She smiled. "I guess not. But if you want the gory details, I need more coffee."

While Joey got her refill, I realized how hungry I was. I toyed with the idea of a falafel burger plate special, but opted for pistachio ice cream with granola on top, which had a healthy ring to it. We settled in back at our table, just as I finished telling Joey about my new job as the *SoapDirt* dating correspondent.

"Good gig," she said. "Easy money, and you'll be charming. Did you know it was Elliot who told Jen Kim she should pitch that show to the network? I wonder if he was sleeping with her too? I'm so frazzled right now, I picture him sleeping with everyone, every business associate, every friend of a friend . . ."

"Back up," I said. "How'd you find out he's sleeping with anyone?"

"I've had little hints for months," Joey said. "If I'm being brutally honest, I saw signs of potential infidelity the day I met Elliot. I didn't bother to read them."

"You were in love," I said. "It comes with the territory."

"It doesn't come with your territory, okay? Don't take this as a cautionary tale. I'm sure Simon, unlike Elliot, is the soul of integrity. He's a government employee."

"Right," I said. "So who's Elliot's Other Woman?"

"Women. Plural. JetBlue flight attendants."

"My God," I said. "How . . . retro."

"The uniforms are cute. The thing is, it's a really good airline. Great snacks. I'd hate to have to boycott it just because it destroyed my marriage."

Vast quantities of falafel arrived at a nearby table, delivered by a large, aproned man.

"Do you have proof of these affairs?" I said.

"Laundry. It was right after I called you yesterday. I was so upset about David. I couldn't call anyone else, couldn't talk about it. I thought, What would my mom do right now? What would Wollie do? And there was a pile of laundry. So I did laundry."

"That is what I'd do."

"It was in his jeans. Elliot's. A printed-out e-mail from one of the flight attendants, a long letter forgiving him for cheating on her with the other flight attendant."

"My God," I said, coughing, as a small piece of granola got stuck in my throat.

"It's very L.A., isn't it? Forgiveness. There's so much therapy here. You don't see Frenchwomen forgiving their lovers like that. Or midwestern women. We know how to hold a grudge." She sipped her coffee. "God, this sucks."

"There's a Starbucks on the other side of Ralphs."

"Too exposed. So anyhow, I stupidly didn't say anything until we were driving to Rex and Tricia's. He didn't even have the imagination to deny it plausibly. So I knew. And he knew I knew. And I knew he knew I knew. And then we walked into the party."

She looked immeasurably sad. The adjacent table was tearing into Greek salads with gusto, and I thought of Sheffo, saying that Greeks were everywhere. I asked Joey if she was sure she didn't want some falafel, or a pita pocket, or maybe some frozen yogurt, but she shook her head. She glanced out the window behind us, then turned back to me.

"Okay," she said. "I'm ready to go, but I have a problem. Can you go over to Rite Aid and buy me a big hat?"

"Yes."

"And can you pay for this coffee I'm drinking?"

"Yes."

"And can we trade cars?"

"I have to drive your car?" I asked, alarm setting in. "Why?"

"See the Mini Cooper outside, parked parallel to us, first row over there?"

I could just make out a person in the driver's seat. "Is it stalking you?"

"Yes," Joey said. "He doesn't know I'm in here, but he's spotted the car."

I didn't need to hear more. I walked to the Topanga Canyon side of the strip mall, past the grocery stores and a dozen odd shops, ending up at an ATM machine. I then retraced my steps, acquiring merchandise as I went: a double espresso, a floppy hat, a cowboy hat, some tangerines, a half dozen protein bars, a previously viewed DVD of *The Great Escape,* three paperbacks, and a hairbrush. I had no idea where Joey was headed, but she wasn't going to die of scurvy, caffeine withdrawal, or boredom on my watch.

Back at the pita place, Joey knocked back espresso and told me her plan. "If I can borrow your car to get home, I should be able to lose the Mini Cooper. I just need my purse and credit cards to check into a hotel."

"I bet you can lose the Mini Cooper on the freeway in your own car," I said. "You're the best driver I know."

"No gas," she said, stuffing her hair into the floppy hat. "No ATM card, no money. And even if you lend me some, I stop at the 76 station, I'll have a camera in my face, and just look at me. A bad angle in direct sunlight? I'll look like a serial killer."

She had a point. Beauty aside, her eyes were bloodshot and she was getting that gaunt look that happened when she skipped meals. I could imagine a photo taken today juxtaposed with one of her *Vogue* covers, with the caption "Former top model stoops to murder and pumping own gas."

"If I'm lucky," she said, "something of national interest will happen soon, and David's murder will get buried in the back pages."

"Until the police arrest someone," I said.

Joey didn't respond immediately. "I can't worry about that. I just gotta get through the next few days. I don't want to be within shooting distance of Elliot, because I swear to God, I could kill him, but I need stuff from the house."

"Let me pick it up for you."

"No, it's better this way, with you in my car as a decoy. Can we trade jackets?"

"Sure." I handed over my blazer and tried on her leather coat. It wouldn't button across my chest. "Take some cash too. And why don't you stay with us? Simon's got room, and—"

"Nope. You're in the honeymoon stage. You don't need me hanging out."

Simon would probably agree. "Joey," I said. "On the news last night, David's housekeeper said you'd had a fight with him."

She looked startled. "When? Oh, Christmas Eve. That was just . . . nothing. A mild argument. Not even a blip on the screen, for us. I was back at his place Christmas morning." She sighed. "I went back again today to pick up some of my stuff, but I couldn't get in. The house is a crime scene, so the whole cul-de-sac is blocked off."

"What stuff?"

"Clothes, books, my Day Runner."

"God, Joey. It sounds like you were pretty much living there."

"I was, this month. He never liked being alone, and now that he was dying . . . And we'd gone so long without speaking, we wanted to make up for lost time."

I'd had no idea. I'd been too wrapped up with Simon. "And Elliot didn't mind?"

"Elliot encouraged it. As it turned out, he was rather busy himself."

I took a deep breath. "Joey, did you—I mean, you didn't . . . shoot David, did you? Not murder, of course, but—did David ask you to help him die?"

Joey's eyes filled with tears. They were wide-set and river green, eyes that looked like they'd stayed up too late and seen too much. "I didn't shoot him," she said. "Not for any reason. But I don't know if anyone in this town will believe that."

"I do." It unnerved me, seeing Joey so vulnerable. "Come on. Let's get you wherever you're going, so you can get some sleep."

Ten

I am not a car person. I'm certainly not an Other People's Cars person. So it was with anxiety that I pulled onto Topanga Canyon Boulevard in Joey's Mercedes.

The gas warning light was on, and I looked for a gas station that didn't require a left-hand turn. The Mini followed. I passed one mall after another, headed for Chatsworth, or somewhere. San Francisco. Anchorage. A phone rang in Joey's coat.

I checked a pocket and pulled out two dimes, some chewing gum, and a parking ticket, on the back of which was printed "**sudstud**," in sloppy pink letters. I turned it upside down and now it read "**pntspns**." I threw it across the seat and tried another pocket, and found the phone.

"Hello?"

"Joey? *Hot Spot* magazine, and we're interested in your side of the story and—"

"What story would that be?"

"How you reconciled with David Zetrakis after he fired you from *At the End of the Day* ten years ago, which was the beginning of the end of your career—"

"That wasn't the end of my career!"

"Really? That disfiguring facial scar wasn't a—"

I hung up.

This was bad. I was shaking with indignation, and I didn't have half the temper Joey did. She could deck someone. She might avoid a murder charge, only to be picked up for assault. I glanced in the rearview mirror. Yes, the Mini was still behind me. What if they took my photo, thinking I was Joey? What if I ended up in the *Los Angeles Times*?

Simon wouldn't like that. He wouldn't be crazy about someone following me home, either.

I'd been followed before, once or twice. By Simon, actually. This should be old hat by now, and I should be able to disappear in traffic. How hard could it be?

A gas station appeared on the corner; I pulled over to the right fast, cutting off a Honda minivan, which caused it to honk at me, which upset me. I missed the entrance, took a quick right on Sherman Way, and pulled into the station's adjoining car wash.

I zoomed up to the attendant, hopped out of the Mercedes, and handed him a ten-dollar bill. "If you can push my car through first, ahead of everyone," I said, "I'll give you another tip on the other side. Big hurry."

"What kind of wash you want?" he asked. "Silver? Gold?"

"I don't care. Whatever. Blue plate special. You pick." I was running toward the cashier when the attendant called me back, waving the invoice at me.

"What kind of air freshener?" he called. "Banana, vanilla, pine, coconut—"

"It doesn't matter. Banana."

"And Armor All?" he said. "On your tires?"

"Anything! Anything!" And I was off again, running into the convenience store to pay the bill. God knows how much this maneuver would cost, and I hadn't even gotten gas. Through the window, as I was talking to the cashier, I could see the Mini pulling into an adjoining parking lot. Out of the Mini stepped a very short man. He looked around, seeming not to see the Mercedes. Good. It worked. Joey's car was now hidden inside the car wash. But car washes are not forever.

The man reached into the Mini and pulled out not a camera, but a yellow legal pad. He climbed over the hedge separating the car wash from the mall and walked right toward the convenience store.

I was about to duck into the bathroom when I realized that a short man with a legal pad posed no clear threat to either Joey or me. I went out to meet him.

"Can I help you?" I asked.

He looked at me curiously. He had a happy, elfin face. "I don't know. Do I need help?"

"Are you following Joey Rafferty's car?"

"I am. But you're not Joey Rafferty, are you? No. Wait—" He looked at the leather jacket and frowned. "Have I been following you all along? From the church?"

"What church?"

"The Church of Religious Science. Toluca Lake."

"No, you've been following me from Ventura Boulevard." Now I was confused. "Are you a reporter?"

"No, I'm a lawyer. Here—" He reached into his sports jacket for a business card. "I saw you pull in here, so I figured you—Joey—was trying to ditch me, so I was just going to leave a note on the car." He wrote numbers on his legal pad and tore off the page. He handed it to me. "The business card's old. But that'll explain who I am. She'll know. Tell her we must speak, that my spiritual survival is at stake. And warmest regards to her. And to you too."

"And to you too." I remained confused. As he moved off, I glanced at his card. "Avram 'Ziggy' Ziegler, divorce attorney. Houston, Texas." I stared. Was this some new form of ambulance chaser, a lawyer who heard rumors of a troubled marriage and stalked the unhappy spouse to solicit business? I was about to call Joey when I realized I had her cell phone.

And, of course, she had mine, left in my Integra. I called myself. Joey answered.

"Never heard of him," she said when I filled her in on Avram "Ziggy" Ziegler. "Hey, some new creep is following me. Either he saw our bait-and-switch routine or you have a paparazzo of your own. Can I take you up on your offer? I just need a few things from home and I don't want to lead him to my front door."

"No problem." Twenty minutes later I reclaimed the now clean Mercedes and found the spare set of house keys she kept in the glove box. Joey kept spare keys everywhere, in anticipation of losing them.

I pulled around to the gas pump in Joey's car, filled Joey's tank with gas, and set out for Joey's house, deeply thankful that I wasn't Joey.

Eleven

The Pasadena residence that Joey and Elliot called home was so serious it had a name: Solomonhaus. It's a place you'd see in *Architectural Digest* and think, What kind of people live there? Even Joey, before she moved in, wondered that.

The answer, we now knew, was: one person obsessed with architecture and one willing to overhaul her lifestyle to go along for the ride. Joey's money provided the down payment, but Elliot was the obsessive, studying up on the 1920s modernist movement to live in it as Rolf Solomon, the architect, had intended. What would happen to Solomonhaus in a divorce? Easy to imagine Elliot fighting for custody of it the way other men fight for the children. Easy to imagine Joey walking away. Someday. Now she was more likely to burn it down.

Elliot's BMW was gone, but when I pulled into the driveway a Jeep drove in behind me.

I got out of the Mercedes as a man and woman got out of the Jeep. Our doors slammed as if synchronized. The man had a camera up and shooting before I could think what to do, and the woman hurried toward me.

"Hi. Miss Rafferty?" she said.

I was so taken aback to be mistaken for Joey this close up, I said, "What?" The man, perhaps taking that as a yes, kept filming.

"We're sorry for your loss," the woman said, with no trace of sorrow in her voice. "Can you tell us how you heard the news?"

"Who are you?" I asked, but it was a stupid question. Who else could she be?

"Have the police questioned you? Are you a suspect?"

I came to my senses and said, "Go away."

They didn't move. I raised my voice. "Go on! This is private property." The camera came closer. Amazingly, I wanted to kick the guy, and contented myself with stopping the lens with my hand. It was a reflexive response. A lifetime of watching news clips where celebrities and defendants put up a hand, blocking out the picture, now made sense. I also had a new understanding of that special L.A. pastime, assaulting photographers. Resisting the impulse, I ran to the front door, fumbling with keys, opened it, and slammed it behind me, locking it.

The house was cold, made of mostly concrete and steel, with wood accents. It was art-gallery bare. In the center of the living room was an unadorned fir tree. Its nudity was due not to post-Christmas undressing but to the fact that Rolf Solomon had not believed in ornamentation and, thus, neither did Elliot Horowitz. For that matter, Elliot didn't believe in Christmas. He'd spent this one in Vegas, on business. The tree was a concession to Joey's cultural sentiments, but it looked lonely and dysfunctional. Still, it had once been alive, which was progress. In their first year in Solomonhaus, Elliot had brought home a "fir" tree made of iron.

I stood, breathing heavily from exertion—I never exercise—and residual anger, and wondered how long this was going to go on for Joey.

Maybe it wasn't so strange to be mistaken for her. It's not that we looked alike, other than being tall and female; it was that those reporters didn't know her. Joey was a star only to people who remembered her acting work, mostly from her last TV gig, *Gun Girl*, but also the old *At the End of the Day* fans. That left out most of humanity. Even those who'd watched the news last night wouldn't know her this morning, so great was the difference between Joey all dolled up and Joey au naturel. She had a strong chameleon quality, going from plain Jane to glamour and back again with a change of lipstick and some pressed powder.

I moved aside a window shade to peek outside. The couple was still in the driveway.

Where could Joey live until the fuss died down? I could hole up any-where, if I had art supplies, but Joey would get cabin fever. I set about in search of creature comforts for her.

Solomonhaus was so bereft of personal effects, it was almost creepy. There were no books, for instance. Built-in bookcases, yes, only they held nothing but an occasional vase. Sans flowers. The house had drama with-out warmth.

What made all this unclutter possible was storage space; I found the cell phone charger in a kitchen drawer, a carry-on bag in a living room cupboard, along with her purse, and Joey's clothes in the bedroom closet, wedged in with surfing equipment. I plugged in her phone so it could get some juice before I left, then called Simon. "It's me," I said.

"Hey, beautiful," he said. "What are you doing?"

"Hiding from reporters."

"Why? What have you done?"

"Nothing, don't worry. They think I'm Joey."

There was a pause, the kind that told me Simon was censoring his immediate response. "Why would they think that?"

"Oh, who can say?" Actually, I could've said, but thought it best not to. "I just called in case you were trying to reach me. Because I have Joey's cell phone and she has mine."

"And the reason for that is—?"

"Complicated," I said. "Look, gotta go. Time is money." And with that aphorism, which no doubt had some applicability to some part of life, I more or less hung up on him.

The phone rang again, but I ignored it. It wasn't absolutely Simon, right? It could've been anyone.

This was going to be a problem. Simon, with an insistence that bor-dered on eccentricity, craved regular phone contact. I wanted to accom-modate him, but if he planned to worry over every unforeseen incident, then wasn't he better left in the dark? I thought yes. He'd disagree.

Joey had told me not to bother with anything except her running shoes, iPod, and purse, that she'd buy what she needed, but I packed two days' worth of clothes and sundry items, including a framed photo of her family that hung on the inside of a closet door. I imagined her brothers handling the reporters in the driveway with a few well-placed punches.

Or gunshots. Her sisters too. God knows what they'd do to Elliot. Judging by the stories I'd heard about the Rafferty clan, Elliot should stay out of the Midwest. Maybe leave the country.

I took forty-eight dollars from a piggy bank to pay the parking ticket I'd found in her pocket. No point in having her car impounded a year down the road, or whatever they do to scofflaws. I peeked outside again, this time from the bedroom window. The good news was, the Jeep was gone. The bad news was, Elliot was walking toward the front door.

I'd make a run for it. Out the back door and into the garden. The last thing I wanted to do was face my best friend's philandering husband.

The front door opened with a groan.

"Joey?" he called.

Damn. He'd seen her Mercedes. In fact, he'd parked behind it. What had possessed Rolf Solomon to design a driveway only wide enough for one car? There was no excuse for it. Even in 1924 people must have gone mad, forced to move cars every time the first person in had to go out. The strain involved in that! No wonder this marriage was crumbling.

"Joey!" Elliot called again, irritable now.

I could fit in the closet. But was social awkwardness sufficient reason to hide among Boogie boards and wet suits? Probably not. I walked out of the bedroom. "No, it's me."

Every time I saw Elliot, I was struck by his handsomeness, even though he had a face that suggested hard playing and late nights. Dissipation looked good on him, made him sexy. He was, by profession, various things, including a television producer, a venture capitalist, and a gambler. According to Joey, he'd made and lost small fortunes three times in two decades. He was currently doing very well. Financially. Emotionally, he'd probably had better days.

"Wollie. Hi." Irritation disappeared, leaving his voice weary. "Where is she?"

"I have no idea."

"What do you mean?" He glanced at the clothes I'd collected. "What's going on?"

"I'm taking stuff to her. She's going to call to tell me where she is. We traded cars."

"Why?"

"The press is stalking her."

He was back to irritation now. He pulled out his own cell phone, an impressive-looking gadget, and dialed. He listened, frowning, as her phone rang in the kitchen. He said, "Call me," presumably to her voice mail, then stuck the phone back in his suit jacket and nodded to my arm-load of stuff. "That's mine, by the way. Volcom."

"What? This baseball cap? I've seen her wear this a dozen times."

He said nothing.

"Elliot, you're not going to nickel and dime her now, are you?" I asked. "Please say you're not. There's no one more generous than Joey."

He had the grace to look embarrassed, running a hand through his close-cropped hair. It was dark, but with more gray in it than the last time I'd seen him. Well, the last time prior to Rex and Tricia's party. There, I hadn't been looking at his hair.

"Just tell her not to lose it," he said. "She loses things."

I thought of what Joey had lost in the last few days. David Zetrakis, anonymity, the freedom to come and go as she pleased, feeling safe in her own house, and illusions about her husband.

"Why did you sleep with other women?" I surprised myself, asking the question. Elliot intimidated me. Not by intent, just by being charismatic. Wealthy. A high roller. If he were a place, it would be Vegas or Monaco, while I was more Burbank. "I'm just curious," I added. "Joey didn't ask me to ask you."

He looked straight at me. "Ever been married?"

I shook my head, startled that he wouldn't know that. I certainly knew all about him, through Joey.

"Be easier to explain if you had. Let's just say it wasn't personal."

"Not personal to whom?" I asked. "Are you saying you don't care about those women, they meant nothing to you?"

He leaned against a wall, folding his arms. "One of them means quite a lot. We go back a long ways. Lotta miles."

"Frequent-flier miles?"

"Before the term was coined. That far back. What I mean is, it wasn't personal to Joey—it had nothing to do with her."

"Except that she's married to you," I said.

He scratched his day's growth of beard. "You're pretty straitlaced. You realize, don't you, that Joey's a little more . . . philosophical?"

"What's that mean?" I was getting defensive, but on whose behalf I wasn't sure.

"I intended to be monogamous. If I'd foreseen this, I'd have asked for an exception clause in our vows. I expect Joey would've agreed to it."

"Exception clause?" I said.

"You know. Where you each get one fling, one old flame. No harm, no foul. No questions asked."

I couldn't argue about what Joey would or wouldn't do. Like Fredreeq, she had a moral code, but it was all her own. "Except there were two flings, right? Two flight attendants?"

He looked away. "Jesus. You women tell each other everything, don't you?"

"Oh, well. In for a penny, in for a pound. Yes, I can see how Joey should just be a good sport and get over it."

He met my eyes again. "You know, Wollie, it's a bad time for everyone. Joey doesn't have a monopoly on grief. Everyone's upset about David."

That stopped me. "I forgot that you knew him."

"Longer than Joey did. He and I were in business together. I was part owner of the soap at one point. Played poker with him in Vegas a lot over the years."

What was that like, to play poker with a man who used to sleep with your wife? Who still loved her, and wanted her at his side as he lay dying? "I'm sorry," I said.

"My point is that decisions made now may not be the most well considered. Joey should keep that in mind."

"Elliot, I shouldn't have gotten into this. If you want to plead your case with Joey, you can do it better than I." I turned to go, then stopped. "Oh—she needs the green checkbook. Do you know where that is?"

He frowned. "What for?"

"She wants to send a check to Tricia and Rex to get their piano cleaned. Repaired. Tuned. Whatever."

"I'll take care of that. Tell her not to worry." He'd been leaning against a wall, but now he stood up straight, restless suddenly, ready to get on with the next thing. Joey described him as having the attention span of an eight-year-old, and I saw what she meant. People like that make me feel boring.

"Okay, I'll go now," I said. "Um, good-bye."

"I'll walk you out," he said, picking up the Volcom baseball cap, which had fallen. "Gotta move the car."

And that would have been that, except that he wasn't the last one in the driveway. A policeman was getting out of a car parked behind Elliot's BMW.

Twelve

I didn't realize he was a cop at first. He might have been an insurance salesman, a man on the far side of middle age, dressed in a suit with a knit shirt and no tie, moving as if his feet hurt, guy ambling into retirement. Elliot and I watched from the doorway.

"Detective Ike Born," he said, shaking hands. "You folks the Horowitzes?"

"I'm not. He is." For a moment, I thought he'd come about Elliot's infidelity.

He squinted at me, then reached into his jacket with a shake of the head. "You're not"—he consulted an index card—"Mary Josephine Horowitz?"

"My wife's not home," Elliot said.

Detective Born zeroed in on the personal effects I toted. "Going on a trip?"

"No. Well, Westwood." I got paranoid suddenly. "Me, not him. He was just moving his car. Elliot here. Horowitz."

"We met," Detective Born said. "You're welcome to tell me who you are."

"I'm Wollie."

"Live in Westwood, Wollie?"

"At the moment." I sounded cryptic, I realized. Perhaps even suspicious.

"How long have you lived there?"

"Three weeks," I said.

"And before that?"

"West Hollywood. Since August." Why did I volunteer that?

"And before that?"

"Los Feliz. Before that, Sunset, east of Highland. That takes care of this year."

An eyebrow went up. He reminded me of someone. Someone famous. "And what is it you do?" he asked.

"Greeting cards," I said. "And murals. Also, I date."

Detective Born's hand went back into the jacket for a pen. He made a note.

"Is there something I can help you with?" Elliot asked.

"When will your wife be back?"

Elliot glanced at me. "I can't really say."

"Where is she now?" the detective asked.

"Good question," Elliot said. "I have a call in to her."

"And what are you?" the detective said, scrutinizing me again. "The girlfriend?"

"Yes."

"No, you're not," Elliot said.

"Yes, I am."

"I believe he's referring to my girlfriend," Elliot said, "not Joey's."

"Oh." I looked at the detective. "Were you?"

Now the detective looked confused. "Joey's his wife, right? Mary Josephine Horowitz?"

"Yes. I'm her friend, not his," I said, which came out ruder than I intended. "If I see her before he does, I'll ask her to call you. Do you have a business card?" As he reached into his jacket once again, I said, "What's this about, by the way?"

Detective Born looked me straight in the eye. "Murder. It's about the murder of a man named David Zetrakis."

Thirteen

sped toward Sheffo Corminiak's in the clean, banana-scented Mercedes. I might've made my appointment on time, as rush hour isn't rush hour on weekends, but an accident on the 134 just past Glendale inspired me to try the 5 South, a freeway I've never really warmed up to, and sure enough, I found myself headed downtown, away from Mount Olympus. I did a fast exit on Los Feliz, only to get caught in a swarm of traffic headed to the Greek Theatre.

The Greeks. There they were again.

I called Uncle Theo. While he didn't drive, he was an excellent navigator. "Oh, my," he said. "You do find the circuitous routes. Go left immediately, dear, then take Franklin to Cahuenga to Mulholland. Go left on Woodrow Wilson, left on Nichols Canyon, right on Willow Glen, left on Jupiter, then left on Hercules, which will turn into Electra."

"Uncle Theo, I'm amazed," I said, jotting it down. This was easily done, as traffic was at a dead stop. "You're a human GPS, aren't you?"

"What is that, dear? Oh! I must tell you, I saw our Joey on the television news."

"What were you doing watching the news?" I'd forgotten my uncle owned a TV.

"It wasn't my idea, although I found those weather maps riveting. But is Joey in some sort of trouble?"

I explained about David's murder and Joey's involvement, how she'd found herself the center of media attention, and how unwelcome it all was.

"Oh, Joey needn't concern herself with that," Uncle Theo said. "Gossip. Tell her to don her metaphysical earmuffs and tune it out."

No toga-attired residents strolled the streets of Mount Olympus. No centaurs. Some houses in the well-to-do subdivision did look Grecian, with columns in front, and many were light-colored and boxy with red-tiled roofs, suggesting the Mediterranean. But others were just ratty, survivors of the sixties, like Rolling Stones album covers.

Not Sheffo's. His home was impressive, with a lawn so perfect it appeared to be vacuumed. White stone statuary lined the driveway, a veritable sculpture convention.

I parked in front of a two-car garage flanked by its own set of Greek columns—Ionic? Doric?—that lent it dignity. I made my way through the statuary to the front of the house, also with a lot of column action, and rang the doorbell, which produced a harplike melody. A lute, perhaps.

The door was opened by a tall man in a white Lacoste shirt. He had lush blond hair, a deep orange tan, and was seventy-five if he was a day. He showed no expression when I introduced myself. However, he mumbled something—it sounded like "stupid," but it might have been "insipid," or "skip it"—then turned and walked away.

Unsure of what to do, I followed. The house, what I could see of it, was antiseptic, with little personal style. We found Sheffo in the breakfast nook of a country kitchen, reading the paper. He looked up with no hint of recognition, but when I reintroduced myself as Wollie, the muralist, he said, "Yes, yes, I know. Navarre! Iced tea, please. Or do you take coffee, Wollie?"

"Oh, whatever you're having," I said.

"I'm having scotch," Sheffo said.

"Iced tea's fine."

Navarre moved, trancelike, to the refrigerator, and Sheffo tossed the newspaper onto a counter and escorted me outside.

The backyard, consisting of a garden, a pool, and a guesthouse, had all the personality the house lacked. The pool was rectangular, thin, built for a single lap swimmer, or as an excuse for more statuary. I did a quick head count: six white, larger-than-life statues faced six others, bordering each long side of the pool, with another statue at the head—I was guessing Zeus—and another—Mrs. Zeus?—at the foot. Fruit trees, vines, and flowers abounded.

To the right, separating Sheffo's property from the house next door, was a concrete wall, stark and ugly, twelve feet high, fifty feet long.

"Your canvas," Sheffo said. "Crying out for paint."

I breathed deeply. "Yes." The wall was an eyesore in its newness, grayness, lack of grace. That much blank space might not set a regular person's blood racing, but to an artist, it's like opening up a new sketchpad, the kind with heavy, textured paper. Impossible to leave it empty. "Yes," I said again.

"I had no choice. We have neighbors. Dreadful, terrible people. We tried reason, letters, casseroles, property owners' association intervention, and in the end, where once was a copse of Italian cypresses—" Sheffo covered his face, apparently blotting out a horrible memory, then got himself under control. I looked again and noticed, in front of the wall, a line of tree stumps scarring the lawn.

"So you built this wall," I said, "to block out the—"

"Wall? Did I call it a wall? My mistake. Erecting a boundary wall over six feet is not allowed on Mount Olympus. This is Art. And it's not on the boundary, it's set back thirty-two inches from the property line. 'Navarre,' I said, 'what shall this work of art be? Let it be a panorama of gods. Let us fill our backyard with numinous beings.'"

"Ah," I said, comprehension dawning. "What's the problem with the neighbors?"

"Don't ask."

We said nothing for a few moments, listening to the chirp of birds and faintly, almost subliminally, a crackle of voices from beyond the wall. Radio static? Navarre appeared with our drinks, my iced tea with a sprig of mint, served in a frosted glass. His orange-tan face remained expressionless, and my "Thank you" went unacknowledged, as did Sheffo's request for some of those white-chocolate Florentines they'd brought home from the bakery at Gelson's. He merely turned and walked away.

"Now," Sheffo said. "Have you read *The Iliad*?"

"No, remember? I'm Wollie, the Ignorant."

"You'll want to do that, of course. Navarre will give you keys, and you may come and go as you please. As long as you're quiet, you can work through the night. Floodlights, whatever you need. It won't bother us, we sleep with nightshades."

"When do you want this done?" I asked.

Sheffo lifted a gnarled finger. "Shall I dictate to the gods? When the story is told, the painting will be done. We do have to appear in court in early March, however, with your work as evidence. Bring your sketches to the set, if it saves time."

"I assume you have a private dressing room?" I said. "Someplace we can work?"

"Oh my, yes. And it's the biggest dressing room, despite the best efforts of a certain diva who shall go unnamed. *Ribbit, ribbit.*" He cleared his throat. "Although now, with David dead, I shall have to rouse myself and court the new regime. A bad, bad business. Did you know David, our producer?"

"Yes. I met him years ago, through Joey Rafferty."

"Joey and David." Sheffo lit up. "Our own Simone de Beauvoir and Jean-Paul Sartre. Tempestuous pair. The passion, the drama, the ménages à trois. Navarre will remember. Decadent, never sordid."

"M—ménages à trois? Threesomes?" This was the first I'd heard of it, and it wasn't the sort of thing Joey would keep from me.

Sheffo waved his hands. "So it was said. One can't be sure. David had an appetite for adventure, but he had to be the center of attention. Losing control of people drove him mad. Of course, he was half mad to begin with. Whom the gods wish to destroy, they first drive mad."

"Mad with power," Navarre said. I turned to see him bearing a silver platter with a lace-paper doily on it, upon which were lacy white cookies. "Whom they wish to destroy, they first drive mad with power."

"There's no power involved," Sheffo said. "It's simple madness."

"Mad with power." Navarre's face didn't move, but his tone intensified.

"I think I know my Euripides," screamed Sheffo. Silence ensued, except for the faint radio static. "In any case," he said, his voice turning sweet as he plucked a cookie from the tray, "David suffered from a need to run things. That's what did him in."

"I understood it was a gun," I said.

"Yes, well." He chomped on his cookie. "They'll discover it had its roots in his need to dominate. His Achilles' heel. He quit acting when he saw he'd have more control as a director. Of course, in television, it's not the director that counts, it's the producer. So then he produced. If he couldn't be on top, he wouldn't play. He dressed it up in talent and geniality, but he needed to pull all the strings. That was his curse."

Sheffo seemed lost in reverie, but Navarre brought him back with one word: "Wall." I broached the question of money, which I'd considered while stuck in traffic. Sheffo had given me the wall's dimensions, so I estimated the time involved in priming the surface, researching the theme, dealing with variables like weather, lighting, and Sheffo's own personality, and came to a completely arbitrary figure of four thousand dollars. Discussing money is my least favorite pastime, so when Sheffo, before I could choke out my proposed fee, offered me ten grand, I grabbed a statue for support—some woman with snakes in her hair—and said, "Great."

We walked back through the garden and out to my car, which was when I remembered my other job. "Are we supposed to be dating?" I asked.

Sheffo did a double take and stopped. "What?"

"Max, your stage manager, said we have a date tonight. A publicity"—I didn't want to use the word *stunt*, but how else to describe it?—"thing."

Sheffo showed no sign of comprehension.

"For the show *SoapDirt*," I said. "Jen set it up. Jen Kim? Your producer?"

"That philistine." He actually snorted. "My dear, I don't do off-site publicity. Haven't done it in years. If they can't squeeze it in on the set, between scenes, then they'll have to live without it." He continued walking.

"Okay, but—"

"You must draw a line in the sand. The world will bleed you dry otherwise, simply bleed you dry. Have you a good agent?"

"I don't have an agent."

"Oh, my dear, you must. Every artist needs one. They're philistines too, of course, but they're *your* philistines. No one respects what we do, you see." He took my arm, steering me past a statue of a man and woman in an embrace that would've felt at home on the porn channel.

"What is it we do?" I said.

"We tell stories," he said, reaching my car and opening the door. "The noblest profession, the only one worth squandering a life on. We are the storytellers."

. . .

Simon sat in the penthouse living room, watching hockey with the sound turned off, cell phone to his ear. I approached him from behind the sofa and planted a kiss on the top of his head. His free hand reached up and caught my neck and brought it down, closer to his mouth.

I thought he was going to return the kiss, but he dropped his phone to his chest and said, "I want to talk to you." Then he let go of me and put his cell phone back to his ear and said, "More teams. Pull Manning and Zhrake off Darvis if you need to."

I was in the bedroom changing when he came in and tossed something on the bed. My own cell phone. How had that gotten here? Joey must've come by.

"Going somewhere?" he said.

"No, just getting into something more comfortable." I struggled out of Joey's leather jacket. I'd spent all day in my Jen Kim interview clothes, and now my body was begging me for flannel or fleece. "Was Joey here?" I asked.

Simon's fax machine started up with a click and a hum. He glanced at it, then back at me. "Yes. And Max Freund called. Twice. Your date is on for tonight. Eight P.M. He asked me to tell you that this message supersedes all earlier messages."

"He . . . called here?"

"Your cell. I answered it. I thought it might indicate how to reach you."

Well, that would account for the attitude. It was that quirk of his, about me being out of communication—forgetting my phone, not answering my phone, not returning calls. It drove him mad. Not mad with power, just mad. His own cell phone rang; he answered with "Yes" and went on to listen, turning his back to me. As if his face gave away anything without authorization.

I stopped unbuttoning the blouse I'd worn all day and zipped my skirt back up. When having a serious discussion with someone, you might be at a disadvantage if they're in a suit and you're in lingerie. On the other hand, it was nice lingerie. Matching, even, and how often does that happen? While I was pondering the clothing question, Simon turned back to me, ending his call.

"When did Joey come by?" I asked.

"An hour ago."

"Did you talk to her?"

"No. She left your phone with the doorman, who gave it to me."

"No note?"

"Wrapped around the phone. It said, 'Thanks. Ex-oh-ex-oh-ex-oh.' Any more questions, or do I get a turn?"

There was a bed between us, a whole king-sized thing with a duvet covered in black linen, and it looked to me like a playing field, and we were opponents of some kind, facing each other, he with his arms folded, not even resembling the guy who slept with me, and I wondered what kind of answers I'd have to give to his questions to turn him back into that guy, the one who called me "baby" and "angel." I was suddenly disinclined to work too hard at it. I didn't like being on the defensive.

"Ask away," I said.

"You're dating a guy named Max Freund?"

"No, I'm dating guys named Sheffo, Rupert, and—Trey. That's it. Like 'breakfast tray.' Max is the guy who set it up."

"Ah. And that would make Max . . . a pimp?"

"Well, if he is," I said, "that would make me a hooker."

"Want to tell me what this is all about?"

"Want to loosen your tie and not look like you're giving me a polygraph test?"

He didn't move a muscle. He had a gift for deadpan. It was probably useful when interrogating drug lords and the like.

"Okay," I said. "I was offered two jobs today, as a result of last night's party. One's a mural-painting thing. The other is . . . well, I guess it falls loosely into the realm of . . . social science."

"How loosely?"

"Very loosely. Okay, it's more along the lines of public relations. Marketing and promotion. Advertising. Well, show business."

"What are you talking about?"

"I'm the dating correspondent for a show called *SoapDirt*. I date soap stars, then dish about them on some talk show that no one I know has ever heard of."

He was no longer deadpan. He looked appalled. "And you're doing this why?"

"Money."

He looked around, made a sweeping gesture. "Are you starving? On the street?"

"I'm about to be broke. Your money and these circumstances don't count. I'm not comfortable being a kept woman."

"But this is comfortable. Some tabloid TV show where you—"

"I'm not sleeping with them, Simon. These aren't real dates."

"In the minds of the audience they are, and you are. Sex, Wollie. What else do you think they're selling?"

"What do you care what some housewife in Spokane thinks about my love life?"

He said nothing.

"I was doing bad reality TV when we met," I said. "This can't be any worse."

"Doing it once is one thing. Twice, it's . . ."

"A character disorder?" I was getting a little heated now, probably because I shared his gut reaction. "What's your problem with this? Personal or professional?"

His phone rang. He answered it, listened, looked at me, and left the room.

I felt like kicking the bed, but I was in bare feet and didn't want to hurt myself, so I put on a high heel, then kicked the bed. I went into my walk-in closet and stared at my suitcase. Changing into sweats was out because that would definitely put me at a disadvantage, homely sweats versus well-tailored suit. How does one dress for arguing? Forget my date; I'd figure that out later. I needed an interim outfit.

I chose jeans and a T-shirt. Black.

When I walked into the living room, Simon was gone. On the kitchen counter was a note. "Emergency at work. Back later," it said. No "xoxoxo." Not even a "Simon."

I crumpled the paper into a ball and threw it across the room. It hit the TV. Hockey played on.

Fourteen

ulio, a uniformed chauffeur, saluted me. A lot of that went on in Simon's condo building, excessive servitude and uniforms that served no function except to announce one's place in the hierarchy. Julio may have been sent by the studio, but he fit right in here at the condo lobby done up in marble with fussy furniture that no one ever sat in and featuring a huge white-flocked faux tree and an electric menorah. I was in the wrong neighborhood. When I dreamed of lovers riding off into the sunset, I never imagined them ending up in a high-rise on Wilshire, being saluted by people. I had to get out of here. But I didn't want to not live with Simon, if living together was what we were actually doing. Simon didn't seem to mind being saluted. I wonder if people did that in his office.

Julio drove me north, to the crowded parking lot scene at Duke's Malibu, on the ocean side of Pacific Coast Highway. Max Freund opened my door, and I stepped out into a squint-inducing light. I could make out a camera, so I worked at not futzing with my tube skirt and a sweater that didn't want to cover my belly button, an outfit approved via phone by Fredreeq.

Then an arm was around my waist and a kiss placed upon my lips by a man I did not immediately recognize. He turned out to be Rupert Ling, my date.

What I hadn't noticed about Rupert up till now was how much taller I was, especially in heels—possibly because we hadn't been kissing before.

Max, himself a veritable Ajax, size-wise, noticed it too. "Let's do a closing kiss," he said, "and then we'll leave these two to their date. Apple box, please!"

A small wooden box appeared at our feet. Rupert stepped onto it.

"Half apple," Max said.

Rupert stepped off. The box was topped with a second one, half its size. Rupert stepped on. He now looked down on me from a height of about six foot five—Simon's size—and kissed me again. It was a fairly aggressive kiss, but he kept his mouth closed, the way I always imagined people kissed in the 1950s, as though tongues weren't discovered until the sexual revolution.

"Good-bye, gorgeous," Rupert said, then turned to the lens and winked.

"Okay, got it," the camera guy said.

"Great," Max said. "Camera's wrapped, and you two have dinner reservations."

"But—" I raised my hand. "What's happening?"

"Oh, sorry. No one explained it?" Max laughed. "We just need a bit of footage for the segment, a visual to play on a screen behind you during the interview with Tricia about the actual date. Like a newscast, to give it all a documentary feel. We film the moment you meet, and then the end of the date. Now you two have dinner off-camera. The check's paid. Rupert, you're on the clock till ten-thirty, but stay as late as you like. Wollie, the car's yours for the evening, so if you want to hit the town, your driver will be happy to oblige, but don't go out of state. Have a good date."

The crew, lights, camera, equipment, and stage manager faded into the night. I turned to Rupert, who now seemed not to know me at all.

"Wollie," I said, extending my hand.

"Rupert," he said, shaking it. "We've met, right?"

"Twice."

This exhausted our conversational repertoire.

. . .

The first twenty minutes were painful. We spent a lot of time looking out Duke's windows onto the dark surf. Periodically, I'd ask questions, and Rupert would answer. Economically, as though he were on a sentence-conservation program. Did he have hobbies? Karate. Ever been married? No. Character on the show? Chief of police. He seemed young for a police chief; had he done any research? No. Favorite movie? *X-Men*—the first one, not the last two. This was his longest sentence.

The problem was, I had only a vague idea of what I was doing, what sort of data I needed for a *SoapDirt* dating correspondent segment, and this had me acting like an uninspired interviewer. Rupert, not surprisingly, appeared to regard me as some dullard foisted on him by his publicist.

When the waiter brought the wine list Rupert came to life and I went to the bathroom. There was a line there, so I stood in the hallway, avoiding tray-bearing waiters and checking out framed photos and press releases of the eponymous Duke. He'd been a renowned surfer who rode mile-long waves in Waikiki, rescued eight drowning men with his surfboard at Newport Beach, and was fantastically photogenic through it all. Even as an old man, his thick hair turned white, Duke Kahanamoku still had it going on. Simon would be like that. I turned on my phone to see if he'd called, maybe wanting to make up or something. The sole message was from my brother, P.B., calling from Rio Pescado, the state mental hospital. I called back, but the ward's psych tech said he'd gone to bed. I called Joey's house and got her machine. Ditto Fredreeq. And Uncle Theo. I went back to studying the wall.

When I returned to our table Rupert was arguing the merits of cool-climate syrahs over the Central Coast pinot noirs the waiter was championing.

"You remind me of David Zetrakis," I said, reclaiming my seat. "The first guy I knew who was serious about wine."

"You knew David?"

"Joey introduced us, years ago. We dated for a few weeks."

Rupert's face softened. "My last conversation with him was about screw tops. Did David ever show you his wine cellar?"

I nodded.

"He must have liked you, then. His brother inherits it. Charles. Along with the rest of David's estate, and just in time. Charles's winery, Artemis, is—or was—up for auction next week. Have you been to it, in Paso Robles?"

"No."

Rupert glowed. "Incredible. Charles tried to get me to invest, but Artemis looked like a sinking ship. And anyway, once I saw it, I wanted my own. There's a parcel for sale to the north, near San Miguel. My plan is, buy now, work one more soap contract, then move there and start my label. Jen and I are looking into export possibilities with Korea. You met Jen Kim, right? We're scouting out backers."

"So Charles needed money?" I said.

"Oh, yeah. Then. Not anymore."

"But couldn't David have helped him?"

"Ah, that's the question." Rupert's eyes lit up. "There's a story there. I just haven't figured it out yet. I'll tell you this: David was generous, but only on his terms, and he always got a receipt. He kept score. Jen was his protégée; she got the receipt part down, but she missed the generosity lesson." He regarded me. "So tell me your name again. You smell good, by the way. When I kissed you."

"Thanks. It's Wollie. Me, not my perfume. Hey, you know who's always looking for investment opportunities?" I asked. "Joey's husband."

He looked struck by this. "You're right. I never thought of that. If Elliot Horowitz backed me, I could leave the show at the end of this contract."

"Are you so eager to go?"

"Eventually. But the money's too good, and the more I want out, the more they keep throwing at me."

"How dreadful for you," I said.

He smiled. "I like you. You remind me of my fifth-grade teacher. Miss Melon."

And just like that, I was his new best friend. We sipped a Riesling from Australia with our spicy sugarcane shrimp, switched to a Sonoma chardonnay with our lobster tail, and by the time we'd arrived at a Napa Valley port and a shared slice of hula pie, I knew about Rupert's mother, who taught jujitsu, and his father, who owned a car dealership. Rupert himself had been a world-class gymnast and still considered himself an athlete rather than an actor, even after a decade on *At the End of the Day*.

"It's like one really long endorsement contract," he said, holding the port up to the light. "Better than coaching. I was washed up at twenty-two for competition. Bad ankle. Actors complain all the time, but they don't know how easy they've got it. Try training for the Olympics."

"I've met actors who'd happily train for the Olympics if they thought it could get them work on soaps," I said.

"Actors are deluded. There's no job security in soaps, any more than in sports. Once you hit forty, you get edged out by the young and the skinny."

"What about Sheffo Corminiak?" I asked.

"Okay, there are exceptions. But Sheffo used to work four out of every five episodes, back in the day. Now they trot him out a few times a month. For February sweeps, they're nuking him."

"What?"

"The Moon Lake nuclear disaster. You haven't heard?"

"Sorry. I don't watch the show."

"Who does? It was David's last big storyline. He planned to kill off six characters for sweeps. Then Jen took over. Now four of them survive. Tricia, Trey Mangialotti, and two noncontract players. Jen doesn't have the balls David did. She won't piss off fans. David was ruthless."

"But Sheffo?" I said, disturbed. "He's really dying? Does he know?"

Rupert shrugged. "He had a good run. Everyone's expendable—look what happened to Joey, ten years ago. If you don't have a Plan B in this business, you're stupid." He sipped his port. "Now. Tell me about you."

I thought of a new greeting card—*Sorry they killed your character*—but decided there was no market for it outside of Hollywood. I turned my attention back to Rupert and the story of me. Which turned into a description of Simon.

"Is he the one?" Rupert asked.

"I want him to be." It was a relief, telling Rupert what I couldn't tell Simon. I hadn't even said *I love you*, being stricken by Single Girl Superstition Syndrome.

"What else do you want?" Rupert said.

"A baby," I said. "And I want my family and my friends to be happy. I want a career with some financial stability. And a house, one I can mess up and fix up. I'm not made for a furnished condo with no room for improvement."

"And this guy—does he have room for improvement?"

"No. At the moment, he is completely perfect," I said, my earlier argument with Simon forgotten, compliments of the wine.

Rupert smiled. He took a forkful of our hula pie and held it up.

"That's your Olympics," he said. "Go for it and don't think about the competition." He floated chocolate and whipped cream toward my lips.

Competition? What competition, I wondered as I opened my mouth and ate it.

At ten-fifteen, Rupert shook the hands of the waiter and the hostesses, autographed someone's menu, and escorted me to Julio's limousine, seemingly unimpaired by the wine. "The trick is to taste," he said. "I rarely finish a glass, let alone a bottle. Save the hangover for a wine that matters." He kissed me on the cheek, told me again how nice I smelled. "By the way," he said. "Who do you think killed David?"

It was such a non sequitur, I blinked. "Not a clue."

"I heard he recently freed up some big bucks."

"What's that mean, 'freed up'?" I asked.

"Liquidation. Turned toys into cash. You've seen his house, all the expensive junk he had lying around? Tricia saw some of his things in the Christie's auction catalog, but said that David got very cagey when she asked him about it."

"What do you make of that?" I asked.

"A couple of things occur to me. Blackmail money. Or a payment, for someone to shoot him."

"You mean like—assisted suicide? Using a hit man?" I said. "How much would that cost? And blackmail? Who'd blackmail him? Why?"

"So you haven't heard anything about this?"

"No," I said, feeling I was disappointing him. "Should I have?"

"Joey's auctioned off things at Christie's. I assumed she gave David the idea."

I shrugged. "Maybe. But why would he hire a hit man if he was dying anyway? Was he in pain? Was he just not dying fast enough?"

"Joey will know," Rupert said, handing me into the limousine. "She knew everything that went on in David's life this last month. Ask her."

And before I could say "But why?" the door closed, and I was transported down the coast toward Westwood.

Fifteen

woke Sunday alone. Hungover. I hit the playback button on the phone machine next to the bed that was connected to Simon's guest line. There were two messages.

"Dear girl!" Uncle Theo said. "Of course you may borrow my books. Come! My library is yours. Delightful people, Greeks. And such good cooks. As you'll see."

Whatever that meant. The next voice was Simon's. "I'm at work, but where are you? Asleep, I hope, because if you're out rescuing friends, then I'm worried, and if you're awake but not picking up, you're in big trouble. . . . All right, look. Let's talk about this job of yours. Do me a favor, just don't sign any contracts. It's Sunday, so that shouldn't be too hard. I miss you."

This was better. That "I miss you" covered a multitude of sins. He wasn't mad anymore, and I was already fuzzy on why I'd been mad. Maybe I hadn't even been mad, merely countermad. The main thing was, we'd averted a major fight, or survived a minor one, whichever it was. It wasn't our first fight, but it was the first we'd had since living together, and working out battle etiquette was critical to relationship longevity. Or so I assumed. I'd never really had relationship longevity.

Although I had had a fiancé earlier in the year. We'd had our share of conflict in our months together but a high compatibility factor overall, until the day Doc called off our engagement. It was nothing personal. He had to go halfway around the world to retrieve his adolescent daughter from his estranged, deranged wife, and he wasn't sure how long it would all take. Six years, at most. Too long for me to wait around, he'd decided. Unilaterally.

I lay in bed, staring at the excessively high ceiling and wondered how Doc would feel about Simon. Not good, probably. Aside from the fact that I was having great sex with him, my new boyfriend was many things my ex-fiancé was not. Tall, for instance. Wealthy. An FBI agent. Doc was an ex-con.

As for Simon, he knew about Doc from whatever sources the Feds use to find out these things, and had expressed the opinion that any man who's got a wife has no business shacking up with another woman. End of story.

It's a philosophy I share in theory, naturally. But stories don't start and stop cleanly, not like crossword puzzles or income tax statements, where answers fit in small boxes. Romance, families, and domestic arrangements—these, in my experience, are sloppy, overlapping, and riddled with exceptions. Still, I'd been an adulteress. Technically. Party to adultery. It's not a highlight on life's résumé. If I'd thought that Doc's marriage had one last gasp in it, any reason that a divorce wasn't immediately forthcoming, I'd never have fallen for him so hard. So . . . consummately.

On these grim thoughts, I got dressed, downed some toast, fussed over six nearly finished greeting cards—since it was December, I was working on Father's Day and Fourth of July—and set out for Glendale.

The Sunday morning traffic was light, and my thoughts turned to Joey, especially since I was in her car and had her phone. The phone's battery had died, though, and there was no charger in the car, so I turned on my own phone, hoping she'd contact me. Almost immediately it rang. It was my brother.

"Wollie, I'm not moving," he said.

I took a deep breath. "To Haven Lane? P.B., what's the problem?"

"They have a different zip code."

"Yes, true, but—"

"I don't like it. I won't like the phone number either."

"But the area code's the same."

"It is?"

"Yes. And if you don't like the number, we'll get you a cell and you can pick the number."

"I can pick it?"

"I think so. Within reason."

"What's the phone number at Haven Lane?"

"I don't have it with me," I said. "I'm in the car."

"Call me when you know," he said. "Or just add up all the digits and tell me that." With that, my brother hung up. Thank God. Another tragedy averted.

I looked for something to write on and found Joey's parking ticket, the one already scribbled on, and wrote as I drove: "call PB: Haven Lane #." Traffic slowed and my phone rang again. Alerting me to unretrieved voice mail.

This was one more thing I didn't understand about technology: why it was that my phone would call at random moments to tell me about voice mails left hours, even days earlier. This one, for instance, had come in last night, from Joey. How could that be? Hadn't I had my phone on all night? "I'm in hell," she said, "although hell's not so bad in a great ho- tel. I met a guy here who knows me, so he put my room on his credit card. I always know someone at Shutters, it's the wildest thing—oh. Didn't mean to tell you where I am. Don't tell the cops. If they ask. I'm hiding."

I called Shutters. They connected me to Joey's room, but there was no answer. I called Fredreeq and repeated Joey's message.

"Delete it," she said. "I don't know why she's hiding from the cops but I don't like the sound of it and—wait! You're in the Mercedes? Look in the backseat, tell me if you see a pair of purple sling-backs."

I turned. "Yes."

"Praise Jesus, I thought I lost them. Where are you right now?"

"The 101, almost to the 134," I said. "Headed to Uncle Theo's."

"Perfect. I'm on Sepulveda, at my cousin's Costco. Franzeen. You've met her. Give me Uncle Theo's address and I'll meet you."

Uncle Theo lived in Glendale near the freeway, on a street with no distinction and no ambition to better itself. I'd been visiting him there for so long I found it appealing. Fredreeq did not. After liberating her shoes from Joey's car, she accompanied me into Uncle Theo's apartment to use the bathroom, against her better judgment. In the elevator, we played Name That Smell.

"Food fried in old oil," she said. "And wet dog."

"Egg rolls," I said. "And diesel fuel."

"Nothing against Uncle Theo," she said upon seeing the fourth-floor hallway, "but if I walked out my door to walls this color, I'd hurl myself out the window."

"Don't worry. Inside the apartment it's wallpapered." My uncle hung wallpaper for a living, and forty years had not dimmed his passion for it. I had my own keys and unlocked the door to No. 411 without bothering to ring the bell, as the bell never worked.

Screams greeted us.

For a moment I thought I had the wrong apartment. A sea of faces, none of them Uncle Theo's, stared at us. One provided the screams and others spoke in a language I couldn't place.

Uncle Theo emerged from the kitchen wearing striped pajamas. "Olympia, what is it?" he asked, then saw me. "Wollie! And Fredreeq. How delightful. Panos, Pericles, calm yourselves. This is not the INS, these are loved ones. INS, no, no, no." Uncle Theo waved his hands in a manner meant to be calming, then gave Fredreeq and me exaggerated, Kabuki theater hugs. "See? No immigration. Not police. No, no, no."

The screaming stopped. I saw that the living room floor was covered with bedding, and the furniture moved aside. "Uncle Theo, who are your guests?" I asked. They were Greek, that much was obvious. *You'll now begin to see Greeks everywhere,* Sheffo had said. Even in Glendale, apparently.

"It's Plato's family. Just a few relatives, the overflow from his apartment."

My uncle's friendship with Plato Nikopoulos dated back to the seventies, meaning his family was . . . our family. "And they're living here?"

He nodded. "For a few weeks, until they find other housing."

"Are they . . . legal?"

Uncle Theo patted the back of the formerly screaming woman. "Apollo is," he said. "Olympia's son. As for the others, their English is not quite up to speed, so it's a bit sketchy. I thought you could open *your* home to two or three of them, but they don't like to be separated."

Thank God for that. I could just see springing on Simon a busload of people whose mastery of the language was limited to the word *immigration*. Fredreeq, bereft of speech, went off to find the bathroom.

"Now, my dear," Uncle Theo said, "I have practically no books on the Greeks, I'm ashamed to say. I must've given some away, because I'm down to a translation or two of *The Iliad*, one *Odyssey*, a *Bulfinch's Mythology*, of course, some Sophocles, a little Aeschylus, Rilke's *Sonnets to Orpheus*, a few Kazantzakis novels, if only I can put my finger on them . . ." He stepped over a prone body watching a tiny television to reach his bookshelves. These were filled to double and triple capacity, requiring a front layer to be removed in order to reach the ones in the back. I envisioned an all-week search.

"That's way more than I need." I explained the mural on Mount Olympus.

"Sheffo Corminiak?" Uncle Theo said. "Years ago, I saw him play Prospero. He seemed quite old then. So he's not dead yet?"

"No. And I've got to finish his wall before he is. What I need most is a general book on mythology, to tell me who everyone is."

Fredreeq came out of the bathroom and said a quick good-bye, whispering that she had to escape before her clothes took on the smell of hummus.

"Lovely girl," Uncle Theo said, putting on reading glasses. "Now, then. Mythology concerns itself with three classes: gods, heroes, and royalty. The definitive story incorporating all these is the *Iliad*."

"Sheffo said so too, but it sounds . . . long. And dull."

"Oh, dear no," he said. "With the proper translation, it's a page-turner."

"It's a war story, right? I don't do well with those. Can't I try the other one, *The Odyssey*? The boat trip. Travel writing. That sounds more fun."

"*The Odyssey*? A classic in its own way, but I strongly urge—"

"How about Cliffs Notes?" I heard the anxiety in my voice. "I'm not a fast reader."

"Cliff? I'm not familiar with the fellow."

Nor did I want to enlighten him. Instead, I accepted the Robert Fagles translation of *The Iliad*, which Uncle Theo said I'd fly through. "While the gods take up residence in you." He tapped my solar plexus. "Keep in mind that the Greeks were concerned with fame, above all. Power too, along with love, revenge, beauty, art, dance, drama, poetry, and wine, but always fame. That's what they lived for, and cheerfully died for."

"It sounds like Hollywood."

"Clever girl." Uncle Theo actually pinched my cheek. "Film, our gateway to immortality, can be—"

My cell phone interrupted us. Joey. "Can you meet me at the corner of Fountain and Fairfax?" she said.

"Speak up," I said. "I can barely hear you."

"Southeast corner. Upstairs room. Only if it's convenient. Can you?"

"Okay, but I'm in Glendale—"

"Gotta go, they're shushing me."

I hung up, kissed Uncle Theo good-bye, stepped over and around his houseguests, and departed, *The Iliad* in hand, along with Dr. Paolo Pomerantz's *Guide to the Pantheon of Greek Gods and Goddesses and Their Roman Counterparts*, the mere title of which exhausted me.

It took forever to get back over the hill and nearly as long to find parking, but within an hour I was on foot, approaching the southeast corner of Fountain and Fairfax.

This was residential Hollywood, with duplexes and apartments, a little grungy, with sad patches of garden, and window boxes putting up a brave front. I reached the corner and a building called the First Christian Church of Christ, which had a sign in front that said GIVE YOURSELF TO HIM AND HE WILL CARRY YOU. For some reason, I envisioned Jesus as a fireman, but erased the image. Nothing like an alternative religious greeting card to offend half your customers.

My own religious feelings were murky. My "conscience" had always been Ruta, who'd taken care of P.B. and me in our childhood. I'd heard her voice years after she'd died, telling me what to do when I least wanted to hear it. Lately, though, she'd been silent, and I didn't know why. Did spirits go on sabbatical? Could I advertise for a new one? Did I want one? Did I even believe in spirits?

On the steps of the church people smoked cigarettes, surrounded by coffee cans full of sand to catch the butts. They didn't strike me as the normal churchgoing public, but now that I thought about it, I didn't know much of the churchgoing public.

"Anyone know Joey Rafferty?" I asked. No one did. I squeezed around bodies rooted to the steps and made my way inside.

The church interior was nearly black after the blinding sunlight, but I stumbled to a bulletin board and found a schedule. As it was now Sunday at noon, church services were over, but I had my pick of meetings: Gamblers Anonymous, Sex Addicts Anonymous, Overeaters Anonymous, and Alcoholics Anonymous. Meeting locations were listed by room number. I went upstairs with a pretty good idea of which Anonymous category my best friend fit into.

The sound of a microphoned voice drew me to a small auditorium. It was packed and sweltering, even in late December. I entered from the back, passing a table laden with industrial-sized coffee machines and paraphernalia, plus trays of cheap, store-bought cookies being picked through by a middle-aged man as though he might encounter a homemade madeleine among them.

A woman in a suit stood at a podium, describing an encounter she'd had with eggnog. People laughed, appreciating a joke that went over my head. Joey emerged from the crowd, greeted me with rolling eyes, and led me out of the room.

"Interminable," she said, chewing gum at a furious tempo. "Horrible place. Thank God you came. Good thing I couldn't find a seat, because I can't sleep standing up, and if I could've, I would've. Did you bring my cell phone?"

I handed over her whole purse. "It's in there, but the battery's dead. Nobody called while it was working except a reporter. What are you doing here?"

"Oh, it's . . . nothing. It's stupid."

"Can we go?" I said.

"Yeah, another ten minutes. I parked your car three blocks away. Did you find parking? I should've warned you about that."

I glanced into the meeting room, where people were clapping again. I wanted one of those store-bought cookies all of a sudden, and a cup of coffee with a lot of sugar and cream in it, and I didn't even know why. "Joey, a detective came by your house yesterday," I whispered. "Elliot was there too. How come you're avoiding them?"

Joey chewed her gum faster and popped it. "I'll talk to them, but I'm putting it off until I can figure out what they already know, which is what I plan to tell them."

"What? Tell them what they already know?"

She looked over her shoulder, toward the meeting. "So I can seem forthcoming."

"But can't you just *be* forthcoming? Joey, have you done something illegal?" I whispered. "You can tell me. It's not like I'd ever reveal it. It's best-friend confidentiality, I'm like a priest. Also, Rupert says that David was selling his stuff—"

"Shh. Not here." She glanced over her shoulder again. The group rose to its feet with a lot of noise and chair shuffling. She turned back to me. "I trust you. I just can't talk about it. Wollie, things are going to get ugly. It might be better for you . . ."

"To disown you?"

She shrugged.

"Better for whom?" I said.

She shrugged again. I looked into the auditorium, where the alcoholics were holding hands. There was a collective drone, and even without hearing the words, I could make out the cadence of the Lord's Prayer. "Is that normal?" I asked, distracted. I couldn't recall the last time I'd heard a prayer. "Do they always do that at meetings?"

"Yeah, there's a lot of praying," Joey said. "So listen, I just mean that because of your situation with Simon, I don't want to put you in an awkward position—"

"Oh, yes, I certainly plan to ditch my girlfriends in order to make life easier for the guy I'm sleeping with—"

A shoulder bumped into my shoulder, throwing me off balance. "Sorry, babe," a man said. A kid, actually. I was about to say "No problem," having a weakness for being called "babe" by men ten or fifteen years younger then me, but now bodies poured out of the room, like they'd just been told to go forth and multiply.

"Hey, aren't you Joey Rafferty?" a voice called from the doorway.

"Oh, hell," she said. "So much for the great principle of anonymity."

I grabbed her arm. "Let's go."

"Yeah. No, I can't, I've gotta get something signed. We've gotta go back in."

We fought our way against the crowd. The room was still full, with some people talking in clumps while others folded chairs and gathered coffee cups. It had the ambience of a successful party, as convivial as Rex and Tricia's at a fraction of the budget. Joey and I joined a sort of receiving line snaking around the room's perimeter.

"It *is* you! I thought it was!" A ruddy-faced man joined us and pumped Joey's hand vigorously. "What are you doing here?"

"Guess," Joey said, letting her hand be pumped.

"Oh! Yeah, right! Of course." The man, who looked to be in his forties, turned ruddier still, then pumped my hand. "Harold Grackie. Alcoholic/addict."

"Wollie Shelley," I said. "Greeting card designer/muralist."

He looked confused, then smiled. "Me and Joey go way back. I did props on *E-Ticket*. Wild times . . ." I saw Joey nod, like she'd just figured out who Harold was. "Hey, how long have you got?"

"Till what?" I said.

"I mean, how much sobriety?"

"I don't know," Joey said. "What time is it right now?"

"And I'm not sober at all," I said.

"That's all right, Shelly," the man said, and I didn't bother to correct him. "Keep coming back. You too, Joey. Hey, there's a guy looking for you."

"Who?" she asked.

"Lawyer dude. Short. Suit and tie. New to L.A. Came up to me at Radford last week, heard I knew you."

"What's he want?" Joey said.

"Make amends. He'd been sharing about looking for this guy who's married to this actress—that's you—and someone else said they just saw you at the Toluca Lake meeting, and someone else remembered that I'd worked with you on *E-Ticket*, so this lawyer guy found me and asked about you. I said I hadn't seen you since the *E-Ticket* wrap party, you and me don't exactly run with the same crowd. Guess we do now . . ." Harold took out his wallet and rifled through it until he found a business card. He handed it over. "There it is. Ziegler's his name. Called himself Ziggy."

"Ziggy?" I said. Harold and Joey both looked at me. "I met him."

Joey looked at the business card, then at Harold. "Can I keep this?"

"It's yours. Know what coincidence is? God's way of doing business."

I glanced at Joey, who rolled her eyes so dramatically they were in danger of spinning back into her head. She saved her commentary until

Harold moved off. "It's those sobriety sound bites I can't stand," she said. "People talking like bumper stickers. Drives me to drink."

"Ziggy's the guy that followed your car to the car wash yesterday," I said. "First I thought he was a reporter, then a lawyer looking for business. Who is he?"

"Some anonymous creep." Joey shrugged. We were at the front of the line now, and she handed a slip of paper to a girl with so much body piercing I wondered if she tarnished. The girl signed Joey's paper and asked how she'd liked the meeting.

"Better than county jail."

"That bad, huh? It gets better. Keep coming back."

"Court card," Joey said by way of explanation, practically running down the steps, with me following. "I had a little incident a month or so ago, and a judge sentenced me to these god-awful meetings."

"What kind of incident?" I asked.

"The kind that involves driving."

"How many meetings do you have to go to?"

"Twelve meetings in thirty days."

"And how many have you been to?" I asked.

"Counting today? Two. But I still have five days to go."

"Or what?" I said. "They send you to jail?"

"Never mind that," she said, studying the business card Harold had given her. "Hey, know what's weird about this Ziggy, who thinks he owes us something? One, I've never heard of him. Two, he's from Texas. Elliot used to live in Texas."

"And three, he's a divorce attorney," I said. "He gave me his card too."

"I'll tell you what I wish he was," Joey said. "A criminal attorney. Because I will very shortly be in the market for one."

Sixteen

he Iliad began problematically. I was back in the penthouse living room, eating pita chips in the hopes that they would put me in the mood, but the book's preface was so intellectually dense, I needed Uncle Theo's advice.

My uncle, according to a heavily accented houseguest, had gone to work, so I called the wallpaper store. At age sixty-three, my uncle was their youngest employee and the only one still nimble enough to actually hang wallpaper, so he was usually out "on location," as they called it, driven by his eighty-year-old colleague, Clive. Since neither of them had cell phones, I left a message at the store with his boss, Pearl. Uncle Theo got back to me in twenty minutes.

"Hello, dear," he said. "Pearl tells me you're having problems with a preface?"

"And an introduction. To *The Iliad*. It's sixty-two pages. Can I skip it?"

"For *The Iliad*? Yes, dive right into the text. You'll be eager to read commentary later, swept away on a sea of adventures with Achilles and Hector and—oh, I envy you, reading it for the first time. An *Iliad* virgin, as it were."

"They sacrificed virgins," I pointed out, having begun Dr. Paolo Pomerantz's *Guide to the Pantheon of Greek Gods and Goddesses and Their Roman Counterparts*.

"Yes. Poor Iphigenia, hoodwinked by her father to get the ships to Troy. And gagged so she wouldn't curse the Achaeans with her dying breath. Dear, you are in the employ of the gods, telling this story. Read it aloud. That's the secret of epic poetry."

I hung up and took his suggestion. " 'Battles,' " I cried, " 'the bloody grind of war. What if you are a great soldier? That's just a gift of god. Go home with your—' "

"Excuse me?" The voice came from behind, sending me springing off the sofa.

"Ilse!" I turned to the cleaning lady. Cleaning person. "What are you doing?"

"I hear you yelling. I think something is wrong."

"I assumed I was alone. It's Sunday," I said irritably. Ilse, through no fault of her own, was young and very attractive, if you went for long, dark hair and lovely, pale skin. That she looked good even in a polyester maid's uniform added to my annoyance. And guilt. Bad enough that she should be forced by the Maids of Merit agency to wear a mustard-colored shirtwaist dress with a white Peter Pan collar, without the client's girlfriend having an attitude about it. But there you go. That's the difference between a saint and a greeting card artist. "Shouldn't you have Sundays off?" I sat back down.

"Yes, but the agency asks me to service a new client tomorrow," she said, "and Mr. Simon does not care if I change my day with him. I have arranged it with him."

The problem with Ilse and me, I realized, was that we were miscast. She had too much confidence for a minimum-wage menial, while I, given that same mustard uniform in a larger size, would feel more at home than I cared to admit. I couldn't even watch her clean without feeling I should be cleaning too. Thank God Simon had no real, full-time servants. I'd have to leave the building just to relax.

I went back to Homer. Twenty-two pages later, Jen Kim called.

"Where are you and what are you doing?" she asked.

"Westwood, reading *The Iliad*."

"Fine. We've got a hair emergency. Can you get over to 2306 Midvale?—north of Pico—cutting out—meet—explain when—leave now!"

What constituted a hair emergency? I wondered, reluctantly sticking a bookmark in Homer with five hundred and fourteen pages to go. I didn't want to go anywhere. It's not that I loved the penthouse, but I loved being around Simon's stuff. Away from it, I felt cut adrift. And his voice mail had a generic computerized greeting, so I couldn't even phone in for a voice fix. Oh, well. Work called. I went to find a sweatshirt.

In the bedroom, I saw an Ilse work-in-progress, a bottle of Windex and a rag on Simon's nightstand, along with a scrap of paper, a button, and a collar stay, debris found under the bed. I looked at the scrap of paper, taken aback to see the word "Zetrakis" scrawled there, and the letters "NV" underneath. And a number.

I dialed the number.

"Hello. You have reached the Las Vegas Division of the FBI. Our menu has changed, so please listen carefully—" I hung up.

Okay, what did this mean? The handwriting was Simon's. Why was he calling the Vegas FBI, asking about David Zetrakis?

I assumed that Simon was working undercover at the moment, although I couldn't figure out how spies could go undercover sixty or seventy hour a week, then come home to regular life under their own names. But undercover or not, Simon's current case couldn't have anything to do with David. The world wasn't that small.

On the other hand, all I really knew about his current case was that I'd know nothing about his current case till it was done and declassified, years hence. Fine. I could live with that. Maybe. But this was moonlighting, this had to do with me, so this was something he'd have to tell me about. Whenever I saw him next.

I wrote a note saying I missed him and had gone to deal with a business-related hair emergency. And added the four words everyone hates to hear: "We have to talk."

●　●　●

Twenty-three-oh-six Midvale was a darling house, jewel-like, with a white picket fence, a tiny garden, and a real Christmas tree showing through the window. Jen answered the door and introduced me to its resident, a woman with tired eyes and mouse-brown hair.

"Gloria is Tricia's very own hairdresser," Jen said. "She's generously given up her Sunday to do this for us, as a personal favor to Tricia. Tricia! She's here!"

Gloria nodded, unsmiling, and led me into a small room that looked like a beauty salon for one. She seated me in front of a wall-length mirror.

"What's the emergency?" I asked.

Tricia appeared in the doorway. "The wildest thing. We just saw dailies of your date with Rupert, and on film, your hair and mine are the exact same color."

"And—?"

Tricia came up behind me and talked to my reflection in the mirror. "We could be *hair twins*."

I was missing the significance of this. "And—?"

" 'And'? The show's host and the dating correspondent with the same hair? The audience will be confused. You don't *do* that to an audience."

"Tricia, I'm twelve feet tall, and you're tiny. We look nothing alike, and—"

"Height is irrelevant on television. Jen? Back me up on this."

Jen, chugging a diet soda, joined Tricia and spoke to my mirror image. "We'll just tone you down a shade. Play up your low-lights. Go warmer."

"You'll love it," Tricia said. "This ice-princess thing you have going on is so unnatural. Who does your color?"

"No one," I said. "This is my color. Also, my hair's very fine and thin and—"

"Gloria's a pro," Tricia said. "Let's let her weigh in. Gloria?"

Gloria put a pink plastic cape around me and snapped it behind my neck. "Color can add body to limp, saggy hair."

"I'm surprised no one's suggested it to you," Tricia said.

Beware, a voice said in my head. "Beware"? Who talked like that?

"Can we back up a minute?" I said. "I'm new to this, but I'm nervous about—"

"Wollie," Jen said. "Hair changes every day in this business. It's a production necessity. How do you think Marilyn Monroe became blond? Production necessity."

Production necessity. Meaning that for a thousand dollars an episode, I was being well compensated for qualms.

"Trust me. It's in no one's best interest to have you look less than fabulous." Jen patted my pink-caped shoulder. "I'll check back later. Wollie, you're a lucky girl. Gloria's the best. Gloria: less is more, okay?"

"She's already mixed the color," Tricia said. "I'm off too. Meeting Rex at Mr. Chow's. See you in a few hours."

"A few hours?" I said.

"Rome wasn't built in a day. Ciao."

And Troy wasn't conquered in nine years, I thought, opening *The Iliad*. I glanced at Gloria in the mirror, but Gloria was focused on my hair follicles. I settled in to read.

∘ ∘ ∘

I realize that most women in Los Angeles, and maybe the world, dye their hair, but I felt as though I had entered the laboratory of a mad scientist. It distracted me from the Trojan War. The smells were noxious and Gloria was not forthcoming, explaining only that my own color had to be stripped in order to absorb the new color. And no point in trying to imagine the final effect, she said, by looking at the goopy paste she was applying. So I went back to *The Iliad*, where the women, with unspecified hair color, were muses, goddesses, or the spoils of war, but the men had all the best scenes. Uncle Theo hadn't mentioned that.

Reading about the wall around Troy, I kept picturing David's gated estate, with his surveillance cameras and alarm system. Curious, I dialed Joey.

"Hey, Joey," I said, sliding the phone around the gray glop covering my ear. "Friday morning: weren't David's security cameras on?"

She paused. "As a matter of fact, they'd been down for days. A guy was supposed to come out Christmas Eve and fix them, but he never did."

"And the alarm system?" I said.

"David didn't like it on when he was home. And he was always home, at the end. Hey, let me ask you something—are you alone?"

I looked at Gloria, in plastic gloves, painting my scalp. "No."

"Never mind. I'll ask you later."

Any fears about my hair color now paled in comparison to my fears about Joey. She was being as tight-lipped as Simon, and very cagey. Why? If she hadn't shot David—and she hadn't—then why all the subterfuge? My head itched. I scratched it, near my temple, and my finger came away stained with brown. "How long have you been doing Tricia?" I asked.

"Three years. I was the show hairdresser for twenty-two years before that."

"You must be very close to her."

"Whose bread I eat, her song I sing," she said. Which wasn't exactly a ringing endorsement, if I understood it properly. And that ended Gloria's chatty moment.

An hour later, she shampooed me in the adjoining bathroom and was towel-drying me when Jen called out, "Hello!" and came to find us, her high heels on the wooden floor signaling her approach. I had not yet seen my hair. But when I moved the towel aside and saw Jen in the doorway, staring, I knew the news wasn't good.

"Holy Christ," she said. "What in God's name have you done?"

Seventeen

There are worse fates than a fluorescent orange head. Wars and natural disasters and world hunger. This is what I told myself, looking in the mirror at the damp strands.

"Change it," Jen said.

"I can't," Gloria said. "Her hair barely survived the stripping process. Anything I do now, she goes to brush it, she'll destroy it."

"My God, she looks like she's on break from clown college."

Tricia waltzed in, doggie bag in hand. "All done?" she said, then caught sight of me. "Why, it's lovely. It becomes her. Redheads are evergreen."

"Red?" Jen said. "It's orange, Tricia. Hi-C. Cheese curls. Construction cones."

I raised my hands in a "Stop, stop" gesture.

Tricia said, "Jen, it's not about any one person's look. My concern is the greater good of the show. This works. I know you'll see that when you're calmer."

Jen closed her eyes and took a deep breath. "Fine. But we have to reshoot her date with Rupert. Immediately."

"Why?" Tricia asked.

"Because she looks like a different person in last night's footage. I can't air that now, it's amateur hour. I'll make some calls, see what I can set up. Nobody leaves."

Leave? I couldn't even speak. I had no intention of leaving, for weeks. Months. However long it took for my hair to grow out. It was the consistency of cotton candy and it did not become me. It was a color that could only become . . . a carrot.

Jen came back into the room ten minutes later with a new plan, a new date. I listened with mounting panic. Dry, my hair was brighter still. A human flare. Radioactive. I knew this because no one was able to look at me.

*   *   *

I'd lived in the greater Los Angeles area my whole life without even knowing about Hollywood Park. Jen's assistant, Sophie, promised to stay in cell phone communication with me until I was safely there. "Turn onto Doty," Sophie said.

"Doty. Yes, here it is." And there it was, across a gigantic parking lot, a pink "Hollywood Park" sign in script letters, with a white Vegasy "Casino" that only the legally blind could miss.

"I'm going to put you on hold now and call Rupert and then call Jen and then get right back to you. It's all gonna be fine."

"Sophie, you're an angel." I was pathetically grateful for the reassurance, even from a nineteen-year-old who'd apparently been told to just get the crazy woman through seedy Inglewood at all costs.

Jen was in the parking lot, waving her arms like I was an incoming plane. She introduced me to a slovenly man who was sitting in a car with a cigarette clinging to his bottom lip. "Hackburg was kind enough to cancel his evening to help us out," she said as Hackburg flicked his car's headlights on and off. "Hackburg, don't screw this up. Sophie," she said to her phone, "get Rupert out here." She turned to me. "Okay. You're a little casual for the shot so I'll lend you my pashmina. This will be fun. Just don't cry or anything. Got lipstick?" She fussed with me, covering my hooded sweatshirt with a pink cashmere-like shawl. "There. A nice cowl effect. Here's Rupert."

I turned to Rupert, who looked like you'd expect a man to look who'd been interrupted during a poker game. He glanced at me with no recognition whatsoever.

Jen said, "We'll make this fast. Hackburg, throw some light on their faces. Rupert, just do what you did yesterday. Kiss her. Couple times, and we're outta here."

"Kiss who?" Rupert said.

"Her. Wollie."

Rupert looked at me blankly. Then his eyes widened and he started laughing. "Jesus. What happened to you?"

"Rupert, shut up," Jen said. "Hackburg? Ready?"

"Gotta use your car lights," Hackburg said, emerging from his car. "Hers too, maybe."

"Fine," Jen said. "Get that casino sign in the background."

"Hackburg," Rupert said. "What are you doing? Working on your merit badge in photography?"

"Rupert," Jen said. "Damn it, just start kissing, would you?"

Hackburg repositioned our cars, shining headlights into our faces for illumination. I closed my eyes and saw a condolence card: orange flames engulfing a hapless woman, with the caption *Sorry your life went to hell in a handbasket.* At which point Rupert started kissing me.

.   .   .

My mother considered poker an educational necessity, and so, like many random lessons from childhood, I had its rules firmly embedded in my head. This took up space that could have been put to better use, because I don't really play poker. Gambling, at even a penny a point, gives me heart palpitations.

Rupert led me through the casino, past the food courts, to the poker area. Beyond a quick glance at a badly done mural behind the deli sector, I kept my eyes focused on the tired blue-and-gold carpet so as not to see people reacting to my hair. "Come on," Rupert said, noticing. "Suck it up. It's not that bad. I'll get you a drink, you'll put in ten minutes, and take off. Just long enough to give a report on *SoapDirt.*"

He had a point. Easier to actually have a date than to pretend to have had one. I risked looking around and decided that if you're going to debut a questionable fashion statement, Hollywood Park Casino is the place to do it. The lights were too bright, but there was such a wide range of what was acceptable appearance-wise, I didn't merit prolonged stares. I did get noticed. Tables held nine players each, mostly men, and there were dozens of tables, with half the players finding time to check out the room. Some ate from TV trays behind them, stretching to stab forkfuls of Korean barbecue or eggs and hash browns, ketchup flying onto their shirts as they turned back to monitor the action. The game, I figured out, was mostly No-Limit Hold 'Em, which my mother had described as hours of boredom marked by moments of sheer terror.

We reached Rupert's table but held back, watching the hand. It was at the river and down to three guys, two of whom I knew. Clay "prop guy" Jakes and Max "stage manager" Freund stared at guy in a Hawaiian shirt with a comb-over, on the button, as he in turn stared at the board, a pair of sevens, a four, a king, and an ace. The Hawaiian shirt bet, Clay bumped it up, Max and Hawaiian shirt called, and Hawaiian shirt showed a pair of kings. Max tossed his cards to the dealer in disgust. Clay smiled slowly, turned over his hand, and said, "I got the boat. Sevens full of aces." The dealer, expressionless, pushed the chips toward him. Rupert patted him on the shoulder.

Max sat back, looked skyward, and shook his head. Then he saw me. "My God," he said. "And I thought *I* was having a rough night."

"Not her doing, Max," Rupert said. "This was the work of Dr. Tricia Frankenstein." Rupert introduced me to Clay, who obviously did not remember me from Tricia's party, and helped me into a chair, as though bad hair constituted a physical handicap. The other men at the table glanced at me, then away. I watched them play another hand, then headed to the ladies' room to call Fredreeq.

"You've done what?" she yelled, hearing about my experience.

"Not me," I whispered into the phone. "Them. Yes, I was duped, I'm an idiot. Listen, you know hair; I need you to tell me if it's fixable, because I don't trust Gloria. Also, how do I handle this vis-à-vis Simon? Can I come over? There's stuff I need to tell you about Joey and I'm not that far, I'm at Hollywood Park with Rupert and—"

"Rupert? *My* Rupert? You're hanging with Rupert Ling? Where, the casino? Don't you move. I'll be there in half an hour. Forty minutes tops."

I spent ten minutes in the bathroom, staring in the mirror, and when I could stand my own company no longer, returned to the poker table. The faces hadn't changed, but Rupert was in the game now and he and Clay seemed to be in excellent moods. Max did not; his good-natured charm was fading along with his stack of poker chips. Focusing on cards kept my mind off my hair, but Clay folded and said something to Max that got my attention. There was a steady stream of ambient noise, and I had to strain to hear. "Cops impounded the guns today," he said.

Rupert looked up. "What guns?"

"From the show. The ones we rent, from ISS. Jen called me at home last night to come in, open up the lockbox."

"I didn't hear anything about it," Max said, watching as the dealer dealt the turn.

Clay wiped his nose on his sleeve. "Jen told me to keep it to myself, till she works out how to spin it."

"And you're doing a heroic job of it," Rupert said. "Very discreet."

"Well, I just realized we got no guns for the Monday hostage scene. We'll have to go with replicas, which don't look right, or Max, you gotta hire a specialist, because ISS won't rent to me anymore. I lost my EFP over a reckless driving conviction."

"Bet," Max said, pushing forward a short stack of yellow chips. "No money for a specialist this month," he said to Clay. "Jen will say to use water pistols. The eighteen to twenty-four demographic won't know the difference."

Rupert laughed. "What's that sound? Why, it's David, rolling over in his grave. Why not borrow some guns from Tricia? She married a Texan— I'm sure he brought firearms into the marriage. Or wishes he did."

I was about to ask what an ISS and an EFP were when I caught sight of Fredreeq in the doorway. She wore a floor-length blue velvet dress and stood staring, fairly quivering. Only Rupert Ling's presence, I suspected, prevented her from screaming. She moved in silently, one hand outstretched. She touched my hair. I was aware of the men looking at us as their conversation faded into silence.

"Oh, please, no," Fredreeq whispered.

"Fredreeq," I whispered back. "This isn't helping. Tell me what I can do."

She gulped. Closed her eyes, opened them, and uttered one word: "Lawsuit."

•   •   •

Fredreeq bore me off to the bathroom to render a diagnosis, as the poker area with its backdrop of TV screens was too distracting. She studied me from all angles, felt my hair strand by strand, and even sniffed it. "Okay, it's bad," she said. "Here's the plan. No one comes near you with an appliance. No blow-dryer, no curling iron. With daily deep conditioning, maybe wrapped in plastic and covered in a wig, in six months you'll be good to go."

"Six months?" I gasped. "What do I do about Simon, take a sabbatical from sex?"

"First, break the news to him over the phone. Phase Two, he sees you dimly lit. Flashlight, candlelight, nothing too bright that evokes Ronald McDonald. Then—"

"Okay, never mind, I'll figure this out. Come on, let's get this date over with."

Back at our table, Rupert pulled up another chair for Fredreeq. Max had just lost a major hand, judging from the reaction he got from Clay, who called him a donkey. "You don't make enough to play junk cards like that," Clay said. Max, in response, hailed a yellow-uniformed chip runner to replenish his supply.

"The cops asked me today about David's medication," Rupert said quietly. "His nurse kept a supply of morphine at the house, and now it's gone. Has Joey mentioned this, Wollie?"

I looked at Fredreeq. "No. Why would she?"

"She's been David's majordomo," Max said, pulling out his wallet for the chip runner. "What did you tell the cops, Rupert?"

"I told them to check Clay's medicine cabinet."

Clay smiled. "I wouldn't turn down morphine. But I haven't been at David's since the first of December, when me and Max put up his Christmas tree for him. Max, what about you? Stockpiling drugs for your knee surgery?"

"Knee surgery?" Fredreeq said. "Do not get it done at Kaiser, whatever you do. My husband's cousin ended up getting his leg amputa—"

"No. Stop," Max said. "Don't tell me, I don't want to know."

Rupert laughed. "Max is a baby. Don't let his size fool you. He tries to dignify his cowardice by calling it a medical syndrome."

"LPT," Max said. "Low pain threshold. I am not making this up. But I don't do morphine; I barely function on Vicodin."

"What do you mean, Joey was David's majordomo?" I asked.

The table went quiet as cards were dealt, then picked up. "David gave Joey his power of attorney," Rupert said, breaking the silence.

Clay tossed down his cards. "She was on the set a lot, I'll tell you that. She got David to reinstate food and flowers in the wedding scene after Jen cut the budget for it."

I thought of Joey spending the Christmas season with David, with access to all of his life and work. Including his morphine, and Joey had a taste for mind-altering substances. Not needles, though. And she wasn't capable of stealing.

Only, would the cops know that? Or the media? And if they were told, would they believe it if the information came from Joey's friends?

Fredreeq was frowning. Maybe she was thinking along the same lines.

Because the answer, of course, was no.

Eighteen

The bedroom was dark when I returned. I'd already pulled off my sweatshirt and jeans in the living room, so as not to wake Simon, and now I carefully slipped under the covers and arranged a pillow over my head, praying to whatever god was on duty at that hour to save me from any more hair reactions until morning.

Simon woke but didn't turn on the light. He asked where I'd been and I said only, "Out with Fredreeq." I was bad at lying, but I was getting better at misleading.

Around midnight, the phone rang. I answered; it was Ali, the doorman, saying a woman named Joey requested my presence in the lobby. I whispered to Simon to keep sleeping, then tiptoed to the living room, threw on clothes, and headed to the elevator.

In the lobby, Joey and Ali were already buddies, eating tortilla chips and guacamole, although Ali stayed on his side of the desk and Joey stayed on hers, with the plastic container between them. I'd have bet that no human power could get Ali to eat on the job, but something about Joey made people let down their hair.

But not dye it orange. When she saw me, she did an audible intake of breath, and even Ali, trained in social discretion, went momentarily wide-eyed.

"You look like you need a walk," Joey said, looping her arm through mine.

"Walk?" I said. "I need a wig, not a walk. It's winter out there."

"Wear this." Joey gave me her heavy biker jacket, and then Ali gave Joey his black wool coat, none of which made much sense to me, but I was busy explaining to Joey how Tricia had deprived me of whatever dignity I'd once had.

"You can handle it," Joey said. "I once shaved my head to play a neo-Nazi. You get used to stares after a while. And look, lots of people have neon hair."

"Yes, fourteen-year-olds, trying to shock their parents." We walked out onto Wilshire. "Joey, this is life-threateningly frigid. It's gotta be forty degrees out here. Come up to the penthouse."

"No. I don't want Simon to know I was here and grill you later. I thought we'd talk in the lobby, but do you know how many monitors there are in that place?"

"A lot?"

"Ali's watching at least twelve." With a glance over her shoulder, she led me south on Thayer, away from Wilshire. We kept our heads down, as if we were making our way through Siberia. "Makes me paranoid. Hey, have the cops called you yet?"

"No."

"They will. They interviewed me today. And they've interviewed Elliot, and now they're going to interview you, checking out my alibi."

"What do you mean, alibi? Why are they using words like that?"

"I'm on their short list for suspects."

"Why?" This was exactly what I didn't want to hear. I put my arm around her, for bodily warmth along with emotional support. "What's your motive supposed to be?"

"I don't know yet. Possibly they think he asked me to shoot him. Assisted suicide. It crossed your mind too. It's not a big stretch. Anyhow, I just need to know—do you remember calling me Friday morning?"

Friday. I'd gotten up, gone back to bed with Simon, then gotten up again and phoned Joey to get the number of her mother in Nebraska, who wanted a boxed set of my greeting cards. There was no such thing as a boxed set of my greeting cards, so I'd wanted to explain to Mrs. Rafferty that there would be a slight delay while I invented one. "I called you around ten, ten-thirty," I said.

"Yeah. Do you remember if you called my home or my cell?"

"Home, probably."

"But you didn't leave a message on the machine?"

I thought back. "No. The machine didn't pick up. So I called your cell."

"So when I answered my cell, you didn't know where I was. I could've been at home. On my cell."

"No, you were in your car."

Joey turned to me. "How do you know?"

"You said your mom was on her way to Croatia on a cruise with your brother and you couldn't look up anyone's cell number because you were in your car."

Joey kicked a stick off the sidewalk and into the street. "Okay, that's bad. Did I tell you where the car and I were?"

"The 134 East. You mentioned it because there was a mattress in the middle lane, causing some problems."

She kicked a rock. "Worse than no alibi. Negative alibi."

"I take it that if you could prove you were home in Pasadena at the time David died, that would be a good thing?"

Joey rubbed her hands together. "A very good thing. It would also be impossible. The next best thing is if no one can prove I *wasn't* home when he died."

"Me, for instance," I said. "What time did he die?"

"Between nine and eleven Friday morning. That's when the cops asked Elliot to verify his whereabouts."

"Why would Elliot have a reason to kill David?"

We stopped as a car's headlights turned onto Thayer from Ashton Avenue, blinding us. "Elliot had no reason to kill David," Joey said. "But then, I didn't either. I have reason to kill Elliot, but that's another story."

I stuck my hands in my pockets, which were actually her pockets. "You and Elliot are on speaking terms?"

"He wanted to give me a heads-up to get my alibi together. He's thoughtful that way." She paused. "I don't want to run into him. I'm not at the top of my game right now, and he'll exploit that."

"Do you have to run into him?"

"I need some things from the house."

"I could pick them up for you."

"Yeah, I'm going to send you to Pasadena now, after giving you hypothermia. Anyhow, it's just Krav Maga gear, my boxing gloves and shin guards. I haven't worked out in weeks. That's probably why I'm out of sorts."

"Oh, yes, that must be it," I said. "As opposed to being a murder suspect. Listen, Rupert Ling said that there was some morphine missing from David's house. And that David auctioned things off to raise cash, to pay a professional to kill him."

"A professional?" Joey stopped and stared at me. Her face was white, her Medusa hair backlit by a streetlight, her body lost in the long wool coat. It was easy to see why she'd had a career in theater. Unexpectedly, she smiled. "That's great."

"Why?"

"Because I don't need money. If these detectives go with that as a motive, they'll have to find another suspect." She started walking again. I followed.

"But is it true? That David auctioned off his stuff?"

"Yeah, a couple of things he didn't care about anymore. He wanted to see how long it took to turn goods into cash; turns out it took too long."

"For what?"

"For someone who needed a lot of money fast."

I thought about what else Rupert had told me. "You mean David's brother?"

Joey looked at me, then away. "I can't talk about Charles. Not tonight."

"Okay," I said, puzzled. "What about the missing morphine?"

"No clue what that's about. Morphine's not my drug. My tolerance is too high."

"So what is your alibi?" I asked. "Where you were at nine or ten A.M. or whatever time it was? Before you got on the 134."

Joey took a deep breath, which turned into a fit of coughing, and from there into a sneeze. "Exactly the wrong place," she said. "I was in Toluca Lake. David's house. I was with David."

Nineteen

Sleep was impossible after Joey's revelation. I was so restless I woke Simon.

"How is Joey?" he asked, his voice low and sexy in the dark.

There was no point in asking him how he knew it was Joey I'd gone to meet. Like magicians, the Feds don't give away their secrets. "You know," I said, "I think she's a lot better with the drinking thing. She's going to AA meetings."

"Since when?" he said.

"I'm not sure. She went to one today, and I know she plans to go to more."

"Court-mandated meetings?"

"I beg your pardon?" I said.

"Was she sent there by a judge?"

"Why would you think that?"

"Is that a yes?" he asked.

"Are you checking out arrest records? Or just making educated guesses?"

"Are you dodging the question for a reason, or in the general spirit of contentiousness?"

I sat up, clutching my pillow to my stomach. "The point is, Joey's facing her problem responsibly. If there is a problem, which I'm not ready to concede. In the spirit of contentiousness."

"Okay." His hand found mine, and held it. I continued clutching my pillow. "Come on," he said, squeezing my hand. "Lie back down and go to sleep."

"I can't." I reached over to his face in the dark and kissed it, somewhere north of his mouth. "I'm wide awake. I think I'll go spend some time with Homer."

The worst thing, I decided, putting on the teakettle, was that Joey had been with David just minutes before someone had walked in and blew him away. I picked up the phone. If I was awake, Joey probably was too.

"I forgot to ask," I said. "What did you tell the cops about where you were? You didn't lie, did you?"

"Not significantly. I said I woke up Friday morning at David's and went home, without looking at a clock. Well before nine, I told them."

"But were you and David alone?" I asked. "What about his staff?"

"He gave them Christmas Day off and half of Christmas Eve. The housekeeper was due back noon Friday. His nurse was coming in around dinnertime."

I found a box of chamomile tea and unwrapped a tea bag, thinking about Joey and David having a last Christmas together. The intimacy in that.

"I cooked a turkey for him," she said, as if reading my mind. "Can you believe that? Me. Patsy—my brother Jamey's wife—talked me through it over the phone. He was too sick to eat, but he liked the smell of it in the house."

I wondered what had become of it, a whole turkey as leftovers. Joey was a vegetarian. Had the housekeeper eaten it? Would anyone want a murdered man's turkey? "Joey," I said, lowering my voice. "Do you know something about his death that you're not talking about?"

"Some things, yes. But not who did it."

"What things?" I whispered, toying with my tea bag.

Her voice was very soft. "I passed someone coming up the back way as I was leaving that morning. You know the dirt road, that shortcut? Anyhow, it was just a glimpse. Stocking cap and sunglasses—I couldn't even say if it was a man or a woman. But longish hair, I think. They took up the whole road, so I had to pull way over and then they raised their arm to kind of obscure their head."

"What kind of car did they drive?"

Joey paused, then said, "I wrote down a license number. But I don't want to use it, and I can't talk about it."

The teakettle screamed. I grabbed it. "But that's a huge clue for the cops."

"Only if I admit I lied about what time I left his house. Otherwise, seeing a car on the road an hour or two before the murder? Not significant."

"You don't know that."

There was a pause. "You know what I can't get out of my head? How yellow he was, from the cancer. Even the whites of his eyes were yellow. And he was so frail, his hair so wispy against his skull. Why can't I picture him like he used to be? That's the worst part. And he was so vain, not wanting anyone to see him looking like a cadaver, he said, so I was really the only one, outside of his staff, the last few days."

We hung up a few minutes later, leaving me more disturbed than ever. What a lonely thing, watching a man die. Keeping his secrets.

But who was she protecting now, with David dead? The killer? She didn't know who that was.

I was energetically stirring my tea bag, getting the string tangled around the spoon. So Joey had gone from her ex's deathbed to her unfaithful husband. I tried to imagine that, Simon sleeping with someone else. The blood rushed to my head so suddenly I had to hold on to the counter.

Toast. That's what I wanted. Peanut butter toast. Comfort food.

I adjusted the settings on the state-of-the-art toaster, then started in on *The Iliad* while waiting for the toast to pop up. I was no longer happy with Homer. The same thing was happening over and over. It had to do with Zeus being beseeched by Thetis, mother of Achilles, to favor the Trojans over the Greeks so that Achilles could be wooed back into battle. I thought maybe I was stuck on the same paragraph, but no, the story was being told three times in the course of three pages. Homer should be writing for the soaps. First the plot was being hatched, then carried out, then it was being talked about by the people hatching it and carrying it out, all of it repeated word for word, with no one even bothering to vary the adjectives.

Murder, war, illicit affairs, revenge, people making spectacles of themselves, gossip—all this was as prevalent in ancient Greece as it was in modern-day Los Angeles.

What ancient Greece did not have was parking tickets. Joey's had migrated from my purse into my book, serving as a bookmark. Forty-eight dollars. A person could go through a fortune just by ignoring residential permit signs. I started reading the fine print—"Do not send cash" then realized the lunacy inherent in preferring the prose of a parking ticket to that of Homer. Uncle Theo would weep. I returned it to its envelope, with **pntspns/sudstud** written in pink ink and my note to myself to call P.B. with the phone number for Haven Lane, which I still hadn't done.

A beeping sound coincided with my toast popping up. I jumped. *The Iliad* hopped out of my hands, onto the granite counter. The beeping continued. I moved *The Iliad* and saw Simon's black personal whatever device thing, that little cigarette pack–sized object that worked as a cell phone, e-mail conduit, and, for all I knew, spiritual adviser. It was plugged into the wall, recharging its battery, and was actually moving around the counter, so powerful was its buzzer. Did it always do that? I picked it up and saw a blinking button. There was something written on the tiny screen. I squinted.

ACHILLES' HEEL FOUND. YOU'RE UP.

I stared, thinking it was talking to me; hadn't I been reading about Achilles? This was Sheffo's theory once more, the idea that Greeks were everywhere. In Simon's kitchen now.

I applied peanut butter to my toast—something I feel strongly has to happen while the toast is warm, or what's the point?—then went to wake up Simon.

He was out of bed, naked but articulate before I'd said his name twice.

"What's up?" he said, reaching for the light switch.

"You are," I said. "Achilles' heel found. You're up."

"What?" He turned to me. "Aaggh!"

I took a step backward, remembering, too late, my hair.

"What in God's name happened to you?" he said. "No, wait. First tell me about Achilles' heel."

"Your cell phone has a text message," I said, trying to act as if my new look was no big deal. "It buzzed and I read it. It's in the kitchen."

He pulled on sweatpants and headed out of the bedroom with me behind, staring at the back of his torso. Pushing fifty, his muscles still rippled, just blurring around the edges in a really appealing way; if he'd been shirtless when we'd met, I'd have fallen for him a lot faster than I did, which was, come to think of it, pretty fast. Would he have looked at me twice if I'd been a tangerine head then?

I took my toast and *The Iliad* out of the kitchen and into the living room, so he could be alone with his call. It didn't take him long. When he found me curled up on the sectional, I knew something was wrong.

"Sorry," I said, reacting to his face. "Should I not be eating on the sofa?"

"What? No, I don't care where you eat."

"Okay, I look a little scary. I know that. But it'll grow. By next Christmas—"

"Wollie, I'm going to need you to disappear for a little while."

"Disappear?" A small alarm, like a kitchen timer, went off in my head. "You mean, sleep somewhere else?"

"Yes, and to stay away during the day. I can make a hotel reservation for you."

"No, that's okay, I can make arrangements for myself. Is it the hair?"

"What?" He smiled. "Yeah, the building has a strict hair code. No, I just have to work from home for a while and it's better if I don't have a houseguest."

"Fine."

He took a seat at the edge of the sectional. "We don't talk much about my work, do we? You're good about not asking. How'd you come to see that text message?"

"I dropped Homer on it." I held up *The Iliad.*

He rubbed his face with both hands. "I hadn't expected my work this month to infringe upon my personal life to the degree it's about to. I may have been . . . precipitous in inviting you to move in."

I was on my feet in a split second. "Oh, that's okay. I can easily just—"

"Whoa." He caught my arm as I tried to move past him.

"No, really," I said. The alarm in my head was now a fire engine siren. "It's better for me to get a place of my own and it's a perfect time, a new year, January first, probably a million apartments for rent and my needs are minimal, and—"

"Stop." He wrested a piece of toast from me, popped it in his mouth, and maneuvered me onto his lap. "This is not about you and me."

"Who's it about?"

"*Who*'s got nothing to do with it. It's work."

I wasn't comfortable on his lap, although it was, theoretically, a romantic position. I rearranged myself. "FBI agents aren't allowed to live in sin?"

He closed his eyes, laid his head back against the sofa cushion, and looked his age. He also looked cramped. It wasn't a sofa on which to lounge or seek refuge from the world. It was a sofa that encouraged good posture. "Wollie," he said, opening his eyes, "I'll be able to explain this to you one day."

"God, you sound like Joey. Let me ask you something." I moved to a chair. "Any of you guys have regular relationships? Or do you wait for retirement? I don't want to bring up J. Edgar Hoover, but there don't seem to be a lot of stable, happy—"

"If I were a fisherman, I'd come home reeking of fish. If I were a doctor, I'd be on call at the hospital at all hours. This is what comes with my territory. I hope you're in my life for a long time, but if you are, you're going to hear that a lot."

"Hear what, the 'reeking of fish' analogy?"

"That there are things I'll tell you about one day, but not today." He paused, watching me. "Today I can tell you that I love you and I'm crazy about your body and I'll kill anyone who hurts you in any way, but I need you to move out for a few days."

"No problem."

"I also need you to tell whoever asks that I work in textiles."

"Textiles?" I did a double take.

"I'm not saying you have to convince anyone, but if someone asks—"

"My friends already know what you do. And my mother, my brother, my uncle, the owner of the gay bookstore in my old neighborhood—"

"I mean chance-met strangers. If it comes up in conversation, I'm in textiles."

"How would it possibly come up? 'Hey, that guy you're never seen with, what's he do for a living?' "

"Okay, let's forget this."

"And anyway," I said, "I'm supposed to lie?"

"Not in a court of law."

"That's part of being your girlfriend? Lying?"

"Occasionally."

There's this thing I have about lying. It doesn't have to do with morality, although it's sometimes that—it's more that I'm lousy at it. I turn red, I stutter, and my eyes go off to the sides, getting all shifty. I'd probably have a seizure of sorts if I had to do it in front of a judge. You wouldn't need a polygraph machine with me; you could just hook me up to a sweat-o-meter. "I'm not sure I can," I said.

"I'll settle for evasive. Don't tell me you can't do that, because I've seen you in action."

That was true. When you can't lie outright, you become adept at vagueness. It occurred to me that within the space of a few short predawn hours, my boyfriend and my best friend had both, in their ways, discussed with me the possibility of lying. The difference was that Joey, who had an occasionally sketchy relationship with the law, did not expect me to lie for her and Simon, who embodied the law, did.

He got up, came over, removed the crumb-filled plate from my lap, and set it on the glass coffee table. "Just so you never lie to me."

"So when do you need me to disappear?"

"Let's talk about it naked." He took my hand and led me toward the bedroom.

*   *   *

I was awakened at nine A.M. by a woman identifying herself on the phone as calling from the offices of Someone, Somebody and Someone Else. She requested my presence in Century City at ten-thirty A.M., for the reading of the will of David Zetrakis.

How strange.

Twenty

nton, Grabayevich & Noswanger turned out to be a management company, on the fifth floor of a Century City high-rise. What, exactly, they managed was unclear to me, but in Hollywood such people abound, so many managers that they beget a subclass, management teams to manage the managers, according to Joey, whose own managers had been merged with or subsumed into her husband's when they'd gotten married. A greeting card idea popped into my head, a lineup of uniformed citizens, formerly known as maid, chauffeur, exterminator, and priest, now known as domestic manager, transportation manager, rodent manager, and religious manager—

"Wollie, how's the hair?" Rupert Ling said as the elevator doors opened. He embraced me like an old friend, which perhaps I was by now, and went on to kiss Joey. I greeted Max, who, dressed in a suit, looked less like a stage manager this morning and nothing at all like a poker player. The lobby was crawling with people, and it seemed that some of them caught sight of Joey and turned away, while others stared at her. I was sure she was the subject of conversation.

Did they all listen to the same news station? Worse, did they believe it? In the car, I'd tuned in to an interview with one of David's nurses, who claimed that David had found Jesus. "That man had me read the Bible to him. He did not want to die. Whoever took his life did it in cold blood." She also pointed out that Joey Rafferty, who did not read the Bible, had been constantly at David's. The reporter seemed to find this a weighty piece of evidence, wrapping up the segment in hushed tones that made me want to pull over to the side of the road and shoot the radio.

On the other hand, there were those, like Rupert, who were openly affectionate to Joey, showing tacit support. Max stood near her, his large frame like a shield, cutting her off from the curious looks.

"Ms. Shelley, we're happy you could make it on such short notice." A man extended his hand to me. He too was dressed in a suit, but his seemed more uniform than costume, suggesting that he was not in show business. "I'm Nelson Grabayevich. We had a bit of trouble finding a phone number for you. And Ms. Rafferty I know from the old days. Very nice to see you again—although I believe it's Mrs. Horowitz now?"

Joey smiled. "I'm still Joey, like in the old days. When I was a working stiff instead of a trophy wife. Nice to see you again, Nelson."

Nelson led us to a conference room, fast filling up with people, many of them soap people. It was like a continuation of Rex and Tricia's cocktail party, minus Rex and Tricia. As we found seats, a couple entered the room and were greeted with ceremony. Joey got up to hug them, then returned to sit next to me.

"David's brother, Charles," she whispered. "And Charles's wife, Agnes."

"Thank you for coming," Nelson said, moving to the front of the room. "Especially Charles and Agnes, who just drove down from Paso Robles. As many of you are aware, David knew for some time that he was dying, although he couldn't know, of course, the unfortunate manner in which he would meet his death so . . . precipitously. The good news, if it can be so termed, is that David had put his affairs in order recently and was quite specific in his end-of-life instructions. This makes my work easier, although losing a client and friend like David is not an easy thing at all." It seemed then that Nelson was at a loss for words, until I saw that he was working to get himself under control. Hard to imagine a group more accustomed to emotional self-expression than the soap opera crowd, but Nelson was not about to give in to sadness. He adjusted his reading glasses, shuffled papers, and cleared his throat.

"David's first wish was cremation. His second, which will explain the haste with which we have gathered, is that there is to be no funeral or memorial service. None. In his own words, here on page three . . . ah, yes. 'Having spent much of my life on television sets where tears—real or manufactured—were mandatory, I've had my fill. I'm also fed up with directing funerals, over two dozen on *At the End of the Day*; as an actor, I've played my own corpse eight times. I won't discourage you from cracking open a bottle of champagne, raising a glass to me, or even getting shitfaced' "—here Nelson blushed—" 'but no audiences for you show-off mourners, no eulogies. Talk to me one-on-one when the spirit moves you, not some Sunday morning at ten o'clock. For God's sake, don't do it in a church.' "

Nelson looked up, as if to take questions from the audience, but no one spoke.

I was disappointed. I believe in funerals. According to Dr. Paolo Pomerantz's *Guide to the Pantheon of Greek Gods and Goddesses and Their Roman Counterparts*, the ancient Greeks believed in funerals too, to save the soul from eternal wandering. I just find comfort in being around other sad people. I believe funerals are for the living, that the dead don't care.

Nelson reshuffled his papers. "Now, to the bequests. My assistant, Evelyn, has copies of the will for everyone, but I'll summarize it here, as was his desire. The estate goes to Charles Zetrakis, with the following exceptions . . ."

This went on for several minutes, an itemized description of individual possessions left to people and sums of money left to charitable organizations. My ears perked up only when someone I knew was named. Jen Kim got a solid gold ingot, for instance, and Rupert Ling a bottle of Domaine something or other, 1985, which seemed to stun him, as well as several cases of wine. Max Freund got a collection of first edition books and some stamps. Nelson himself got a desk from David's library. Sheffo Corminiak got a Cartier-Bresson photograph, Trey Mangialotti got a share in a racehorse living at Santa Anita, and some assistant got David's Emmys, which produced a sob. Clay got David's prized collection of props from old forties movies, and a Maserati Quattroporte Sport GT on top of it, which drew gasps.

I got three original illustrations from a version of *The Jungle Book* that

I'd gone into raptures over years before, when I'd dated David. The thought that he'd remembered that and bequeathed them to me, an old girlfriend he hadn't dated in two presidential administrations, touched me deeply.

Joey got the Klimt.

The silence around the room was broken by a shout of laughter and the words "Good work, Rafferty" from Clay.

Beside me, Joey hid her face in her hands. I couldn't tell if she was laughing or crying, but I put my arm around her and felt her body trembling. I heard Jen Kim behind me say, "He got it appraised last year. It's only worth two million, if that. It's a very minor Klimt." Possibly she thought she was speaking sotto voce; possibly she didn't care.

Joey's body shifted and she looked to the front of the room, where Charles and Agnes Zetrakis were seated. I became fixated on Charles, trying to find his resemblance to David. From this range it wasn't an obvious one. Charles was smaller than David had been, and bearded. From a distance, at least, he had none of David's magnetism or life-of-the-party insouciance. But no doubt grief was taking a toll on him. He leaned toward Agnes, a large woman, who whispered to him. He whispered back.

He glanced at Joey and gave her a thumbs-up. It was a small gesture. Surreptitious. He stood and walked around the crowd to the back of the room.

"Well, that's . . . some bequest," I murmured to Joey, at a loss for something more meaningful to say. A new greeting card popped into my head, along with amazement that I hadn't thought of it till now. *Congratulations on that inheritance.*

"Yeah," Joey whispered back. There was the faintest scent of alcohol about her, and mint mouthwash. "God help me. The Klimt comes with the one thing I don't need."

"Inheritance tax?"

"Motive for murder," she said. "Excuse me."

I sat, stunned, watching her follow Charles Zetrakis out of the room. I looked around. Agnes was buttonholing Nelson Grabayevitch. Rupert Ling gave me a smile and exaggeratedly raised eyebrows, which could have meant anything. Max Freund was deep in conversation with Jen Kim. I was about to follow Joey out of the room when Jen called out to me.

"Wollie," she said, hurrying over. "Can you come by the studio right now?" As I mentally ran through my schedule, she said, "Good. See you there. Max, don't dawdle, I don't want C.G. running things alone, not this week. And did you see the *Variety* piece on me this morning? Good article, bad head shot. See if hair and makeup can do me and get the stills guy to shoot me, in case there are follow-up articles." Then, cell phone to her ear, she was gone.

"I guess I'm coming to the studio," I said to Max.

"I'll get you a drive-on," he said, taking his own cell phone out of his breast pocket. I was about to ask what a drive-on was, but Max was already talking to his phone, heading to the elevator. I'd ask Joey, my human showbiz glossary. Realizing I'd never make it to the Valley without a bathroom break, I headed down a long hallway, then stopped.

Hidden in an alcove, Joey and Charles Zetrakis were face-to-face, well into each other's personal space. They were holding hands. I couldn't hear the words they were speaking, but there was no mistaking the depth of feeling between them.

I was feeling like a voyeur and just about to drag myself away when Joey reached out and touched his beard, then leaned forward and kissed David's brother gently on the mouth.

Twenty-one

There are all kinds of kisses. The kiss I'd witnessed was not exactly sexual, did not involve tongues, and wouldn't merit even a PG-13 rating in a movie. But there was something so intimate about it that I backed away and left the building without using the bathroom.

The sun shone on Century City, on the Christmas decorations still adorning Avenue of the Stars. Around me people hurried, bustling with corporate energy, while I stood, uncertain of what to do next. The day was perfect: cloudless and warm. Then a motorcycle raced by, gunning its engine, shaking me from my stupor.

Joey was in trouble.

I am not by nature a meddler. With the possible exception of my little brother, I try to let people live their lives as they see fit. But a strange confluence of events was making my innocent friend look increasingly suspicious. I kept waiting for things to come to light that would exonerate her, or for the real guilty party to emerge and draw off the media and the cops. This was not happening.

A voice popped into my head, so loud I looked around for its source. *You must do it.*

"Excuse me?" I actually said it aloud.

Look around you.

I looked. In front of me was a small crowd of people, one holding a microphone. I looked toward Avenue of the Stars and saw a news truck from a local station, defiantly double-parked.

Perhaps the media was learning what we'd just learned, that Charles and Agnes Zetrakis had hit the inheritance jackpot. David's estate was worth a few million, and there were rumors of a huge life insurance policy. That should deflect some attention.

I went around the back of the building and found a fire exit. The door was locked, but I figured it would open on the inside. I returned to the entrance and took the elevator again to the fifth floor and started looking for Joey. She was no longer in the hallway, so I went to the reception desk of Anton, Grabayevich & Noswanger to ask if anyone had seen her.

Behind the desk, a woman had her back to me, filing, talking to someone through her headset. ". . . called here last week. The day before Christmas Eve. Made me get Mr. Grabayevich out of a meeting, did that whole 'Don't you know who I am?' thing. And I didn't know. Not till I heard about him on the news—I thought he was just some repulsive client. . . . I'm not kidding, it's right here in the book for Friday, Mr. Grabayevich was going to make a house call. I should erase it. Morbid."

I couldn't resist. I leaned over the desk and turned the desk calendar a few degrees clockwise. Friday. Noon. "David Zetrakis" with his street address and "amend will" written underneath.

"*Excuse* me," the woman said. "May I help you?"

I jumped back, mortified. "Is Joey Rafferty still around?" I asked.

She pointed to the conference room.

Joey was talking to Nelson Grabayevich, and Charles and Agnes. "There's a news team outside," I said. "We can avoid them by taking the stairs."

"Good Lord," Nelson said. "We're certainly not accustomed to that."

Agnes Zetrakis spoke up. "Could we talk to them about the Syrah?"

"Agnes, they don't care about the Syrah," Charles said. "They want—"

"But you said you want to get the word out," Agnes said, picking up her purse. She was dressed well, but with no discernable style. "And I have press kits in the car."

"We'll catch you later, then," Joey said. "Wollie and I will take the stairs."

Except that I still had to use the bathroom. I excused myself, and when I returned to the conference room, Joey and Nelson Grabayevich were alone.

I took a deep breath. "Mr. Grabayevich, I know David was planning to change his will last week. I'm just wondering—did he tell you what the change was?"

Nelson and Joey both looked at me in surprise.

"Because," I went on, "I'd feel bad accepting my bequest if he'd had second thoughts about it."

"Ms. Shelley, I'm comfortable saying that David intended those lithographs for you. *The Jungle Book* woodcuts, weren't they? He died without telling me the change he had in mind, but my impression was of something with greater monetary value."

Joey said, "An impression based on—?"

Nelson hesitated. "His state of mind, when I last spoke to him. He was agitated."

"Did you mention this to the police?" I asked.

"Oh, yes. My partners and I considered the issue of privacy, but in these circumstances we feel the duty of confidentiality dies with the client."

This gave Joey and me fodder for conversation down five flights of stairs. "It opens up the field of suspects," Joey said, over the echo of our footsteps in the stairwell. "The big winners today are Charles and Agnes, me, and then a tie, probably, between Clay, Max, and possibly Trey, if that racehorse starts racing well. Big long shot."

"You mean that someone shot David to keep themselves in the will?" I asked. "If so, you should get bumped from the list. You don't need a Klimt."

"True," Joey said. "But I know wealthy people—millionaires—who'd kill each other over gift cards to Sizzler."

I let a few stairs go by, then said, "I don't mean to get personal, but how well do you and Charles know each other?"

"I haven't seen him in years," Joey said. "But we were very close at one time."

"When you say 'close,' do you mean . . . ?"

"Let's not talk about Charles."

"Okay," I said, getting dizzy. Every eight steps we did a ninety-degree turn. "But what's the big deal? I mean, obviously you don't have to tell me, but if you had an affair, what's the big deal?"

Joey took a moment to answer. "For one thing, Agnes. She gets jealous. Even though it was before her time. Charles is sensitive to that."

"I doubt I'll be mentioning it to Agnes," I said.

"And God, I hope the media never picks up on it."

"No kidding." I imagined the headline: TWO PEOPLE WITH A MO-TIVE . . . AND A PAST. I said, "So you never had a ménage à trois?"

Joey looked up at me from half a flight below. "With Charles and Agnes? Are you out of your mind?"

"No, with Charles and David. Sheffo said that you and David—"

"Sheffo's an incorrigible gossip." Joey continued down the stairs at a reckless pace. "I expect Charles and Agnes to absorb some of the media attention, based on how rich they just got, but their alibis are airtight. They worked all day Friday. They couldn't drive to L.A., shoot David, and drive back to Paso Robles without their staff noticing."

"Joey, wait." I was too winded to talk and racewalk simultaneously. "So David did or didn't think about suicide, about having someone shoot him?"

She stopped. "I'm trying to figure that out."

"You can't just let LAPD figure it out?"

Joey shook her head. "I like cops. I respect what they do. But they're looking at me, Wollie. I feel them looking. They're saying, If she walks like a duck and quacks like a duck, she's our duck. That's what I'd be saying, in their shoes. I think they're coming up with a theory, and if no one better comes along, they'll do their best to make me fit it. You think innocent people never get arrested?"

"So wouldn't it make more sense to cooperate with them? Tell them everything you know, so they can see you've got nothing to hide?"

"But I do have things to hide. It's just that what I'm hiding isn't what they're seeking."

"Well, that's reassuring."

"I can't reassure you, Wollie. It's all I can do to persuade myself."

"About what?"

"That what I'm doing is the right thing to do. And that everyone's going to come through it okay."

With that, Joey continued going down, her footsteps clattering, drowning out all the questions I wanted to ask.

Twenty-two

On the way to the set of *At the End of the Day*, I compiled a worry list, a habit that falls under the heading of "car therapy."

Joey topped the list. However, I was also anxious to the point of obsession about Simon and me, my brother, my Greek mural, my dating-correspondent job, and L.A. traffic congestion, which showed no sign of ever getting better and every sign of becoming truly unbearable in the very near future. Which meant that by the time my children were grown, Southern California would be nothing but sand, sky, and freeway on-ramps. If I ever had children, which was doubtful. A few hours earlier I'd been living with my boyfriend. Now I was headed for Motel 6. This was not progress.

I was in the middle of alphabetizing my worry list when my cell phone rang. I was fuzzy on the L.A. talking-while-driving statutes, but I decided to live dangerously and answer it. In case it was Simon.

The screen read RESTRICTED. Aha. Simon.

"Simon?" I said, answering it.

"No. It's Elliot. Hey, Wollie, do you happen to know Rupert Ling's number?"

"No."

"Oh. I was under the impression you and he—. Anyhow, he was

pitching me a great idea, and we got cut off. I'm trying to call him back but his number's blocked."

"How come every guy I know has a blocked number but none of my girlfriends do?"

"Couldn't say. By the way, thanks for suggesting he contact me. He's on to something with this vineyard thing, and I want to see his business plan."

This was the most excitement I'd ever heard from Elliot. He was talking fast, and I got a glimpse of why he was successful. He had boundless enthusiasm for business, any business, apparently—TV production, computer chips, winemaking. "Sorry, I don't know Rupert's number," I said. "Try Max Freund. He's the stage manager for—"

"Yeah, I know Max. Another poker buddy. Good. I'll try that. Let me ask you . . ." He seemed to slow down. I imagined his car exiting a freeway. "Seen Joey lately?"

"Yes."

"She doing okay?"

"No."

"Yeah. All right," he said, "you don't need to confide in me. But do me a favor? Tell her the milk steamer on the espresso machine is screwed up and I'm wondering if it's still under warranty. Or if I should throw it out and get a new one."

"That's it?" I said.

"What do you mean?"

"How about that you're deeply depressed and can't live without her?"

Elliot laughed. "What's going to get her home faster, corny dialogue badly delivered or me throwing out her four-thousand-dollar Pasquini?"

"Okay, I've underestimated you. There's nothing wrong with the milk steamer, is there? But if I'm going to do you a favor, you might think twice about calling me corny."

"I do need a favor. Keep an eye on Joey. She shouldn't go all psycho with the whole town watching, but she won't listen to me and her shrink's in Europe."

While not sure what "psycho" meant in this context, I told him I would and hung up. How irresponsible of Joey's shrink. Shrinks are supposed to leave town in August, not over Christmas, Hanukkah, Kwanzaa, New Year's—all the emotional-overload holidays when patients need them. Even I knew that, and I'd never had a shrink.

I got to the studio in Burbank and pulled out identification for the guard at the entrance gate, who studied it as if committing it to memory, then checked my trunk and handed me a parking pass—my "drive-on"— and waved me through. I drove to the set, where I parked, as instructed, in a red zone, and left my keys with C.G., the co–stage manager, once again in pigtails. She graciously avoided staring at my hair and pointed me toward Max, still dressed in his reading-of-the-will suit.

Max gave me a hug. "Feel like family yet? Come meet Laurie, our costumer."

Laurie was round, with buzz-cut hair, all in black except for a red tool belt. She looked me up and down and asked if I knew my measurements. I said I didn't. She shook her head, pulled out a measuring tape, and got to work, barking out numbers as an assistant, also in black, wrote them on a clipboard. These were not your standard bust-waist-hip statistics. Laurie made me stand with arms out, then legs apart, putting her tape measure in places that have never been measured in my life.

Rupert Ling walked by in a Speedo swimsuit and boat shoes. He stopped to kiss my cheek for the second time that day, undaunted by the sight of me being fitted for a crucifix. "You make out okay?" he asked. "At the David Zetrakis Giveaway?"

I nodded, which drew a reprimand from Laurie and an order to stand still.

"Oh, right," Rupert said. "Lithographs. I got some outstanding wine. Laurie got a brooch that once belonged to Coco Chanel, and she didn't even show up."

"Working," Laurie said, making furious notes on a chart. "Some of us do that, rather than leave things to our assistants, not to mention any names, *Max*."

"Associate, not assistant," Max said. "And C.G.'s very capable."

"And Max got books and stamps—geeky, yet valuable," Rupert said. "Good work, Max. But not as good as Joey, once fired by David from this very show."

"Speaking of Joey," I said. "Elliot Horowitz needs you to call him back."

"Already done, thanks. We got cut off and then I was stuck for an hour here inside the building, where one is not allowed to talk to the outside world."

"Laurie, if you're finished, I'll steal Wollie." Max pointed across the cold and cavernous sound studio to an oasis of light.

"I'm curious to know," Rupert said, walking with us, "if anyone else finds it strange that our current diva got nothing from our producer's death. Except a new contract. And a reprieve from nuclear disaster."

"You mean Tricia?" I asked.

"That's not quite accurate," Max said. "Tricia renewed her contract days before David died."

"But no one told David," Rupert said. "Not even Joey, his spy. He wanted Tricia gone last year. She was hanging on by her fingernails when Jen took over the show."

"Why didn't anyone tell David?" I asked.

Two crew members walked past, transporting a stained-glass window. We stopped to let them by. "Rupert, can we spare Wollie our in-house gossip?" Max asked.

"No, really," I said. "Happy to be part of the team. Whatever it takes."

Rupert smiled. "No one told David because David would've fired Jen if he knew she was bringing people back from the dead. Jen was show runner on a conditional basis. But she's safe now. She made *Daily Variety* this morning. Right next to David's obit. 'Temp Ex OK'd by Net.' "

"Excuse me?" I said.

"Interim executive producer approved by network," Max said. "*Variety*-speak."

"But how could David not know what was going on?" I asked.

Max looked at Rupert, then said, "It was a bit of a conspiracy. We have four weeks' worth of episodes in the can, instead of our usual two, by working six-day weeks and cutting corners. So we're up to the February storylines, which deviate somewhat from the scripts David signed off on; he planned on several more characters dying."

"Wouldn't he have found out eventually?" I asked.

Max nodded. "If he'd lived three more weeks. But it would've been too late. The episodes were shot; we haven't got the time or money to reshoot them."

"Why would everyone go along with this?" I asked.

"Only department heads and a few actors knew, and we stuck to the spirit of David's scripts. No one was crazy about the bloodbath he envisioned. And to be very pragmatic about it, David's reign was over. The consensus, I believe, was that Jen deserved a vote of confidence. She did, after all, sign the paychecks."

"Unless David withdrew his support," Rupert said. "Whatever alliances Jen's made with the network, she's still seen as David's protégée. She's the first to admit it. If he started yelling 'foul,' they'd very likely have replaced her after the sweeps."

How convenient for Jen, I thought, that David died ahead of schedule.

We'd reached a living room, eerily real, messy with newspapers and coffee cups, and someone napping on a sofa. All it lacked was a TV. And its fourth wall.

"Trey, wake up." Max shook the shoulder of the napping person, covered in an afghan. "This is Wollie. You're taking her miniature golfing tonight."

Trey's eyes flew open. "Why?"

"She's the dating correspondent on *SoapDirt*. Didn't Jen talk to you about it?"

"I don't know." Trey rubbed his eyes like a toddler grumpy with sleep.

A clicking alerted us to the arrival of Tricia, careening onto the set. She wore heels so high they might have been stilts, under a yellow chenille bathrobe. One pink hair curler sat on her forehead like a third eye. "What's she doing here?" she asked.

"Wollie? Wardrobe fitting for *SoapDirt*," Max said. "Jen wants—"

"What I want also counts," Tricia said. "Am I not coproducing? Coordinate her fitting with my schedule. We need to minimize her height; she's a giant."

Max, expressionless, made a note on his clipboard.

"Also," she said, "what's the show doing for the memorial service? Flowers? I'm thinking a full page in *Variety*. And when is the memorial service?"

"David's?" I asked.

"No, Joseph Stalin's." Tricia threw me a withering glance. "Of course David's."

Max answered, "No service, Tricia. David's express wish."

"Says who?"

"His last will and testament," Max said.

"Which you," said Rupert, "were not written into, Tricia. No bequests for you, darling. I can't imagine why not. All the other ex-girlfriends made out like bandits."

The silence that fell along with Tricia's face was chilling. I cleared my throat. "I wouldn't say *bandits*."

A scream from across the set broke the silence. This was followed by lamentation, in the voice of Sheffo Corminiak.

"And this is how I'm told?" he cried. "I read of my demise in Tuesday's script? Not even a death scene. My body discovered in full rigor mortis. Have the inmates taken over the asylum?"

Max moved across the sound stage fast, even with his limp. "Sheffo," he called. "Sheffo, calm down."

Rupert took my hand and led me to where the action was. Trey, roused from his stupor, followed, leaving Tricia with her clicking heels to catch up as best she could.

"A pox upon you!" Sheffo Corminiak wore a ruby-red smoking jacket with black velvet collar and cuffs. With one hand he waved a script. In the other was an old-fashioned shaving brush. He held it aloft like a sword or a magic wand.

"Sheffo, my dear man," Max said. "I thought Jen had told you."

"You knew you were scheduled to die, didn't you?" Rupert asked.

"When David was alive, yes," Sheffo bellowed. "But he's gone. I was told the nuclear disaster was canceled."

"No, my death was canceled," Tricia said. "Yours was not. It's February sweeps. Someone's got to die."

"Me? Die?" Sheffo opened and closed his mouth in the manner of a fish, then found his voice again. "Fired? One who trod the boards with Gielgud, Richardson—"

"Oh, get over yourself," Tricia snapped.

"You." Sheffo's shaving brush pointed at Tricia. "You shallow bitch, you toy poodle of a woman, you married a network executive to survive, while I'm to be sacrificed like Iphigenia at Aulis, to a ratings period—"

"I survive because fans love me. Your fans are dead, you aging fag."

I was shocked into silence, as was everyone else. After a moment, Tricia turned to Max. "Don't forget, I want to be in on Wollie's costume fitting." And with that, she walked off with a clicking of heels and a swaying of chenille.

Sheffo, his face ashen, watched her go. "Hell is stoking its fires, waiting for her."

＊　＊　＊

As I was leaving the set twenty minutes later, I thought I saw Joey's car pulling onto the lot, but I might have been mistaken. When I called her on her cell phone to ask her, we got cut off, right after she'd noted that a Mercedes on a soap set was practically a cliché.

Which wasn't really an answer.

Twenty-three

returned to Westwood to pack up my life. I was feeling both belligerent and shy, having just left a message on Simon's answering machine
explaining that I was about to get my worldly goods out of his closet. I
wanted to give him notice, in case he thought I'd already vacated the
premises.

Simon was not home. Ilse, the cleaning lady, was. But she wasn't
dressed for cleaning.

"Hi, Ilse," I said, causing her to jump. "I didn't recognize you in street
clothes."

Ilse had a hand to her heart as she wheeled around to face me. She
recovered, smoothing the jacket of her suit. It was a nice suit, steel gray,
well cut and showing a lot of leg. "Nor I you," she said, in her slight ac-
cent, "in orange hair. I did not expect you to be here, Miss Wollie."

It was pointless, I'd discovered, to ask Ilse to call me plain Wollie. I'd
drawn the line, though, at Madame Wollie, which highlighted the fact
that Ilse was in her twenties, whereas I could see, in the distance, the big
four-oh. "I just came to pack up my stuff," I said, wondering why she
wouldn't expect me there. I mean, I lived there. Or had.

"I have packed for you," she said.

"You've what?"

"Your suitcases are ready."

"You went through my stuff?"

"This is a problem for you?" she said.

"Well, yeah," I said. "You're not my valet or lady-in-waiting, or—"

"I did not mind."

"I mind." It was not just Gothic, it was intrusive. My art supplies, minimal though they were here at the penthouse, were my stock-in-trade, and I was finicky about them. And Ilse, looking at me with something approaching boredom, wasn't trying to be helpful. I like to take people at face value, but there was something off-key about Ilse. "Okay," I said. "Then I'll just check out the closet to make sure—"

"I have already—"

"Do you mind?" I asked, moving past her.

Ilse stepped aside. I entered the bedroom and saw my suitcases near the door, side by side and stuffed. I went from there to my walk-in closet. It was as empty as a hotel room, awaiting the next guest. I fought back a bizarre impulse to sob, looking at the bed where I'd . . . felt the earth move.

I went out to the living room. It too reeked of cleanliness. And impersonality. Ilse had lowered the blinds, something I'd constantly asked her not to do while I was living there. I like natural light. Simon had said he liked it too.

In the kitchen my refrigerator magnets were gone, along with my raisin bread, peanut butter, I Can't Believe It's Not Butter Spray, and my ice-cream sandwiches.

"Ilse, where's my food?" I said.

Ilse appeared in the doorway. "I gave it away."

"What?"

"Except for the perishables."

"Are you nuts?" I was now shaking.

"Mr. Simon does not eat the food you eat, so there was no need for it. Your coffee mug is packed in your suitcase."

"What were Mr. Simon's instructions about ridding the place of my presence?"

A look I'd seen before descended upon Ilse's face.

"Come on, Ilse. Anyone who uses the word 'perishables' in context can understand that question."

"Mr. Simon has a meeting here today for business."

"And this business meeting is to take place in the refrigerator? Are people bringing their own snacks, forcing you to evict my ice-cream sandwiches?"

"Perhaps I did not understand his instructions."

She was more than off-key, I decided; she was positively eccentric. She was also more attractive than ever, in makeup and a suit that probably cost more than anything I owned. Moreover, she seemed to have no fear about losing her job, which is what I imagined happened to domestic help that did not please the boss's girlfriend.

Which meant that she had some sort of tenure situation. Or that I was no longer the boss's girlfriend.

"Are you in love with him?" I asked.

She looked startled, at least. "With—whom?"

"With Mr. Simon, that's whom." And where had she learned her English? *Masterpiece Theatre?*

"No, I have a boyfriend," she said calmly. "Not Mr. Simon."

There was nothing more to be said. It took me several trips to get my bags to the elevator, but I refused Ilse's offer to help, other than letting her prop open the door.

Dragging my stuff through the parking garage, I wondered how many other girlfriends of Simon's had vacated the premises in this manner. I felt rotten enough without also feeling like part of an assembly line.

Although I was now in my own crummy car, I couldn't help but notice, as I left the parking garage, that I was being followed.

Twenty-four

talked to Simon's machine.

"Hi, it's me. Wollie," I added, as if he'd no longer recognize my voice. "Okay, I've moved out. The coast is clear. Nice doing business with you." I sounded like a perky bank clerk and tried a different tack. "The thing is, I'm being followed by some guys and I'm wondering, Can they do that? Have we no anti-harassment laws in this country?" Now I sounded like a disgruntled political activist. "Okay, that's it. Bye."

I hung up, annoyed with myself. What a stupid question. Of course harassment was legal. People far more rich, famous, infamous, beautiful, notorious, powerful, important, sleazy, and suspicious than I had discovered this. Probably it had to do with the First Amendment. Possibly those newspapers in the checkout line at the grocery store had powerful lobbying forces in Washington, ensuring that paparazzi would never face unemployment. And why had I never met a paparazzo socially? Where was the random conversation on line at the post office—"What do I do for a living? Oh, I work for the tabloids, making people's lives hell . . ."? I knew prostitutes, but no paparazzi.

The car that followed me, eastbound on Wilshire Boulevard and northbound on Westwood, right on Le Conte, left on Hilgard and left again on Sunset, was a red SUV. It finally pulled alongside me at the stoplight at Bundy.

"Hey, Wollie, how about a smile?" said the passenger-side person, and stuck a camera out the window.

I stuck out my tongue.

My cell phone rang. "Hello," I answered, and stuck out my tongue again.

"Mrs. Shelley?"

"Call me Wollie. Maybe," I added, not sure I wanted to talk to someone who didn't know my name.

"Detective Ike Born. Like to ask you a few questions pertaining to an investigation. Shouldn't take more than half an hour." He had a careless way with his consonants, like maybe he was on medication, or he had a mouth full of cotton candy.

"We've met, Detective. At the Horowitz house." Was this some kind of test?

"How's four-thirty this afternoon?"

"That's not convenient for me. I have a business appointment then." The appointment was with myself, at the public library, reading *The Iliad,* but still.

"Six?" he said.

"No, at six I have a work—thing." Miniature golf.

"Until when?"

My call-waiting beep sounded.

"Um, can I just put you on hold for a minute until—"

I hit TALK. P.B.'s voice came through. "Wollie," he said. "Eunice says if I go to Santa Barbara my life will be in danger."

"From what?" I asked.

"Unspecified disaster," my brother said.

"Who's Eunice?"

"A psychic."

"Staff or patient?"

"Psych tech. She's new."

"Great," I said. Had it occurred to anyone that hiring staff that gave psychic readings to psychiatric patients might not be the wisest choice? "Okay, here's the deal," I said. "In an unspecified disaster, who's more useful than you? No one. What if it's your destiny to help out? Suppose your girlfriend was up there, for the Chalk Festival or something, and disaster struck? Where do you want to be? Down the coast? Or down the street? You're not going to be much good to her from Rio Pescado."

There was a pause. "Lunchtime," he said, giving no indication of whether I'd made an impact. "I have to go."

P.B. hung up on me, and then I hung up on Detective Ike Born. Oops. Well, that could happen to anyone, pressing END instead of TALK.

The red SUV was no longer stalking me. That was one nice thing. I called Joey's cell and got voice mail. "Okay," I said, "what exactly am I supposed to say to the homicide detectives about your—" Wait. Did I want to say "alibi" on a recording device? "Never mind. Are you still staying at—" Was I still not supposed to say "Shutters"? "—that hotel you're staying at? And might I stay there too?"

Detective Ike Born called me back and was so gracious about being hung up on that I agreed to meet at nine P.M. Not that I had a lot of choice. I skipped the library, drove to a bookstore, bought the Cliffs Notes for *The Iliad*, and, exhausted by the events of the day so far, got back in my car, locked the doors, and napped.

Miniature golf ranks right up there with full-sized golf as a sport I have no real interest in. Along with hockey, bowling, drag racing, curling, and sumo wrestling. I'm not a sporty type. I'm an arty type. Joey's a sporty type. Well, she's an arty type too, but that part is not always immediately evident, whereas my nonathleticism is instantly noticeable to anyone trying to engage me in anything involving balance, coordination, balls, sticks, or wheels.

I drove myself to the Green's GolfLand, since I had no home from which Julio, the chauffeur, could fetch me. I'd been too melancholy to explain that to Max, telling him only that it was more convenient to drive myself. He was waiting in the parking lot, along with the camera crew, who were sitting in their minivan with the windows open, smoking. The back of the minivan featured a LIVE FREE OR DIE bumper sticker, a sentiment somewhat undercut by a vanity license plate saying DRUDGE2. There was no sign of Trey, but Max phoned him frequently for updates on his ETA.

"He's close," Max said. "And once he shows, you'll see, he won't be the, uh—"

"Slug?" supplied the cameraman.

"—slacker that he appears to be." Max made notes on his ubiquitous clipboard. "I tried to think up an activity that will appeal to him. It's all paid for, so have fun."

"Max," I said. "What kind of training did you go through to be a stage manager? Were you a butler in a previous life? Or a psychiatrist? A babysitter?"

Max smiled, his face relaxing into comfortable creases. "Only half the job is corralling actors. And yes, it's true that many creative people are—"

"Psychopaths?" the cameraman said. "Flakes?"

"—operating on a different frequency," Max said. "I try to provide a calm environment so they're free to focus on art."

Once Trey showed, we went through the same drill I'd gone through with Rupert. A lingering hello kiss hinting at an advanced degree of sexual interest on Trey's part, despite the fact that he could not have picked me out of a lineup as someone he'd ever met. There was one key difference: I was now kissing a man young enough to be my offspring. It was something Simon would notice when he saw it on TV. Not only that, Green's GolfLand brought out Trey's inner child, which was not, admittedly, deeply buried.

"Whoa!" he said as the crew packed up to leave. "Check this place out. You can get fake tattoos. And draft root beer? No way."

"Amazing," I said, joining him in line to pick out a putter.

"Man, I love this stuff." Trey's body went through a snakelike hip-hop movement that I took to signify joy. "We used to do miniature golf with my dad when he had us on weekends. This place rocks. I wonder if I could get one for my backyard. How much do you suppose it would cost?"

"A miniature golf course? Sounds like a custom job. Not a big market for—"

"Yeah, but you know, how great would that be, to come in from the clubs and you can't sleep and you go in the backyard and sink some putts till the sun comes up?"

"Do you get insomnia a lot?" I asked.

"Oh, yeah, every night. Till I fall asleep. Yesterday the cops were like, 'Buddy, where were you when David Zetrakis got whacked?' and I'm like, 'Are you kidding me? Before noon? A day off? Where do you think?' "

"The cops questioned you?" I asked. "The homicide cops?"

"Yeah. Like, where's anyone at ten in the morning? If I'd known I was supposed to have an alibi, I'd have brought home a girl to sleep with me. You know, like a witness. But the problem with girls is, then in the morning, there they are. And then you're supposed to remember their names and stuff."

"How come the cops questioned you?" I said.

He picked out a putter. "Not just me, everyone on the show. I don't know why they think it's one of us. Well, except Tricia. I could see her shooting someone."

I smiled. "I won't quote you when I talk about you on *SoapDirt*."

"You can. They're always trying to get me to shut up—my publicist, and Jen, our producer, like when *Soap Digest* calls and I rag about my storyline or whatever, but then why even answer the phone?" He looked at me. "Got a favorite putter?"

I chose a blue-handled one because it matched my sneakers and a green golf ball that complemented my gauze skirt, then followed Trey to the first hole. "So you like nightclubs. And do you play poker like everyone else on *At the End of the Day?*"

Trey smiled. "*At the End of the Payday*. That's what Rupert calls it. I went one time to Vegas with them, but I always get carded, so it's kind of a drag."

I had not, I suddenly remembered, asked Simon about his Las Vegas FBI research. "Did David go to Vegas a lot?"

"Like every weekend. David, four or five regulars, and then whoever else wanted to." Trey hit his ball easily through a miniature windmill.

"Who were the regulars?"

"Jen and Max and Clay, and then crew guys, like grips and whatever. Rupert, about half the time. Tricia once, but I don't think she was into poker, I think she just worked on her tan and did the spa thing. The whole operation shut down once David got sick. He had some deal going at the hotel, because it was a really cool place and he got us rooms super cheap."

"So David was . . . well-connected?"

"In Vegas? He knew everyone. He was Mr. Important. Hey, mind if I give you some pointers? I can help you improve your game."

At the third hole, Joey showed up.

"What are you doing here?" I asked. "Are you all right?"

"Moderately. Max told me you were here." To my surprise, Joey gave Trey a kiss. "Hello, monkey. Wollie, do you have the key to your storage place on you?"

"In my car. I think. Why?"

"I sewed some money into that chaise longue I foisted on you. Mad money."

Trey blinked. "You know how to sew?"

"I grew up in Nebraska," Joey said. "4-H. Anyhow, Elliot canceled the credit cards. He said he'd put money into our checking account, then he went surfing and now I'm down to spare change. And the hotel evicted me over the canceled credit card."

"Why would Elliot cancel credit cards but transfer money into your account?" I said. "And why don't you have your own bank account?"

"Because I'm an idiot. He canceled the cards over our last fight and he's putting money back into the account because we made up."

"Well, that's good news," I said, thinking what an odd marriage they had. "Are you moving back in?"

Joey shook her head. "No. But we did have sex this afternoon."

"Dude," Trey said. "You had sex with your husband?"

"With my probably future ex-husband," she said. "There's a difference. Hey, you guys have to do all nine holes?"

Trey looked at me. "What's this for, again? *SoapDirt*?"

"Yes," I said. "I think I have to play enough miniature golf with you to be able to say you're one of the hottest men in daytime. I can say that now."

"Cool. I'm gonna finish up here and hit the Roxy. Want to meet up?"

Joey declined, dragging me away. On the way to the car she explained that she and Trey went way back, to presoap days. "He was my little nephew in an episode of *Murder, She Wrote*. I could no more go night-clubbing with him than I could go skinny-dipping with him." She looked at her watch. "I should drop in on an AA meeting. There's one in Toluca Lake, pretty close by, but I'd rather go to the storage place."

"We'll do both. I'll come to the meeting too." That would ensure she got there. "I have to go talk to this homicide detective, but not till nine."

She looked momentarily scared, then shook her head. "I'll skip the meeting. I'm a little hungover. Elliot and I shared a bottle of Cristal."

"I bet you're not the first person to go to a meeting hungover."

She sighed. "True. Okay. Maybe I can nap through it."

But it didn't come to that. In a church parking lot, we ran into Avram "Ziggy" Ziegler. And Joey's life changed.

Twenty-five

Ziggy remembered me from the car wash and greeted me happily. The sight of Joey made him rapturous. He looked like a man pleased with all of life, except for the item of information he had to impart to Joey.

"I moved to L.A. last month," he said. "Great town, by the way. So I've been trying to track down Elliot, but he's a hard man to get ahold of, and then I remembered his sister in Palm Springs. Camille. She said he was out of town, but then I realized that it wasn't just Elliot affected by my actions, it was you too, only Camille had no number for you, but then I heard you were turning up at AA meetings, someone said Toluca Lake, and so I started coming here too and that's how I came to be following you the other day—probably scared you, huh?—and I knew then that God would throw us together. Don't you love it when those promises come true?"

"I'm sorry," Joey said, "have we met?"

"No. But didn't Elliot tell you about me? His divorce lawyer?"

Joey glanced at me. "I wasn't aware he was divorcing me, as a matter of fact."

"Divorcing you?" the little man said. "No, no. He's not married to you."

"Yes, he is," Joey and I said simultaneously.

"No, he's not. That's my point." Ziggy stared, his smile faltering. "Uh-oh. Oops. Deep breath here. Joey—can I call you Joey?—Elliot was my client years ago."

"During one of his divorces, I assume," Joey said.

"Ziggy!" A woman hailed him from across the parking lot as she opened the back of her van. "How about a hand with the coffee machine?"

"Uh . . . sure," he called back. "Give me a minute."

"Now," she called. "Or it won't be ready for meeting time."

"Do you mind?" he asked us. "I'm co–coffee person for December." Without waiting for an answer, he took off across the parking lot.

Joey and I followed. "Look, Ziegler, Ziggy, whatever," she called, "you gotta finish that thought."

"Well, it's delicate," he yelled over his shoulder. "There may be some confidentiality issues here. I thought you knew already."

"Pretend she does know," I called, "and you're just reexplaining it."

Ziggy reached the van and lifted out a coffee machine the size of a small child. The coffee lady handed Joey and me boxes of coffee, creamer, sweeteners, and Styrofoam cups. "It's attorney-client privilege," Ziggy said. "At least, I think. I'll look up the statutes. I never practiced in California, so I don't know the laws here—"

"We won't report you to the state bar association," I said.

Ziggy and his coffee machine turned to us. "It's not about getting caught, it's about doing the right thing. I'm sorry, I thought I was just going to apologize, not break the news to you. What a moral dilemma. I have to consult my sponsor."

"Will you please," Joey said through gritted teeth, "tell me what you're talking about before I go and drink myself into a frenzy?"

"Ziggy!" The coffee lady unearthed two cans of coffee and slammed shut the van door. "I'm appointing myself your interim sponsor. You tell this girl whatever it is you're not telling her. Make your amends and get on with it. Nowhere does it say you're allowed to torment people. Only start the coffee while you're at it."

We followed the coffee lady into the church. She turned on the lights in a meeting room. We dropped off our supplies, then followed Ziggy as he lugged the coffee machine to the men's room to fill it with water. The men's room was empty.

"Okay. About eight years ago," Ziggy said, "Elliot came to me to handle his divorce from Mary Lou, his second wife."

"I know about Mary Lou," Joey said.

"Well, it was pretty straightforward, no kids and not much money to split up. There'd been money at one point, but Elliot had made investments that didn't pan out, which was one reason Mary Lou didn't care to stay married."

"Another reason she didn't care to stay married was that he was cheating on her," Joey said. "But go on."

Ziggy looked over at her from the sink. "He told you that?"

"We have a very honest relationship. With some glaring exceptions. Go on."

"So. They signed the papers and Elliot gave me money to file them, but I put it in a special account I had for clients' money, and one day I took all the money and headed for Tijuana."

"Excuse me?" Joey said.

"I took everyone's money and went to Tijuana. It wasn't a fortune, but then, Tijuana's quite a bargain. Have you been?"

Joey just stared at him. I noticed how pale she looked in the bad bathroom light, the white scar running down the side of her face more prominent.

"Wait," I said, putting it together. "That means there are people out there thinking they're divorced and, in fact, they're still married."

"Exactly. Until last year, when I started to make amends." Ziggy tried to lift the filled coffee machine, grunting from the weight. "So there I was," he said, still grunting, "living high on the hog south of the border—. Sorry, can one of you help me here?"

Better me than Joey. I took one end of the coffee machine and walked in mincing steps with Ziggy as he talked. "—until I got sober. Want to hear that story?"

"No," Joey said.

"We'll just call it a miracle. So then I had to clean up my past. Which is gonna take a while. Years, even." He sounded cheerful about this. "Also, I had to do a little jail time, which is why it took so long to get to you. Elliot and Mary Lou were last on the list." We reached the meeting room, where people were beginning to congregate.

"So you got everyone redivorced?" I asked.

"Well, not Mary Lou, obviously. She died two years ago in a small plane crash. I figured that was the end of it, till I heard Elliot had re-married *three* years ago. None of the other couples had remarried, so, Joey, you're the only instance of what I call collateral damage. One couple even started dating again. Isn't that fascinating?"

"Not to me," Joey said. "You're telling me Elliot's still married to Mary Lou?"

"Well, he's widowed from her." Ziggy and I hoisted the coffee machine onto the table. "He's definitely not married to you, though. I explained all this to Elliot's sister."

"Yes," Joey said, "and *my* question is, How come you were so eager to tell Camille, and had to be tied down and sat on to tell me, whose business it actually is?"

Ziggy nodded. "Good question. Bottom line, I'm a coward. I knew it would be easier to tell her than to tell him, let alone *you*. I don't like to upset people. Now, can I assume that you'll fill in Elliot, if in fact he doesn't already know, or should I call—"

"You do it," the coffee lady said, overhearing. "As your interim sponsor, I'm making an executive decision."

"Good idea," Joey said. "You do it. And Ziggy? Have a nice day."

"Thanks," Ziggy said. "Oh! I'm happy to pay for a new marriage license, when you two tie the knot again. I'd like to pay for the whole wedding, but it'll take me about seventy years to settle up with Uncle Sam. But you're not leaving, are you? The meeting hasn't even started, and we have a great speaker tonight."

"I can't imagine anyone topping the speech you just gave," Joey said.

"Joey," I whispered on the way out, "don't you have to attend meetings?"

"Yeah, but I don't have to attend that one. I'll go to four or five tomorrow. What I have to do right now is find Elliot and marry him."

"Are you sure?" I said. "Under the circumstances, why not just—"

"Wollie." She turned to me. "I don't have a choice. I'm flat broke."

Twenty-six

Broke?" I yelled. "How can you possibly be broke?"

"Shh." Joey looked around the parking lot. "Let's not feed the paparazzi."

"You're exaggerating, right?"

"Well, there's still the cash I sewed into the chaise longue."

"I'm serious," I said.

"I am too. All the money I ever made is tied up in Elliot's companies, which are in his name, not mine."

"But that's so—feudal, Joey. It's not like you."

She rubbed her eyes as if she was allergic to the topic. "Three years ago, I had assets and he had . . . ideas. I provided seed money, and he quadrupled it. Quintupled it. He's a genius of sorts. Anyhow, this is California, it's community property, so half of what he made is mine, which is a lot more than I came into the marriage with. Not a bad deal." She was talking like she was legally married, which was only natural.

"But you assumed all the risk. Years of savings, to subsidize a gambler."

"A husband, Wollie. That's the horse you back. I believed in him and he never screwed me."

I was growing agitated. "He cheated on you."

"In bed. Not at the bank. There's a difference."

The parking lot was full now. I looked around for reporters, but how could I tell them from the alcoholics? "Joey, what if he was, though? Screwing you?"

"What do you mean?"

I hesitated, then plunged in. "Ziggy told Elliot's sister about the non-divorce, thinking she'd tell Elliot. What if she did? And what if, instead of telling you, he . . ."

"Decided to dump me? To stiff me?" Her arms wrapped around herself like a straitjacket. "I *know* him. It's not in him to do that to me. He's tough, but he's not mean. David was mean. Elliot's not mean."

David was mean?

I wanted to pursue that, but Joey was moving off, distressed. I ran to catch up with her. "Okay," I said. "You know Elliot, I don't. Sorry. Come with me."

"Where, to the police station? I don't think so."

I put my hand on her arm. "But you shouldn't be driving, you're upset, and—"

"I'm fine. And I've sobered up, believe me. I've gotta find Elliot. I've got no money, but I've got a full tank of gas. I'll catch up with you later."

I tried every argument I could come up with. I pleaded. I offered to cancel the cop interview and accompany her. If I could've thought of a plausible threat, I'd have threatened her. But she did seem sober, and short of physical force or calling the cops, neither of which I was willing to do, I couldn't think of a way to stop her. I did extract a promise that she wouldn't drink anymore tonight, and that if she did drink, she wouldn't drive anymore.

I watched her pull out of the parking lot, which she did with precision. I went back to my own car and drove slowly to the police station.

Twenty-seven

En route to the North Hollywood police station I remembered to turn on my phone. There was one message, from Simon.

"Ilse called me," he said. "I can't talk now except to tell you that we're not breaking up—I hope to God we're not breaking up—" Simon's voice crackled, in imminent danger of losing the signal. "Look, I'm breaking up. My cell phone, not us."

Good, we weren't breaking up. Yet. After hearing Ziggy's tale, could I take anything for granted? I considered returning the call. We'd been parted for more than twelve hours, and my body ached for him—probably due to dopamine withdrawal, Fredreeq would say. Just a phase, I told myself. Three years hence I could be Joey, spending Christmas with a dying ex while my significant other was off in Vegas.

Better not to call Simon. He'd ask tough questions about Joey, which would be like a bad dress rehearsal for the cop interview. Instead, I dialed Fredreeq. She'd also ask tough questions, but her response would be less frightening.

"Not married?" Fredreeq shrieked. I had to pull the phone away from my ear. "Joey's been living in sin all these years?"

"It gets worse," I said, and told her about Joey's financial problems.

"At least she's got the Klimt. Angel Ramirez did a special report on *News at Noon*. Is Joey there with you?"

"No, she went looking for Elliot. That worries me too. She seems sober, but her record hasn't been so great lately, and—"

"Yeah, I know about that DUI. What does Simon think about all this?"

That stopped me. "Fredreeq, gotta go. I'm at my police interview. Bye. Wish me luck." I couldn't tell her I was no longer living with Simon. Easier to confess to murder.

The North Hollywood division of LAPD at Burbank and Colfax was clean and snappy looking, with a library-like quiet. A slow crime night, I figured, providing little in the way of distraction. I read the community service posters and checked out various trophies, and waited. Eventually, the officer behind the huge circular reception desk told me Detective Born had phoned in, asking me to wait more. I went out to my car, brought in *The Iliad,* and tried to settle in on a bright orange chair the exact color of my hair and get some reading done. But reading about death made me think about . . . death.

The assisted-suicide theory no longer seemed so plausible, if David's pain had been rendered manageable by a generous supply of morphine—although what *about* that missing morphine? It was more likely that someone wanted him dead—but fast, since he was dying on his own pretty quickly. Who?

There was Jen, of course, whose job would've been in jeopardy if David had lived another few weeks. But there were also actors who'd narrowly averted Death by Nuclear Disaster, characters now anticipating a ripe old age in Moon Lake. Who were they, other than Tricia? Trey. And two noncontract players, Rupert had said.

But would someone really kill David over a job?

An acting job? A producing job? In Hollywood? Yes.

And then there were the people who'd inherited money, one of whom had been on the verge of being written out of the will. As motives go, this was a time-honored classic. Except that the category included Joey.

My phone rang and I answered it without thinking. Bad move.

"How are you, where are you, and when were you planning to call me back?"

Simon sounded more like a boss than a lover, something I'd have to address soon. "Ah, the lost art of conversation," I said. "I'm in a safe place. The North Hollywood police station. And not even under arrest.

Waiting for some homicide detective to interview me. No need to worry."

"It's only half worry."

"What's the other half?"

"Lust."

I smiled. "That's much better. So what are you wearing?"

"Later," he said. "Look, for the interview, just answer their questions and don't get creative."

"Why would I do that?" I asked, watching a pair of cops leading a pair of teenage boys past me and down a hallway.

"Because Joey's face is all over the news and you want to protect her. If the cop's any good, he'll see through it. Even if he's bad, he'll see through it, in your case."

My heart started to thump loudly. "Simon. Do you think Joey did it?"

"It doesn't matter what I think. They won't arrest her unless they have a case. There's nothing you can do to help Joey except—"

"You don't know that—"

"Wollie." He was getting testy. "What the hell do you think I do for a living?"

"Textiles."

Silence. We were still getting the hang of the relationship thing. Except the lust part.

"Mrs. Shelley?"

I jumped up, looking into the face of a man I hadn't seen approaching. "Gotta go, my date's here," I said to Simon and hit the END button. "It's Ms. Or Miss. Not Mrs." I shook the outstretched hand. "Hello again, Detective Born."

He frowned. "You sure we've met?"

"It's the hair. I used to look normal."

He asked the desk sergeant about an interview room but was told they were both in use. He led me through a hallway into a large area crowded with desks and settled us right under a sign suspended from the ceiling that read HOMICIDE. The desk belonged to a Jakov Gloom; Born explained that his own office was downtown, but this division was easier for most of the case's witnesses to get to. As he spoke, I figured out who he reminded me of. George Washington. His hair was white, long enough on the sides to do a little flip at the nape of his neck. He had a hooknose and large, tired eyes. In profile, Detective Ike Born looked exactly like a quarter.

He started by asking standard questions, starting with my name.

"Wollie," I said. "Short for Wollstonecraft. As in Mary Wollstone-craft Shelley."

He looked up from his note taking.

"She wrote *Frankenstein*," I said. "Named for her mother, Mary Woll-stonecraft, a famous feminist. *Vindication of the Rights of Women*. Not that you asked."

He went back to writing, without comment. "Address?"

I cleared my throat. "That's a tough one. I'm between residences."

"Where does your mail go?"

"Post office box."

"Where do you sleep at night?"

"Last night? Westwood. Tonight's up in the air."

He looked at his watch, the implication clear.

"I'm a night owl," I said. "Sometimes."

"Occupation?"

"Greeting card designer, muralist, and dating correspondent."

He looked up again. "What's a dating correspondent?"

"I date soap opera stars and talk about it on television."

"And you're paid to do this?"

"Yes. But there's no sex involved. Although I'm still new at it." That sounded a little odd, but then the whole interview was not going as I'd have liked.

"How'd you come to know David Zetrakis?"

"We had a short relationship ten years ago. It didn't really pan out, romantically, but we remained friends."

"Why didn't it pan out?"

"Oh, you know. Chemistry. Destiny. That sort of thing. Wasn't in the cards."

"How did you meet?"

"My friend Joey introduced us. She thought we might hit it off."

"That would be Joey Horowitz? She was sexually involved with him too, right?"

This was making me wary, for some reason. "Later on, yes. She was just friends with him when she fixed up the two of us."

"And why'd they break up? Same chemistry-destiny deal?"

"I couldn't say. You'd have to ask her."

"Come on." He leaned in. "Close friends and you don't know why she broke up with the guy?"

"Joey's good at keeping secrets." As soon as the words were out of my mouth, I regretted them. It made her sound . . . secretive.

"When did you last see David?"

I stared at George Washington's wrinkled hands. I knew his name wasn't George, but I suddenly couldn't recall what it was, because I was flooded with a memory of David. I'd run into him six months earlier, at a sushi place in Tarzana, a favorite with my ex-fiancé and me. He'd given me a big kiss and told Doc that he'd gotten lucky and should treat me well. Doc had said, "I know. I will."

Ha.

"This past summer," I said. "He looked a little fragile. I asked him if he was okay, and he said he'd gone vegan. I guess that's code for 'cancer.' "

"Where were you last Friday morning?"

I didn't have to think about this. "I slept late, then made phone calls from my then-residence. In Westwood."

"Were you alone?"

"My boyfriend was with me until about ten. Until he went to work. At the—" I took a deep breath. "Textiles . . . textile factory. He's in . . . textiles."

Ike Born looked at me and squinted. "You okay?"

I nodded, then shook my head. I was red, breathing heavily, and sweating. My hands were clammy. I felt like throwing up. This is what lying does to me.

"His name?"

"Whose?"

"Your boyfriend."

My antiperspirant gave out. It wasn't up to this job. "Simon Alexander," I said. "He's in textiles." How many times was that going to pop out of me?

"Phone number?" he asked.

"Whose?" I said.

"Boyfriend."

I told him.

The detective turned the page in his notebook and continued taking meticulous notes. "Did you talk to your friend Joey on Friday morning?"

"Yes, on the phone. I don't know the exact time. After Simon left for work."

"You called her or she called you?"

I couldn't lie about this, right? They had phone records. "I called her."

"Home phone or cell phone?" he said.

"C—cell."

"Where was she when you called her? At home?"

I gulped. This was it. Sweat was flying off my forehead. I was a geyser, the Old Faithful of witnesses. I had to protect Joey, if I could, but could I?

"I think so," I whispered.

"You think so?"

"Um, yes. I do. Think so. Not a hundred percent sure."

"What percent sure are you?"

"Ninety-three? Low nineties. Maybe high eighties."

"Would you go as low as eighty-three percent?"

I shook my head, unable to speak. My mouth would no longer cooperate. I held up a thumb, in a "higher than eighty-three" gesture.

"Do you own a gun?"

"Me? Hell, no. I mean, heck no."

"You can swear. It won't count against you."

"What will?" I asked. "Count against me, I mean."

Detective Ike Born peered at me over that hooknose, the eyes looking more tired than they had even four minutes ago. "Perjury," he said. "Lying on a sworn statement will count against you."

I nodded. "Okay."

"Does your friend Joey have a gun?"

"Haven't you asked her?"

"I'm asking you."

It was probably easily verified that Joey had a gun. "Yes. She has a— I can't remember the name. Kind of cute-sounding. One syllable. Plastic-looking."

"Glock?"

"That's it."

"I understand that David Zetrakis left you something in his will."

"Yes, some lithographs. Illustrations from an edition of *The Jungle Book* that hung in a guest bathroom."

"What would you say their value is?"

"No idea. Great framing, though. Twenty-two-karat water-gilded closed-cornered frames. Abe Munn."

"And the painting your friend Joey inherited. By—?"

"Klimt. Gustav Klimt."

"What would you say its value is?"

"Framed or unframed?" I said.

He just looked at me.

I looked back. "It's not a major Klimt. It's a minor Klimt. A cheap Klimt."

He said nothing. Then: "How are you set financially?"

"I'm not set. I'm wiggly. I have four thousand dollars in the bank that's gotta go to first and last month's rent on a new apartment, which I have to find soon. I drive a car that's had six previous owners, one of whom smoked cigars in it. I have a couple jobs at the moment, but they won't last. My greeting card income is both erratic and small. I have no real debt, but I have a brother who's on medication and can't hold down a job and is my responsibility. I don't gamble or smoke or shoot heroin, and I'm a cheap date. I have no outstanding parking tickets. That's my life story, Detective."

He took no notes. Maybe he was saving paper, hoping his notebook would last till retirement. It was so old, the spiral was coming out of its tiny holes. "And your friend Joey?" he asked.

My heart pumped faster. "What about her?"

"What's her financial status? And I realize I can ask her, but I'm asking you."

"I haven't seen her tax statements, but she does fine."

"What's that mean?"

"She picks up the check at restaurants, she gives tens of thousands of dollars to charity, and she's always been that way, even when she was single. She was an actress for twenty years—a working one, not a wannabe one—plus a model, with magazine covers, and now she and her husband produce TV shows and computer chips, and they own a landmark house built by Rolf Solomon in the 1920s and they do a lot of traveling and that's what I mean by doing okay."

He put down his pen and sat back. "Well, I seem to have hit a nerve."

"I'm just saying they're not going to hawk the Klimt to pay the gas bill. They already have a Kandinsky."

Detective George Washington did not react to this.

"I'll be honest," I said. "The Kandinsky depresses me. I wouldn't want it. But Elliot did and Joey bought it for him on their first anniversary, so there you go."

"There I go," he said. "A historic house. Bunch of paintings. Sounds like these people are pretty serious about their art." He wrote on his notepad. From upside down I could read his handwriting: "Art nuts."

"Waitaminute. You're not thinking art acquisition as motive for murder."

"Shouldn't I?" he said.

"Joey's the last person who'd commit murder over a painting."

He kept on writing. "And what would she be likely to commit murder over?"

"Nothing. She's as likely as your own grandmother would be to kill anyone."

"Do you know my grandmother?"

"No." It wasn't hard to imagine. Like Martha Washington, but older. I felt the first stirrings of a greeting card but squelched them.

"Let's go back and revisit Friday morning," he said. "You were at home. Your home of the day, anyway. Your boyfriend goes to work. You call your friend. Do you happen to remember what it was that made you think she was home, if in fact you called her on her cell phone?"

The sweat that had begun earlier was recurring. New sweat on top of old sweat. I heard of someone once who was allergic to their own sweat. If that were me, I'd be covered by a rash by now. Maybe I was. George Washington, the father of our country, was scrutinizing me.

"No. I don't remember."

He continued looking at me. I wanted to tell him everything: how bad I felt about lying, what a nice person I often was, and how the day was going for me. But it wasn't about me. It was about Joey.

"Maybe," he said, "she wasn't home, she was talking from somewhere else?"

"You know, I'm not very good at this. I'm disappointing you, aren't I?"

"You do okay when you stick to the truth." Detective Born stood. "You'll most likely be hearing from me again."

"Anytime. Aren't you going to tell me not to leave town?"

"Don't leave town."

.   .   .

I'd told Simon that the police station was a safe place to be, but when I reached the door I heard a "Hey!" and saw a stranger emerge from a taxi, flagging me down. He was a slight man, not visually threatening, but still. Paparazzi. I didn't want to talk to him. I covered my face, in case he had a camera, and hurried across the parking lot.

"Hey, *you*," he called, like that would sell me on him.

I ran. When I reached my car, I looked back to see him entering the police station. I unlocked the Integra and scrambled in. Then I screamed. Simon was in the passenger seat.

"What are you doing, scaring the life out of me?" I yelled.

"This," he said, leaning over to pull me into him. He kissed me.

I thought about not kissing him back, but it was the end of a long day and resistance is exhausting. Strangely, once into the kiss I couldn't remember what I had to be resistant about.

After a few minutes of that, we stopped and sat back, staring at each other. How beautiful he was, even in the near dark. I reached out and touched his jaw, and then he took my hand and pulled me toward him again and we kissed some more.

"How'd it go in there?" he murmured after a while.

"Lovely," I said. "How's work?"

"Couldn't be better. Would you consider getting naked in a parking lot?"

"My car or yours?" I said.

"You think I'm kidding?"

I reached for his belt buckle. "Not at all. I know how serious you are about sex."

His hand caught mine. "Not this parking lot. Across the street. Where are you staying, by the way?"

"Haven't figured that out yet," I said.

He leaned back against the passenger door, regarding me. "It's after ten. When were you planning on thinking about it?"

"It's no big deal. I can stay with Uncle Theo." I suddenly remembered his apartmentful of illegal immigrants. "Or Fredreeq, or . . ."

"Call her."

"Later."

"Now. I want to know you're set for the night."

"Later."

"Okay," he said, losing patience. "I'm calling a hotel."

"Make it the Bel-Air. It's my favorite."

"Fine."

"I'm kidding, Simon. Look, I'm not one of your junior operatives, so you don't get to give orders and you don't have to worry about me."

"Don't I? Do you know your friend David was killed execution-style, suggesting a mob hit? Except that—"

"Is that the theory at the Vegas office?"

He frowned at me. "Except that there are no indications that David had a problem with the mob. Which suggests there's a killer out there with a cold-blooded manner and some planning skills. If I were LAPD, I'd take a hard look at Joey, because she was close to the victim and that's where you start. And she profited from his death—yes, I've watched the news. If she's innocent, the detectives eliminate her. But from what I can tell, they're not doing that. Probably because she's not acting innocent, she's behaving erratically, and she's involving you at every turn—"

"No, she's not, she's—"

"You've driven her car and answered her phone. You've been mistaken for her. The killer's watching the news too, which means the killer's watching Joey. And, by extension, you. So you'll forgive me if I want to know where you're spending your nights."

My mouth went dry. "I'm not abandoning Joey just so you can sleep better. As to where I'll be staying, when I know, you'll know."

Simon said nothing for a long moment. "Ever hear the phrase 'pick your battles'? Because you're not going to win this one. Call Fredreeq."

I hit REDIAL.

Fredreeq answered on the first ring. "Wollie?" she yelled, causing me to pull the phone away from my ear. "I was just going to call you. I've got Joey in my car, heading to her place. Can you meet us in Pasadena?"

"Okay, but—"

"And don't tell Simon what's going on. Make something up." With that, Fredreeq hung up.

"Oh . . . kay," I said slowly to the dead phone, then turned it off.

"Go ahead, make something up," he said. "Entertain me." He folded his arms, managing to look relaxed even in the Integra's small passenger seat.

I sighed. "Fredreeq is not the most soft-spoken of my friends."

"If she thinks you're capable of inventing a story I'll buy, she's not the smartest one either."

I climbed over the console to get right in his face. "Have I told you that I'm in love with you?"

He breathed heavily, unevenly. We stayed that way, face-to-face, breathing heavily, both of us. Not touching.

"No," he said finally. "You hadn't gotten around to that."

I whispered it a few more times, just to make sure he got it. Then I drove him to his car. As he opened the door, I said, "Rain check on the car sex."

He turned to me. "You're going to do whatever you can for Joey. I understand that. But if you get in too deep, I'm coming in after you. You're what I care about. I'll shut this down if I see you getting hurt."

And without waiting for a response, he climbed out and closed the door.

Twenty-eight

The drive to Pasadena was beautiful, meaning nearly traffic-free, but I didn't rush. I didn't want to get to Solomonhaus first, because the place gave me the willies in the dark. And in daylight. Also, I was not happy about Simon's parting words. It wasn't just the Gary Cooper delivery; he thought I was in danger. I couldn't focus on that, because I'm a natural coward. To be of any use to Joey, it was better to stay in denial.

But something else bothered me too. Simon talked like he had the power to stop me from helping her. It brought to mind Zeus on the sidelines of the Trojan War, staying out until he didn't like how things were going, then jumping in. It wasn't just autocratic; it made me wonder, How did he plan to do it? Would he use his resources to monitor my activities? Should I check the Integra for bugs? On one hand, it was nice to know someone had my back, but I had little experience with men who rode to my rescue. In my family, men read poetry. Unless he was also planning to ride to Joey's rescue, I wasn't interested. Also, did that macho chivalry thing ever work? With Mr. Right guarding the door, wouldn't the bad guys just come down the chimney?

Fredreeq's car was under the carport when I pulled into the driveway. "In the kitchen," Fredreeq yelled, in answer to my knock. I found her frowning at a hot-air popcorn popper, speaking loudly to be heard above a whirring noise. "This is it for food. This and three bottles of capers. No wonder their marriage is on the rocks. They better have butter, or this popcorn is going to taste like packing peanuts."

"Where's Joey?" I asked, finding a stick of margarine in the refrigerator.

"Bedroom. Setting up the TV. They keep it in a closet. How can people live like this?" She lowered her voice. "I brought her home because she's broke and *he* should check into a hotel, not her. She's not well. I don't suppose you have any sedatives on you? Never mind. But one of us needs to stay here tonight." Tentative pops emerged from the hot-air popper. "I vote you because I've got in-laws coming tomorrow. And it won't hurt Simon to know that a king-sized bed without you in it is a sad thing."

"I'll stay." I went into the bedroom and found Joey cross-legged on the bed, with a remote. On a steel shelf was a small TV. On the floor was an open bottle of champagne.

I sat on the bed. "What's up?"

"I went to Malibu to find Elliot. His surfing haunts. The last place I tried, one of the guys had seen him in the parking lot with a woman. The bastard."

"Arguing with her!" Fredreeq yelled.

"Immaterial!" Joey yelled back.

"A woman who looked like you, don't forget!" Fredreeq yelled. "At least he's consistent."

Joey clicked the remote at the TV with a certain ferocity. "Fredreeq showed up and we found his car parked at Zuma. I assaulted it with my purse."

Fredreeq appeared in the doorway. "I got it away from her before the strap broke. So then she starts in on the car with her hands. Rafferty, I'm signing you up for anger management. I understand beating on a husband, but when you start terrorizing a car with your own purse—that's a Dolce & Gabbana."

"But Joey," I said, "if Elliot and this woman were arguing, why would you assume they were romantically involved?"

"It's Elliot's M.O. He likes makeup sex."

"Well, you ought to know," Fredreeq said, retreating to the kitchen as the popping sound slowed. "Channel Nine!" she called. "Seconds to go."

"So Fredreeq hauled me out of there, because I was attracting a crowd." Joey reached for the champagne. "Bottom-feeder," she added, referring not to Fredreeq but to Angel Ramirez, in a "Channel Nine Special Report."

Angel, microphone to her pink lips, announced that the bulk of David's estate was going to his former girlfriend Joey Rafferty and his brother, Charles, implying that the police need look no further for suspects. Angel also mentioned the early rumors of assisted suicide, but only in order to refute them. Jen Kim appeared on the small TV screen, caught outside the Century City office building that morning.

"David was living for February sweeps," Jen said in her rapid-fire delivery. "We have a hot storyline coming up, which he created before he got too sick to work. I'm not saying he wouldn't orchestrate his death, but not till March at the earliest."

Tricia appeared next, in a tiara and a strapless evening gown, presumably interviewed from the set. "As a Christmas present, I sent David my acupuncturist," she said, "and he brought David to a very good place mentally. So suicide just wasn't an option. He's excellent. Chinese. The acupuncturist, I mean."

Next up was a nun. "Just after Thankgiving," she said, "David heeded a call to return to the faith, which prohibits suicide. I began coming to the house, doing visits and so forth, part of a parish-patient outreach program. David was very determined to make his peace with everyone before meeting his Maker."

"I'd say that's overstating it, Sister," Joey said to the TV.

"And so," Angel said, returning to the screen, "perhaps we can lay to rest the theory that David Zetrakis had a hand in his own death. As for those reports that the murder weapon was a gun from his own soap opera, *At the End of the Day,* LAPD has not yet confirmed them, but we'll let you know the moment they do."

We stared at the screen as a car commercial appeared.

"Oh, God," Joey said. "Tell me I didn't just hear that."

Fredreeq passed the popcorn. "What's the problem? It's not like you're on the show anymore."

"I was there constantly. The set. The whole month. David put me on the list at the guard gate, I had my own parking place. He was trying to produce the show from his deathbed, so he had me running back and forth all the time. I humored him. We all did."

"You didn't tell him about Jen's rewrites, though?" I said. "About the people she saved from nuclear death?"

"No, but he found out—about Tricia, anyway. Her new contract. That's what we fought about on Christmas Eve. He was mad that we were keeping things from him, and I told him to let it go, to let Jen find her way, give her some breathing room. He was a micromanager. It was at odds with this newfound spiritual thing, this spirit of forgiveness that came over him at the end. I just wanted him to relax."

"Back up," Fredreeq said. "I don't understand this gun business. If the murder weapon was a prop, how could it kill someone?"

"Shows use replicas and real guns both," Joey said.

"Clay Jakes was talking about this last night," I said. "Now I understand it."

Joey silenced the car commercial with a click. "Clay's another problem. I've known him for fifteen years. We're buddies."

"So?" Fredreeq said.

"I hung out in the prop room a lot. At the holiday party a few weeks ago we were in there doing shots of tequila. Clay was schnockered. Showed me the current arsenal. He locked it up afterward, but the keys were lying around all night."

"So everyone had access to the gun," I said. "Anyone working on the show."

"You're missing the point," Joey said. "I'm not anyone. I'm now the trifecta of homicide suspects. I've got means, motive, and opportunity."

"Have the cops figured that out, do you suppose?" I asked.

"Yeah." Joey reached for her bottle of champagne. "There's a message on the machine, wanting to know if I'll take a polygraph test. You know, to 'rule me out as a suspect.' "

"And?" I said. "Are you going to?"

Joey downed the last of the champagne, then lay back on the bed, closing her eyes. "Hell, no."

Twenty-nine

woke the next morning to the sound of a doorbell alternating with frantic knocking. It took me a second to realize whose door and bell it was; I was in a bedroom so austere it might have been a space module. Once I figured it out, I waited for Joey to answer her front door. When that didn't happen, I wrapped a gray cashmere blanket around myself and padded across gray concrete floors to the foyer.

The man seeking to enter Solomonhaus was athletic and tan, with gelled hair and irritation wrinkles on his face. "Who are you?" he said.

"The butler," I said. "Who are you?"

"Where's Elliot?" he asked, and brushed by me, displacing my blanket. I wrapped it more firmly about me.

"No idea," I said. "But Joey's here someplace. I smell coffee."

"This is one goddamn peculiar house," he said, heading for the kitchen quadrant. "I keep telling him, 'Guy, get a flat-screen TV. Hang some pictures.' Here, I brought the mail in. It was falling out of the box." He handed me a clump of letters and magazines as though I were in fact the butler, then helped himself to coffee. He took a sip and grimaced. "Stuff could fuel a jet. Hey, Joey!"

He continued on his way through the house, with me behind him. Joey wasn't in her room, but the bed was rumpled. There weren't many places to hide in the house, and when we went through the sliding doors to the backyard, there she was, lying in the sun on a stone chaise, eyes closed, coffee mug resting on her concave stomach. She wore the clothes she'd been wearing the night before.

"Hey, Rafferty. Wake up," the man said, grabbing one of her cowboy-booted feet and wiggling it.

Joey's eyes opened. She looked at him, at me, then back at him. "Hi, Van Beek. Where's Elliot?"

"That's what I'm here to ask you."

Joey frowned and sat up, setting her coffee mug on the grass beside her. "You really don't know where he is?"

"I really don't. We were supposed to do a conference call with our accountant this morning and he didn't show. What's up with that?"

"Your accountant?" Joey said. "Why was he talking with an accountant?"

"Calm down. We had to do year-end stuff. Who cares? The point is, he didn't make the call, and where the hell is he?"

Joey stood up, rubbing her face with both hands. "Sorry. I don't know where he is. Obviously. Did you two meet, by the way? Wollie, this is Drew Van Beek, Elliot's partner in all his nefarious enterprises. Drew, this is my best friend, Wollie."

We shook hands. "Pleasure," he said.

"Wollie, help yourself to my clothes," Joey said. "I've got sweatpants and stuff in the bottom drawer in the bedroom."

I thought of Achilles lending his armor to his friend Patroklos, inadvertently causing his death. This was Simon's doing, putting thoughts like this in my head—

"Hey!" Van Beek was staring at me. "You were in Elliot's reality show, weren't you? Didn't recognize you in a blanket. Did something to your hair too."

"Yes, I know, I—"

"Okay, I'd love to chat, girls, but here's the deal. I need him to sign off on two documents by the end of business today, because tomorrow's New Year's Eve, after which options lapse and two projects fall off the table. Get it?"

I said, "Can Joey sign stuff on his behalf? Since she's his wife?"

"You mean forge his signature?" He looked at Joey. "You any good at that?"

"Not great." Joey glanced at me. "Wollie doesn't mean forgery; she means legally, as his wife, could I—?"

"Is there a Mrs. Horowitz on the letterhead? Are you at the board meetings? No. What are you talking about?" Van Beek was irritated, but he wasn't questioning her marital status. If Elliot knew about Ziggy's perfidy, he hadn't told his business partner.

"Okay, just trying to be helpful." I headed into the house to change.

Joey got up to follow, saying, "We better call what'sername, the flight attendant he's been sleeping with."

"Wha . . . who?" Van Beek asked.

"I believe her name is Debbie. Is it Debbie? From JetBlue."

"I don't—uh—" He was visibly disturbed now.

"Oh, save it. I know you know. Was it you that gave him the Viagra I found in his jeans?" Joey reached the kitchen and opened a drawer. "Here it is," she said, pulling out a piece of paper. "Yes, it's Debbie. The other one he's sleeping with is Daryl Ann, but Debbie's the main squeeze."

"Maybe Mr. Van Beek should call," I said. "She may be more forthcoming with him."

"Good point," Joey said, handing him the phone. "Drew, you're on."

"You are two lunatic chicks," he said, but he dialed. He introduced himself to Debbie and asked if she knew where Elliot was. "I'd never bother you," he said, "except I'm worried about him, and he's always spoken so highly of you—" He turned to Joey and shook his head, mouthing the word "bullshit" to show where his loyalty lay. There followed a lot of "uh-huh"s and then a quick hang-up.

"Debbie hasn't heard from him," he said. "And he didn't give her a Christmas present. She's unhappy about that. Now she's worried, on top of unhappy. Happy?"

"No," Joey said. "Because now you've gotta call Camille."

"His sister? She called me this morning. She has no idea where he is and I got her worried too. Anyone else we can get worried about it?"

Joey turned to her espresso machine and emptied out the used grounds, dumping them into the garbage can and banging on its side, as if doing a drum solo. "He was here yesterday afternoon. We had sex. Then he went surfing. He said he'd call me. He said he'd put money into the checking account. He hasn't done either one. Goddamnit, this is pissing me off."

"Surfing or skimboarding?" Van Beek asked.

"Surfing. Night surfing." She filled the spoonlike apparatus with ground espresso, taking time with it, tapping it into place.

The doorbell rang, startling all three of us, but Joey most of all. She spun around, sending her ground espresso flying across the kitchen. We all went to the door.

It was Rupert Ling.

"What are you doing here?" Joey asked.

"Appointment with Elliot," Rupert said, indicating a portfolio under his arm. "To show him my business plans, for a vineyard just north of Paso Robles. Hello, Wollie. Nice blanket."

"Elliot told me about you," Van Beek said, shaking Rupert's hand. "Wine has unbelievable cachet right now. We're potentially very interested. I'm his partner."

"Rupert," Joey said. "You were meeting Elliot here? Right now?"

"As a matter of fact," Rupert said, glancing at his watch, "I'm twelve minutes late. Ugly traffic."

"Shit," Joey said, with a look to Van Beek. "Elliot doesn't miss appointments."

"Who'd he go surfing with?" Van Beek said. "You know any of those guys?"

"He was alone. I talked to Clammy, Suds, and Stoner last night."

"Night surfing?" Rupert said. "This time of year? That's pretty high risk. Ten-foot waves, the radio said."

I picked up the phone and dialed Simon.

"Hey, little girl," he said. "What's up?"

Being called "little girl" when you're neither little nor a girl is a strange and wonderful thing, coming from someone with whom you're having a grown-up affair. I wanted to tell him this, but I stuck to asking how to find someone last seen surfing.

"It hasn't been twenty-four hours," I said. "I think that's how long you wait before reporting someone missing, but won't they make an exception if there's surfing involved?"

"Probably," Simon said, his voice wary. "Who's missing?"

"Elliot. Joey's husband."

"Describe him."

This was surprisingly hard. I had to hand off the phone to Joey. Forty-six years old, she said, five eleven, one hundred and seventy pounds, salt-and-pepper hair, brown eyes. Appendectomy scar, silver wedding ring, Tag Heuer diving watch. Driving a BMW that he'd left parked in the Zuma Beach parking lot. The laundry list had a bad sound, reducing Elliot to body parts and possessions. Judging from Van Beek's facial expression and Joey's tone of voice, I wasn't the only one to feel this. A cold air blew through the room, and I went to close the sliding door.

When I returned, Joey had hung up, her hand still on the phone.

"What'd he say?" I asked.

"He'll get back to us."

"And what do we do in the meantime?" Van Beek said.

Joey rubbed her eyes. "That thing I hate. Wait."

Thirty

We did our waiting on Mount Olympus, Joey and I. Rupert and Van Beek had gone off to discuss Rupert's vineyard over breakfast, with instructions to let them know the minute we heard anything, and a promise to do likewise.

"That's some wall," Joey said. We stood in Sheffo's garden, staring at the expanse of gray. "What on earth are you going to do with it?"

"Oh, that's easy," I said. "I'm putting everyone from the Trojan War in a sort of line dance, illustrating the chain-reaction relationships: Achilles pulling a spear out of his heel with Paris behind him, with his bow and arrow, and Helen holding on to Paris, and Menelaus reaching out to Helen, and Agamemnon holding hands with Menelaus. . . . I'll do the same thing with the gods, but they'll be in the back row, in more muted colors. I think. Not to sound sacrilegious, but the whole *Iliad* story works just as well without the divine elements. I can't get a handle on these guys at all."

"That's your Catholic upbringing. Polytheism makes you nervous." Joey plopped herself onto the grass near the pool. "And the gods make it more like a soap opera. So I guess you have to like soaps. But what I'm asking is, What will you paint it with? And do you have to treat it with something or clean it first, or what?"

Navarre came into the garden from the house, bearing a tray with a single glass on it. He'd greeted us at the door with a sigh and an ag-grieved air, but he'd seemed even more displeased when we'd turned down refreshments, so I'd said yes to iced tea.

"I have to consult a graffiti artist," I said to Joey. "Who else paints on cement?"

"Concrete," Navarre said. "Number five rebar."

"Pardon me?" I said.

"I refer to the thickness of the reinforcing bars," he said, sounding de-pressed. "That which gives the wall its rigidity. You'll need a concrete-bonding primer, then acrylic or an oil-based enamel. After washing it, of course."

"Of course," I said. "Thanks. You're very knowledgeable about . . . concrete."

"I'm gay. I'm not ignorant," he said, and made a slow march back to the house.

"What an odd man," Joey said. "On my worst day, I'm not that un-happy."

From a second-story balcony came a cry. "Do you see? This new de-bauchery?"

Sheffo stood in a brocade dressing gown, pointing a shaking hand to his neighbors' yard. I looked up and saw antennae visible above the wall, like wire tree branches. "I build my wall high," Sheffo said, "and his eye-sores go higher. The property owners' association shall hear about it! Is it not enough to massacre my Italian cypress? Now this?" With that, he withdrew into the house.

I wondered what the maligned neighbors had done with their side of the wall, in terms of decor. Perhaps nothing, since it was thirty-two inches from their land. I walked over and felt it with both hands. Cold. Just what you'd expect in winter. It smelled like . . . rocks. But what was on the other side? Paint? Ivy?

At the wall's north end stood a statue of Poseidon. He leaned on his trident, a husky god who looked like he could bench-press at least . . . well, whatever constitutes a lot of weight for a seven-foot guy. He was solidly planted in the ground, solid enough that I was able to climb him. He was much easier than a tree, having a lot of footholds. Standing on his shoulder I could see over the wall.

The world looked vastly different from up here, with an intimate view of the neighbors' backyard. It was a jungle of wires, antennae, and electronic devices, the antithesis of Sheffo's garden, and there was the soft hum of radios just audible, like a distant beehive. Amid the general buzzing came the syllables "double-you-eight-dee-ex," repeatedly. The top of the wall was at least two feet across. The neighbors had a wooden fence on their property line, about four feet high.

My cell phone fell out of my breast pocket.

Damn.

Now what? It was in the thirty-two-inch gap between wall and fence. I wasn't nearly agile enough to get myself the rest of the way up the wall and over, into enemy territory, and there were no statues of Poseidon on that side to help me back up even if I did. I could get the phone only by reaching through the slats in the neighbors' fence. I looked down at Joey, deep in conversation on her own cell phone.

And then, far below me, my phone rang. I stared down at it.

There was only one rational way to handle this. I did "be right back" hand signals to Joey and then went out front, took a left, and rang the neighbors' doorbell.

No answer. I waited and tried again. No answer. I looked around. A mailbox announced their names as Myrtle and Elmer "W8DX" Whistler.

I'd sneak into their backyard. Fast. Nothing illegal about that, right? Well, except trespassing. But just past the front of the house, a gate barred my access, possibly to protect the equipment. Were these people building their own nuclear reactor? Contacting aliens? I tried the gate. Locked. At knee level, though, there was a pet door, sized for a large dog. I crawled through it easily.

And encountered, on the other side, gardening clogs. And a pair of knees.

"Why hello," a woman said, and squatted.

She had frizzy gray hair and wore a bulky plaid shirt.

I would've stood, but it seemed more polite to squat along with her. "Hello," I said. "I'm very sorry, but I think my cell phone's in your back-yard."

"Yes," she said. "It was ringing. I didn't know how to answer it. Here." She handed it to me. She wore a fishing cap that said w8dx. She seemed pleased to see me. "I'm Myrt. You're Betty, aren't you?"

"Betty?"

"Buckley. I could tell by your hair. So distinguished."

Betty Buckley. She was an actress, wasn't she? Surely not orange-haired, though. "Actually, my name's Wollie. I'll just be off now. Thanks for rescuing my phone." I started to stand, but she leaned in, putting a hand on my shoulder, pulling me back to a squat.

"I know you stars like to be left alone. You're visiting"—she gestured with her chin toward Sheffo's—"them?"

"Yes."

She pulled me closer and lowered her voice. "Just so you know. Muffler got into their yard and that was the end of her."

"Really?"

She nodded. "Just so you know. Rat poison."

"I'm so . . . sorry."

"I know you are, dear." She patted my arm and reached past me, holding open the pet-door flap, assuming that I'd want to leave in the manner I'd come.

I made my way back to Sheffo's, wondering if it could possibly be true that Sheffo or Navarre was capable of poisoning the aforementioned Muffler. It seemed unlikely. And so was the idea that Myrt or her husband would chop down a copse of Italian cypresses. At least as unlikely as someone mistaking me for some actress.

I checked my cell's voice mail for the missed call. It was P.B., saying there was a comic-book crisis at the hospital and, also, did I know where his Pink Floyd shirt was, because he was trying to pack. "I'm not really willing to leave it behind," he said. "None of this is working out. Call me." A comic-book crisis sounded suspiciously like a hair emergency, I decided, and as for Pink Floyd shirts, I'd never seen one in my life, certainly not on my brother. I'd deal with it later. If at all. Sometimes it was best to let things slide until they disappeared from view.

Joey stood at one end of the statue-lined pool, looking into its depths. She was so still she might have been a stone goddess herself, except for her hair blowing in the breeze. Her hand reached into her pocket and brought out her phone. I watched, thinking about how even the goddesses and the gods were always dealing with spousal infidelity. What was the point of immortality if eternal jealousy went along with it?

Joey looked over at me, then walked toward me, holding out her phone, saying Van Beek wanted to talk to me.

"Hello?" I said, taken aback.

"Hi," he said. "Listen, I know we just met, so I hate to dump it on you, but I can't do this to her on the phone. I need you to do it."

"Do what?"

"They found Elliot. In the water, south of where his car's parked. He drowned."

I became aware of my own breathing, in and out, in and out. I looked at Joey, who was studying me with a furrow between her eyes, no doubt wondering what Van Beek could possibly have to tell me. I whispered, "Okay" and pressed END and handed the phone to Joey. Her hand was cold. Her face was a question mark. I started to shake.

I didn't know how to word it, so I opened my mouth and said, "Elliot's dead."

She kept looking at me, as if I hadn't spoken. I was almost going to say it again when she nodded. Her eyes closed, and for a moment I thought she was going to smile, and then every muscle in her face contracted, as if squeezing something inside her skull. She put a hand up to stop me from coming closer and, with the other hand, reached out to the statue. She lowered herself to the ground, using Poseidon's trident for support. She knelt on the grass, sat, then let her whole body collapse forward, touching her forehead to the ground like a supplicant. No sound came out of her.

Minutes passed. Navarre came and stood in the doorway of the house, looking at us. I didn't move, having no idea what to do except stay close to Joey. After a time, Navarre walked to us in unhurried steps. I felt caught in some slow, silent ballet. He came to a stop and spoke. "Is she all right?"

"No," I said. "Her husband died."

He bent down and put his hand on her back, between her shoulder blades. We stayed that way, no one moving, for a while. Birds chirped.

Sometime later, Joey raised her head from the ground and said, "I want to see him."

Thirty-one

We headed to Zuma Beach, where Elliot's BMW was parked. Van Beek, over the phone, had suggested it as a place to meet while he tried to get more information from the police. Then Simon called.

"I'm waiting to hear from the sheriff's department in Malibu," he said.

"They found him," I said.

"Alive?"

"No."

Simon let out a long breath. "I'm sorry."

"Me too," I said. "Who was it that reported him missing, besides us?"

"Another surfer, a friend of his, noticed his car parked on the beach all night. His sister called it in too. The sheriff sent out a lifeguard boat midmorning to start looking. How's Joey doing?"

I turned to look at Joey, behind the steering wheel of my Integra. She'd insisted on driving, and whatever grief was doing to her, it wasn't affecting her skill. She zoomed west on Sunset Boulevard, swerving in and out of traffic, passing cars whenever possible. "Stoic," I said.

"And you, my love," he said. "How are you doing?"

"Okay."

"I miss you."

"Me too," I said, and hung up.

Joey said, "It's all right to tell him you love him in front of me."

"He knows."

"Tell him anyway."

"It's not like rubbing salt in your wounds?"

"I can't feel my wounds," she said. "I just have to get to the beach. I have to see Elliot. How long was he in the water, do you suppose?"

"Apparently some surfer last saw him around midnight, and it sounds like they found him an hour or so ago, so maybe as long as twelve hours. Why?"

She didn't answer for a moment. Then, "When I worked in the morgue, we fished someone out of the lake who'd been dead for a day. She didn't look good. Of course, I don't know what she looked like alive. Most of the drownings that summer, we got to them a lot faster. And there's no ocean in Nebraska. I don't know if seawater's different, what it does to people. I want to prepare myself."

I didn't point out that she need not see the body. It made sense to me that she'd want to. It would give substance to an event that seemed impossible to absorb.

I kept thinking, First David, and now Elliot. Maybe Joey was thinking it too, so I said it aloud: "First David, and now Elliot."

She nodded. "You should get a grace period between deaths. It doesn't seem fair. They're not connected, one's got nothing to do with the other, but it feels like an epidemic. Of two. I'm trying not to take it personally."

"Shall I call Fredreeq?" I asked.

"Yes. But I can't talk to her yet."

I nodded, dialing, and left a message. Fredreeq would want to mother Joey, and I saw how that could short-circuit the compartmentalization process that was allowing Joey to function. She hadn't let me touch her. No hugging. Unsure of what else to do, I let her set the tone and steer the conversation, along with the car.

Van Beek and Rupert were in the parking lot, staring at the BMW convertible. The top was down, which Rupert explained was for the surfboard. The car looked vulnerable, as if it was waiting for Elliot to return.

Joey had an extra key and opened the trunk. Hot air emanated from it, despite the winter beach wind swirling around us. The interior of the car itself was clean and empty, but the trunk was packed, like the closets in Solomonhaus. Joey was bent over, collecting mail, when a police cruiser pulled into the parking lot.

"Ma'am," a voice called. "Step away from the car, please."

I jumped back, thinking the police officer was talking to me. I always do. If there's a siren anywhere, a black-and-white in the vicinity, I always assume it has to do with me and that I'm in imminent danger of arrest.

But I wasn't the "ma'am" in question. "Are you talking to me?" Joey yelled.

"Yes, ma'am." He had to yell back, because of the wind on Pacific Coast Highway. Maybe he'd sound less contentious if he weren't yelling, I thought. Maybe Joey would too.

"It's my car," Joey said. "My husband's. I'm not breaking in."

"Step away from it, ma'am."

"Why?"

"Ma'am, I'm not going to tell you again—"

"Oh? What are you going to do, arrest me?"

Rupert, Van Beek, and I went from spectator to participant at the same moment, moving forward to shield Joey from the cop, with Van Beek taking her arm. She shook him off impatiently.

"She's got a key," Rupert said to the cop. "It's her car. What's the problem?"

"This car's part of an investigation. It's my job to secure it. You're not allowed to touch it or remove anything." He was a young cop, and good-looking—a surfer himself, probably, stuck in a cop suit.

"What are you talking about?" Joey asked. "What kind of investigation?"

"I can't tell you that."

"Because you're at the bottom of the food chain, and no one tells you anything. Here. Take the damn car and the contents of it, such as they are, which is nothing. Happy?" She slammed the trunk closed with more force than was necessary.

The cop moved in between us and the car. "You didn't touch anything?"

There was mail under her arm, but her body was positioned so that it wasn't visible to him. He turned away for a moment and I closed in on her and took it, slipping it under my sweatshirt.

Joey held up both hands. "Nothing." Her voice cracked. "My husband's dead and I have nothing. Okay?"

The cop looked miserable. "Okay. I'm sorry, ma'am."

"Fine. Quit calling me ma'am. Where's my husband's body, do you know?"

"Topanga. I mean, that's where the boat brought it in. But the coroner might've taken him away by now."

.   .   .

It wasn't hard to spot them. Official government vehicles on the beach, especially when they're clumped together like a little village, have high visibility. The dress code of the people gathered at Topanga and Pacific Coast Highway ran the gamut, from the tan-and-green sheriff's department uniforms to wet suits, business suits, and swimsuits. As we approached, Joey broke into a run. Rupert took off too, catching up, with Van Beek and me hurrying after. "Where's Elliot?" she called. "Where's my husband?"

A camera appeared alongside me and began clicking photos. Instinctively, I jumped in front of it to shield Joey and found myself walking backward, face-to-face with a jean-jacketed man. He stared at me, then aimed his camera at my face and continued shooting.

Joey was now engaged in a heated discussion with a thin, uniformed woman, who informed her that Elliot—"the deceased"—was on his way to the coroner's office.

"But who ID'd him?" Joey said. "I need to see him. How did—"

"I identified him!" The announcement cut off Joey in mid-sentence.

I turned to see a petite woman marching toward us. She wore a wool suit and pumps, dressed more for the boardroom than the beach, and those in towels and swim trunks cleared a path for her. It wasn't until Van Beek left my side and started toward her that I recognized her as Elliot's sister, whom I'd met years before.

"Camille," Van Beek said. "I'm so sorry—"

"I am his next of kin," she said, ignoring Van Beek and addressing Joey. "I identified him, and your presence here is unnecessary and unwelcome." She wasn't quite yelling; it was more like giving a valedictorian speech. The crowd hung on her words.

"Next of kin?" Joey said. "I'm his *wife*."

"No, you are not." Camille turned to the police. "They weren't married. She's not next of kin, she's nothing. If anything, she's a murderer."

Van Beek touched her shoulder. "Camille. For God's sake—"

"They were never married. They lived together, but they were breaking up and she wanted him dead."

It was a shocking thing to hear. The photographer who'd been in my face swerved his camera toward Camille. Joey, to my surprise, kept it together, confining herself to a restrained "You bitch."

It was enough for Camille. She walked up to Joey, getting in her face as much as possible, given that she was half a foot shorter. "How dare you? How dare you?"

"Hey, hey, now—" Van Beek said, and one of the policemen stepped in, but the women were oblivious to everyone but each other.

"You better back off, Camille," Joey said calmly. "You get any closer and I'll drop-kick you to Catalina."

"She could," Rupert said to me. "I've been to her martial arts class."

Camille, apparently, had not. She held her ground, veritably hissing. "I don't know what you did to him, but you won't profit from his death. Not one penny. Not his house, not his cars—"

"Okay, ladies, let's take it easy," one of the policemen said, inserting himself between them. "I'm sure you're all in shock, and it's very hard to—"

"She's not in shock," Joey said. "She's always like this. Hostile and hysterical. You need to refill your Prozac, Camille."

"You trashy, gold-digging—" Camille made a move as if to hit Joey, but the cop was on top of it, wrapping his arms around her. She was so small, he easily lifted her off the ground and deposited her several feet away from Joey. I let out a breath.

A burly man in the tan shirt and green pants of a sheriff approached Joey. He introduced himself as a deputy and asked when she'd last seen Elliot.

"Ask her where Elliot got the black-and-blue mark on his neck," Camille said. "Go ahead. Ask her if she threw a Wedgwood crystal candlestick at him yesterday."

The deputy squinted at Joey. "Did you?"

"Foreplay," Joey said. "Look, I'll answer anything, I'll tell you whatever you want to know, but I have to see him. Can I see him? I don't care what he looks like, I just have to—"

"When the coroner's done with him, when they establish cause of death, they'll release him to you."

"Not to her," Camille said. "To his family, not to her."

"But aren't you his wife?" the detective asked Joey. "You're his wife, right?"

"I am," Joey said. "Of course I am."

"She's not. I'm telling you!" Camille said.

"Camille, relax, would you?" Van Beek said. "Look. Detective. Officer. Whatever. I'm his business partner, and I can vouch for the fact that this is his wife."

"Okay," the deputy said, "I may need some information later, Mrs.—"

"Horowitz," Joey said, and told him her phone numbers.

"And what about my statement?" Camille said. "About how this woman has tried to kill my brother on more than one occasion?"

The deputy asked one of his crew to take down Camille's phone number and escort her to her vehicle. He waited until she was out of earshot, then said, "You're Joey Rafferty, right? The actress?"

"Yes," she said.

"*Gun Girl,*" he said, referring to the old TV series she'd starred in. I expected him to comment on that, but he just looked off toward Camille. "I'd keep my distance from her. Dealing with a death in the family can make people—"

"Psychotic," Joey said. "I've been trying to keep my distance for years. When can I have my husband's car back?"

"Once we determine the cause of death. As soon as we hear from the coroner, we'll be in touch."

"Elliot was Jewish," Joey said. "Nominally. I'd like to bury him according to tradition, meaning fast—"

"Yes, his sister said the same thing. The coroner will try to accommodate that. They get pretty backed up over there, but they'll do their best."

Joey nodded. The deputy was a red-nosed guy with a sloppy face and a humane manner. And piercing eyes that hadn't stopped sizing up Joey since he'd arrived.

"How'd he die?" Joey asked.

He shrugged. "Drowning? It happens. Even with a full moon, it's hard to see those waves coming at you. Had he been drinking?"

"Drinking, fighting, screwing. The works."

"With you?"

"With me."

"Sounds like a full day."

"He liked to pack a lot of living into a day," Joey said. "Did you find his surfboard?"

"Attached to his ankle, they tell me. He was wearing one of those—"

"Leashes." She nodded. "He'd like that. Dying with his surfboard on."

The deputy kept looking at her, maybe wondering what was going on inside her that her grief was so controlled.

Eventually, he turned away, finished with us. He was all the way to his car before Joey lost it.

Thirty-two

I waded through seventy pages of *The Iliad* while Joey walked on the beach. I sat in my car with the windows rolled up, cold. California is rarely as warm as people imagine. Especially at the beach. Especially on the second-to-the-last day of the year.

Homer, in a perverse way, was cheering me up. Well, perhaps "cheering" wasn't the exact word. Helping me put things in perspective. *The Iliad* is short on comic relief, but there is so much fighting in it—fighting and talking about fighting, about fighting that is to come, fighting that's already happened, fighting from long ago, and fighting that happened five minutes earlier—and, thus, so much dying that it reminded me that even survivors eventually perish; in fact, it's remarkable that any of us last as long as we do. I thought of a condolence card—*Sorry your time ran out*—but if there was ever a card with a limited audience, it was that.

Joey had to be alone, and I understood that, her need to talk to the ocean or whatever it was she was doing. As long as she wasn't drowning herself, and I could see that she wasn't, I didn't care how long she stayed there. I closed my eyes and thought about my own grief. This was complicated. Disbelief was still my predominant emotion, followed by sadness, and then anger. "Damn, Elliot," I said. "It wasn't enough to cheat on her? You had to die too?"

And what a nightmare Camille was. Would the police, not to mention the media people, be swayed by her insistence that my best friend was a murderer? Or would they just thank their lucky stars they weren't related to her?

Joey, in the distance, was kneeling in the sand, facing the ocean. I thought of sailors' wives waiting for the boats to come across the water, bringing their men home. I thought of Demeter, the mother of Persephone, waiting for her daughter to return after being stolen by Hades. One thing you could say for the Greeks: death didn't always get the last word. Sometimes the dead came back.

I picked through the stuff I'd held for Joey, taken from Elliot's trunk. Except for a tiny gadget with earpieces attached, it was all mail. Nothing of interest aside from a padded manila envelope with the return address of Dressed to Kill: Frannie's Feminine Firearms Accessories.

And a letter, in Joey's sprawling handwriting, addressed to Elliot.

Joey stood as someone approached her. Her body language changed, arms gesturing, and then she turned and jogged toward me. I threw the mail into the backseat of the Integra and had the car started up by the time she reached it.

"Take me home, would you?" she said, slamming the door. She curled up in the passenger seat in a near-fetal position. "My car's parked across PCH, from last night, but I can't go pick it up now, I just—"

"Of course you can't. I'm going to take care of you."

"They'll never leave me alone now, will they? Reporters. Photographers. I just want to be home with the doors locked. Someplace no one can get at me."

I pulled out of the parking lot and onto Pacific Coast Highway. She looked through the mail, coming to a stop on the letter she'd written to Elliot. She stared at it, then ripped it into halves, quarters, and eighths, and shoved the pieces in her pocket.

I drove to Pasadena, glancing at her as she made herself smaller and smaller, a little ball hugging her knees to her chest. I broke my own rule, not to mention California laws, by not making her wear her seat belt. I knew that lightning, which had struck her twice in one week, wouldn't touch her again. Not today.

Still, I drove carefully.

. . .

On a structure as old as Solomonhaus, no matter how modern it is for its time, new hardware stands out. In this case, the hardware was a fresh lock on the front door.

Another shiny lock adorned the gate leading to the backyard. Joey scaled the fence, and her scream of frustration told me that the back door also had new locks.

Camille.

Who responds to tragedy by changing the locks on someone else's house?

I thought I'd seen Joey in all her moods, but I was wrong. I watched through the fence as she banged on the back door, then picked up a rock from the desertlike garden and hurled it against the side of the house. Her screaming continued, a combination of weeping and hysteria.

There were sliding doors in the back of the house, but maybe they were too strong to break, or maybe Joey didn't want to find shards of glass in her living room for the next two weeks, or maybe she didn't want to set off the alarm and have the security company harass her, along with the rest of Southern California.

After a while, she wore herself out, climbed back over the fence, and let me drive her away from Pasadena.

. . .

We were heading toward We-Store-U in the west Valley when I remembered that the key to my storage locker wasn't in my trunk but in the custody of Simon "Mr. Security" Alexander. Specifically, in his wall safe, along with my passport and other odds and ends. Like anyone in the world would care about my stuff. I didn't even care about my stuff at this point, but I did care about Joey's money, since her credit cards had been canceled and her bank account cleaned out.

"How come you have cash sewn into your chaise longue anyway?" I asked.

"Habit," she said, repositioning her visor to shut out the setting sun. "In my waitress days, I had a roommate with a heroin problem, so I'd hide my tips. Later, when I started making real money, I always kept a stash there. Rainy-day money. It was a superstition of sorts, like if it stayed there untouched, I'd never need it."

"How much is it?"

"Six grand. Kind of Ma Kettle of me, isn't it?" She was calmer now and wearing her seat belt. "Speaking of my family, how do I tell them about Elliot? They'll all come to the rescue. My mom will leave her cruise and beg me to come home to Lincoln."

"Would that be so terrible?" I asked.

"Ever been to Nebraska in the dead of winter? Anyway, LAPD wants me to stick around. We won't tell her that, though. The idea of her kids in jail upsets Mom."

I froze. "Joey, they've got no evidence, right? How could they arrest you?"

"Sweetheart. I was at David's when he was killed or, as we say, close enough for TV. I knew his house, his alarm system, I had access to the murder weapon, we had a tempestuous history, and in the end, I got a two-million-dollar painting out of the deal. Pick the alternative scenario, assisted suicide, and I was a good enough friend to shoot him, if in fact he wanted to be shot. If they don't suspect me, they're stupid."

"Then why not take a polygraph test so they can go suspect someone else?" I asked. She didn't answer. "Joey, whatever it is you know about David's death, tell the cops. If you don't want to tell me, okay, but tell them."

She looked out the window. "In those AA meetings, they have these corny sayings. Things you're supposed to tell yourself when you want a drink. There's this one I keep hearing: We're as sick as the secrets we keep. And I think, Okay, but what if the secrets aren't ours to tell? What if they belong to other people?"

"To David?" I asked. "If these 'other people' are dead, does it matter?"

"Everything matters," Joey said. "Death just means you can't renegotiate. I didn't know it would be this hard, though. I could never be a priest. Or a lawyer. Which reminds me . . ." She looked up a number on her cell. "Hi, this is Joey Rafferty calling for Rick Slepicka. . . . Sally, you're still there after all these years? . . . Listen, I have a legal problem. Is Rick taking new clients? Well, old clients." After a moment, Joey rattled off her phone numbers and hung up. She leaned back. "He'll be in touch. I can't imagine how much that phone call will cost me."

"Joey, listen to me. Whatever David asked you to keep to yourself, he couldn't know you'd be suspected of killing him. And after years of not speaking . . . you said yourself, he was mean. If that's the case, how can—"

"He was only occasionally mean. If you did his bidding and recognized his genius, he was great. Professionally, we were great. My job as an actor—everyone's, on the set—was to carry out his vision. And I did that. I inspired him. We all did."

"But he fired you."

"Yeah, but that was personal, it had nothing to do with my work. He got mad at me. He couldn't kill me, so he fired me. Anyhow, that was all nearly ten years ago."

"What was he mad about?"

"I can't talk about it. It's not my story to tell."

"Whose story is it to tell?"

Silence.

"Last name, A to K or L to Z?"

More silence. Then, a tiny buzzing sound from the passenger seat.

"Zzzz. Zee?" I said. "Z? Zetrakis? David? But that's who we're discussing."

Joey shrugged.

"Z. Ziggy?" I asked. "No, he didn't know David. Wait . . . Charles Zetrakis?"

"I'm not confirming anything."

"Okay. No problem. But if you told the cops this thing about Charles Zetrakis from ten years ago, would it help their investigation?"

She considered this. "Maybe, maybe not. But if I find out what happened to David, I may not have to tell them."

"Joey. Your husband died today. The last thing you need to deal with is—"

"Wollie. The only thing standing between me and a rubber room is that I have things to do. You have to let me do them. Everyone's just going to have to let me. I can't fall apart until next week anyway, when my therapist is back in town. Okay?"

"Sounds like a plan," I said.

Thirty-three

have a horror of showing up where I'm not wanted, so it was with trepidation that I rang Simon's doorbell. But he hadn't answered his phone, and now he wasn't answering his door, so that was good.

I was letting myself in with the key I still had when the door opened. Damn.

Simon stood there, wearing a blue silk shirt that matched his eyes and navy trousers, not his usual at-home attire. Music played, and there was the smell of cooking, and the sound of a crackling fire in the fireplace.

None of that had gone on during my tenure. Simon didn't cook.

"Wollie." Simon looked surprised to see me. Not the good kind of surprised. "Is Joey with you?"

"Waiting in the car." A dark parking garage, Joey had said, suited her interior landscape. "I need the stuff I left in your wall safe."

He glanced over his shoulder.

"Can I come in?" I said, craning my neck to see what he was looking at.

"It's better, actually, if you—"

"Simon?" A head appeared in the hallway. "Shall I warm the focaccia?"

"Hello, Ilse," I said, walking past Simon. "Whatcha cooking?"

Ilse, seeing me, looked thunderstruck, as Homer might say. She had in her hand a spatula, which she raised as if to threaten me. She wasn't dressed in her cleaning lady attire, or in the business suit I'd last seen her in, but in a maid's outfit, unnecessarily short, complete with white, lace-trimmed apron. And, God help me, stockings. And shoes. Not your basic orthopedic waitress shoes, either.

"Nice outfit," I said, walking past. I was in the bedroom, moving the painting that hid the wall safe, when Simon caught up with me and touched my shoulder.

I shook it off, and he took me by both arms and turned me around to face him. I twisted myself out of his hold, as angry as I'd ever been at him, and I'd been angry once or twice before.

"Okay," he said, hands raised in truce position. "But it's not what you think."

"And what is it you think I think?"

"That Ilse is here to—that we're romantically involved. We're not."

"Fine."

"No, it's not fine. You're obviously upset."

"Yes, because you have a cleaning person who changes costumes like she's a Vegas showgirl and she's in here cooking a candlelit dinner and I'm out driving around with my best-friend-the-widow, who got kicked out of her house this afternoon, so yes, yes, I'm upset. And no, don't touch me. Don't hug me. Just let me get my stuff and I'll be outta here." I turned to the wall safe.

"Here, let me do it," he said, stretching past me to work the combination. It opened with a soft click. I reached in and took out everything that was mine.

"Come," he said when I was finished. "I'll walk you out."

He put his hand on the small of my back, despite my express wish that he not touch me. I let it go, not wanting to let Ilse, wherever she was, hear us argue any more than she already had. When we were out the front door, I said, "I can take it from here."

He ignored this, steering me down the hallway away from the elevator, glancing at his watch. He stopped in an alcove and, very close to me, said, "Can you really think me capable of that? Being with another woman while I'm doing what I do with you?"

"I don't know what you're capable of."

"You know what I do for a living."

"Yes."

"Think about it. Has it occurred to you that there might be a specific reason for you moving out? That hosting a dinner might be something other than social pleasure?"

"Yeah, it occurs to me, along with other scenarios." I bit my lip. "I don't want to be had. I've been had before, and it's no fun. You're telling me not to believe what's in front of my face, while you feed me lines so old they don't even use them in the movies anymore."

"What lines?"

"What you just said. 'It's not what you think.' "

"What if that's true?"

"Convince me," I said.

Simon threw a glance over his shoulder, at the elevator. "It's going to require touching you. Think you can handle that?"

"Maybe."

He took my face in his hands, softly, and when I didn't resist, kissed me, hard. I kissed him back harder. I wasn't done being mad, but I was finding it possible to simultaneously do two things that had once seemed mutually exclusive.

When it ended, he brushed my hair out of my eyes. "Where are you staying tonight?"

"No idea," I said.

"Will you call me when you know?" he asked.

"If you're lucky."

*　*　*

There are many ways to measure lifetime achievement. It's not always about material possessions. I realize that. Still, to see one's worldly goods fit neatly, if tightly, into an eight-by-twelve space is not wholly uplifting.

And the ride to We-Store-U had not helped. A limousine had blocked our exit from Simon's parking garage while a visitor took her sweet time getting out of the car. She was an ice blonde wearing a full-length fur coat and enough jewelry to satisfy a family of muggers. Joey pointed out the fur. I couldn't see past the beauty. There was no reason to think she was visiting Simon, but naturally I was convinced she was visiting Simon. I was still obsessing an hour later, in my eight-by-twelve cubicle.

"Good packing job," Joey said, lifting out a Don Quixote standing lamp. We were working our way to the back, to the chaise longue she'd lent me long ago.

"Doc did it," I said. "A last act of love before leaving me. I've lived four places in eight months. My Year of Living Transiently." I thought about the Greeks parked outside the gates of Troy for ten years. At what point had their wives and girlfriends back in Sparta and Athens moved their stuff into storage or hauled it off to the Goodwill?

Joey handed me lamps, pictures, and boxes of books, which I set outside one by one, clearing space. We were sweating, even though there was a cold wind blowing in the Valley. The storage facility was lit by a single lightbulb, augmented by flashlights.

"Look," Joey said, "there's a little space right here, between your drafting table and the ironing board, for my Klimt."

"I keep forgetting the Klimt," I said, wrestling with blankets. "So even in the worst-case scenario, you're not exactly broke."

"No. But I don't want to sell the painting. And anyhow, when you sell something because you need the money, you never get what it's valued at. If it's worth two million, I'd be lucky to get one. A lousy million. Yeah, like that's gonna last." She dragged a box of photo albums across the floor. "And if I have to take my sister-in-law to court so I can live in my house, I may as well hand the Klimt to the lawyers."

"But isn't Solomonhaus in your name, along with Elliot's?"

Joey sighed. "No, we used what's called a house trust. So my name wouldn't show up on the title, as a matter of public record. People do it all the time in Hollywood, so the yahoos don't come over for autographs or . . . whatever." She touched the scar on her face. "It's in the name of the microchip company—but it was my money that bought it. Oh, well." She went back to burrowing. "I did one thing right," she said. "I told him I loved him."

"Elliot?"

"Yeah. Along with all the bad things I said this week, I at least said that. When he left to go surfing." She blew her nose. "If he'd known he would die, I know what his last words to me would have been. 'Take care of the businesses, Joey. And wax the BMW.' "

"If you're going to take care of the businesses, you do need a lawyer."

"I need a lawyer, an accountant, a shrink, a rabbi, a fifth of Jack Daniel's, a lot of money, and a black dress."

My phone rang, loud in the silence of the storage space. "If someone's looking for me, I'm not here," Joey said.

It was Fredreeq. "Are you watching the news?"

"Nope."

"Well, don't. Elliot's death is all over the place and they're milking it like crazy. Someone called Joey a black widow. At least they still think she's married to him. Oh, and it's official—the gun that shot David came from the *End of the Day* prop department. And they found some plastic sheeting in one of the Dumpsters on the lot, with David's blood spattered all over it. And they know that Joey was on the set all the time. Don't tell her any of this tonight. Bye."

I hung up and watched Joey, now flipping through a photo album. She pointed to a shot of a picnic at the Hollywood Bowl. There we all were—Fredreeq and her husband, Francis; Joey and Elliot; and me, dateless. Everyone was laughing.

"Look at us," Joey said. "We're like a beer commercial. You know, it only started to go bad for us this year. I think he was bored with how stable the businesses were. He started to take other kinds of risks—sex, night surfing, hang gliding."

"Check this out," I said, flipping through another album. "David's fortieth birthday. Morton's restaurant."

Joey looked at the photo. "I wasn't dating him then, was I?"

"No. You took me to the party and introduced me to him. Look, there's Rupert. And who's this woman?"

Joey studied the photo, then handed it back to me. "You don't know?"

I looked again. "She looks like . . . is it David's sister? Does he have a sister?"

Joey was still looking at me. I looked back at her, puzzled. She shrugged.

"Are you okay?" I said.

"Can I borrow this photo of Elliot?" she asked.

"Of course," I said. "Take any of them. Tell me something. Why'd you spend Christmas with David, after all those years of not speaking?"

"Because he asked me to," Joey said, clearing off a love seat and lying down. "Everyone deserves a second chance. And because I got to live and he didn't."

Within minutes she was asleep. I covered her with a moving blanket.

Next to her was a case of wine. It belonged to Doc. I had no idea what wine went best with grief, but cabernet sauvignon sounded fine. I had no corkscrew, but I used the small blade on a Swiss Army knife, slowly and painstakingly, to open it. I drank right from the bottle, feeling it warm on my tongue and all the way down to my stomach, flavored by pieces of cork. I covered myself with packing blankets and settled on the floor with a flashlight, looking through old photos until I fell asleep.

Thirty-four

New Year's Eve is a holiday popularly assumed to be spent in crowds, maximum flesh packed into minimum space and forced to stay until midnight, blowing on noisemakers and exchanging wet kisses with total strangers.

I suspected, on waking, that this would not be my experience tonight.

A muscle cramp hit. I was between a file cabinet and a hat rack, illuminated by a dying flashlight. I opened the storage cubicle door to daylight, waking Joey. We got to the chaise longue, retrieved six thousand, eight hundred dollars, moved everything back, and went in search of coffee.

An hour later we were in Pasadena, with a locksmith.

"You girls got proof you live here?" he asked, getting out of his van.

Joey pulled a driver's license from her purse and pointed to the address.

The locksmith studied it, scratching a goatee. "Hot picture," he said, then scrutinized Joey. "This isn't you."

"Oh, for God's sake, it is too her," I said. "What, you think she stole some woman's purse, and now she's going to steal her house?"

"This doesn't look like her."

Joey said, "It looks like me on a good day, with makeup and my hair combed. Not on the morning after the worst day of my life, no."

"Well, I can't open that door until I have some—"

"Look, you heartless moron," she yelled, "my husband drowned yesterday, so my keys are at the bottom of the ocean and I need you to open up my goddamn house."

The locksmith stared at the awful beauty that was Joey at full volume, and then, despite being called a moron, opened up the front door.

The house had a musty smell, as though being alone for one day had aged it, as though it knew Elliot was dead. It had been his house, in all its concrete and steel sophistication. I wouldn't be sorry to see Joey sell it and live in a place that suited her.

"Espresso?" Joey said from the kitchen.

"Yes, please," I said, hugging myself. The house's open floor plan, every room but the bathroom flowing into the next, made it hard to regulate the temperature. Plus, the wiring and heating had been installed in the 1920s, so Joey stayed warm by way of sweaters, space heaters, and a fire in the fireplace. Now it seemed colder in the house than it was outside, and outside was cold enough. Forties, the car radio had said. Beyond the sliding glass doors the sky was a funereal gray, a shade lighter than the house's concrete floors.

I sipped my espresso, considering whether jumping jacks might be in order to get my blood flowing, as Joey gathered personal items and stuffed them into a duffel bag. "For the car," she said. "In case this happens again, Camille locking us out."

"But how can she change the locks? She doesn't have proof that she lives here."

"Pays off the locksmith, maybe. Damn it, where are my bullets?"

I stood, scared. "Your what?"

"Bullets. I had my box of bullets somewhere. Just now. I set them down and . . ." She disappeared into the bedroom.

In the kitchen, the phone rang. And rang. And rang.

"Wollie, can you get that?" Joey called. "The machine's not picking up. But I don't want to talk to anyone, unless it's the morgue, about Elliot."

I answered the phone distractedly, my mind still on a box of bullets. "Hello."

"It's Charles. Sorry to call so early."

"Hi," I said. For one strange moment, I thought it was Charles Kuhlmann, a greeting card rep I knew, from the days when I had a card shop.

"Have you talked to that detective yet?" he asked.

It was Charles Zetrakis. I don't know what evil genius came over me, but I found myself saying yes, trying to infuse the word with Joey's gravelly quality. I had, in fact, talked to the detective, so it's not like I was lying.

"And—?"

"What?" I said.

"Just a minute—" His voice grew muffled. "Honey, I thought you'd gone . . . okay, let's meet back here for brunch." His voice returned, full volume. "Joey? Sorry. You know we're staying in town, right? The Bel-Air. It was David's favorite. I keep sending Agnes out to shop, she keeps ending up at church. It's like she's got post-traumatic stress disorder, inheriting all this money."

"Hmm."

"Joey," he said, "you didn't—?"

"Hmm?"

There was a pause. "Tell the police about me?"

I stopped breathing. Tell the police what? That Charles Zetrakis . . . spent money? Kissed Joey? Shot his brother?

"Although they're going to find out, if they're looking. If they're good. So the question is—are you all right? What's going on with you?"

"Call you back, gotta go," I choked out, and hung up. I stood there holding on to the phone, as if to make sure it stayed hung up. The machine blinked out the number 25. Twenty-five unplayed messages?

"Found 'em." Joey came out of the bedroom and set a box on the counter. It said "Winchester Ranger SXT Controlled Expansion 9 mm Luger, Law Enforcement Ammunition." As opposed to Bad Guy Ammunition, I supposed.

"Joey," I said, "that was Charles Zetrakis on the phone."

"Oh."

"He thought I was you. He's staying at the Bel-Air."

She nodded. "Great hotel, the Bel-Air."

"He didn't seem to know about Elliot."

"No, he's probably avoiding newspapers and TV right now."

"He wanted to know if you'd told the police about him."

"Ah."

"You're not going to call him back?"

"Not right now. I don't want to explain about Elliot yet."

I took a deep breath. "Joey, if Charles killed his brother, if it was as-sisted suicide or whatever, I'm sure people would be understanding about that, that's different from garden-variety murder, so if you're protecting Charles—"

"Charles and Agnes were in Paso Robles all day Friday. With wit-nesses."

"Oh. Right."

Joey sat at the dining room table, a wood-and-steel affair jutting out from the wall. "What's problematic about suicide," she said, "assisted or otherwise, is that the family can't collect life insurance."

"True," I said slowly.

Joey's green eyes looked right into mine. "If you want your survivors to cash in on a big policy, if you go to all the trouble of passing an insur-ance physical before cancer even shows up, if you're that prescient, you don't then kill yourself in a way that looks like suicide. If you need to die faster than nature's killing you, you might get a very tough-minded per-son to help you."

"But why would you need to?"

"Maybe someone you love needs money right away. Maybe you try selling off stuff to raise the money, but that's slow and inefficient, you take a loss, and that bothers you. And maybe your quality of life's not so hot anyway, so what the hell. I'm just guessing here, you understand." She grabbed a sweatshirt from her pile of stuff and pulled it over her head. "Can you drive me to my car? It's way out in Malibu."

I nodded, but suggested she listen to her unplayed messages. "Be-cause if Camille has access to the house, I wouldn't want her listening to them."

Joey moved to the kitchen. "I should've thought of that. I'm getting careless."

"You're tired."

"I'm tired, I'm sad, I feel like shit. But that's no reason to set aside paranoia."

I went outside to give her privacy, but not fast enough to miss the first words of the first message. This was what she'd been avoiding. The messages would sound like this for a long time to come. "Joey, I just heard about Elliot. I'm so sorry . . ."

. . .

I drove Joey to her car, parked in a lot off Cross Creek, near Pacific Coast Highway. The Mercedes appeared unmolested and Joey was sober, so there was no reason to stick around. Yet it was hard to leave her.

"I'm okay," she said, leaning over to give me a kiss before getting out of my car. "You've got things to do, and so do I. But come back to Solomonhaus tonight and stay over. Saves you from getting a hotel room. And it will make me sleep better."

The minute I saw Joey start up her car, I peeled out of the parking lot. I was off to the Bel-Air, where I intended to find Charles Zetrakis and persuade him to talk. I didn't have an exact plan as to how. I'd figure it out en route. But I was still on Pacific Coast Highway when Max Freund called, saying I needed a date with Sheffo ASAP.

"But it's New Year's Eve," I said.

"Yes, so early afternoon is best. That way I get my camera crew off the clock before traffic gets bad. Sorry about this, but I did leave the schedule with your doorman. Oh, and you'll have to go to Sheffo's. He won't leave his neighborhood on holidays."

"That's fine."

"Good. We need to wrap up our dating footage before Friday."

"What's Friday?" I said.

"*SoapDirt*. Didn't you get the call sheet? Check with your doorman. You've got an early call. We tape five episodes and you're in three, and you'll need extra time in hair, makeup, and wardrobe, since Tricia has some opinions on your look."

My look. I didn't know I had a look.

"Don't lose your drive-on," Max said. "Security's tight because we're prepping the building for the Moon Lake explosion. Makes everyone nervous. They should let you park next to Sound Stage D, but let me know if they give you any trouble."

I said okay, happy that I at least knew what a call sheet was, having done time in show business on a bad reality show. And I now knew what a drive-on was. Unfortunately, both items were at Simon's. I did not want to see Simon. I wanted to see Charles Zetrakis. Now I'd have to stop in Westwood en route to the Hotel Bel-Air, but I could make it fast. Run in, run out.

Yet I hadn't told Max I was no longer living at Simon's. How come? Because part of me believed I'd be back there soon, and part of me wanted to be.

I skipped the underground garage and parked on Ashton. Only one block south of Simon's condo building, it was a different world, small, older homes suggesting stable families. One week earlier, Christmas trees or Hanukkah menorahs had showed in nearly every window, brightening the twilight. Simon's penthouse had neither. I slunk into his building with my head down, trying to look invisible. But Ali was working. He explained that he'd traded shifts so he could go to a party that night, then handed me a manila envelope containing the call sheet and drive-on. I wished him a happy New Year and left, reading as I walked. The call sheet was a taping schedule, with lots of information squeezed onto front and back in cramped handwriting. I found "W. Shelley" with "6:30" written after it. There was a drive-on to tape to my windshield.

I was about to take a left on Ashton when I heard a "Hey!" I turned.

Simon loped toward me in sweatpants, a white T-shirt, and stocking feet. Good God. There must have been a natural disaster to get him out on the street without shoes. I looked around for smoke, flooding, or aliens disembarking spaceships.

"Hey," he said again, catching up to me and catching his breath.

"Hey," I said. "What are you—"

"Come here." He took me by the hand and led me into an alley, behind a row of poplar trees. There we necked like teenagers for a minute or two. I couldn't believe how much I'd missed him in the hours since I'd last seen him, despite the fact that I was still mad about something or other. My body was practically climbing onto his when I felt something hard sticking into my leg. I pulled back.

"You're carrying your gun?"

"Yeah," he said, pulling me toward him again. "Why?"

"You've got no shoes but you've got a gun?"

He breathed into my ear. "What's the problem?"

A car pulled into the alley, forcing us back into the poplars. "Damn," Simon said, hopping on one foot. He leaned over to examine the other and pulled some kind of thorn out of his sock. "Okay, come on, where are you parked?"

I pointed toward Ashton. "What'd you do," I asked, "have Ali alert you when I showed up to pick up my call sheet?"

"Yes. How's Joey doing?"

"Okay. Not great, but . . . okay."

"Where'd you stay last night?"

"My storage unit."

He stopped. Since he was attached to my arm, I stopped too. "God-damnit," he said. "That's it. I'm getting you a hotel room."

"No, you're not."

"You're really making me nuts, you know that?"

"Likewise."

"Is it money? Can you not afford a hotel? Because I've got—"

"No, it's not money, and this isn't your problem, and I—"

"Wollie. Everything that concerns you is my problem."

"I'd like to think that my defining characteristic is something other than 'problem'—just a minute," I said, feeling my cell phone pulsate. "Hello."

"Wollie, there's a problem."

I sighed. "What is it, P.B.?"

"I have to give back all my comic books to Boyd," my brother said. "The whole collection. He said I can't take them with me to Santa Barbara."

"Who's Boyd?"

"Bipolar."

"Oh, right. Wait," I said. "I thought Boyd gave you his comic books when he got released from the hospital."

"He's back in. Relapse. Now he wants his comics."

I was aware of Simon, controlling his impatience. "P.B., we'll scout out comics in Santa Barbara. Santa Barbara has everything."

"No, I'm not showing up there empty-handed. It doesn't feel right."

"Uncle Theo can—"

"No he can't. He's working today. There's no time."

I felt the beginnings of hysteria taking root near my feet and crawling up my ankles. "What do you expect me to do, re-create the whole collection, issue by issue—"

"Not every issue. I just need one representative of each series. It's the characters I need, not the stories. I don't care where they are in their history."

"Okay, but—"

"If you pick up Apollo at Uncle Theo's and take him to Earth 2 he'll handle everything, but they close at noon today because it's some holiday."

"Yeah, New Year's Eve," I said, glancing at my watch, "but—"

Too late. My brother, his objective reached, had hung up.

Simon was now on his cell phone apparatus, answering e-mail or something with his little sticklike pen. Gun and cell phone, but no shoes. Interesting priorities.

"P.B. okay?" he said without looking up.

"Relatively," I said. "But I have to run."

"Wait." He finished with his cell phone, pocketed it, and then turned the full force of his attention on me. "It's New Year's Eve."

I nodded. "I know."

"One request." He took my shoulders in his hands and drew me closer.

How silly I'd been. Of course he wanted to ring in the new year with me, of course he was taking the night off, putting his personal life—me—before business, whatever business he was engaged in right now. Textiles. "Request away," I said.

"Take your cell phone off vibrate and check your voice mail," he said into my ear. "I swear I'll pay you money if you'll just stay in communication with me. Especially tonight. There's a lot of crazy, drunk partying going on. And promise never again to sleep in storage units."

I pulled back, shocked at the depths of my disappointment. I wasn't going to be with him at the stroke of midnight, arguably the most significant moment of the year.

"What?" he asked, frowning.

"That's three requests," I said. "But don't worry. I'm sleeping at Joey's. And just like you, she's got a gun."

"Christ," Simon muttered. "That's reassuring."

"Isn't it?" I said. "Happy New Year."

Thirty-five

lendale was cold, being north of Westwood, of Bel Air, of all civilized society. In many places in the United States, cold is below zero, but in L.A., anything less than fifty is arctic. I found parking just three blocks from Uncle Theo's apartment and nearly injured an SUV in the process. Actually, I wanted to set the SUV on fire, just for being so big. What earthly need was there for all these cars the size of barns? Were they transporting troops? Relocating cattle?

Yes, I was grumpy. I understood that Simon was out there on assignment, saving the world, probably assisted by the mysterious Ilse, that it was a job and not necessarily the fun-fest it appeared to be. But understanding this did not cheer me up. Glumly, I entered Uncle Theo's apartment.

There was no screaming this time; the assorted houseguests remembered me, greeting me with smiles and a plate of baklava. I counted three women, two adolescent girls, and four children running around. One woman was ancient and wore a head scarf.

"Hello," I said, nodding at everyone. "Anyone know where Theo is?"

After a flurry of Greek, a woman answered, "Your uncle, he is at work."

"No problem," I said. "Is there an Apollo among you?"

"Apollo!" another woman called.

From the kitchen came a boy who looked to be around fourteen, in a

Superman T-shirt, with the scrawniest arms I've ever seen. His elbows looked like they were trying to push their way through his skin. I said to him, "You're the guy who knows a place called Earth 2?"

He nodded. "You're Wollie?"

I nodded. "Let's go."

． ． ．

I'd never been in a comic-book store, although my brother had been a lifelong devotee of the literature. It had been Uncle Theo's job to provide comics when P.B. was in the hospital, in the same way it was my job to keep him in socks and shirts and lotion for sensitive skin, a division of labor we'd never discussed. P.B. and I had a mother, but she was of the opinion that she'd done quite enough bringing us into the world.

I expected a place run by Archie and Veronica. But Earth 2 was hip, a hole-in-the-wall joint just east of Kung Pao Bistro, with White Stripes music filtering out the door and a life-sized cloth-sculptured Spider-Man in the window, beckoning us in.

Apollo led me around the store. He'd been talking nonstop, volunteering that he was fifteen and pretty good at math, having been accepted at the California Institute of Technology. Since he was too young to live in the dorm or survive without his mother's cooking, she'd accompanied him to America, on a visitor's visa. The extended family had followed. I wondered how long visitors' visas were good for—not as long, I suspected, as the program at Caltech.

He certainly knew his comics—not just the flimsy ones I recalled from childhood, but graphic novels as well, glossy publications printed on high-quality paper. I'd seen books like these in P.B.'s room but had never paid attention. I picked up one called *Olympus,* happy to see that even on Earth 2, the Greeks prospered. The drawings were violent and erotic, with sound effects reminiscent of Batman: *Kraakkooom! Blamm Blamm Blamm!*

"You guys need any help, or you doing okay?" a salesperson asked.

"What do you have by Craig Thompson that's new?" Apollo asked.

The guy beckoned. "Check this out."

I followed them, still carrying *Olympus.* "Your brother will like these," Apollo said. "We talk on the phone each day and I can extrapolate from what he reads now."

"But will my bank account survive these?" I mumbled, checking the prices.

"Consider," Apollo said, "that P.B. will not want to keep these in the hospital, where others will borrow and not return them. And spill orange juice on them."

"You mean it's incentive for him to move to Haven Lane?"

Apollo nodded.

I looked at him with newfound respect. I had not liked having my morning disrupted, schlepping to Glendale, shopping with an adolescent boy at Earth 2 when I wanted to be at the Bel-Air, but perhaps I shouldn't look a gift horse in the mouth. I repressed sticker shock, watching the register add up the prices of *Watchmen, 300, Planetary,* and *Orbiter,* and on and on and on. I told Apollo to pick out a couple books for himself. What the heck? It was only money.

My phone rang. It was Detective Ike Born. "Like a word with you, Ms. Shelley, check out a few facts about your friend Joey, if today's convenient."

"Gee, I've got a tight schedule today, Detective. Maybe tomorrow?"

"Maybe," he said, and put me on hold.

Or maybe never, I thought, hanging up. I had no facts that would help Joey. Opinions, yes. Convictions. But Ike Born probably had plenty of his own.

I left Earth 2 nearly three hundred dollars poorer. On the plus side, Jud, the owner, told me to bring in my greeting card samples. If there was one place that had "unorthodox artwork" written all over it, it was Earth 2.

On the way back to the car, we were hailed by a friendly "Hello, Wollie!" A woman in a vintage letter jacket and beret, red-faced from the cold, walked up and held out a hand. "Monica Pulliam. From *Southern California Magazine.*"

I shook hands, then realized this was the enemy. "Not interested," I said.

"Monica Pulliam," she repeated, shaking Apollo's hand. "Okay, here's the deal. I want an exclusive interview with Joey Rafferty."

"You won't get one," I said. "Come on, Apollo."

"Don't run off. You're her friend, I'm her friend. Hear me out."

"Talk fast," I said.

She did. "I'm on Joey's side. Everyone else wants to see her arrested because A, she's an actress slash model and everyone hates beautiful; B, she sleeps with high-profile guys; C, two of them died this week; D, leaving her richer; E, she's been spotted in AA meetings and also spotted drunk, so someone's gonna get it on camera soon." She paused for breath. "F, her dead husband was sleeping around and now his grieving mistress is about to sell her story to the tabloids; and G, I don't have to tell you what that means."

"Actually, you do," I said.

"Two words: Scott Peterson."

"Who's Scott Peterson?" Apollo asked.

"Guy who murdered his pregnant wife on Christmas Eve. His mistress told her story to the tabloids, and he got put away for life."

"It's hardly an analogous situation," I said, wondering if the term *mistress* was still in fashion, and if it was Mistress One or Mistress Two selling her story. I hoped it was Number Two, the nonmeaningful one. "And no one believes tabloids."

She took off her beret and fluffed her hair, blond with black roots. "Tabloids don't need to be credible. People remember faces, not facts. If it's the right face, they develop a taste for it, then a craving. Then mainstream media jumps on it, because that's what their audience wants. Tabloids have influence."

"And you're saying you can turn it in Joey's favor."

"I can. I like to go against the tide."

"She won't go for it," I said. "Nothing personal, but she has a higher opinion of earthworms than she has of the press."

"Take my card." She pulled out a worn leather wallet and thumbed through it. "If she doesn't come around, I can interview you. That can be very effective, having a friend speak for her. A lot of celebrities do that if they don't want to be quoted."

"She won't go for that either," I said.

"Here's incentive: they finished the Horowitz autopsy. Guy didn't just drown. Toxicology report says he had chemical help. Now, if it wasn't a self-administered recreational drug, who's the first person the cops are going to look at?"

I stared. "How could you know information like that?"

"Sources. Here's more bait: Joey had a juvenile rap sheet. The record's sealed, but you can bet people in Hometown, Nebraska, remember what's in it."

"That doesn't prove anything."

"Proof isn't the point. Perception is. In the world of perception, I can make Joey Rafferty innocent."

Or guilty, I thought.

Monica Pulliam pressed her business card into my hand. "You think about it."

Thirty-six

A date with anyone but Simon right now sounded as appealing as having my teeth cleaned, but it wouldn't be the first time a person had to go to work during a crisis, so I dropped Apollo in Glendale and pushed onward to Mount Olympus.

My mind was reeling. The possibility that Elliot's death was other than accidental—how, by the way, does one chemically encourage drowning?—shocked me. Two murders in one week, both of them men I knew. But many people knew them both, since they'd run in the same circles, so why should suspicion point to Joey? Just because she was married—sort of—to one and inherited a Klimt from the other?

On Electra Drive I parked behind the camera crew's DRUDGE2 minivan. Sheffo stood in the driveway, chatting with Max, while Navarre lurked in the background, as if holding up the—Doric? Ionic?—column.

Given my previous *SoapDirt* dates, I was prepared for Sheffo to plant a kiss on me for the camera. However, after determining that my left profile was the more aristocratic, he gave a critical glance at the sun, positioned us, and raised my hand to his lips. "Welcome, flame-haired goddess," he said. "My domicile is graced by your presence."

He repeated this twice more, same words, same actions, same intonations, then told the camera guys we were finished. "But as you're here,

Wollie, you may begin work on my wall," he said. "What better way to celebrate New Year's? We shall bring our libations and join you. Navarre has made cosmopolitans."

I glanced at my watch. I'd hoped to make it to the Bel-Air, as I was determined to find Charles Zetrakis, but there was no guarantee he'd be there, and I was already traffic weary. "Okay," I said. Sheffo was, after all, not only my date but also my boss.

"Navarre, fire up the heaters and bring cleaning supplies for Wollie. Max, join us. Who knows when we shall drink again, you and I, as my days are numbered."

I gasped, thinking, *Not Sheffo too,* then realized that he was referring to his soap character.

Max agreed, in deference to Sheffo, perhaps, rather than a thirst for cosmopolitans. Despite his limp, he insisted on helping me carry a ladder from the garage, with Sheffo shuffling along behind, asking questions, and Navarre behind him, bearing a tray of drinks. The faint static greeted us from the other side of the wall, and a voice was heard repeating, at intervals, "W8DX." One of Muffler's people? An image of Sheffo and Navarre strewing their lawn with rat poison entered my mind, and left.

"According to the rumor mill known as Tricia," Sheffo said, "related to me by the voluble Rupert, the police are about to make an arrest. And is it true that the gun that shot David came from our own prop department?"

"It is," Max said. "Jen handed Clay his pink slip over it. Clay's assistant Renée will become department head. I think she'll prove less—"

"Drug addicted," Sheffo said.

"Careless," Max said. "Clay had a casual attitude about locking up. David would never have fired him, though. They'd been friends since their New York days."

"Theater people," Sheffo said, nodding, "value loyalty. My impending death was not David's idea, you know. That Korean woman. Jen Kim. This dreadful nuclear storyline is her brainchild. And destroying Building Twelve for it? Disgraceful."

Max accepted from Navarre a drink in a frosted highball glass. "Building Twelve's been scheduled for demolition for years, Sheffo. It's coming down, whether we film it or not. Jen had nothing to do with it; that comes from higher up."

Sheffo shook his head. "Does no one value history? The pictures they cut in Building Twelve! Back when editors were king, before these special effects people took over. Using silver nitrate film—that took guts. Remember, Navarre? We knew an editor who lost an arm. At Paramount. Or was it the old ABC lot?"

Navarre had fetched a pail of water for me, and I was halfway up the ladder with it when this stopped me. "Lost an arm?" I said. "Editing film?"

"Nitrocellulose," Sheffo said. "That's what film was made of, back in the day. Highly flammable. Editors worked in rooms of reinforced concrete, veritable fortresses, bunkers, stronger than that wall you're climbing. That's Hollywood's past, my dear, and there's no one left to honor it. When the buildings go, memory goes with them. And the gods weep." Never mind the gods; Sheffo had worked himself up to tears.

"Wollie, how's Joey doing?" Max asked, in a transparent effort to distract him.

Sheffo perked right up, recalling Elliot, the most recent tragedy. "Poseidon, claiming one of his own," he said. "Live for the surf, die in the surf."

I said, "There's a rumor that Elliot may not have simply drowned, that something else showed up in a toxicology report. I heard it from a reporter, so I assume it's on the news by now."

"Two murders," Sheffo said. "Fascinating. I wonder who would want Elliot Horowitz dead. Besides his cuckolded wife. If a wife can be said to be cuckolded. What is the proper use of the word, I wonder? Navarre, do you know?"

Navarre expressed no interest in the etymology of *cuckold*, but Max and Sheffo argued about whether it was gender-specific, applying only to husbands.

I said, "Joey had no reason to want Elliot dead, and some very good reasons to want him alive. Not the least of which was that she loved him, cuckold or not." And that she was totally dependent on him financially, I didn't bother to add.

Sheffo stood, moving to refill his drink. "Excellent girl, Joey. Expectations of marital fidelity are both unreasonable and bourgeois. As to these two deaths," he said, raising his voice as if playing to the back row, "must they be the handiwork of one murderer? No. The first kill may have led to the second, for reasons not yet illuminated. Consider the Greeks: Agamemnon sacrifices Iphigenia, Clytemnestra slays Agamemnon, Orestes kills Clytemnestra. 'And they seemed like such a nice family,' the neighbors would've told reporters." Sheffo wobbled and I feared for his newly refilled cosmopolitan, but Max reached out to steady him. "Modern man likes to segregate these propensities, putting all of our bad eggs into one basket and calling them Hitler or Pol Pot when, in fact, murderous impulses abound. Have we less rage than our forefathers? No. We are less comfortable with our passions."

"Except in the soaps," Max said. "A more likely possibility is that Elliot Horowitz died by accident or by ingesting something that shouldn't have been ingested while night surfing. Occam's razor, Sheffo."

Sheffo snorted. "What is that, that the simplest theories are preferred? Rubbish. I'm surprised that you'd subscribe to that, Max, you, who've spent a life in the theater."

"What's that got to do with it?" Max said.

"It's too Apollonian. We are ruled by Dionysus. Revelry, man. Wine. Debauchery." He settled his chair under the patio heater, an orange glow of hot air.

"Actors serve Dionysus," Max said. "But stage managers serve actors. We stay sober so you can become intoxicated with your muse."

"The designated drivers of showbiz," I said.

"It wasn't us you served," Sheffo said, "but David. It was for him we all jumped through our hoops. I never knew such a man for making people want to please him. The performances he would wring from actors you'd swear were made of wood . . . and have you felt it? Life draining out of the show now that he's gone?"

I knew what Sheffo was talking about. David had had an effect on me too, making me feel glamorous and adventurous and just . . . special. A silence settled on us. Navarre came around the side of the house with a scrub brush and a sponge the size of a soccer ball. I descended the ladder to meet him, then returned to my perch, implements of hygiene in hand. This made me think of Hygeia, goddess of health, and the beginnings of a greeting card rose up in my mind: a Greek maiden bearing an electric toothbrush in one hand, a jug of Clorox in the other. But for what occasion?

I swabbed the top of the wall with my sponge, causing water to drip down the other side. I leaned over and satisfied my curiosity from the day before: Myrtle and Elmer's side of the wall was as bare and gray as Sheffo's. Talk about an eyesore. Maybe they could encourage ivy or bougainvillea to grow up from the ground and obscure it, but their yard was all dirt and patchy grass. No green thumbs there, I guessed.

A man in a reindeer-appliquéd sweater came out of the garage and looked up. He frowned. I smiled. He held a paper bag that said BIG BAD BURGER and wore a cap that said W8DX. Myrtle's husband, I guessed. Elmer. Co-owner of Muffler.

I descended the ladder to exchange my bucket of dirty water for the clean one that Navarre had standing by. "Don't take this personally, guys," I said, "but since the murder weapon came from your show, doesn't that make all of you suspects?"

Sheffo smiled. "Exciting, isn't it? And such weak alibis we all have. Everyone at home on Boxing Day, lounging about in dishabille, in a post-holiday stupor."

"Not everybody," Max said. "There was an all-morning production meeting, planning Friday's explosion. Twenty-three department heads and staff share that alibi."

"But no actors?" I said.

"No actors."

"And no one could've slipped out after the meeting started?" I said. People were always leaving the set to make phone calls.

"I would have noticed," Max said.

So that left actors as suspects, along with other people not at the meeting. Joey, for instance.

"Let us hope," Sheffo said, "that David was not murdered by some below-the-line crew person unhappy about overtime. Wait. Was Jen Kim at this meeting?"

"She came in for the last half hour," Max said.

"Aha! A quick holiday murder, then on to work." Sheffo lifted his glass in a toast.

"And what if neither death was murder?" I said, ascending the ladder again. "What if David's was a form of assisted suicide?"

"What would be the point?" Max said.

"The point," Sheffo said, "is that pancreatic cancer is gruesome. Not an actor's death. It has a yellowing effect. Bile. Exceedingly unbecoming."

Max shook his head. "No doubt. But if I were a betting man—"

"But you are." Sheffo gave a shout of laughter. "All of us. Gamblers. Everyone in this business. Some unluckier than others, eh, Max? How's that leg, by the way?"

"Fine, Sheffo. How's that prostate?"

While the men discussed ailments, I wrestled with the question Joey had posed. Assisted suicide or murder? "Sheffo," I said, "if vanity was an issue for David, would he go for a head wound? Those aren't pretty. I hear they found blood-covered plastic in a Dumpster. Are blood and brains an improvement over bile?"

Elmer, on the other side of the wall, glowered at me. I may have spoken louder than I intended. I smiled apologetically. He glowered more, then returned to his own activity, stringing up Japanese lanterns.

"Gunshots," Sheffo said, "cure boredom and impatience. David was prey to both." He held out his glass to Navarre for a refill. "To whom did the estate go?"

"His brother, Charles," I said.

"Then perhaps Charles is the one we should ask."

"Why ask anyone anything?" Navarre said, refilling Sheffo's glass.

It was startling to hear Navarre voice an opinion.

"Why?" Sheffo said. "Why? Because these are unanswered questions."

"Is it your business to answer them?" Navarre said. "Are you the police? Are you the insurance investigator? Will the answers bring back the dead?"

Sheffo stood, his drink sloshing dangerously in the highball glass. "Knowledge, you cretin. The thirst for knowledge fuels the world. Especially knowledge of the dead. And this was our friend, our David!"

Sheffo was nearly screaming. I looked down at the neighbor, who stared back with such malevolence, I thought it might knock me off the ladder. "Mouths crying out from the grave, Navarre, do you not hear them?"

The man with the reindeer appliqué may not have heard crying from the grave, but he'd heard enough from his neighbors. "Myrtle!" he called. "Crank up the music!"

"You're drunk," Navarre said loudly. Which could hardly have come as news, given that he was the one doling out the cosmopolitans. Max sat back, knee elevated, staying out of the fray.

"Now you've roused the natives, idiot!" Sheffo yelled. "Now we'll have their infernal cats coming over the wall."

Dear God, I thought, looking around for trained felines, then back at Sheffo, who attempted to exit with grace. He held his highball glass like a banner and set off to the house, weaving in a manner strange for one who had been completely lucid and relatively stable only twenty minutes earlier. He was slight, and perhaps that was the problem. Navarre started after him.

"Stay away from me, philistine!" yelled Sheffo. But Navarre, with the air of a man who's been called worse, followed anyway.

Max stood. "I better take off if I'm to beat the traffic. You too, going all the way to Westwood."

Westwood. I was actually growing nostalgic about it, something I'd never have thought—

A burst of music assaulted us. It was so loud Max dropped his cosmopolitan onto the grass, and I grabbed the wall for support.

Midnight . . . not a sound from the pavement . . .

It came from the neighbors' yard. It was not cats coming over the wall, but *Cats*. The musical. I had dated, briefly—although, as Fredreeq had pointed out, not briefly enough—a man who called himself the world's foremost *Cats* aficionado. Max picked up his glass, calling something to me, but I was too close to the music to hear. I gestured back, pointing to my ear, and he nodded and mouthed, "Happy New Year."

Touch meeeee . . . it's so easy to leeeeeeeeave me . . .

Max left.

I stayed on the wall for one more verse before realizing that Sheffo couldn't compensate me for hearing loss. Or insanity. I packed up my stuff as the sun set and dragged the ladder back to the garage, cutting my hand along the way, drawing blood.

Happy New Year.

Thirty-seven

let myself into Solomonhaus with my own brand-new key and called Joey.

"Where've you been and how are you doing?" I asked.

"I've been to the set on a fruitless mission, and now I'm on Ventura Boulevard, in traffic," she said. "Can you meet me here? We can drive together to La Baguette."

I didn't want to drive anywhere. I was beat. "What's La Baguette?"

"Little French restaurant on Little Santa Monica. They're having a party."

"I've never understood that, a restaurant having a party," I said. "Besides, don't you find parties overrated? How about a nice AA meeting instead?"

"Are you insane?" Joey said. "I'd rather drink lighter fluid."

"I don't know. Could be entertaining." I moved to the kitchen, eyeing the espresso machine. I was going to need lots of caffeine.

"But this is business and it's important. Only I can't make it home to change."

"What do you need?"

"A black cocktail dress. And an evening bag. And borrow anything you need for yourself. I'll wait for you at the Vons parking lot on Ventura and Laurel Canyon. Oh—the dress can be sleeveless, but no spaghetti straps. There's a Valentino that should work. Oh, and shoes. Flats. I have to charm my ex-lawyer into taking my case, but he's put off by tall women."

"Your case? What case?" I asked, panicky. A murder charge? Already?

"Calm down. This problem with Camille. Van Beek thinks she's trying to become executor of Elliot's estate. Rick, my lawyer, goes to Telluride tomorrow for a month, so I have to corner him tonight."

"So you need a lawyer to get your money so you can pay your lawyer?"

"Yes."

"Okay, then." I hung up, made espresso, found the Valentino and a pair of patent leather Chloe flats, then threw on the clothes I'd worn to Rex and Tricia's cocktail party. What fueled me, along with the espresso, were fiscal considerations. A murder trial, if it came to it, would be murderously expensive, and not the place to economize. Not in L.A., where a star lawyer can mean the difference between spending the rest of your life in golfing attire and spending it in an orange jumpsuit.

I'd just found a clutch for Joey, a Fendi, when someone knocked on the door.

It was Detective Ike Born. With a search warrant.

While his minions fanned out around the house, Detective Born chatted with me. No, Joey didn't need to be here, he said; in fact, it was probably less stressful for her to avoid witnessing it. No, there was nothing I could do to help. The crew would make themselves at home. No, I didn't need to know what particular thing they were looking for. Nothing interesting, his tone of voice suggested. He treated me courteously, and as if I were a little slow. I kept nodding while trying to determine my best course of action. I was interrupted by a ringing phone.

Should I answer it? Yes, because it might be Joey. I headed to the kitchen, only the phone wasn't in its cradle. I dashed through the house, bumping into a cop in the dining room, but too late. The machine clicked on, then a voice.

"Joey. Charles. Look, this is crazy, what we're doing. I'm thinking of talk—" I ran back to the machine and turned down the volume. Detective Born came into the kitchen and regarded me with raised eyebrows.

Well, let him wonder. I hovered, I lurked, I studied the search warrant, which looked scary, I called Joey's cell phone and got no answer. When I ran out of ideas, I told him I was late for an important engagement, and he told me to go, that he'd lock up and leave the key under the mat.

I didn't go. On TV, at least, cops didn't get search warrants without probable cause, something sufficiently dramatic to get a judge to sign it, usually in the middle of the night in his pajamas. I wanted to know what it was. And I wanted to grab Ike George Washington Born by the lapels of his unremarkable sports jacket and shake him, telling him that he was barking up the wrong tree, suspecting Joey. But since I knew she was innocent, what did I fear they'd find?

Well, drugs. Pot, at least. Would they hold that against her? Arrest her? Was pot still illegal? God, why had I never taken a course in criminal justice?

And then, as abruptly as they'd begun, they were done.

They'd found something, but what? Laundry, from the looks of it, being put into paper bags. They wore latex gloves, which made it look sinister.

When they left, I checked the house. Things were stuffed back into closets and drawers, looking more or less like they always looked. The phone showed up in the bathroom. I took it back to the kitchen, replaced it in its cradle, and hit the REPLAY button on Jocy's machine.

"Joey. Charles. Look, this is crazy, what we're doing. I'm thinking of talking. The fallout's going to be bad, but what's the alternative? I think it's better for you, but it's your call. You could be screwed either way. Hell. Call me."

I'm an upbeat person, but there was no way to interpret that call in a positive light.

I locked up Solomonhaus and hit the road.

Thirty-eight

Traffic was hideous. I felt myself going gray by the time I got off the 101. Joey's Mercedes was parked in front of Vons. She hopped out and into the backseat of the Integra with her backpack, saying, "Give me a second to change."

I'd moved my stuff into the trunk, anticipating this, but the car was not roomy. "I'm used to it," Joey said. "Stage training. I went to the Emmys one year with six people in a van. Coming from a location shoot. You could tell who'd been in theater—Max, David, and Clay changed into black tie in under ten minutes, in the backseat, and I got myself into a full-length Oscar de la Renta. But Rupert and Tricia made us stop at 7-Eleven so they could do it in the bathroom. Hey, *Promethea*," she said, discovering the comic books. "And *Planetary*? Pretty hip. Are these P.B.'s?"

"Yes. Apollo picked them out. The Caltech student Uncle Theo adopted." I looked in the rearview mirror. Joey had pulled off her shirt; underneath she had on a spandex tank top. "You're wearing a jogging bra under the Valentino?"

Joey met my eyes in the mirror. "This camisole? It's not for jogging, it's . . ." She lifted one arm, revealing a hidden pocket, and pulled out a gun.

"Joey!" I yelled. "What kind of party are we going to?"

"I'm not gonna use it, I just don't want to lose it. It's from Elliot. It's got sentimental value."

I found this ridiculous, but I couldn't dissuade her. She was wearing a Glock to a French restaurant. She finished dressing and climbed up front to put on makeup.

I headed west to the 405, wondering which bad news to break first. Joey took time with her face, covering the scar that ran down her cheekbone. If there was a trial, would they let her wear makeup? Out on bail, yes. But in jail? Because she'd look a lot scarier with her scar and the haunted look she gets when she loses her appetite.

"Charles Zetrakis called again," I said. "He says he's thinking of talking."

"Why is everyone so garrulous these days? Okay, I'll call him later."

"And the cops came to the house with a search warrant and took away some clothes." I hadn't meant it to come out that baldly, but how else to put it?

She froze. Then she went back to her makeup. "Okay. Nothing to worry about. Probably they found David's blood on my clothes. Everyone who took care of him got blood on them. He had IV tubes. That happens. So what?"

She was talking a good game, but she was scared. "Joey, I met a reporter today. Monica somebody. She wants to do a feature article on you, something favorable. Free PR is how she described it."

Joey snorted. "That's what they all say."

"But it might be a good thing. Couldn't you meet with her, and see if—"

"I'd rather sunbathe on an anthill."

"Okay, clearly there are creepy reporters, but there must be ethical ones too."

"There are. But the times I've been burned? They'd have to kiss my ass for the next thirty-four years to even the score. I don't see that happening."

"I kind of liked this woman," I said. "And she seemed to like you."

"I'm sure she likes her grandfather, too," Joey said. "But you think she wouldn't sell him out for a good lead? Not even a whole story, just a good lead."

"Okay, so what about Charles Zetrakis?" I said. "Him talking—to the police, I assume—that's good, right?"

She began moving stuff from her big purse into her clutch. "No. It's premature."

"Oh? When would be a good time?"

"After I talk to the person who shot David."

"You know who shot David?" I yelled.

"I've narrowed it down to two people. Maybe three. I've been trying to check it out."

I forced myself to glance back at the road. "What's that mean, check it out?"

She was quiet for a moment, then said, "Well, there's the license plate I saw."

"Yes," I said. "But you can't just look up a license plate like it's a phone number. Do you know anyone with access to the license-plate database?"

"A cop, you mean? I know a lot of cops."

"Yes, but will any of them help you?"

Joey was quiet again. Then: "I haven't asked my brother. He's out of the country. And he'll say I have to tell the detectives, let them handle it. He's like that."

"I'm like that too," I said. "So you have this license number, but it's no help. What's Plan B? You walk up to the top three candidates and ask if they shot David?"

"Not 'if.' Why."

"But why?"

"Why what?"

"Why 'why'?" I honked my horn, blaming a poor bus for my frustration.

"Because." Joey put down her lipstick. "David was shot. In one sense, it doesn't matter what the intention behind that bullet was. It doesn't matter to the cops; either way, it's a crime. But it matters to the insurance company. And it matters to me. Because if David planned it, I want the shooter to get away with it."

"Joey, this is just getting worse and worse—"

"It was David's death, nobody else's. Not the state of California's. If he wanted it on his terms, a fast bullet rather than a slow eating away by cancer, okay by me. I couldn't help him do it, and he wouldn't ever ask me; he wouldn't want it on my conscience. But I won't turn in anyone who did."

"You'll stand trial instead?"

"It won't come to a trial. I've thought it over. I had means, motive, and opportunity, but there's no physical evidence."

"His blood on your clothes? That's not physical?"

She frowned but said, "I can't start to panic over every little thing. It's a game of chicken. They're welcome to frame it any way they like; it's still circumstantial."

"And if it wasn't assisted suicide?" I asked. "What if someone actually murdered David?"

"Then all bets are off. I'll tell the cops everything I know."

"But otherwise, LAPD will just have to fold up and go home?" I asked.

"Yep. Unsolved case. Too bad."

I kept my eyes on the traffic lights around me, eight lanes of freeway in the growing darkness of New Year's Eve.

I had faith in the police, maybe naively. More faith than Joey did. But even I could see that if their minds were set on her, they might not waste time on their second-string theory, or their third, the one that might be the right one. Because they were human and how many hours were in a day, after all?

What I didn't see them doing was throwing in the towel, if only because this was such a high-profile case. If Joey was their pick, I believed they'd take what they had and run with it, exploiting every detail that might work in their favor. "There's one more thing to consider." I swallowed. "According to this reporter today, there's a toxicology report— from the coroner, I guess—saying that Elliot had something in his body, that it wasn't a simple drowning or heart attack. Maybe it's just a rumor, but if his death looks suspicious, along with David's—"

"Jesus Christ! Are you serious?" She stared at me in disbelief. "What an idiot! Stupid, risk-taking, thrill-seeking—" She pounded on the glove box, which fell open, and then on the passenger door of my previously owned Integra, punctuating her diatribe.

I flinched, thinking a flailing arm might fly into me or hit the steering wheel. I also worried she'd break her hand. That would be bad. Unless she banged the door right open and went flying out onto the freeway. That would be worse.

I leaned forward to make sure she was wearing her seat belt and the next thing I knew, the whole freeway seemed to be honking. Okay, so maybe I was swerving a little.

I saw other cars swerve too, possibly in response to my swerves. Oh, dear. Oh, well. No harm done.

Except that when I looked in the rearview mirror, I saw the flashing lights of a police car.

Thirty-nine

My arms turned to fettuccine. Everything I'd eaten somersaulted in my stomach.

"Joey," I said. "There's a cop behind us. What do I do?"

She turned in her seat. "Shit. You've got to pull over."

"I know that. How?"

"A lane at a time. Not yet. After this car. Turn on your signal."

It amazed me, how fast she pulled herself out of an emotional frenzy to help me through my driving crisis.

"You're slowing down," she said. "Don't. It's dangerous." She turned to watch the flow of traffic behind us. "Now. Change lanes. Go, go, go."

By the time I reached the shoulder of the 405, I could have gone another fifty yards and gotten off the freeway altogether. The Sunset exit ramp was right there. But I wasn't sure what the protocol was; I'd never been stopped on the freeway, only on surface streets. Well, too late now. I didn't want to look like we were fleeing. I focused on slowing my breathing, and turned off the engine.

"Damn," Joey said. "Damn. Damn, damn." She was trying to reach her right hand through the left armhole of the sleeveless Valentino, but the dress was too tightly fitted.

"What are you doing? What's wrong?"

She gave up on that and gathered the dress from the hemline and pushed it up till it was bunched around her waist, trying to reach under it from the bottom. Valentino would have keeled over, watching this. "I should've rehearsed before wearing it. Damn." She glanced behind her, then straightened up and pulled her dress back down. "Listen, Wollie. I don't have a license to carry concealed. So you never saw this gun. Got it?"

"Okay, but—"

"Or they'll haul us both in and—"

"Okay, but—"

And there was the cop.

He just materialized, on Joey's side of the car. Had he heard her? Joey rolled down her window. The Integra was so old, the windows still rolled down manually.

"Hello, there," I said. "Happy New Year."

He aimed a flashlight at me, blinding me, which was probably intentional, to throw me off my game. Not that I had a game. I was too distracted, thinking about Joey's gun.

"Both of you put your hands on the dashboard."

We did this. On Joey's side, the glove box popped open. The flashlight went there and he said, "License and registration. Where are they?"

"The registration's in the glove box there and the license is in my evening bag. Purse. Small purse," I said, as though "evening bag" were an esoteric term.

"Keep your hands on the dash." His light went to Joey. "You all right, miss?"

"Yes."

"You seemed to be having a problem a few miles back."

"No, that was me," I said. "I was weaving. In and out of my lane, just a little bit. Weaving. The driving kind of weaving." As opposed to hair weaving, I supposed.

"Are you high?" he asked Joey.

"No, sir."

He shone the flashlight into the glove box, which held the usual assortment of vital minutiae, including nail polish, cuticle scissors, pens, index cards, Kleenex, coins, paper clips, magnified makeup mirror, hairbrush, hair spray, and registration.

"Reach in there and pull out the registration," he said.

"Are you talking to her or me?" I said. "I mean, me or her?"

"You."

I complied. Stuff fell out in the process, which Joey and I crammed back in.

"Where's your purse?" the officer asked.

"Trunk," I said.

From what I could see, he was on the young side of thirty, in a sand-colored California Highway Patrol uniform, and not bad looking. Okay, he wasn't good looking either. Not that it mattered. It's not like I was going to turn on the charm, because honestly, whatever charm I possess has no on/off button.

"I'll need to see ID for you too," he said to Joey while looking at my registration.

"Okay," she said. "But I don't even know this chick. She was just nice enough to give me a ride."

I stared at her, wondering what I was supposed to make of that.

He was writing now, still holding the registration. "You girls been drinking?"

"I had espresso," I said. "An hour ago. A double."

"I've been drinking, Officer," Joey said. "In fact, I might need to throw up. Is it okay if I step outside the car to do that?"

He moved back, as if she might hurl all over him. "Hold on," he said, and talked into his radio. "Requesting backup."

Backup? Just how sick did he expect Joey to be?

He repeated his request, asking for a female officer to assist in a search of two female suspects. Then he told Joey to stay where she was, but to vomit out the window if necessary. He stepped back but kept talking to me from her side of the car. "This vehicle is registered to a 'Thomas Flynn,'" he said, referring to the registration. "Who are you?"

"Wollie Shelley," I said, my mind reeling from the prospect of getting searched. "Doc—Thomas Flynn—was my fiancé. By now I was supposed to be Mrs. Thomas Flynn, but it didn't work out."

"But he gave you the car?"

"Yes. He felt it was the least he could do."

"Can he verify this?"

"Yes, if you can find him. Certainly."

"Where is he?"

"Asia."

"For how long?"

"Five, six years. I have proof of insurance, though. In my purse. Handbag."

"All right, when you can safely exit the vehicle, do so, and open up the trunk."

I glanced at Joey, who nodded at me and smiled almost imperceptibly.

How could she be so calm? Even a halfhearted frisk would reveal the gun under her arm. Then what?

I got out slowly, unnerved by the cars whizzing by, and walked to the back of the car slowly, as though I might grow more intelligent with time. The officer stood by the right rear fender and kept the flashlight on me while I sorted through trunk junk. Perhaps he thought I'd emerge with a submachine gun or a vicious dog. Probably that happened all the time in Los Angeles, the birthplace of road rage.

I stalled as long as I reasonably could, but I had no inspired thoughts on what to do, so finally I turned to him, evening bag in hand. Which was when I saw movement twenty feet ahead of the Integra, streaking toward the exit ramp.

It was Joey, sprinting into the night.

Forty

The thing about Joey is, she's a runner. She's got small breasts and long legs and no body fat, and to her, jogging is a good time. She's one of those people out doing it at midnight or in the midst of a rainstorm, making you wonder if she's got an Olympic event coming up. So it didn't surprise me that she'd try to outrun a cop.

Why she chose to was another story, but she must've considered it to be in my best interest, because she'd never just ditch me.

I saw her a full six seconds before he did, and by the time it occurred to me to stop gawking, it was too late. He spotted her. She was now a flash in the distance, at a full-out sprint, disappearing down the exit ramp.

"Stop! Halt!" he yelled.

Run, Joey, run! I screamed, but had the good sense to keep it in my head.

She was on the shoulder, thank God. The cars must've appreciated that, as no one wanted to end the year by mowing down an overdressed jogger.

I had to give the cop credit—he started after her. But after a dozen or so yards he slowed, then stopped. He was a little on the chubby side, and fully clothed, in heavy shoes, holding a big flashlight, while Joey had a good head start, a runner's body, and carried nothing but a gun in her lingerie.

The cop headed back to me, talking into his radio. He was not happy. His gait was heavy and aggressive now, and his words came in angry sound bites: "long red hair" and "mid to late twenties." It was nice of him to underestimate her age by ten years, but the fact was, police everywhere were going to be looking for her now.

"Up against the car," he yelled at me.

I complied.

He didn't frisk me. He did something truly unnecessary. He handcuffed me.

I don't suppose anyone really likes to be handcuffed—unless her taste runs to bondage, which mine doesn't, although I try to be open-minded—but my problem was not with being restrained. It was that I'm well endowed. With no arms, I felt exposed, like two breasts with a head attached. Like I was practicing for my *Playboy* centerfold shoot. Not that this cop had any prurient interest in me, but there was a lot of traffic on the 405, and I could only hope that I wasn't distracting. I sure as heck was cold.

I didn't bring up these concerns, because the guy was hopping mad. He made me perch on the guardrail rather than have me sit in my car, which I found mean-spirited. When another California Highway Patrol car parked behind us on the shoulder of the freeway, he pushed me into the passenger seat of his own car and buckled me up, still handcuffed, which meant I was effectively straitjacketed. He walked back to his colleagues, and after a time I heard his voice raised in indignation. Maybe losing a suspect—what we were suspected of I didn't know—wasn't going over well with the other cops. Especially a suspect on foot, in a cocktail dress and patent leather shoes.

And how would I protect her? If fleeing the scene of a routine traffic stop was against the law, then Joey would see in the new year from jail. If they found her. So it was imperative they didn't find her. L.A. county jail is a place people talk about the way they used to speak of that prison where they kept the Count of Monte Cristo. Not that jail's ever a good time. Mug shots. Strip searches. Hanging with a bad crowd.

The three officers approached me. One was a woman, and it was she who helped me out of the car, patted me down, uncuffed me, gave me a

Breathalyzer test, and held up a finger, instructing me to follow it with my eyes. Then I was rehandcuffed, put into the backseat of the squad car, and shoulder-harnessed, which was as comfortable as lounging in a rock quarry.

"Okay, who's your friend?" The original cop, whose name tag said KRANSLAUER, got in the driver's seat, poised to write down my full testimony on a small notepad. He'd been nice enough on first meeting me, but that was then, and this was now. Maybe his belligerence was for the benefit of the woman officer, who sat in the front passenger seat.

I took a deep breath. "Officer Kranslauer—am I pronouncing that correctly?—I'm often the designated driver at times like these, because, as we've legally established, I'm not much of a drinker. That being the case—"

"What's her name?"

Evade, evade, evade. Obfuscate. Conceal. Becloud. Perplex. There was that voice again, and whoever he was, he had access to a thesaurus.

"You see," I said, "we met tonight in a parking lot in front of Vons, in Studio City. I had no plans for New Year's Eve, and she had a party to go to, and I didn't intend to drink, and she did, and what with the price of gas, carpooling always seems to be—"

"You don't know her name?"

"Not absolutely." This was true. Until Joey's marital status was sorted out, was she or wasn't she Mrs. Horowitz? "Well, her first name is Mary. What struck me about that is, my mother named me after Mary Wollstonecraft Shelley, and so it was something we had in common."

Blood was rushing to Kranslauer's face. "Are you telling me you have no idea who she is?"

"I'm bad at names. Isn't everyone? The trick is, you're supposed to repeat someone's name immediately after they—"

"Whose party were you going to?" This came from the woman officer.

"A little French restaurant on Little Santa Monica was what she said." I was discovering something extraordinary: if I stuck to the truth—not the whole truth, of course—I could do this. It was pouring out of me, in fact. I wasn't even breaking a sweat.

"Who's giving the party?" Kranslauer barked.

"Hold on. Let me just adjust my handcuffs—there. The party? Hosted by—not sure. A law firm, maybe. As I said, she was the invitee."

"Let me get this straight," Kranslauer said. "You were going to a party you weren't invited to, where you wouldn't know anybody, giving a ride to a total stranger." He leaned over the front seat to get in my face. "Are you a lesbian?"

"No. Well, not to my knowledge. I mean, I'm currently in a hetero-sexual relationship, and I'm pretty happy."

"Where's he tonight?" the female cop asked.

"Working. He's in—textiles." Okay, not so good. Must stick to truth.

"Where's this woman live?" Kranslauer asked.

"Her? Not sure." This was also true, in the sense that Joey might not be the actual owner of Solomonhaus. Hadn't the locks been changed re-peatedly? "I'd probably have just dropped her back at Vons, where she left her car."

"I thought you said she'd been drinking, that you were the designated driver."

"Yes, true. I mean, assuming she was sober. Naturally."

Kranslauer glared at me, but I was able to look him in the eye. I kept my expression limpid. One thing I had going for me was orange hair, which, even more than blondness, had to lower people's expectation of my intelligence. And judgment.

Kranslauer checked his clipboard. "This your current address, on your license?"

"No, I've had a few since then."

"Where do you live now?"

"Pasadena."

"With your boyfriend?"

"No. Uh . . . no."

"You don't live with your boyfriend?" the female cop asked. This was making me nervous.

"No. Although I've spent a lot of time there lately. Wilshire, in West-wood."

"What's his name?" she asked.

"Whose?"

"Your boyfriend."

"Why do you need to know his name?" I was suddenly panicked. What could they possibly want with Simon?

"Does he know you're driving a car registered to your old lover?" Kranslauer's tone was rude now. Anger's one thing, but is rudeness ever necessary?

"Yes, he knows," I said. "It's not a problem."

"Well? What's his name?" The woman cop wouldn't give up. She obviously had boyfriend issues. Happily, her cell phone rang, and she stepped out of the car to answer it.

"Well?" Kranslauer asked. "What's his name?"

"S-simon."

"What? Suss-simon?" Kranslauer asked. "What kind of name is that?"

"Hebrew, I think."

"Suss-simon what?"

I coughed and mumbled, "Alexander," which came out, approximately, "Bubgeezer." Kranslauer didn't even take a crack at that.

"Back to this situation. What was going on with you two when I pulled you over?"

"What do you mean?"

"With you driving erratically and her waving her arms."

"Have you ever heard of car dancing?"

"No."

"When you hear a song that just makes you want to dance, but you're in a car, so you have to pour all your moves into your upper body? You've never heard of that?"

He stared at me. "Lady, I saw a car swerving like a potential accident hazard, and a woman carrying on like I don't know what. Maybe she was being held against her will."

"Against her will?" I said, mildly shocked. "Wouldn't she have asked you to rescue her, if that were the case?"

He had no answer to that. "Did I see a bungee cord in your trunk?" he asked suddenly.

"You saw my bungee cord? That's great news. I thought I'd lost it."

He glanced at the woman cop, still on the phone, then back to me. "All right, what do you think made her run off like that?"

"Officer, the world is so filled with disturbed people following strange impulses, it amazes me that most of us still manage to get out of bed and make it to work. Maybe she hears voices. I know I do."

That did it. Kranslauer clearly did not hear voices, and he didn't want me hearing them either. He leaned back, away from me. "What kind of voices you hear?"

"At first I thought it was Agamemnon. Lately I've been thinking Zeus."

At that point, the woman opened the car door and told him that she and her partner were taking off to check out a possible 23-152 northbound on the 405. Her manner made me think she was higher up in the food chain than Kranslauer. He told her he might book me on a 207. She stared at him, then asked him to step out of the car.

I couldn't hear it all, because of the freeway traffic, but the woman said the watch commander would not go for a 207 based on a bungee cord. A radio squawked. A minute later Kranslauer came back, undid my cuffs, and told me it was my lucky day.

"If I wasn't just called in on an eleven seventy-nine, you'd be on your way to getting booked for kidnapping and maybe even car dancing. Get out of here."

"Thank you, I—"

"Don't thank me, that really pisses me off. Go. Just go. Because can I tell you something? I don't like you. And I really don't like your hair."

Forty-one

got off at the next exit and took surface streets back to Sunset, looking for Joey. It would be an exercise in futility if Joey didn't want to
be found, but what if she did? I would, if I were out there in a little black
cocktail dress, without even a sweater. At least she was in flats. Thank
God for Chloe and the lawyer who didn't like tall women.

I turned on my phone and found hers in her Fendi clutch under the
seat and kept them close, in case Joey found a way to call. Unless she
thought I was still under the watchful eyes of Kranslauer, in which case
she'd call someone else. I dialed Fredreeq.

"Heard from Joey?" I said.

"No. What's up?"

I told her. Everything. The traffic cop, the gun, the search warrant,
Joey's wild idea of confronting the killer, the cryptic call from Charles
Zetrakis, the toxicology report on Elliot. It took a while, as I had to
pause for Fredreeq's periodic screams. But by the time I told her about
the party we were supposed to go to and the lawyer who was going to get
Joey back all the money she'd handed over to Elliot, Fredreeq had had
enough.

"Where is this party?"

"La Baguette," I said. "Little Santa Monica, near Century City—"

"I'll find it. Meet you there in twenty minutes."

"But—"

"Joey will show. She dressed for it, she needs a lawyer, she'll hitchhike if she has to. So we'll show too. If she thinks we'll let her waltz on up to some gun-happy killer—"

"I've had this conversation with her, Fredreeq—"

"Over my dead body," Fredreeq said. "You hear what I'm saying? Over my dead body. I expect full backup from you. If we have to organize an intervention, we will."

I agreed, hung up, and headed to La Baguette, listening to voice-mail messages on the way. Two were from Simon, a restrained sort of "Happy New Year" that suggested he didn't care to be overheard sounding amorous.

The third was from P.B. "I just want to know if you got me the *Planetary* where they fight for the future of Man in the Spawning Caves of the Neo-Arachnid Variants bred by the Murder Colonels," he said. "But I guess it can wait till I see you tomorrow."

I wasn't going to see my brother tomorrow, and I didn't know the answer to his question, but whatever it was he spoke about sounded so much more relaxing than the night ahead. I don't love parties. But Joey was on foot, with no money, credit card, house key, or phone, and if helping her out meant partying, then party I would.

.   .   .

La Baguette was small, and everything in it had an undersized element, from the chairs to the serving sizes. "Very French," Fredreeq said. "They're a petite people."

But it was also meticulous in its attention to detail, and the candlelit beauty was reflected on the faces that filled the rooms. I imagined this restaurant and all its guests in Europe, where things were soft and a little worn and comfortably old. Much more appealing than the steel hardness of Solomonhaus or the matte, neutral tones of Simon's penthouse. It struck me that Simon's condo didn't really suit him, any more than Joey and Solomonhaus were a match. Only Fredreeq, in Mar Vista, seemed at home in her own home, with its yellow kitchen and literal picket fence. Where would I feel at home?

Joey's lawyer, Rick Slepicka, was fashionably thin, wearing a thin tie, holding a thin champagne flute, and sporting a thinning head of hair. The hostess of La Baguette pointed him out to Fredreeq and me. Joey had not yet shown up.

"Let me take a stab at him," Fredreeq said. "Since he doesn't like tall women. I never heard of that, by the way. Must be some wacko lawyer thing."

I let Fredreeq collar Slepicka while I moved to a buffet table to befriend his date, Daphne. She was a young and pretty thing—and short—who said she was a first-year associate at Sawyer, Slepicka & Sloane, Rick's law firm.

"What kind of law do you do?" I said.

"Torts."

I had a greeting card image take shape, of lawyers working alongside chefs, doing torts and tortes. And tarts. This got me to wondering about the difference between tortes and tarts, which then got me to wondering if I knew what a tort was. I didn't.

"What is a tort?" I asked.

Daphne wrinkled her nose. "Geeky sounding, isn't it? I wasn't looking forward to the class, in law school. But a tort's just a wrongful act, an injury other than by breach of contract, for which you can seek legal redress. So it's pretty interesting."

"That is pretty interesting," I said. "So, if you give a bunch of money to someone and you think you're in business together fifty-fifty and they do too, but then they die and it turns out you were mistaken, would that be a tort?"

"Depends. If contracts are involved, no." Daphne poured champagne into my glass. "And since one party is dead, it might get into estate law. Wills and probates."

"The reason I ask is, my best friend has a situation—"

"Joey Rafferty?"

"Yes."

"Oh, you're *Wollie*," Daphne said. "Joey was talking about you. You're going to be on *SoapDirt*. Anyhow, Rick had me looking into Joey's problem. Interesting case."

"Daphne, could you tell me what you found out—I mean, unless it's privileged? Because Joey may not make it here tonight, and—"

"No problem," Daphne said, nibbling a bread stick, "since we're not taking the case. Tell Joey that Elliot, her putative husband—he's got this sister—"

"Camille Horowitz," I said. "I know her."

"Camille. Right. She's going to post a bond to try to get herself appointed administrator, first thing Monday. Joey needs to show up at the courthouse and try to block that. She may not succeed, but Camille's doing an end run around her by not telling her. That's not cool."

"But it's legal?" I asked.

"Technically."

"But couldn't Joey and Elliot be considered common-law husband and wife?"

"Nope. Not applicable. Trust me—our firm's estate guy says this has the makings of a long story. Like the siege of Troy. Endless billable hours."

The Trojan reference gave me pause. And who would pay for all those billable hours? I asked Daphne about that.

"Well, that's the problem. Rick doesn't do contingency cases. None of the partners do. Or even pro bono, unless there's some major PR angle."

"Oh, there's plenty of PR with Joey," I said. "Believe me, Daphne, the coverage you'll get—"

"But not the kind we need. We have tons of celebrity clients. We had David Zetrakis, you know. The thing we look for is prestige, some noble political or charitable cause, the kind they give awards for. Joey may be broke, but the perception is, she's just another Hollywood bitch who can buy her way out of trouble. Situation sucks."

"It does suck," I said. The news was bad, but you had to love a lawyer who looked like a cheerleader and talked like one too.

"I'll tell you," she added, "if I thought I was married to a guy and he did that to me, I'd blow his balls off."

I was just revising my cheerleader impression when Rick Slepicka appeared and whisked Daphne onto the tiny dance floor, leaving me with Fredreeq.

"Dinner," she said, "will be morel mushroom soup and tuna *tartare* to start, then tournedos of beef with baby carrots and fingerling potatoes, and green salad at the end, in the European style. Tarte tatin for dessert.

The menu. That's all the information I got out of that skinny-ass lawyer. Talk about a—"

But someone was coming in the front door. I put my hand on Fredreeq's arm, thinking it was Joey, but it wasn't.

It was Charles and Agnes Zetrakis.

Forty-two

Charles and Agnes stood uncertainly, their coats still on, looking around. François, the chef-owner, hurried to greet them, followed by Rick Slepicka and Daphne.

"What is it?" Fredreeq said. "Do you know them?"

"That's David's brother and his wife. The ones who inherited the entire estate, except for a few tchotchkes, like the Klimt." I knew I was rattled when I started using Yiddishisms learned from Ruta, my long-ago babysitter. What rattled me was the synchronicity of Charles showing up when I'd been trying to get to him all day. "Fredreeq, he knows something about David's murder. I've got to talk to him."

"Right behind you, sister. Let's go."

"But how do we get him alone?"

Charles and Agnes seemed to have inherited David's celebrity along with his wealth, judging from the swarm of people gathered in the foyer. Rick, in particular, was standing quite close, as if Charles might need legal advice while checking his coat.

Agnes disengaged herself from the coterie. I was struck again by the contrast: Charles had a certain style, while Agnes, large-boned and wide-faced, was as chic as a minivan. She wore a beige suit, matching pumps, and a string of thick pearls, all of which were too old for her. Her straight hair was in a ponytail, with blunt-cut bangs, like a fifth grader. "She's going for the food," I whispered. "Let's befriend her."

. We followed Agnes to the buffet table, where she piled food onto her plate in a businesslike manner.

"Try the soup," Fredreeq said. "So creamy, yet not a drop of dairy in it."

"But you've run out of hands," I said. "Let me fill a bowl for you."

If Agnes found it odd that two strangers were pressing soup on her, she gave no sign, allowing us to accompany her to a free table. Once there, she applied herself unself-consciously to her dinner. Fredreeq nabbed a bread basket from an adjoining table and urged her to sample the sourdough.

I introduced Fredreeq and reminded Agnes that she and I had met, in a cursory way, at the reading of the will. "I'm very sorry about your brother-in-law," I added.

"David?" she asked, breaking off a piece of bread. She had a nice manicure, but the nails were short and her hands were thick and rough, like someone who gardened. "Thank you. He's in God's care now. But we weren't close."

"No?"

She shook her head. "He didn't like me. I'm not creative."

"Oh." What an odd thing to say. Wasn't everyone creative?

"But I'm grateful, of course. All that money. The estate. The insurance."

Fredreeq and I nodded. Yes, millions of dollars probably merited gratitude. "David must have loved his brother very much," Fredreeq said.

"In the end." Agnes cut into a tournedo of beef. She held her knife in her right hand as she ate and her fork in her left, a way of eating I always associate with either old money or a European upbringing. "Not for years before that. They had a falling-out. David came around just recently. A shame it took so long." She chewed methodically. "All this money would've come in handy over the years, but now the IRS will circle like vultures. People just never think."

I didn't point out that life insurance money isn't usually available until one's life is terminated. "I understand you and Charles have a winery," I said. "That's gotta be a tough business."

She looked up at me and I noticed how green her eyes were, blindingly pretty in an otherwise plain face. "Artemis Vineyards. Have you heard of us? Five generations in my family. We were facing foreclosure next week."

"Next week?" I said. Fredreeq and I looked at each other.

Agnes nodded. "We couldn't pay the back taxes and one of our neighbors has had his eye on the property, and next week was the auction. But Charles was able to take out a loan, just before Christmas, based on the inheritance we were expecting, and he settled everything. Of course, the interest is outrageous."

Fredreeq and I nodded vigorously.

"David almost didn't tell us what he was leaving us. Imagine if we got all that money, but too late to save Artemis Vineyards? Father Bob thinks it's a miracle. People say, 'Well, you could just buy another vineyard,' but it's not the same at all. It's *land,* for goodness' sakes. It's like when your dog dies and people tell you to just get a new one."

"Absolutely," Fredreeq said. "And I bet it's the same house you grew up in. You can't replace those memories."

"Yes. And David almost didn't get to see it. Charles was always writing to him, inviting him up for Christmas, et cetera, but David never answered, not till he got cancer. He could have lent us money anytime, but he waited till he was dying. And then the foreclosure news, and then the loan application; everything was such a rush job—it's been just crazy. We're exhausted."

"That's death for you," Fredreeq said, rummaging through the bread basket. "Very fatiguing for everyone."

Agnes forked another tournedo of beef. "The last months they were very close—that's when David came up to visit. His assistant drove him. He was impressed by the vineyard. Had no use for me, of course. But he was show people. They're like that."

"Like what?" I asked.

"Showy."

I frowned. That made David sound shallow. He wasn't. Theatrical, yes, a man who functioned best in a crowd. It was easy to see that Agnes wouldn't hold his interest and that she, in turn, wouldn't appreciate him. I was curious about Rupert's friendship with Charles and what he thought of the unshowy Agnes.

"I imagine you and Charles tried to get other investors interested in your vineyard," I said.

Agnes dipped a spoon into her soup, raised it, sniffed it, blew on it, then sipped it, holding it in her mouth before gulping audibly. It was as though she'd learned to eat at wine tastings. "No one's got that kind of money. None of our friends from church."

"How about the soap opera?" I said. "Charles must've known some of them, from before his falling-out with David. Like Rupert Ling."

"Or Joey Rafferty," Fredreeq said.

Agnes harrumphed. "Show people. They think grapes are glamorous. Grapes are crops. You say 'soil samples' or 'migrant workers,' those people start yawning."

I looked over at Charles, standing at the fireplace with Rick and Daphne and other well-dressed party guests, champagne flutes in hand, light glinting off the golden liquid. That was the ad campaign; Agnes was the one with dirt under her fingernails.

But how much was that dirt worth to her?

Fredreeq kicked me under the table, wiggling her eyebrows in a "Go ahead, squeeze her for information" look. I wiggled mine back, then said, "Who do you think shot your brother-in-law, Agnes?"

"Mugger," she said. "David should've kept a gun in the house. Or a dog."

There was no trace of doubt in her voice, despite the fact that her opinion was not shared by anyone I'd yet met.

I stood. "Good luck with your vineyard," I said, and shook her hand.

"Try the tarte tatin," Fredreeq said, adding, "Nice suit, by the way. It's got that new-suit smell. St. John?"

"Chanel," Agnes said. "Charles has been after me to shop since the loan came through. I hadn't bought clothes since our honeymoon. But things sure are pricey here."

Fredreeq took my arm, waiting until we were just out of earshot before whispering, "She did it."

"Did what?"

"The murder. Remember the Menendez brothers? Out buying cars and tennis rackets with their parents' blood still wet on the family room carpet."

"You heard her," I said. "It was Charles's idea."

"Chanel was not his idea. Men do not like Chanel. It costs gobs of money and has zero sex appeal."

We sidled over to the fireplace to join the group surrounding Charles. The conversational topic was basketball, as was always the case where four or more were gathered for any length of time in L.A. As I knew little about the Lakers, I stood by awkwardly, waiting for the subject to change.

Not Fredreeq. "I'm not saying you're wrong," she said to the group, "but Phil Jackson—or Dr. Phil, as I like to call him—had his moment in the sun and that was the golden age of the Lakers, if you don't count the Pat Riley years, but you can't go home again, so let's just all move on. Charles, my friend Wollie here needs to talk to you in private for just a moment. Will the rest of you excuse us?"

Charles looked perplexed, as did everyone else, but what Fredreeq's tactic lacked in grace it made up for in effectiveness. He mumbled an apology and let me lead him to the end of a hallway.

"We're friends of Joey Rafferty's," I said, "and—"

"I know. From the reading of the will. And I saw you coming out of the police station the other night when I went in for my interview."

"Oh, was that you?" I said. "I thought you were paparazzi. Look, Joey was going to be here tonight, but she's in trouble. She needs your help. I know that you know something the police should know, something Joey won't tell them." I dropped my voice to a whisper. "I also know that you two had an affair years ago."

Charles raised his eyebrows, then looked over his shoulder.

"Which is none of my business, of course," I said, "except that Joey's out there confronting the killer, which is something the police should be doing."

His eyes widened. "Shit."

"Exactly," I said. "She has a good idea of who the murderer is. Do you?"

Charles lowered his voice. "I don't know what the legal definition of murder is. I believe my brother paid someone to shoot him in the head."

Here we go again, I thought. Murder, suicide, murder, suicide. Why was there no consensus on this? "Who?"

"Well, that's the question, isn't it?" Charles said. "Several weeks ago, Joey drove to the edge of the property at night and left a laundry bag full of money there. Over a hundred grand. She counted it. David had tried to drive it down himself, but he was too weak, so she did it for him. So the 'who,' I would say, is whoever picked it up."

Which David's surveillance cameras wouldn't reveal, as they were conveniently not working. "Okay, forget who. How about why?" I asked.

Charles scratched his beard. "My brother was on heavy medication. Drugs had a strong effect on him, his whole life. He was the guy on acid who thought he could fly. So maybe he was just out of it. Maybe there was no rhyme or reason."

I didn't buy that. There was always a reason; you just had to find the context where the reason felt at home. "Joey didn't tell the cops about the laundry bags, did she?"

"No. If David arranged his death, the life insurance wouldn't kick in. She wanted Agnes and me to have that money. It's all David talked about, she said. Expiating guilt."

"Guilt about what?" I asked. When he didn't answer, I said, "Your affair with Joey? Did David break it up?"

Charles looked at me steadily. "Did Joey tell you we had an affair?"

I thought back. Hadn't she? Before I could answer, Daphne came down the hallway toward us and excused herself, squeezing around us to a door marked LES FEMMES. She said, "Charles, your wife's looking for you."

He nodded. When she'd gone into the ladies' room, he said, "This isn't a good time. Or place."

"Where?" I said. "And when?"

"Tomorrow. Agnes is going to noon Mass. She'll have the car, but if you don't mind coming to the hotel—we're at the Bel-Air—I could give you an hour."

"I'll be there," I said.

"Bring Joey with you," he said.

I took a deep breath. "I will if I can."

Forty-three

Fredreeq, to my great relief, decided to spend the night with me at Solomonhaus, despite my lame attempt to dissuade her, on the grounds that she had family in town and it was New Year's Eve.

"Are you kidding?" she said from her car, talking to me in mine via cell phone. "My kids are poppin' champagne. Francis lets 'em stay up till all hours watching horror movies with their cousins. As long as I'm home tomorrow in time to drive to the reunion in Fresno. What we've got to do now is gang up on Joey. History shows us that you can't do it alone. Your heart's in the right place, but you're a pushover."

But Joey was not home to be ganged up on. Neither, thank God, was her evil lock-changing sister-in-law.

"Now what?" I said, moving through the house, turning on lights.

"Now we use our brains," Fredreeq said. "The one thing that skinny-ass lawyer of hers told me is that his firm doesn't do criminal. If he has a client looking at a prison sentence, he sends them to Howard Weitzman."

"Howard Weitzman? He must be hideously expensive."

"Slepicka's clients do not need to clip coupons," Fredreeq said. "Joey's deluded if she thinks he'll take her case against Camille for old times' sake. For a big, fat check, yes. Speaking of auld lang syne, where's Simon?"

The question I'd been dreading. "Working," I said, moving to the kitchen to plug Joey's phone into the battery charger. "Spy stuff."

"On *New Year's Eve?* What in the Sam Hill—"

"Do criminals take holidays off? No. Neither do federal agents."

"They do," Fredreeq said, "when they're in the Dopamine Phase, so—"

"Irrelevant, since I wasn't about to leave Joey alone anyway."

"All right, one crisis at a time." Fredreeq came up behind me and hit the PLAY button on Joey's blinking answering machine.

"Joey, this is your mother. Happy New Year, dear." Mrs. Rafferty's voice was like warm oatmeal. "We're off the coast of Croatia, and it's exactly the way you picture Croatia, just like the postcards—oh, your brother's telling me to keep it short, as I've got all the other kids to call. I went youngest first this year. I'm sure you and Elliot are out celebrating. Have a lovely time, dear. Miss you. Bye."

"Damn," Fredreeq said, taking the word out of my mouth. Mrs. Rafferty didn't know about Elliot's death—did any of Joey's endless family?

There were three messages from journalists—one of them Monica, the one I'd met—asking for interviews, and seven from miscellaneous friends, expressing shock and sadness about Elliot.

"Okay, nothing interesting there," Fredreeq said. "Let's search the house."

"For?"

"Clues."

"You start," I said. "I'm getting into jammies first."

The mere thought of going through someone else's stuff was exhausting, but once I was in my signs-of-the-zodiac pajamas, things seemed less daunting. Especially since Solomonhaus was so clutter-averse. Fredreeq attacked the kitchen drawer that held a manageable assortment of paperwork, bills, and correspondence, and I focused on the master bedroom. I started with Joey's backpack, brought in from the car.

The first items of interest were photos borrowed from my storage space: the picnic at the Hollywood Bowl and David's fortieth-birthday at Morton's. This justified the endless hours I'd spent pasting photos into albums. Maybe that was the whole point of that exercise, that one day the subjects die and the photos become priceless. Until all the people in all the photos are dead and there's no one left to recognize them, at which point they become worthless.

The woman in the background at the birthday party caught my eye again. Her facial features had Zetrakis written all over them, perhaps because I'd just seen Charles. But if she was a sister, or even a cousin, why had she been left out of the will? Maybe she'd been estranged from David, like Joey and Charles, but surely Joey would've known about it.

"Okay, what is this?" Fredreeq said, appearing in the doorway. She held packaging and operating instructions for a piece of clothing called the All-Caliber Camisole, manufactured by Dressed to Kill: Frannie's Feminine Firearms Accessories.

"It's an undergarment that Joey's currently wearing, and it's holding her Glock."

Fredreeq stared at me, then walked away without a word. I didn't know whether she was shocked speechless by this sartorial choice or relieved that Joey was armed, albeit with a gun she couldn't get to without removing her dress.

I returned my attention to the backpack and all its detritus, including sunscreen, sunglasses, Kleenex, chewing gum, dental floss, a small book of Zen meditations, and a thimble-sized carved Buddha.

"Wollie! I've got a clue!" Fredreeq yelled.

I hurried to the dining room, where my friend triumphantly held up a trio of DVDs in plain cases. "*At the End of the Day*," she said. "Future episodes. These must be significant, or what's Joey doing with them?"

"She's not doing anything with them," I said. "They're mine. Jen Kim gave them to me when she hired me to do *SoapDirt*. She thought I should watch the show."

"Oh." Fredreeq's disappointment was short-lived. "Well, I think we need to take a break and watch them right now. Wait'll my cousin Zonya hears that I've seen the future of Moon Lake. Too bad I have too much integrity to sell them to the tabloids."

We all had our addictions, and who was I to interfere with Fredreeq's? We went into the bedroom and I cleared off Joey's bed, scooping stuff back into the backpack. The TV, with a built-in DVD player, was still set up on the dresser, Joey's jean jacket tossed over it. Fredreeq handed the jacket to me. I was about to hang it up, then remembered that Joey had been wearing it the day Elliot died. I checked the pockets.

In one was a letter and its envelope, in small pieces.

We laid it out on the bed and pieced it back together.

E—

What I hate most about all this is being a cliché—the wife who's so blind she thinks she's happy. And now what? My current plan to drink myself into a stupor isn't working out that well and isn't exactly original either. I think I should just kill you. It's proactive, within my capabilities, and requires thought and planning, which is good for someone with time on her hands. If I see you in person, I might be too mad to fire a warning shot, so this is it. The warning shot. Stay away from me.

J.

P.S. No kidding. That's how much I hate you.

I went to a dresser drawer. Inside was a book of matches and a few mar-ijuana stems on an ashtray. I thought about the police with their search warrant seeing that, but I didn't dwell on it. I took the pack of matches and the ashtray to Fredreeq and we set the pieces on fire, one at a time.

Then we settled in to watch our soap.

Forty-four

*A*t the End of the Day's opening sequence was hip, snappy theme music accompanied by windswept glamour shots of a dozen cast members. Everyone looked merry and adventurous and intriguing and sexy—all at once—and I saw each one as a potential murderer.

It was lucky Fredreeq was there to provide commentary, along with hot-air popcorn, or I'd have been lost. Every character in the show seemed related to every other character in multiple ways: cousins were also lovers, in-laws, and former stepchildren, since anyone over the age of twenty had been married at least four times. Offspring, Fredreeq explained, were shown briefly as babies, then whisked away, returning a few short years later as teenagers, victims of Soap Opera Sudden Growth Hormone. There was neither homelessness nor homeliness in Moon Lake, and certainly no obesity, but an astonishing number of citizens had, over the years, experienced temporary blindness, amnesia, and multiple personality disorders.

Fredreeq described the two major families, the Wrensides and the Trents. There were also the Reggianos, but they were recent arrivals from Vegas, mostly loan sharks and enforcers. The Wrensides were old money, with mansions and faithful servants and coats of arms; the Trents were nouveau riche. They had hotel chains and construction companies and a shopping center they were trying to build atop a failed vineyard they'd acquired from the Wrensides by foul means. They also owned the notorious nuclear power plant.

Toward the end of the first episode, an environmental group led by Tricia's character, Lilac Grant Fabian Wrenside Trent, was conducting a sit-in at the plant. Lilac's archenemy was Rupert Ling's character, Rocket, who was a Wrenside and also the chief of police. Lilac was holding Cruise Trent, her former stepson—played by Trey Mangialotti—hostage. She wore rubber gloves and held a gun to his head.

August Wrenside came charging onto this scene in a white limousine and persuaded his former daughter-in-law to enact a hostage exchange. She let go of Cruise, who, in any case, had lapsed into a diabetic coma, and put her gun against the white-haired temple of Sheffo/August, who, I noticed, walked with a limp.

Fredreeq stopped the show at this point to discuss the possibility that this was the gun that had shot David, which led me to wonder what had made the police think to look in the prop room of the soap opera for the murder weapon in the first place, something neither of us could answer. Fredreeq hit PLAY.

"I'll shoot him, Rocket," Tricia/Lilac shouted to Rupert's character, who could be seen through a picture window, on a plank, wearing a window washer's harness. "Don't think I won't." She turned to her captive. "Sorry, August, but I have nothing to lose. Either way, I'm going to prison for this. Or to hell. Besides, you're old."

"But you're young. That's what you have to lose, Lilac," Sheffo/August told her, limping toward her. "Sleep. Innocence. Sweet dreams."

"My dreams aren't that great," she said.

"You're looking out over dark water, child," he said, and music began to play under his words. "If you take my life, you cross a bridge from which there is no return. No round-trip tickets. On the far side are all the people who have killed their fellow man. It's their company that awaits you. Is that really your social scene, Lilac?"

"I'm tougher than you think," Tricia/Lilac said, tossing her well-coifed hair. "Who masterminded this break-in, who kidnapped the cleaning crew and showed up in their place?"

Fredreeq spoke up. "That explains the rubber gloves."

"The old cleaning-crew-as-Trojan-Horse scenario," I said.

"Lilac," Sheffo/August said, "you don't know the torment that killing brings."

"But my mother died from radiation poisoning. Someone's got to pay for that."

"I'm paying," Sheffo/August said. "I fired her as my museum curator, and there was nowhere for her to turn for work but the nuclear plant. I suffer for that every day. But not for much longer; this damn testicular cancer is eating me alive. So have patience. Wait three weeks and I'll be dead. Shoot me now, it will haunt you forever. And you lose your inheritance; I've left precise instructions in my will."

"What inheritance, August? Why would you leave me anything?"

"Because, Lilac, I have always loved you. Since before you were born. As I once loved your mother."

"My . . . mother?"

The music swelled, alerting us to the Significant Moment looming.

"That's right. I loved her. Lilac, I am . . . your father."

"What?!" Fredreeq and Lilac shrieked at the same moment. In the background, Rupert/Rocket was so shocked that he lost his balance and disappeared from view. The camera moved outside, showing him dangling from the window washer's harness. He wore tight-fitting gymnastics attire, an outfit worn by neither police chiefs nor window washers, in general. But perhaps things were different in Moon Lake.

The scene faded to black.

Unlike Fredreeq, who actually dabbed at her eyes, I couldn't summon up the concern I was evidently supposed to feel. The elements of impending death, failed vineyards, and guns held to the heads of people who were dying of cancer anyway hit too close to home. "The parallels here to David's life are a little scary," I said.

"That's vintage David, using his life for his art. He was writing up till the day he died," Fredreeq said. "Tricia told me that at her party. They'll be shooting his ideas right into the summer. Some details will change, of course."

"Yes, like the reprieve from death given to Tricia and Trey. But how does Tricia know what David was doing till the day he died? They weren't exactly close."

Fredreeq shrugged. "If Sheffo's still getting nuked, I guess we cross him off the short list of murder suspects."

"No, because Sheffo thought he was getting a reprieve too. He was simply mistaken. But I'll be very depressed if it turns out to be Sheffo. The thing is, all three actors could conceivably get another job, right?"

Fredreeq nodded. "Happens all the time. Actors soap-hop."

"And Jen Kim? If she was fired, couldn't she work on another show?"

"Not executive-producing. She'd be lucky to associate-produce. Soaps are dying off—those jobs just aren't that plentiful, and she doesn't have the experience. This one fell into her lap."

"How on earth do you know all this?" I asked.

"*Inside Soaps,* plus my favorite soap blog. I'm a very well-informed viewer."

We watched two more episodes of *At the End of the Day,* which more or less recapped and replayed the bombshell that Sheffo/August had just dropped regarding his paternity. Fredreeq explained that in the olden days, before TiVo and VCRs, the average viewer was a housewife who watched two or three times per week, often while ironing. She depended on the writers to fill her in on what she'd missed, which explained why characters spent time telling each other what they already knew. It also explained *The Iliad.* Greek women probably brought along darning to the acropolis and tended to their children while watching Troy fall.

After the soaps, we popped in an episode of *SoapDirt.* It was not the worst half hour of television I'd ever seen, but it made the Top Ten, lacking charm, wit, or any redeeming social value. And I was shortly to be a part of it. "It's not too much worse than *Biological Clock,*" Fredreeq pointed out, referring to my erstwhile reality show, a remark that certainly brightened my day.

I gave Fredreeq the guest bedroom and stretched myself out on the modernist sofa in the area euphemistically called the living room. Neither of us wanted the master bedroom. We didn't know when the sheets had last been changed and agreed that, in any case, sleeping on a dead man's pillow should be reserved for his widow.

I tossed and turned on the angular sofa, wondering whether I should move to the inner city or an underdeveloped country and offer myself up for missionary work—anything more meaningful than painting murals or dating for dollars. I slept badly, keeping one ear open for a knock on the door, telling me that Joey was back.

It never came.

Forty-five

eep. I was awakened at seven A.M. by Uncle Theo, wondering when I was coming over. *Beep.*

The beep came from my phone, which in my disoriented state I found puzzling.

"*Am* I coming over?" I asked. *Beep.* "I planned on painting my wall today." This, I knew, would clear my mind so I could figure out what to do next about Joey.

"Why, yes. New Year's Day, you know." *Beep.* "If you're here by eight, we'll be right on schedule."

"For what?" I asked, but there was no answer. Or another *beep.* My battery was dead.

My battery charger was in the car, so I went to find Joey's phone, which rang as I reached for it.

"Hello?" I said, praying it was Joey.

"Happy New Year, sweetie pie," a hearty voice yelled.

"Happy New Year to you, but this isn't Joey," I said. "It's her friend Wollie."

"Well, hi, Wollie. This is her brother Jamey."

"Oh, hi, Jamey," I said. "You're the one living in—Iowa?"

"Nebraska. You're thinking of Skippie."

"Oh, right. I'm not sure where Joey is, Jamey, but I'll tell her you called."

"Thanks. Uh—how's she doing?"

"Oh . . . you know . . ." My heart pounded. How much did he know? That her ex-boyfriend was dead? And the man formerly thought to be her husband? That she was broke? And a murder suspect? With a drinking problem? And a gun? "She's . . . hanging in there. One thing about Joey, she's . . . intrepid."

"Well, here's the deal. Our mom's on a cruise—Joey may have told you."

"Yes. Croatia."

"We haven't told Mom yet about Elliot," Jamey said. "It's her first vacation in fourteen years. We don't want her cutting it short, flying right from Zagreb to L.A. Joey was adamant about that."

"I think that's a good call," I said, vastly relieved that they knew about Elliot.

"You think I should fly out, though?" Jamey asked. "Joey told us all to hold off, but it doesn't feel right to leave her alone right now. I thought of just catching a plane, but the kids' wrestling team is going to state finals this weekend—it's a bad time."

"If Joey told you not to come—"

"And our sister M.J. is snowed in in Pittsburgh, the airport's shut down, and Sweezie can't travel, she's nine months pregnant, and Patrick's family is with Mom—"

"Jamey," I said, hoping I was about to do the right thing, "Joey seems to be dealing with this by keeping busy. By next week, when it all quiets down, that's when it will really hit her, I think."

"Oh, we'll all get there by next week. Well, not Sweezie, but Sean, me, Skippie, and, later, Mom and Patrick . . . helluva thing. Guy dies surfing. I've never liked oceans."

"Yeah. I'm not a surfer either." To put it mildly. I didn't even swim.

He paused. "I heard things were dicey between them, but I thought Elliot was an okay guy. Not like the yahoos some of my sisters married. Anyhow, tell her to call. She needs us, we're here. Next week, we're there."

"I'll tell her," I said. Assuming I ever found her again.

I tried to call Uncle Theo, but there was a busy signal, and, of course, he had no call-waiting. Too newfangled. I roused Fredreeq and told her I was driving to Glendale, as I was expected there for some reason or another. She had to get home herself, she said, to gear up for Fresno. We left a note for Joey, and I took her cell phone. I didn't want to think about what I'd do if she didn't return by nightfall. I'd sooner stay at the Bates Motel than alone at Solomonhaus after dark.

All the way to Glendale I tried to calm my nervous stomach and remind myself that Joey was the most resourceful person I knew. But she had few resources now beyond brains, imagination, a gun, and a capacity for running. If I'd let on to her brother just how worried I was, he'd already be at the airport.

I entered Uncle Theo's apartment and was hit hard by the scent of lamb.

My uncle's apartment was even more cramped than it had been a week earlier, as Apollo's entourage, as I'd begun to think of them, had spread out. They'd hung prints on the wall, put down a rug, and strung fabric to act as room dividers in a space that had no room to be divided. Four of them were watching a woman sell diamonds on the Home Shopping Network. The scent of spices hung like the L.A. fog layer. Apollo greeted me excitedly and introduced me to Olympia, his mother and the head chef, who I'd seen but not formally met. She clasped my hands, offered me food of some sort, and spoke excitedly, either in Greek or English too heavily accented for me to understand. I nodded a lot.

Uncle Theo was playing a board game called Sorry! Madagascar with a couple of the younger houseguests, but he hopped up at the sight of me.

"Ready to go?" he asked.

"Where?"

"Rio Pescado," he said. "It's moving day."

"P.B.'s? I don't think so," I said. "Nothing happens on New Year's Day."

"Oh, yes. They were very clear about it at the hospital, that P.B.'s bed is to be given to another patient on January first. It has to do with accounting, and the paperwork is all done, so P.B. must vacate this morning. They hinted that they preferred him to leave yesterday, but he wanted to ring in the New Year with his friends. Very understandable."

"Are you telling me," I said, "that today is literally moving day? That we're moving boxes and—P.B.—today?"

"Sorry!" said the two boys he was playing with, laughing uproariously. I thought they were talking to me, then saw that it had to do with their board game.

"Yes, of course!" Uncle Theo looked like a child himself, faced with a trip to the zoo. "A new home for a new year. Well, nearly. I spoke to the Santa Barbara people, but Haven Lane won't be open for business until Monday. So we'll just drive to Rio Pescado, pack him up, and bring him here for a few days. Give me a moment to find my gloves and hat and I'll be ready. I'm not as good as I used to be at finding things."

I resisted pointing out that this was because he now had numerous illegal aliens living with him. Who was I to find fault with anyone who chose to take in those with nowhere else to go? I took several deep breaths and then headed outside with Apollo to empty my trunk. I left *The Iliad* and my purse on the front seat and added the rest of my belongings to those already cluttering the apartment. Apollo was coming along; P.B. had specifically requested it, and regardless of how cramped the car would be, whatever P.B. wanted, on this day of days, I was inclined to give him.

We drove up the 101 freeway to the Pleasant Valley exit and found my brother waiting for us in the reception area. He stared at my hair, which, until recently, had been exactly like his, blond, straight, and fine. He was thin, pale, intense, and wore clothes I'd never seen before, traded or inherited from God knows whom. I hugged him, and he touched my hair with both hands in an accordion-like gesture, as if testing it for a force field.

His clothing, books, and sundry items were stuffed into two gym bags and three shopping bags. After months of struggle and planning, he appeared to be, if not seizing the day, at least holding it limply.

I picked up a duffel bag. P.B. took it from me and handed it to Uncle Theo, indicating a need to orchestrate every move of the move. A nurse I'd never seen before, large and Asian, came over to cluck at him, and then began to weep.

"You take care of my boy, now," she said, addressing either God, Uncle Theo, or me, crushing my fragile brother in an embrace. "Take care of my little angel boy sweetheart." She kissed him on both cheeks, back and forth, in a manner that reminded me of an obsessive-compulsive; in fact, I wondered if she was a patient dressed in a nurse costume, because she showed no signs of stopping. Just as I was considering intervening, she let him go.

P.B. bore all this in a distracted manner, but once we were all organized with what we were carrying, he allowed the nurse to take the last shopping bag from him and walk us to the car. There, he surprised me by kissing her on the mouth and saying he'd meet up with her again. "And you know where I'm talking about," he said. "Right, Tiki?"

I worried that he'd made elopement plans with a woman who had twenty years and eighty pounds on him. When she finally walked away, I asked about the nature of their future meeting.

"String theory," he said, then got in the car and buckled up without a backward glance at the place that had been his home longer than any place he'd ever lived. Uncle Theo and I, however, clasped hands all the way down the long driveway to the main road, stricken with nostalgia for the place we'd visited weekly.

"Apollo, did you get my comics?" P.B. asked.

Apollo handed him the stash from Earth 2, and my brother responded with inarticulate noises, like a monk presented with a Gutenberg Bible.

"May I look at one?" Uncle Theo said. Apollo passed one up to the front seat, and my uncle studied it. "*Olympus.* Wonderful title. Suggested for mature readers," he said. "I wonder why."

"Sex," Apollo said.

"Speaking of Mount Olympus," I said, "I'm not going to finish *The Iliad.* I'm barely making it through the Cliffs Notes at this point."

"Who is this Cliff fellow?" Uncle Theo said.

"You don't know about Cliffs Notes?" Apollo asked, and explained the phenomenon of distilling classic—i.e., dense and/or long-winded—works to their essential points. I was amazed to learn that Cliff was an international celebrity, and Uncle Theo was amazed, period.

"Merciful heavens," he said, picking up *The Iliad* from his lap. "It's like paying someone to make love for you and tell you about it later."

The idea of my bachelor uncle making love, by proxy or otherwise, was as shocking to me as Cliffs Notes were to him, but I pulled my thoughts back to the subject at hand. "In whatever form I read *The Iliad*," I said, "I'm not going to finish it in time. I've got to get these Greeks on a concrete wall before my client has a nervous breakdown."

"Let's see," Uncle Theo said, flipping through the book. "Is this where you are? Your bookmark?"

I glanced over and saw the parking ticket of Joey's I'd been carrying around. I saw the writing on it—"sudstud" or "pntspns" and my own handwritten note, "call PB: Haven Lane #." Which I'd forgotten to do. "Yes," I said. "See, I'm not very far along. Only three hundred pages."

"As long as you keep reading," Uncle Theo said, "—the real thing, and not Cliff's condensation—your good intention will carry you through. The very act of committing yourself to a god will call forth his—or her—power, and give you transcendent knowledge. The universe delights in reciprocity."

"Will the god put the primer on the retaining wall?" I said. "The sealant? Will the god come to Home Depot with me and pick out—"

"Why, yes," Uncle Theo said. "You mustn't think it's all your doing. If you consider yourself a conduit, it's much more pleasant. It's what I do, hanging wallpaper. Imagine the stress of my work otherwise."

Stress? In my youth, tagging along on summer vacations, I'd found it immensely satisfying to cover a stained surface, or even a plain surface, with wallpaper. Of course, anything involving glue is a wonderful thing. Even when the wallpaper was dreadful, I found comfort in knowing that for every customer with what I considered bad taste, there was a designer who shared it. It made the world less lonesome. "I had no idea you found it stressful," I said.

"Matching plaids. Making the corners work."

"Apollo," P.B. said, "is the god of wallpaper."

"Do you think so?" Uncle Theo strained to turn and face P.B. "I would say Hestia. The hearth, and so forth."

"Hestia? Second-rate. One temple away from being a demigod. They all bug me anyway. The Greeks. Eating their own children. That's just crap."

Uncle Theo said, "That's not the whole picture, P.B. I admit, it takes a special person to love a Cyclops, but every Olympian had goodness. It is those shades of gray, lost with the advent of Christianity—"

"Who likes gray?" P.B. yelled. "Nobody."

"There is not so much gray in Greece," Apollo said. "We like color."

"Hector?" Uncle Theo said. "Who can fail to admire Hector? Odysseus! Achilles! Flawed, rash, marvelous. The prototype for every modern hero, right down to the vulnerability. Consider Superman with his—what was the stuff that weakened him?"

"Kryptonite," Apollo said.

I missed Simon suddenly.

"Kryptonite," Uncle Theo said. "Now take Eros, for instance—"

"Eros?" P.B. said. "The guy's a lightweight! A quack!"

My brother's reaction to Eros alerted me. "P.B.," I said, "are things okay with your girlfriend?"

"I'm not talking about it," he said. "In fact, I don't want to talk at all. Eros is overrated, that's all."

Definitely a girlfriend problem. P.B. would restore Eros to Mount Olympus if Eros straightened things out with P.B.'s beloved, a girl with body dysmorphic disorder. Whether or not she could pull herself together sufficiently to travel to Santa Barbara for visits had been a touchy subject weeks earlier, and apparently still was.

Which led me back to Simon. I ached for him, with a holiday poignancy that was especially acute. Well, I could call him, couldn't I? Even if he was working, even if he was Textile Man right now, whatever that entailed, I could let him know I was thinking of him. No. I had to have a reason to call him.

But I did have reason. It was a new year. I called.

"Yes, hello," he said, answering his phone. Which was a strange way to address me. Ordinarily, he'd see my number and say, "Hello, beautiful" or "What are you wearing?" or something along those lines. Oh: I was calling from Joey's phone.

"It's Wollie," I said, perhaps unnecessarily. "Happy New Year, Mr. Textile."

"Happy holidays to you. I trust you had a good celebration?" He could've been addressing his tax preparer.

"I've had better," I said. "Sounds like you can't talk."

"Tomorrow will be a more appropriate time to discuss the project," he said. "I plan to take today off from business."

"Ah, so I'm business. And what constitutes pleasure for Mr. Textile?"

"A great American tradition. College football."

"Well, okeydokey," I said. "I'll talk to you later."

"Fine. Tomorrow, then. I'll be reachable during business hours."

I hung up without saying good-bye, so he wouldn't have to strain himself crafting a farewell that sounded computer generated.

By this time, P.B., Apollo, and Uncle Theo had moved on from the Greeks to string theory, on which they found themselves in agreement. I was about to ask what exactly string theory was when Joey's phone rang.

It was Charles. "Joey?" he said.

"No, it's Wollie. Joey hasn't turned up."

"Really? I mean—God, that's not good."

"No, it's awful. I just don't know what to do about it."

"Well, look. I've been trying to reach you too, but your phone—"

"Yes, out of battery power. What's wrong?"

"Agnes's going to the ten-thirty Mass instead of noon. Can we meet earlier?"

"Well, that's tricky," I said, glancing at my watch. "I have—people with me. And I'm a little underdressed. I'd planned to go back to Glendale and change—"

"There's certainly no dress code here, and perhaps the people with you could walk around the grounds while we talk. Really, I'm sorry, but I can only meet you when Agnes isn't here; I can't pretend it's business, not on New Year's—"

"We're on our way." I certainly understood subterfuge around a significant other.

My passengers were fine with the new plan. As long as there was a bathroom, P.B. said, and I assured him that the Bel-Air was full of them.

"The Bel-Air?" Uncle Theo said. "I love the Bel-Air."

I was surprised that my uncle knew the place, but he told me he was older than he looked—I refrained from telling him he'd always looked old to me—and had been around the block once or twice. He also told me that the alpha swan on the grounds of the hotel was named Homer, which was just the sort of thing Uncle Theo would know.

The Hotel Bel-Air was not the most dramatic in L.A., nor the most glamorous, but it had a magical quality to it, marked by lush gardens, gurgling creeks, tranquil ponds, rustic footbridges, and twinkling lights. The rooms were on the small side, many of them freestanding cottages, whitewashed and simple. And expensive. I'd never stayed there, but I'd attended weddings there costing twice my annual income.

I pulled up to the main entrance and waited in line for a valet parking attendant.

"These cars!" Apollo said. "Jaguar, Porsche, two BMW convertibles. What are they all doing here?"

"Showing off," I said. "Business establishments always keep the nice ones out front. Although here, it may be just a cross section of what's in the parking garage."

"It's like we are in *Car and Driver* magazine."

I was just envisioning a new greeting card—*Congratulations on entering the highest tax bracket*—when Apollo's next words froze my brain.

"Is that the Bentley Continental G.T.?"

"Where? What color?" *Dear God, let it not be silver,* I prayed.

"There," Apollo said. "Silver."

This couldn't be. I stared at the car parked prominently under a palm tree. What was Simon doing here? He didn't know Charles and Agnes, did he? I had a panicky urge to hide. What if he saw me and thought I was stalking him? What if—

The voice interrupted me. *This is a free country.* Not that innovative, as sayings go, but it gave me courage.

"Ma'am? Here for lunch?" The valet held open the door.

"No, just visiting," I said. "And walking. We'll be taking a walk. Some of us." It wasn't until we piled out of my sad preowned car that I saw what a motley crew we were.

P.B.'s pants-of-uncertain-origin were several sizes too big and rolled up at the waist. Uncle Theo sported a T-shirt that said "got pot?" and a serape slung over his shoulder, suggesting membership in a mariachi band. He also wore a multicolored crocheted beanie atop his head of fluffy white hair. Apollo, in jeans and his Superman T-shirt—again—

looked normal, if dwarfed by three tall, albino-pale Shelleys. The best I could say about myself was that I was clean, in tie-dyed overalls and a baseball cap over my depressed hair.

Which didn't bother me, really, until I saw Simon walking across the rustic footbridge toward the lobby.

In the company of an extremely beautiful woman.

Forty-six

'd last seen her going into Simon's building, she of the white-blond hair. She wore the same full-length mink. It was the kind you see in old movies, and sometimes in real life, in Chicago, maybe, or New York. Reykjavik. The kind you don't see much in Southern California, in Bel Air, particularly, where it hasn't snowed since the Ice Age.

My first impulse was to run screaming back to the parking lot. But I couldn't figure out how to get P.B., Apollo, and Uncle Theo to run with me. In fact, they'd already dispersed, in search of a men's room.

Then I got curious. Who was this woman? What was she to Simon? I hurried across the footbridge after them, with a sudden need to study the architecture of her French twist. I moved closer as they reached the far side and turned right, as close as I could get without setting off Simon's eyes-in-the-back-of-his-head radar.

They reached the restaurant. Simon turned. I bobbed to the right, looking for a plant or doorway to hide behind. Was I supposed to pretend not to know him?

But he didn't see me. She called to him, the mink woman, a single "Simon?" in a very high—perhaps a bit whiny?—voice. So he was using his own name. Interesting. He helped her take off her coat, but some restaurant person jumped in to lend a hand as though Mink Removal were complicated, beyond the capabilities of a mere guest. Then Simon's hand was on the small of her back, guiding her around the enclosed patio tables dressed in their pink table linens. Perhaps she was blind.

She wore a red dress—silk crepe was my guess, but I'm not in textiles—a dress far too dressy for brunch. A backless halter dress, which explained why she'd kept her coat on earlier, as the day was not warm. She had a lovely back. And arms. Simon must've thought so too. His fingers touched her shoulder and slid down to her wrist.

They stopped to confer with the maître-d' mid-room, perhaps seeking the best possible location in which to . . . brunch. I moved in, alongside a potted palm—not hiding, of course, just . . . okay, hiding. I got a good look at her face as she got a good look at my boyfriend, which quashed any doubts about her eyesight. A word leapt to my mind, a caption to go with the way she studied him.

Prey.

He was a marked man.

Simon slipped something to the maître-d'. Money? For what, a strolling violinist? A private room? Was this a good use of my tax dollars?

As the maître-d' walked away, Simon glanced at the woman, and her look changed from predatory to sweet. Well, to the extent that someone who wears her hair in a French twist can look sweet. Someone who wears dead animals next to her bare skin. Now I knew why it was that people threw buckets of blood on fur-wearing humans. Not that I wanted to do that, of course. Not a bucket of blood. A cupful, maybe. Eight ounces. Twelve at most.

"Why, that's our Simon, isn't it?" Uncle Theo said, making me jump.

I turned to him. "Where? No—well, I mean—"

Too late. Off went my uncle, the world's friendliest human being, to say hello.

I caught up with him and grabbed his arm. I told him Simon was having an important meeting and should not be disturbed. Uncle Theo's eyebrows, white and fluffy, rose high. "But we can't not say hello," he said.

"We can. We must."

"Why?"

"He's here on a . . . job," I said. "He's not himself."

"Heavens. Who is he?"

And then Simon was walking toward us. "Hello, Theo," he said. "Wollie."

"Ah, my friend," Uncle Theo said, beaming. "A very happy New Year to you. We stopped in to use the bathroom."

"And now we have to leave," I said.

"We must wait for P.B. and Apollo," Uncle Theo said.

"I am here," Apollo said, joining us.

The mink woman slithered up on Simon's right. In the background hovered the maître-d', holding menus.

"Hi. I'm Simon." Simon shook hands with Apollo, who remained quiet. "And you are?"

"Legal," I said. "He has a visa."

"An H-one-B," Apollo added.

Simon smiled. "Have you a name?"

"Apollo."

Uncle Theo said, "The sun god. My own name is also from the Greek. Theo: gift of the gods. You probably knew that."

Simon smiled. "Simon: he who hears. Or 'is heard.' I don't remember which."

The woman looped her hand through Simon's arm. She was prettier close up. No wrinkles. Cosmetic surgery, I decided. Actually, I have no radar at all for that sort of thing, but I preferred to think she'd paid for her looks.

"A pleasure to meet you, Apollo. Theo, good to see you again." Simon turned to me. "Please give your brother and mother my regards."

"Simon?" the woman said. "Are you going to introduce me to your friends?"

"Lucrezia, this is Wollie, Theo, and Apollo. And here comes P.B."

"Yes, never mind," I said, my voice shrill. I didn't want her meeting my brother, engrossed in his comic book as he walked toward us. "We have to go. Good-bye." Lucrezia. What kind of a name was that?

I got my trio out the door and had just given them instructions on where to rendezvous in an hour—the swan pond, not under any circumstances the restaurant or lobby—when Simon came up behind me.

"Wollie."

I turned. How beautiful he looked against the blue of the sky. He was wearing the brown Gianfranco Ferre silk shirt I'd given him for Christmas. Was it a flaw in our relationship that he always outdressed me? It happened in the animal kingdom, the males upstaging the females, the birds with their plumage, the lions with their manes. But we were humans, in Western civilization, and maybe Simon belonged with the Lucrezias of the world, their hair in French twists that implied a hairdresser on call or a talented housekeeper, and, of course, money.

"What are you doing here?" he said.

I wanted badly to tell him that Joey was missing. He'd know what to do, and what a relief it would be to let him do it. But Simon was sworn to uphold the law, and Joey was breaking it, running around with an unlicensed gun. She wouldn't thank me for involving him, and neither would he, putting him in that kind of conflict. "Nothing of interest," I said. A breeze stirred in the trees. I wanted him to open up his shirt so I could burrow into him and soak up his warmth. "How about you? Of all the gin joints in the world, why here?"

"I needed a place that served brunch. You'd said it was your favorite hotel . . ."

"I'm happy to have inspired you. Doesn't it blow your top-secret cover to gambol about in famous places? Running into people who know what you do for a living?"

"Let me worry about that."

"And what shall I worry about? Lucrezia?" I stretched out her name as far as it would go, *Loo-creeeet-zeeeeee-ah,* just to show I wasn't frightened of it.

He looked around casually, hands in pockets. "I imagine this is hard for you."

I put my hands in my pockets too. In case Lucrezia came waltzing out to check on our body language. I was about to ask him how hard it was for him when over his shoulder I spotted Charles coming down the path to meet me.

"Really, Simon, I have to go," I said. "And you have to get back to work. I mean pleasure. *Bon appétit.*"

"Wait. Did Joey ever mention that she had a juvenile record?"

Charles had spotted me. He stopped, waiting. He'd want to talk to me alone. "Uh—no," I said, completely distracted. "I'll ask her about it, though."

"I'll save you the trouble. It was an assault charge. In tenth grade, she put a boy in the hospital. Broke his nose and his wrist."

"Oh, hell." This made me want to cry. When was the news going to get better? "I'm sure she had her reasons." I tried not to look at Charles, but I didn't succeed. Simon glanced over his shoulder. "That man's looking at you. Do you know him?"

"Yes."

He looked back at me, eyes narrowed. "Are you all right?"

"No," I said. "I'm not. But there's nothing you can do about it at the moment except walk away."

For a guy like Simon, whose instinct to rescue was so strong, those words were hard to hear. I could see it in his face. But after a moment he turned and moved off, back down the path. Part of me was sad to have caused him pain.

Part of me wasn't.

Forty-seven

Charles found us a stone bench in a secluded area dense with foliage, then went in search of coffee. I had a raging headache.

I might have been in another country, it was so extravagantly green. Rushing water drowned out every mundane thought, and part of me marveled at what money could create, this tropical rain forest in the midst of an urban desert. Another part of me just felt alone. How could I be lonelier now than when Doc had left me, months before, or when I'd moved out of Simon's penthouse? It wasn't just about Simon and the dreadful woman he was—whatever it was he was doing with her. It was that Joey was gone.

Joey was my foul-weather friend. Fredreeq too, but Fredreeq was a mother, with car pool and Little League and trips to Costco, and strong opinions on acceptable behavior. Joey was the least judgmental person I knew, which meant I could tell her anything.

She was also enterprising. If someone else had exited the 405 on foot, Joey would've found them by now. It wasn't a situation that came up a lot. Nowadays. The Greeks, of course, were always running after one another. Menelaus going after Helen after she ran off with Paris, Jason chasing his Golden Fleece, Demeter following her daughter Persephone into the Underworld. And Orpheus going there after Eurydice, armed

260 HARLEY JANE KOZAK

only with his lyre and his voice. Not many of those rescue attempts had happy endings.

Charles approached, carrying a single cup of coffee on a saucer. "There's more coming," he said. "This is just to tide you over."

I swallowed it with a couple of Tylenols. He said, "When did you last see Joey?"

I filled him in on the situation, not bothering to put a positive spin on it. Then I said, "Your turn. And your secrets are safe. As soon as we find Joey and keep her out of jail, I'll forget them. I have a terrible memory."

A waiter arrived. "I hope this will do it," Charles said, and I didn't know if he was referring to the croissants accompanying the pot of coffee or the promised information. The waiter asked if we'd like champagne to ring in the New Year and Charles asked what he had. While they discussed it, I studied him, trying to understand his appeal. Because he was appealing. Maybe it was the part of him that evoked his brother, making me feel I knew him well, even intimately, when I barely knew him at all. Maybe it was the beard.

"Sorry," Charles said, after the waiter left. "Professional curiosity. I'm always doing research, seeing what sells. You know my wife and I have a vineyard?"

"Artemis. Yes, Agnes and I talked last night."

Charles looked at his hands. "It thrived, once. Not so much in recent years. We had some bad luck. An earthquake. A fire. When we married, I tried to drag it into this century. Agnes's family is old-school. They feel that if the product is good, it will sell itself. Our balance sheets show otherwise."

"But you'll do okay now, won't you? I mean, since David left you—"

"Millions?" He smiled. "Yes. But he didn't foresee the fallout, the scrutiny from the police and the insurance company. There was a theory afloat that Agnes and I hired someone to shoot David, but it's fallen out of favor. Maybe they took a look at our truck. Last week we couldn't afford a plumber, let alone an assassin."

"And the fact that the gun came from *At the End of the Day*—I don't see a professional borrowing a gun from a soap opera. Don't they bring their own tools?"

"Never having hired one, I wouldn't know." He toyed with the croissant basket, then moved it aside. "Let me tell this backward. When my brother suspected he had cancer, he didn't go to a doctor, but to an insurance agent. He took out a twenty-million-dollar policy—not an easy thing to do, by the way, even after he passed their physical. I didn't know it at the time. At that point, David and I hadn't spoken in nine years."

"How could he know he had cancer before any doctors knew?"

Charles looked up. His eyes were David's, a blue unexpected with the dark hair. "Pancreatic cancer can go undetected a long time. But David had intuition. That's Joey's theory. She says it's an actor thing, being in touch with your body to that extent."

I thought of David's yoga and massages, his faith in vitamins and antioxidants and Chinese medicine. Alternating with heavy partying. "And is it your theory too?"

Charles shrugged. "I just keep thinking about his hypochondria. The headache you have? For David, that would be a brain tumor. Indigestion was an ulcer. That his cancer was really cancer is . . . ironic."

The waiter appeared with champagne. Charles examined the bottle, then handed it back for the ritual, the steps done in the proper order, suspense building to the satisfying pop of the cork, and the deluge. The waiter was assured and self-possessed, and I wondered who he was when not waiting on the rich and famous. He poured, bowed, and retreated.

"David and I were close growing up," Charles said, "but temperamentally different. Our parents had problems, which drew us together. David was very big-brotherly. Loved to fix things. If he couldn't, or I didn't take his advice, it enraged him."

Joey would've driven him mad, I thought. She wasn't much for taking advice.

"Giving made him happy," Charles said. "And surprises. I didn't know about the life insurance and rest of the estate until a few weeks ago. Joey talked him into telling us."

A rustling in the bushes across the walk got my attention. Was there an animal in there? I imagined a mink waddling around the Bel-Air. Did minks waddle?

"Last night," I said, "you implied that—look, I'm sorry, but did you or didn't you have an affair with Joey?"

Charles studied his champagne flute. I tried to read his face, but his beard covered half of it, and hair is not very expressive. "It doesn't matter. David believed we did."

"While he and Joey were dating?"

He nodded. "Living together. One Friday, instead of Vegas, David invited several of us up the coast." The rustling in the shrubbery continued. It had to be something big. A coyote? Charles noticed it too. "We ended up in Big Sur," he continued, "where he'd enrolled us all in a consciousness-raising weekend. A tantric sex seminar. Are you familiar with it?"

"Big Sur, yes. Tantric sex, no. Powerful stuff?"

"No idea. The teacher came down with pneumonia. But there we were—"

"Ouch. Damn it." The creature in the bushes spoke.

Charles and I stood.

A man crashed through the bushes, shaking his head and brushing something from his face with both hands. From his neck hung a video-camera on a strap. "Killer bees," he said. "Are those killer bees?"

I don't know killer bees from bumblebees and was about to say so, but Charles said, "They are. If you come into contact, you need first aid. See the concierge." He pulled me away. "Reporters. Ever since Monday. Relentless." He led me down a walkway, past a fountain. We passed a trio of men in tuxedoes. A New Year's wedding.

"So," I said. "Tantric sex."

"Yes," he said, slowing. "By Saturday night, David had been drinking heavily, and disappeared with a local waitress. Joey was understandably unhappy. She was going to hitchhike back down the coast, so I gave her a ride. She crashed at my place that night. And the next. For a week or so. I was new to L.A., and Joey became my first real friend."

A woman hurried by, armed with two cameras and a light meter, chasing not us but a bride, I guessed. "Carlotta!" she called to someone ahead.

Carlotta, I thought. *Charlotte*. And then I remembered. The woman in the photograph, from David's birthday party. Charlotte. That was her name.

"Charles?" I said. "Who's Charlotte?"

He turned to me and said nothing, watching me figure it out myself.

"Oh," I said. "You were."

.   .   .

"You've never met a transsexual?"

"No," I said. We were at the swan pond now.

"Male to female is more common than female to male."

"Oh." I realized I was speaking in monosyllables. "I'm sorry," I said, trying to reorient myself to the man next me, to picture him as a woman. But there was nothing feminine about him except that his hands were small, and his feet too. Smaller than mine. But that was true for three-quarters of the world. "I'm sure you're used to talking about this, but for me it's a first-time conversation."

"As a matter of fact, I never talk about it. In the transsexual community I'm strictly e-mail. Otherwise, almost no one knows. I left the East Coast after the surgeries, and started over here. Joey met me briefly as Charlotte."

"Did you always know this about yourself?" I asked. "That you were—"

"It's called gender identity disorder. I always knew. I did not find life easy as a child. David was alternately protective of me and frustrated by my social ineptitude. Once I stumbled onto a name for my condition and a therapist, and started to reconcile body and soul, David paid for all of it, including the surgeries. He felt guilty, being the normal one. As if the life of a child star is normal. But I didn't begrudge him anything; I wouldn't have been happy being him. I just wanted to be who I was."

"So he was okay with it?"

The biggest swan—Homer, presumably—spread his wings, as if threatening liftoff. Something appeared to be pissing him off.

"Initially, no," Charles said. "He didn't like losing his little sister. But he could put himself in my shoes; the thought of living in a woman's body, for a man, is . . ."

Never having wanted to be anything but a woman, I tried to imagine that. I couldn't. I tried the reverse, picturing myself caught inside a man's body. Oh.

"Then it captured his imagination," Charles said. "He began to see it as an act of invention. And he was very interested in the logistics of it."

"I admit to some curiosity myself."

Charles met my eyes and I saw David's face again, and felt myself blush. He said, "I function sexually. Is it an experience identical to that of a man who's had all his body parts from birth? No. Am I complaining? No. My life, relative to what it was, is a miracle. That's not hyperbole."

I nodded. "So the weekend in Big Sur—?"

"I was Charles by then. And when he got back to L.A., David found out that Joey was staying with me. He drew his own conclusions."

"I imagine he was upset."

"He was enraged," Charles said. "To think that I could be a rival, that Joey and I had something just between us, distinct from him. He felt— not to sound melodramatic—that he'd created us. And we betrayed him." He stared at the pond. "He fired Joey from the soap, cut me off financially. I repaid him over the years. He didn't cash the checks, so I sent cash. And letters, but he never responded."

An image came to mind, of one hundred thousand dollars stuffed in a laundry bag. "That's it?" I said. "That's why he felt he owed you twenty million dollars?"

Charles nodded. "He said if he'd helped me years ago, we could've built up Artemis Vineyards to something spectacular. He didn't owe me a thing, but he believed he'd ruined our lives—because he'd wanted to ruin our lives."

"And Joey?" I said. "How was he supposed to have ruined her life?"

"If she'd stayed on the show, she wouldn't have been working in Canada the winter of that incident. He said he was responsible for the scar on her face."

I shook my head and realized that my headache was gone. I looked at the swans, their necks like the letter *S*. I'd loved "The Ugly Duckling" until I'd heard that swans are unfriendly. Now, thanks to Dr. Paolo Pomerantz's *Guide to the Pantheon of Greek Gods and Goddesses and Their Roman Counterparts,* I'd learned that they're sexual too. Zeus impersonated one to seduce Leda, who gave birth to Helen of Troy. Looked at that way, a swan was responsible for the Trojan War. "Charles," I said, "how—oh. There's Agnes."

She was walking our way, but she hadn't seen us.

"Come on." Charles took my arm, pulling me toward the far side of the pond.

"Okay, but why do we need to—"

"Agnes doesn't know."

I struggled to keep up. "Doesn't know what?"

He kept moving. "That I was once a woman."

"What? That's not possible." I caught up to him.

"She was sheltered," he said. "Convent school. I was her first boy-friend. I knew she couldn't handle it when we met, so I waited." We were practically running now, as though just seeing me would reveal it all to Agnes. "I waited for her to notice things, to ask questions. She never did. She was a virgin until our wedding night, so she had nothing to compare me to . . . and she didn't want children, so that wasn't an issue."

"She knows," I said, breathless. "She can't not know."

"It's occurred to me. But if she's not asking about it, is it right to force it on her? Even if she could accept it, her family couldn't. So then she either keeps my secret or becomes estranged from them. For what? It's a small sin, to protect her from that choice."

"But is it a marriage?" The vehemence in my voice startled me. "I'm sorry. Obviously, it's none of my business. But to have such a huge thing between you—"

He turned to look at me. "Have you ever been married, Wollie?"

Elliot had asked me the same thing. "No." Was I socially deficient, having neglected to bag a husband? "So what it is that only married peo-ple understand?"

"Was that condescending? I'm sorry."

"No, go ahead."

"You take those vows," he said, his arm in mine, leading me past a gushing fountain. "You shoot for one hundred percent honesty, or fidelity or kindness or whatever your ideal is, but you come up short. Everyone does. So then you ask, Do I live with that shortfall or do I cut my losses and look for something closer to the ideal?"

"But you're living a lie—well, an omission. A rather large one."

"No. Living all those years as a woman was the lie. This isn't a lie. This is me. How I got here, the story of that, that's the only thing I'm withholding. The backstory, as David would say."

I was disturbed by this answer, but I couldn't figure out why.

"What about you?" he asked. "When the choice is between honesty and kindness, do you always tell the truth?"

I saw Uncle Theo and Apollo and P.B. ahead, watching a bride getting photographed with seven scarlet-attired bridesmaids. "If I were better at lying, I'd probably lie more. But this is about Joey. She's risked everything to keep your secrets."

"The police really suspect her?"

"Yes. If she'd laid it all out for them at the outset, maybe they'd have moved on to other suspects. But she's been protecting you and your insurance settlement. Wanting to keep your history out of it too, I guess. She hasn't done anything wrong, but she's acting so cagey, it reads like guilt."

He slowed, finally. "All right. I'll talk to the detective. Whether it will make a difference to him, I don't know, but I can't sacrifice Joey for an insurance settlement. I have my own protective instincts."

"And Agnes? How will she react to that?"

We came to a tree and stopped. Charles looked at me. "Maybe she'll surprise me," he said. "Women often do."

Forty-eight

W hat do you mean, get over to Royce Hall?" I said into the phone.

"Don't you check messages? I phoned *and* faxed the Westwood numbers, along with your cell phone." Jen Kim talked at her usual lightning speed as I drove down Stone Canyon Road. "Anyhow, meet us at Will Call. You're just minutes away. As God is my witness, I wouldn't ask you if it weren't life and death. Don't dawdle."

Jen had found me via Joey's phone, because I'd given it to Sophie as my emergency contact number. I addressed my passengers. "Guys? Slight change of plans. We're going to swing by UCLA."

"Delightful," Uncle Theo said. "Apollo will enjoy that. It's no Caltech, but a nice little campus nonetheless." Apollo nodded. P.B. continued to read his comic books.

I didn't know many people who'd describe UCLA as "little," but the good news was, it was New Year's Day, and for the first time in history, I had no trouble parking. I left the boys locking up the car in Lot 4 and ran—okay, racewalked—across the pastoral green grass to Royce Hall, campus map in hand. I had no idea what was going on at Royce Hall, but I thought of Gloria, the hairdresser, saying, "Whose bread I eat, her song I sing." Jen was certainly getting her bread's worth out of me.

"At last," Jen said, finding me at Will Call. People were piling into the concert hall, but some, like Jen, waited for latecomers, pacing up and down the walkway, cell phones to their ears. "Oh, Jesus, you weren't kidding—you're *not* dressed for this. What *are* you dressed for?"

"Wall painting," I said.

"Whatever. Here, take my jacket. These little rhinestone buttons dress it up. Shit, it won't fit. Hackburg, cut her off at the neck. Don't let those overalls show."

I said hello to Hackburg, with his camera and cigarette and the facial expression of one recently raised from the dead to come to work. "What are we doing?" I asked.

Jen yelled, "Rupert!," which caused a dozen people to turn to her in displeasure. "Okay. We have to reshoot your date again, because Hackburg sent the film from Sunday night to a special rush-job el cheapo lab, where it got eaten up by their machine. Let's go."

Rupert sauntered over, looking like Hackburg in the "Why am I here and not home sleeping off a hangover?" department. Jen positioned us on steps, Rupert higher up, told Hackburg to try to get the stained glass windows in the background, and said, "Action." Rupert and I kissed, which by now felt as routine as flossing my teeth. When we finished, but before Jen could yell, "Cut," I heard a familiar voice.

"Why, another beau?" Uncle Theo said. "Goodness, Wollie, you are quite the—"

"Cut! Cut, cut, cut, cut," Jen said. "Who is this guy, and Hackburg, did we get enough before he walked through the shot?"

"Yeah."

"Okay, let's move inside," Jen said. "Wollie, Rupert, you take the F-row tickets, and Hackburg and I will be right behind you. I want to get the backs of your heads watching the show. An art shot. Hackburg, hide the camera going in. I saw a sign saying you can't photograph anything."

I gave Uncle Theo money in case they were hungry, apparently a chronic condition with Apollo, and told them to look for vending machines. I promised to rejoin them as soon as humanly possible. Then Rupert and I entered Royce Hall, through a doorway that bore the words, etched in stone, THEY SHOULD LEARN BEFOREHAND THE KNOWLEDGE WHICH THEY WILL REQUIRE FOR THEIR ART. PLATO.

They should also learn beforehand the kind of art they've just been handed tickets for, I thought. But Plato, of course, had never been a *SoapDirt* dating correspondent.

. . .

Tibetan Monks draw a certain crowd. It was not the poker-playing casino crowd or the Duke's surfer-bar crowd; it was the *Yoga Journal* subscriber/Mensa member/senior citizen discount crowd. Rupert, Jen, and Hackburg looked fine, but I, in orange hair and tie-dyed overalls, drew stares. "This," Rupert whispered, "is gruesome."

The houselights dimmed. Onstage, in front of a blood-red curtain, a few dozen monks gathered, bald and dressed in crimson and saffron robes, off-the-shoulder numbers that showed more bare skin than you generally see, for instance, with Catholic monks. On cue, there was a tinkling bell, and then a deep guttural noise that I eventually realized was coming from the monks themselves, microphoned. Chanting. I listened in fascination, wondering how they were going to follow an act like that, only to find they weren't. That was the act.

Jen, however, in the row behind us, provided her own drama. She stage-whispered to Rupert and me and then reached forward to force our heads into just the right position for Hackburg to focus his lens between us. This drew *Shh*s. I began to wilt from embarrassment.

"Got enough light?" Jen whispered loudly.

"No," Hackburg whispered back. "But what do you expect me to do?"

The *shh*s around us became more insistent and, when Hackburg turned on his camera, with its tiny little whirring motor, grew into frenzied whispers of "Shame on you!" and "I'm telling the usher!" I clutched Rupert's arm, but when I looked at him, I saw that he was sound asleep. I squeezed his arm hard.

"WHAT!" he said, waking.

Until now, I had not realized that *Shh* could carry such gradations of hostility. Or that I could be this mortified and still remain conscious. An usher did indeed come down the aisle to confer with Jen and Hackburg, and a minute later they left.

The monks chanted on.

I sat in place, frozen, too socially terrified to leave. Rupert went back to sleep. He wasn't the only one in the audience to do so. I tried to use the opportunity to calm myself, but sitting still merely intensified my worry about Joey, and my curiosity about Charles and Agnes, and whether their insurance would come through, and the whole murder versus assisted suicide debate. I took a pen out of my purse and jotted notes on my program: "Gun vs. $100,000."

The gun from *At the End of the Day* suggested garden-variety murder, but the hundred grand pointed to murder for hire. Especially as David's surveillance cameras were turned off—intentionally, I assumed. Unless the hundred grand was to pay off someone for some other reason. Blackmail? Someone who knew about Charles having once been Charlotte? Would David pay to keep someone quiet about that? And what about David wanting to change his will? But did I really need to figure out all this, or did I just need to find Joey?

I just needed to find Joey. But maybe they were the same thing.

"Rupert," I whispered, bracing myself for more *Shh*ing. His eyes flew open, and I leaned in close. "That's all the enlightenment I can handle. I gotta go."

.   .   .

Once outside, I took Joey's phone from my purse and turned it on. Rupert was right behind me. "Well," he said, "I got a nice nap in."

"Rupert, any idea how to access Joey's most recent calls on this phone?"

"No, I only know how to work my own. What are you doing with Joey's phone?"

"She's missing." I was telling him about it when P.B. came running across the lawn toward us from Powell Library, calling my name. "What is it, what's happened?" I yelled, seeing Uncle Theo and Apollo in the distance, trying to catch up.

"Something very big," he said breathlessly. "Huge. We've been to the physics department. I talked to some students in the lab working on genomes, and guess what?"

"What?" I said.

"Guess who lives in Santa Barbara?"

"Who?" I said.

"Joseph Polchinski."

"Who's Joseph Polchinski?" Rupert asked. "I'm Rupert Ling, by the way."

"Joseph Polchinski," P.B. said, oblivious to Rupert, "delves farther into M theory than anyone in the field today, and he's in Santa Barbara. I have to live there."

"You're *going* to live there," I pointed out. "What a remarkable coincidence."

"That's the whole point," my brother said. "There aren't coincidences. There are just connections you haven't made yet. The thing about Polchinski—" P.B. clammed up, seeing people pour out of Royce Hall for intermission. Uncle Theo and Apollo reached us, bearing candy bars, as excited as P.B. about Joseph Polchinski. I was introducing them to Rupert when a woman tapped me on the shoulder.

"Do excuse me, won't you," she said, "but I believe I've seen you on the news."

I turned to find myself face-to-face with a nun. Or a paparazza disguised as a nun, I thought, then chided myself for excessive cynicism. She wore a modified habit, with a shoulder-length veil and just-below-the-knee skirt. "Wollie Shelley," I said, shaking hands with her. "And this is Rupert, Theo, P.B., and Apollo. Have I been on the news?"

"The newspaper, perhaps? I'm Sister Genevieve. It's the unusual hair-color. That's how I recognized you. You knew David Zetrakis."

"Yes," I said. "Did you know him too?"

"No. He made a wonderful donation to our order, though. One of our sisters took care of him just before his passing. She's been on the news, so we follow the story. Aren't these monks marvelous? So inspiring. So virile, somehow."

"Very," I said. "Sister, I'd like to meet your sister—is that possible?"

"Why not?" Sister Genevieve said, and pulled out her cell phone.

. . .

"I wouldn't miss this for the world," Rupert said, walking south with me, nearing the UCLA Medical Center. P.B. followed at a distance, engrossed now in a comic book called *Promethea*. Apollo and Uncle Theo were back at Royce Hall, in our seats for act two of the Tibetan monks. "I'm insatiably curious. Also, I like your company."

I looked up from the campus map, amazed. "Rupert. Are you flirting with me?"

"Why, do you have a rule? No flirting until the—what is this, our fifth date?"

"Fourth," I said. "But is this a date? Interviewing a nun?"

"It could be considered an extension of the monk date."

"Well, I guess it's okay to flirt, since you've slept with me," I said. "Or fallen asleep next to me. Not exactly the same thing, I guess."

Rupert laughed. "Not remotely the same thing. I'd like to think. Maybe we should ask my girlfriend."

I looked at him. "Aha. I thought you had a girlfriend. Where is she?"

"Vancouver, shooting a TV series. I don't think we're going to last. And I know you have a boyfriend, but it can't hurt to know there are other men out here turned on by orange hair."

This was an interesting wrinkle but one I didn't pursue, because we walked through the automatic doors to the UCLA hospital, and there in the lobby was our nun.

Sister Perpetua, despite working with the dying, was as cheerful as a kindergarten teacher. This was partly due, she said, to having just been given a box of chocolates by one of her "families." She got us settled on a sofa, then unwrapped the plastic from a Whitman's Sampler and offered us first pick. I declined. Rupert and P.B. accepted.

"Oh, you're dark chocolate men," Sister Perpetua said, nodding approvingly. "Antioxidants." After consulting the flavor guide printed on the inside of the lid, she chose a milk chocolate coconut and nibbled at the edges delicately, mouselike. "Now then," she said, "your relationship to David was—"

"Old girlfriend," I said.

"Friend, poker buddy, employee," Rupert said.

P.B., chewing, said nothing. He'd gotten a caramel, was my guess.

"Here's my question," I said. "Was there a turning point, along with David's, uh, newfound religious feeling, that convinced you he wouldn't arrange his own death?"

She nodded happily. "Yes, I know just what you're asking. A turning point? Yes. It was the point where I helped him figure out an alternative."

"An alternative to—? Can you tell me about it? It's not confidential, is it?"

"Do I look like a priest?" She chuckled. P.B. looked at me. *Nun humor,* I could see him thinking. "You see, David had planned a kind of suicide— now, that's a sin. In order to provide someone with a financial windfall— now, that's insurance fraud. It weighed on him. That's where my job comes in. I help people unburden themselves. It can be easier for them to talk to me than to family. I busy myself with their care, changing the sheets, feeding them, things their mother used to do. And they come out with all sorts of secrets." She reached out to pat P.B.'s shoulder, which surprised him. It surprised me too.

"So he told you his suicide plan," Rupert said, "and then what?"

"I asked why he would take such a drastic step. And it was to help out his brother. His brother needed money by such and such a date. David thought maybe he could sell off everything he owned, but that wasn't feasible, so this life insurance policy seemed the only way. And I asked him, Why can't your brother take out a loan on the expectation of this inheritance? David didn't know such a thing was possible. He had managers to take care of his money; any of them could've told him this, but he was very secretive about his plans. Except with me." She carefully transported the top layer of chocolates, in their gold plastic tray, to an end table, then sat back down. "So after he'd looked into the loan situation, he said to me, 'Sister, you've saved my life,' and I said, 'David, I'll be happier if I've saved your soul.' " She pulled off a quilted liner to reveal the underlying layer of her Whitman's Sampler. After scoring the second milk chocolate coconut, she offered the box to us.

"When did all this happen?" I asked, picking what turned out to be a truffle.

Sister Perpetua frowned, trying to remember. "Around the third week of Advent," she said, passing the box to P.B. "Maybe the second week. Mid-December."

"And he was happy after that?"

"Yes, indeed. Very much so."

"No arguments that you knew about?" I asked. "Something that would make him want to change his will?"

"Oh. Yes, others have asked me about this," she said, watching P.B. pass the chocolates to Rupert. "Yes, something did happen just before Christmas, something he was very agitated about, but he wouldn't discuss it. I heard him on the phone one day when I arrived. Very displeased with someone. Here, dear boy, take a Kleenex. Those chocolate-covered cherries are always messy." She pulled a folded square of tissue from her pocket.

"Who was it that displeased him?" Rupert asked.

"He didn't call them by name, you see. But he said, 'Well, then that's your inheritance' or 'That's all you're getting' or something of that nature." She pulled a second Kleenex from her pocket to dab at her mouth. "I liked David very much, but that's not to say he wasn't human. We all are. And dying can be thorny. There's powerlessness at the end of life. And those who had a lot of power in their day often have a tough time with that part of it. Do you see what I mean?"

"I do," P.B. said, startling us all. "I won't have that problem, though."

"Or me," Sister Perpetua said, eyeing her Whitman's Sampler.

"Sister," I said, "was Joey Rafferty there that day, the day you heard that phone call?"

She smiled. "Oh, no. Except for Mrs. Valladares, the housekeeper, he was quite alone. In fact, I thought it might be Joey he was talking to."

"Why?" I asked.

"Oh, he'd tease her about that very thing, threatening to cut her off without a penny. Or to leave her his collection of soap opera scripts. That made her laugh. They were always having fun with each other. But I must say, this time he did sound serious."

Rupert and I looked at each other.

"Did you tell that to police?" I asked. "That you thought it might be Joey he was talking to?"

Sister Perpetua nodded. "Of course. I don't know if they paid any attention to me, though."

"Sister," I said, "I'm sure they did."

Forty-nine

We drove by my post office box in West Hollywood to collect my mail, then pushed on toward Glendale. I felt like I'd been on the road for weeks. Uncle Theo could not stop talking about the Tibetan monks, and I listened with half an ear, driving and randomly pressing buttons on Joey's phone.

"Wollie, may I use your phone to call my mother?" Apollo asked suddenly.

"Sure." I passed it back to him. "But it's not mine, it's my friend Joey's. Hey, I don't suppose you could figure out how to find the last calls she made, could you?"

"Of course."

It took six minutes for Apollo to reassure his mother in Greek about something or other. It took him sixty seconds to figure out Joey's phone, with P.B. looking on.

"Here you are," he said, passing it back. "Your friend's call history, incoming and outgoing. I was able to make it go back only three days, however. Also her address book, but for that I had to break a code. I hope that's okay."

I looked into the rearview mirror and smiled. "Apollo, you're a genius."

"Yes," he said. "But do not tell people, please. Especially girls."

I asked Apollo to see if any of Joey's recent calls matched people listed in her address book. Several did; excluding Fredreeq, me, and her lawyer, Rick Slepicka, each was from *At the End of the Day*. One of them, it occurred to me, was probably the killer.

I phoned Clay Jakes, Joey's most recent call. I had to remind him who I was, and I told him Joey was missing.

"Shit," he said. Was this surprise, concern, or simple crabbiness?

"Clay, something's been puzzling me. How'd the cops think to look in your props room for the murder weapon? Why would that even occur to them?"

"Joey asked me that too. It occurred to them because I told them to look there."

"Really?" I said, excited to be on Joey's wavelength. "But how'd you know?"

"I didn't know. I guessed."

"How'd you guess?" I asked. "Look, this isn't general nosiness—I'm trying to figure out what was in Joey's head, to learn whatever it is she learned."

"Okay. Saturday morning I checked the lockbox, had three guns in there: Beretta 92F, SIG 226, Glock. Shoulda been four. I was missing a Colt 1911. Later that afternoon, I went to pack 'em up, send 'em back to the rental house, and the Colt was back in place."

"So that's . . . odd. And you're sure? You didn't just overlook it earlier?"

"No, I did not overlook it." He was now crabby. "I had my EFP revoked—"

"What is that?"

"Entertainment firearms permit. Rental house—ISS is their name—found out and called the set, said they'd need their guns back. So bad enough I lose the EFP, but now I lose a gun? Uh-uh. Me and my assistant tore the place apart. Nada."

"Joey said a lot of people had access to the props room and—"

"Props room, yeah, people go in and out, actors use the kitchen—which is why the guns are in lockup."

"And who's got keys to that?"

"Me, my crew—three of them—and head of security. Also some network suit."

"Not the producer or director or—"

"Nobody. I don't know the security guy or the suit, but I know my people."

"So what's your theory, Clay?" I asked. "How'd the killer get the gun?"

"Anyone with three hundred bucks can buy a kit, make duplicate keys."

"But why would anyone want to?"

"If you need a gun, rental's a good one to use. Lotta prints on it, no traceability. Smart move. If the shooter'd got it back a couple hours sooner, or if ISS hadn't called me on my EFP that morning, they woulda pulled it off. Just a case of bad luck."

"Any thoughts on who did it?"

He snorted. "The clowns on that show? Nothing would surprise me. There's bad blood there. Little producer bitch fires me for incompetence? Let me tell you, I was never once drunk on the job. They fired me so they can promote one of my crew and pay 'em less money. It's all about money. Doing things on the cheap. Skimming off the top."

"Really?" I said. "Skimming off the top?"

"Oh, yeah. They allot money for a storyline, two weeks later they cut it in half. They say, Oh, we forgot, we blew the year's budget on last sweeps period. Right. A year ago, things weren't run this way. If they were, I'd've looked the other way. For David. But I owe nothing to this bunch. Bet your ass I called the cops."

"But none of this points to Joey, your theory."

"Rafferty? Hell. She wanted to shoot David, she'd a plugged him with her own gun. Sneaking around is not her style."

Clay was bitter, hungover, and unpleasant, but he was on Joey's team. So I liked him. I crossed him off my suspect list. Why would he shoot David, then alert the cops to the gun he'd used? It sounded like Clay thought Jen Kim was the guilty party, but was this based on reason or simple animosity? I tried to picture the tiny producer shooting David. She'd have to stand on an apple box to do it, but I didn't doubt her ability.

Uncle Theo studied me from the passenger seat. "It's rude of me to eavesdrop," he said, as though he'd had a choice, "but am I to understand that Joey is a fugitive?"

"They haven't printed up wanted posters yet, but she's in trouble. There are people who think she killed a friend of ours, a soap opera producer."

"A soap opera?" Uncle Theo asked. "My mother—your grandmother—listened for years to her programs, as she called them, on the radio while doing laundry. I remember the mangle she used to press the sheets, and the organ music, and the mellifluous voice of the narrator, as I ate my bread and jelly after school."

"I don't like daytime TV," P.B. said. "Except for *At the End of the Day*." I turned to look at him. "You *watch* it? At the hospital?"

"Yeah. Two o'clock. It's my soap." My brother then launched into a detailed and barely comprehensible synopsis of the story for the last several years.

"This is much like the *Watchmen*," Apollo said. "I would like to see this, but my mother and aunts watch *Emeril* at two."

"We missed it today," I said, "but how'd you like to see next week's episodes?"

*   *   *

We dropped Uncle Theo in Glendale and continued west. I had only one reason for taking P.B. and Apollo to Solomonhaus: either the place had defective feng shui or it was just plain haunted, but I couldn't stay there alone. And I had to stay there, because that's where Joey would return. When she returned.

My key still fit the lock, and P.B. and Apollo settled in front of the TV as though they'd lived there for years. I popped in the first DVD and went to the kitchen. Joey had called Clay, Jen, Rupert, Max, Laurie, and Tricia in the past three days, so I would too. I wasn't sure why; the killer was unlikely to say, "Why yes, Joey did come by asking questions today, so I murdered her. She's in the trunk of my car." But I couldn't see a downside. I left messages for Jen, Max, and Tricia. As for Laurie, the costume designer, her number was answered by a beleaguered-sounding assistant who told me Joey had called the previous morning, asking about wigs.

"Wigs?" I said.

"Yeah. Hair and Makeup had sent over some wigs we sewed into stocking caps for a dream sequence. I described them to Joey. Don't know why she wanted to know."

"Were any of them missing recently?" I asked.

"Funny," she said. "I don't know, but Joey asked the exact same thing."

From the bedroom came the *At the End of the Day* theme music, luring me to the doorway. Onscreen, Trey Mangialotti's character was still in his coma, with Sheffo's character limping around the room, talking to him. I watched for a minute as if it would illuminate something, give me a sign, but perhaps my faith was insufficient. A god who'd communicate through a daytime drama was a god I couldn't put a lot of stock in.

I went back to the living room, torn. Was Joey in more danger from the police and jail or from the actual murderer? If it was the former, I should do nothing. If it was the latter, I should be calling everyone from the National Guard to her mother in Croatia to help look for her. But look where?

It all came back to the person who shot David. If Detective Ike Born was as good as I wanted to believe LAPD was, he was on the killer's trail. But if he'd decided the perpetrator was Joey, then Joey was the only one on the killer's trail, and Ike Born was on her trail. As was I. But I had more clues than Ike Born—or at least, different clues. If only I could decipher them.

I found Ike Born's business card and dialed the number, and to my surprise, Ike Born answered his own phone. On the first ring.

"Detective, it's Wollie Shelley," I said. "Listen, I forgot to ask yesterday when you came by with that search warrant, but do you still need me to answer any questions?"

"No, I believe we've got everything we need from you. Thanks for asking."

"Okay," I said. "I'm also wondering, are you zeroing in on Joey Rafferty in the David Zetrakis murder case, or is the field still wide open? Can you talk about that?"

"Why do you ask?" he said.

Of course he'd say that. Like a therapist, never answering a question. "Curiosity."

"Can I put you on hold for a moment?" he asked.

"Yes," I said, and hung up. What was I thinking? Ike Born wasn't going to confide in me. And I wasn't going to confide in him either, until I had something that could help exonerate Joey. He was not, at this point, on her side.

The phone rang again, and I let the machine pick up. Ike Born left his number and told me to call him. Fat chance.

I looked around the kitchen. Fredreeq had left all of the Solomonhaus paperwork on the counter, and I flipped through it. There was little correspondence and fewer bills. Possibly Joey and Elliot used a business manager for that, or maybe they did it via computer, like many residents of the twenty-first century. At least I could pay the parking ticket I'd been carrying around. No point in Joey coming home to that along with one or two murder charges. I wrote a check, copying the Mercedes license number onto the bottom, and saw once more my note to myself to call P.B. and the letters scribbled on the envelope. Sudstud. Pntspns. And then I put two and five together.

SUDSTUD. Seven letters. It was a license plate.

Like DRUDGE2 on the camera crew's minivan, a vanity plate. Belonging to someone on the soap, of course. Joey had jotted it down while driving, the license plate of the car she'd seen come up Elliot's driveway as she came down, the morning after Christmas. Then she'd stuck it in her pocket. How could it have taken me so long to figure this out?

And she'd gone to the set in the last few days—at least once, maybe more often—but she'd been cagey about it. Was this why? Was she looking for that license plate?

I went to my purse, found my address book, and dialed Pete Cziemanski. My cop buddy. "Pete, it's Wollie," I said. "Listen, I'm—"

"Where's your friend Joey?"

"I don't know."

"Because I'm hearing some stuff today that doesn't sound good for her."

"What?" I asked, heart sinking.

"Never mind. But if you see her—"

"Pete, Joey knows who killed David Zetrakis. At least, she knows the license plate on the car the killer was driving. You have to tell me who the car's registered to."

"What? Slow down."

I took a deep breath and explained it again.

"Talk to the detective assigned to the case," Cziemanski said.

"Ike Born. I know. But I can't. Because Joey told him she was far away when the murder happened, which would mean she couldn't have seen the car and—"

"She lied in her statement?" Pete asked.

"I think so, but can't you just call the DMV—"

"Are you out of your mind? I'm a cop. You're talking about breaking laws. Prison time. Jesus, woman, I'm not even sleeping with you."

"You're right. I wasn't thinking. Sorry, Pete. Happy New Year. Bye." I hung up, with him still yelling at me to call Ike Born. Stupid move. Stupid, stupid. He was right. If I was going to ask some public servant to commit crimes, it should be one I was sleeping with. But not Simon. He was far too ethical, not to mention nosy, to be of any use. Was it too late to have an affair with Ike Born?

Anyhow, I thought, looking in the kitchen drawers for a stamp, was the SUDSTUD driver necessarily the killer? Hard to imagine any of my favorite suspects sporting a vanity plate like that. In the case of Jen or Tricia, impossible to imagine. Too unsophisticated. I found a roll of stamps, near the tablet on which were written the numbers for Debbie and Daryl Ann.

Ah, yes. Elliot's JetBlue flight attendants. No help there.

Maybe I was approaching this from the wrong angle. Let's be realistic, I told myself. I couldn't be expected to pull a murderer out of my hat. If it were that simple, everyone would be doing it. What if I could show that Joey wasn't the killer, though? Shouldn't that be easier? Then I could call the police and say that she was missing and probably in trouble, and get them to go find her.

But wait! Maybe the cops would expend more energy on finding her if they still thought she was the killer.

Only then they'd toss her in jail, where she'd rot, waiting for some cheap public defender, since she didn't even have the Klimt yet and it would take time to turn it into cash once she did. Which was still better than being killed by the killer. It wouldn't be a home run, though; more of a base hit. On the other hand, base hits won games too. Even I knew that, I, who wasn't much for baseball.

I was back to my original plan. The most direct route to Joey was to follow the path she'd taken, based on the clues she'd left. But how?

I made a list.

Joey was a suspect, I wrote down, because she had access to the murder weapon, she benefited financially from David's death, and she was near the crime scene at the right (wrong) time. She also had a history with David that had had its ups and downs, a small assault charge back in her teenage years, a gun she wasn't supposed to be running around with, some possibly blood-spattered clothes that the police were in possession of, and a husband—at least, a man she'd thought was her husband—who'd died under mysterious circumstances shortly after she'd expressed a desire to murder him.

Okay, it was a long list. Perhaps I should just start with clues.

I looked again at Debbie and Daryl Ann's names and wondered if there was any mileage, so to speak, to be gotten out of them. Debbie had already told Van Beek she hadn't seen Elliot since before Christmas. Daryl Ann, though: might she be the girl he'd met on the beach the night he'd gone surfing?

This was a job for Fredreeq, but Fredreeq was in Fresno. That left P.B. and Apollo. I went into the bedroom. "Can either of you call someone and pretend you're a journalist?" I asked.

Apollo could, he assured me. Had he not met Monica Pulliam, a real live journalist, the day before? P.B. put the soap on pause to join us.

I explained my idea, dialed Daryl Ann, and put her on speakerphone.

"Hello," Apollo said. "I am John, writer for the *Planetary Orbiter*. We understand that you were the last to see Elliot Horowitz alive, you had a special place in his life."

"Yes, but I've already told my story to *California Celebrity*," Daryl Ann said. "I saw him in Malibu the night he died."

"How was he, please?"

"He was good. Elliot was a man full of vitality and life."

"Was he drunk?" Apollo was enjoying this. I began to write a hasty note.

"No," Daryl Ann said. "He was going surfing."

"Yes, I see. Did you fight with him? I understood you were fighting."

"No. We were having a passionate discussion. We were two highly passionate people. I feel things deeply, and he was under a lot of pressure. At home. His wife was putting him through hell, because the marriage was over. We were deeply in love."

I passed my note to Apollo. "I have heard," he said, "that you look like his wife, Joey Rafferty. Is this true?"

"Well, I'm actually a lot younger. And I've been told I have a really hot body. And my hair is more of a strawberry blond."

"She's not in love," P.B. said, loudly. "That's a lie." He must not have understood the concept of a speakerphone.

"What?" Daryl Ann said.

"High. You're sure he was not high?" Apollo asked.

"Oh, no way. I have way too much self-respect to be with someone who needed to do drugs."

I felt I needed to do drugs just to listen to her. I made the cutoff signal to Apollo, and he ended the conversation, hesitating only when Daryl Ann asked him his name again. "Paul," he said, then corrected himself. "John. John Paul. Like the pope."

That was enough for me, Daryl Ann saying it was she and not Joey who'd last seen Elliot, and that he hadn't been drugged. Of course, Daryl Ann was no pharmacologist, but if Elliot had been given something, it was neither obvious nor fast-acting, unless it was administered after his rendezvous with Daryl Ann, while Joey was miles away at Green's GolfLand. Whatever else the cops could pin on Joey, I didn't see how they could get her for this.

A loud knock sent Apollo, P.B., and me to the front door. I opened it. There stood Simon.

"Hello again," he said. "Wollie, I'd like a word with you. It's about Joey."

Fifty

led Simon into the backyard, heart pounding and limbs shaking.

"Where is she?" Simon asked.

I let out a breath I hadn't known I'd been holding. "Thank God. I thought you came here to tell me that she's . . ."

"What?"

"You know. Dead." I sat on a stone chaise and told myself not to do anything ill-advised, like crying. "I don't know where she's gone. I'm so worried."

"You should be. There's going to be a warrant for her arrest."

"What? For Elliot's death?"

"No. Zetrakis. Don't ask how I know, just see if you can get her to come in quietly and avoid a media circus. Have her lawyer come with her."

I looked at him, drained. I couldn't begin to explain that there was no money for a lawyer and that Joey wasn't just gone for the evening but *gone*. All I could do was stare at the man in front of me, remembering that one week earlier we'd shared Christmas dinner. Pizza. In his bed, because we liked the dress code there.

"Is that what brought you all the way out to Pasadena?" I said. "You could've told me this over the phone."

"You didn't answer your phone, as usual. Or Joey's. Theo said you were here."

"But I've been answering Joey's phone all—oh." Her cell, I realized. Not her land line. I'd forgotten about that one, and the answering machine along with it.

I jumped up and ran into the kitchen and hit the machine's REPLAY button. Simon followed. We listened to the first message, from Joey's mom. Worried. This was followed by a belligerent message from Camille, a terse one from Rick Slepicka on his way to Telluride, and then one from Simon, for me. After that was a second one for me, from Max, changing my call from six-thirty to six A.M. for the following day, in order to keep on track with the *SoapDirt* schedule. And, finally, the message from Ike Born. No message from Joey; that was the only thing I cared about.

"*SoapDirt*? At least I'll know where you are tomorrow." Simon crossed his arms. "Shall I check in with them when I need to find you? They seem well-informed."

"You're as well-informed as anyone. I'm camping here until Joey shows."

"Great. So *you'll* be the focus of the media circus. Did I tell you I saw a photo of you in a newspaper at a checkout stand? Not your best, by the way."

"Well, sorry to disappoint you. I've got bigger things to worry about." I walked past him, through the sliding doors, to the outside again. He followed and slid the doors shut behind us. The sky was cement-colored. I shivered.

"What's wrong, Wollie?"

"It'll take too long to get into it. I'm sure you have to get back to . . . whomever. Work." I hated the note in my voice.

"I've gotta tell you," he said, running a hand through his hair, "I find this attitude of yours tiresome. I've been honest about who I am and what I do. You don't like it, I can understand that, but don't treat me like I've betrayed you in some way."

There was truth in what he said, which made it the last thing I wanted to hear. "Can I just ask, how friendly are you expected to get with Lucrezia Borgia?"

"Let's not get into this."

"You won't answer that," I said, "because you don't talk about work. As a matter of principle. You'll have sex with her, though, right? If you have to. For God and country. You'll hate it, but you'll do it. And I'm supposed to disappear, yet be available. And understanding. And now you're even asking me to play cop, turn in my best friend, tell her to roll over, give herself up to the system that wants to hang her, even though she's innocent. That's your job, Simon. But it's not mine."

He stared at me, breathing deeply, his face dark. "Let's leave me and my value system out of this, shall we, and stick to the matter at hand before I tell you where to take your low opinion of me and what to do with it. I'll tell you one thing. You don't know what you're doing. You may have guts but you've got no training, experience, or even intelligence, at the moment. With the best intentions in the world, you are going to screw it up for your friend."

I was so mad now I was starting to cry, which made me exponentially madder. "Joey would rather I screw it up in good faith than stand back and sell her down the river to a bunch of men who think they know what's good for her. She'd rather die."

"And she may." Simon walked toward the back gate, delivering a parting shot over his shoulder. "I've heard the gods watch out for drunks and fools. I hope it's true."

Fifty-one

"Way I come with you?" Apollo said when my alarm went off at
four A.M. "I have never seen a television studio."

It took me a moment to orient myself. The three of us were camped
out in the living room, due to having opened a window in the guest bedroom that we were then unable to close, so that that room now doubled
as a walk-in freezer.

I left the light off, looking out into the backyard, lit by the moon.
"The thing is, Apollo, this is my first time doing the show and I'm not
sure about bringing visitors."

"I am small, so no one will notice me."

"I wouldn't go," P.B. said, yawning. "Too many power lines. Signals
going in and out. Broadcasting. Wires. You won't like it."

"I will," Apollo said. "I will meet some of the actors from your soap
opera."

"No point. They're never as interesting as their characters."

I thought about the dream I'd had, laying coins—or poker chips?—
on the closed eyelids of a man who morphed into Joey. "Tell me something, P.B.," I said. "Was there ever a transsexual character on *At the End
of the Day*?"

He was quiet for a moment, then said, "No. Gays, lesbians, angels, vampires, neo-Nazis, aliens, priests, nuns, and conjoined twins. No transsexuals. How come?"

"Just curious." I liked that, that the one thing David hadn't exploited for the show was his brother. "David used bits and pieces of his life in the storyline. Do you think there are clues in there about how he died?"

"His character, Zeke Fabian? His death was caused by the aftereffects of his exorcism, which had happened years before. But this was back in the 1980s."

"That's when he was just an actor. I'm talking about now, as a writer-producer."

"There's death all over the show," P.B. said. "But it won't tell you who did it."

"Why not?"

"Because he didn't care about 'who.' He cared about plot and theme. Characters to him were foot soldiers, carrying out the orders of the writer. He sacrificed people all the time. There are no stars on *At the End of the Day*, not like on other soaps."

"You know this about David, just by watching his show?" I asked.

"You can tell. He was an egomaniac. That's what made it fun to watch. Once his scripts run out, you'll see. It won't be anything special anymore."

I couldn't see anything special in it now, but I was apparently in the minority. What my brother said fascinated me, though. "P.B., where do you think Joey's gone?"

"You don't want to know."

"Yes, I do."

"She's gone underground," he said. "Seeing if she wants to stay there. She's been doing it for a while now. Maybe you should leave her alone, Wollie."

"I can't." I didn't know exactly what he was talking about, but I knew that much. "I can't."

   .   .   .

I dropped my brother in Glendale at Uncle Theo's and took Apollo along with me to Burbank. At worst, he could stay in the car reading comic books.

I was a wreck. I'd spent half the night awake, awaiting a knock on the door and Detective Ike Born with an arrest warrant. That wasn't the only thing that drove back sleep—it was my fight with Simon. I could not, like Daryl Ann, describe it as two highly passionate people under pressure. I might describe it as two people calling it off.

And I didn't have guts—where had Simon come up with that?—because even now, with all my other concerns, there was still room for stage fright. The prospect of doing *SoapDirt*, of saying the wrong thing on TV, nearly paralyzed me.

Apollo was another story. It was still dark when we pulled up to the guard gate, but his excitement was palpable. "Wow. The technology in this booth," he exclaimed, craning his neck for a better look. A small screen showed an image of my Integra, its license plate in sharp focus. My face was there too, clearly enough to show how tired I looked.

Something occurred to me. I waited for the guard to check the trunk and wave us through, then read his name tag and said, "Hello, Leroy. Tell me, do you guys keep the footage of all the cars going in and out?"

Leroy frowned, like it was a security breach to discuss operations.

"Hey!" Apollo said. "That's a great PTZ. Does it have built-in IR illuminators?"

Leroy smiled, revising his assessment of us from threats to tourists. "Just keeping our stars safe," he said. "We record hundreds of thousands of cars going in and out, all stored on a little microchip. You folks enjoy your day."

We drove up to Sound Stage D and I told Apollo to keep his eyes open for a license plate that said SUDSTUD.

"Since *SoapDirt* is produced and staffed by the same people who do *At the End of the Day*," I said, "SUDSTUD could belong to one of them. Also, nearly every phone call Joey made recently was to people on the lot, which suggests that the killer works here."

"That's fantastic!" Apollo said, with what I considered an unnecessary degree of enthusiasm.

We were met at the door by C.G., taking the early stage manager shift. "Max is sleeping in," she said. "The big explosion's tonight, and he'll be here till all hours overseeing that." She told Apollo that he was welcome to sit in the *SoapDirt* audience.

"What audience?" I said.

"The studio audience," C.G. said, oblivious to the blood draining out of my face. "Not a big one, because of the holiday. A hundred or so. Meanwhile, Apollo, I'll give you a tour while Wollie tries on clothes. This way." She led us outside to a clump of trailers, pointing a flashlight to one with my name on it, written on masking tape.

My trailer was homier, if not roomier, than anywhere I'd lived recently. While I checked out the beige-and-blue main room, bedroom, kitchenette, dining area, and bathroom, Apollo inspected the television, tape deck, CD and DVD players, and telephones. Everything was new. Plaids matched. All was clean, with the happy scent of vanilla air freshener. A gift basket "To our guest star!" sat on the table. C.G. turned on the heat, and I bumped it up to eighty degrees and immediately felt it kick on.

"C.G.," I said. "I want to spend my life here."

She smiled without looking up from the clipboard she was scribbling on. "By the time you're done today, you'll feel like you have. Leave your stuff here and I'll take you to Tricia's trailer. She wants to okay your wardrobe. Ready?"

She unclipped a radio from her belt. "Give Tricia a heads-up, please," she said, talking into a small burst of static. "We're walking."

Tricia's trailer was fifty yards away, the one closest to the sound stage. If mine was cozy, hers was Buckingham Palace. I guessed by the look on Apollo's face that here, at last, was the real America. We entered to the beat of techno music and the smell of coffee. The furnishings were those of a high-end yacht. One woman was steaming milk with a cappuccino machine. Another was doing Tricia's makeup while a third, Gloria, put soup can–sized curlers in her hair. Tricia herself, swathed in a pink velvet dressing gown and fuzzy slippers, lounged in what looked like a dentist chair, eyes closed.

"Is that you, Max?" she asked without looking. "Listen, I want a new cappuccino machine. This might have been state-of-the-art eighteen months ago, but I was reading in *Los Angeles Magazine* about a titanium one that goes for six grand. Get in touch with them and tell them I'll mention it on the air if they'll send me a free one."

"It's C.G., not Max," C.G. said, writing. "If they say no, want me to order one?"

"Not if I have to pay retail. Can the show buy it?"

"No. We're over budget. I have Wollie here."

"Who?"

C.G. looked at me and smiled encouragingly. "Wollie. Your dating correspondent. You wanted to approve her 'look.' "

"Tell her to wait."

"Okay, Wollie," C.G. said, "I'll take you back to your trailer, and—"

"No," Tricia said. "Wait *here*. God. I can't have her running back and forth and wasting everyone's time."

C.G. looked at me, her face blank, but then allowed herself an infinitesimal eyebrow raise, conveying sympathy. I took a seat on a plush swivel armchair and picked up an entertainment magazine, dated a week ahead. There was already a feature story on David, with extensive photos and a sidebar on Joey captioned "The Millionairess Heiress"; it included a tiny photo of the Gustav Klimt painting. I squinted to get a better look, but all I could really see of the painting was a half-naked woman with red hair in a sensual pose. It might have been Joey.

Tricia kept up a steady stream of chatter with her hair and makeup artists, about the likeliest candidates for Daytime Emmys. She informed her assistant that the cappuccino was cold, and that a new one would be required. "And could you keep the racket down while you're doing it?" she asked, as if there were a volume control on the milk steamer. Perhaps on the six-thousand-dollar version, there would be.

I wondered what had become of the Tricia whose frog mural I had painted, whose house I'd visited, the charming, affectionate, laughing woman. Party Tricia. Perhaps she was not a morning person. Perhaps she was at her best . . . drinking glögg.

Jen Kim came into the trailer and walked past without seeing me. "How long?" she asked, standing over the dentist chair.

"Seven minutes," said the makeup woman.

"Thirty for me," Gloria said. "I have to blow her out."

"I wouldn't dream of rushing you," Jen said. "But we have tons of work to get done and we leave at three for the Elliot Horowitz funeral."

I stood. "What?"

Jen turned to me. "Oh, hello. Is that your wardrobe?"

"No," Tricia said. "I need to be in on her wardrobe."

"You don't have time to be in on her wardrobe," Jen said.

"I can look at the rack while I'm getting blown out," Tricia said.

"What did you just say about the Elliot Horowitz funeral?" I asked.

"It's at Mount Sinai," Jen said. "Geographically convenient, and Tricia, you'll be camera-ready, so we'll shoot some segments there afterward. Twilight. Very dramatic."

"Who arranged this funeral?" I asked.

"Did you know Elliot?" Tricia said, addressing me for the first time.

"I knew him very well," I said, with more vehemence than I'd intended. Everyone froze, then turned to me. It may have sounded like I was having sex with him.

"Well, it's a private service," Jen said. "Family and close friends, his sister said. Which would include all of us, but . . . okay, this is very awkward. Were you invited?"

"Was his wife invited?" I asked.

"What's the story with Joey?" Tricia asked. "Has she been arrested yet?"

"Oh, is Joey going to be arrested?" Jen asked.

"No!" I said. All eyes turned to me again. "Given the fact that she's innocent."

"As if that matters. Ow." Tricia swatted at Gloria, who was removing her curlers. "Angel Ramirez says that Joey is Suspect Numero Uno, not just in David's death but Elliot's too."

"Elliot!" Jen said. "Elliot was murdered? Why would Joey kill Elliot?"

"Joey didn't kill Elliot," I said. "And unless Angel Ramirez is moonlighting in a toxicology lab, she can't know if he was murdered or not. And Joey did not kill David."

Tricia turned her head and gave me a look I couldn't interpret. "I don't see how you're in a position to say that, unless you were with her when David was shot."

"Whether or not she killed him," Jen said, "she could still go down for it."

"They have no other suspects," Tricia said, with the assurance of the totally uninformed.

"Yes, they do," I said, goaded beyond endurance. "A car was seen driving onto David's property right before his death and—"

"That's absurd." Tricia sat up so fast she gave Gloria a form of whiplash. "How could you know that?"

"Whose car?" Jen asked.

"Is this something Joey told you?" Tricia demanded.

"What kind of car?" Jen said.

I looked back and forth at them, as if I were at a tennis match. "I don't know, but Joey got a license number."

"Oh, come on," Tricia said dismissively. "Nobody notices license numbers. She's making it up."

Jen opened Tricia's refrigerator. "Joey won't be at the funeral. Elliot's sister mentioned it rather pointedly. How are these grapes? They're not sour?"

"I haven't tried them," Tricia said. "I have the appetite of a bird."

"How does Elliot's sister know she won't be there?" I said. "Does she know where Joey is?"

Jen shrugged. "Wherever she is, it won't be at Mount Sinai today. That alone is news. You lose media points, not attending your spouse's funeral." She stuck a grape in her mouth and made a face. "If the color is too good, never trust them."

Static from C.G.'s radio filled the room. She'd been so quiet I'd forgotten she was there, sitting in the back of the trailer with Apollo. "Tricia," she said, "if you're going to be in on wardrobe decisions for everyone, we'll have to adjust your call. We can't keep the studio audience waiting."

"Of course we can," Tricia said. "Builds anticipation."

"No, it zaps their will to live," Jen said. "They sit there like corpses, waiting for food and prizes. By the third episode, we have to use cattle prods to get them to clap."

"So order cattle prods," Tricia said.

I was getting worked up and was just about to walk out for some air when Laurie, the costumer, walked in, flanked by assistants bearing clothing racks, safety pins, and dressmaker's chalk. Laurie was strangely intimidating, and within minutes Jen was gone, with C.G. and Apollo leaving soon after.

All attention was now on me. I tried on clothes with tags displaying designer labels and name brands from stores like Neiman Marcus and Saks Fifth Avenue, the kind of things I bought only when they'd made their way to Ross Dress for Less a season or two later, marked down by 75 percent. These were full price. I was whisked in and out of pants, sweaters, suits, and dresses, zipped and buttoned by Laurie's assistants as though I were in preschool. I changed in the bedroom, then walked out to the main living area to have each outfit—and my physique—critiqued by Tricia.

"No, no, no," Tricia said, having her hair blown out with a circular brush. "Laurie, do you want her to look like a complete slut? That blouse! Get her a bigger size, would you?"

Laurie glared at Tricia. "She's busty. She's already in a large, and it's far too big across the shoulders." The short costumer demonstrated this failing by plucking the excess fabric on each of my shoulders. She had to stand on tiptoes to do this. I tried to accommodate her by bending my knees, but she snapped at me to stand up straight.

"Oh, it's ugly anyway," Tricia said. "How about a turtleneck? That puce one wasn't too bad."

"I'm not nuts about puce," I said. "Or leg-o'-mutton sleeves. In theory, they're fine, but—"

"Sweetie," Tricia said. "I think I've been in this business a little longer than you."

"Tricia, she's anemic in puce," Laurie said. "And the angora will make her look plump on camera. It's texturally interesting, but on her it's wrong."

"Nonsense. Who's the coproducer here?" Tricia said. I felt like a spear carrier in the Trojan War, torn between Hector and Achilles. "I have an eye for what works. She'll wear the puce for the Monday episode. Let's move on."

Laurie snarled under her breath. Perhaps she had a professional mandate to "do no harm" and had ethical issues about turning a not-unattractive, albeit orange-haired woman into someone plump, furry, and neckless who appeared to have recently eaten a bad oyster.

I put my vanity to one side and focused. I would attend Elliot's funeral as Joey's proxy. Maybe Laurie could lend me something black to wear. I'd leave the tags on, so she could return it. Returning worn items was morally corrupt, but these were desperate times.

I walked back to my trailer in my original clothes, while three homely outfits were hauled off to the wardrobe truck to be steamed and altered. I'd no sooner settled into my own cozy armchair than Max came by.

"I thought you were sleeping in," I said.

"We're behind schedule, and it's barely daylight," he said. "Thought I better help out. I'll take you to Nero and Noel, hair and makeup. They do everyone but Tricia, who's got her own people. I hope Tricia hasn't terrorized them into doing her bidding. Can I ask what've you done to offend her?"

I sighed. "I met Tricia for the first time at her party, where I was hailed like a long-lost sister. I've spoken all of seven words to her since, and now I'm . . . the Antichrist."

"Well, you're good friends with Joey, aren't you?"

"Very."

Max shook his head. "As the saying goes, 'The friend of my enemy is my enemy.' They've never gotten along, going back to the days when Joey was a star and Tricia wanted to be Joey. We called her Joey Junior."

Max left me to the ministrations of Nero and Noel, who were friendly and encouraging until Tricia popped her head in to offer aesthetic advice. I emerged an hour later with false eyelashes so large it looked like spiders had died on my eyelids. My hair had been teased and sprayed and bullied into a do that resembled a basketball, if a basketball could be made of hair.

I went into my trailer, fell asleep sitting up, so as not to disturb the basketball, and was awakened twenty minutes later by Max.

"I'd thought there'd be a script or talking points for you," he said, frowning at my hairdo, "but now I'm told you're good at extemporaneous speaking, so we'll just wind you up and start you talking."

I stared. "Who said I was good at extemporaneous speaking?"

"Tricia." One thick gray eyebrow shot up. "I take it that's not the case."

"Oh, God." I closed my eyes again.

Among the particular hell-on-earth experiences human beings endure, public speaking, when one lacks aptitude, enthusiasm, and experience, ranks right up there with stomach flu. Not only did I face an audience that had been kept waiting for two hours and had no interest in me to start with, but these hundred-plus faces represented only a fraction of the television-viewing audience who'd eventually witness my pain. Not that any of them mattered. All I cared about was Simon. One single viewer. Even if we had in fact split up, he'd watch. Unless the entire West Coast underwent some kind of natural disaster that shut down the power grid for several weeks. That might be nice. Or he could die before the episodes aired. That would be sad, but at least he'd be spared the hair.

Tricia was a big favorite with the audience. She combined confidence with heart, like a drum majorette who volunteered at homeless shelters. She introduced me as a professional escort and a contestant on the canceled reality show *Biological Clock*, suggesting a second-rate celebrity hooker. At Max's signal, I walked onstage to tepid applause. Max waved his arms like a frenzied orchestra conductor, trying to muster a show of support from the audience, who clapped with more gusto.

Tricia and I were seated on bar stools flanked by plastic palm trees. She looked lovely, in an enchanting pink sundress. I tried not to think of how I looked, in my puce turtleneck, basketball beehive, and false eyelashes. I mumbled a hello and traded air kisses with Tricia, then settled in to watch a monitor showing footage of me exchanging close-contact kisses with Rupert Ling. This brought oohs and ahhs and wolf whistles from the audience. Even I was struck by how intimate it appeared. We looked ready to procreate.

"So tell us, Wollie," Tricia said, "is it true what they say about Asian men?"

"What's that?"

"You know. NWE." She gave the audience a conspiratorial wink, then whispered into the microphone, "Not well endowed." This evoked more catcalls and applause.

I was appalled. "It was a Buddhist monk event, so it didn't really come up."

"So to speak." Tricia winked again at the audience. And to think I'd once found winking attractive. "But you're among friends now, Wollie, so . . . dish! What about *après* the monks?"

"We . . . talked to a nun."

"Fascinating," she said, in a tone of voice that assured me it wasn't. "What about?"

I went blank. You know how that is, when you have a hundred people waiting for you to say something entertaining? The silence got longer and Tricia just sat, watching me. "Cat got your tongue?" she asked finally.

"Well, we wondered, naturally, who killed David Zetrakis."

"Aha. Now we're getting somewhere," Tricia said. "Our audience may not realize that the murder weapon was a gun used on our own show, *At the End of the Day.* Which meant oodles of people—cast or crew— could've walked off with it, as we had the world's most incompetent drunk, Clay Jakes, in charge of props. How*ever*—" Tricia held up a hand while she sipped from a glass of ice water, creating suspense. "As the crew was in a meeting the morning of the murder, guess who's left without an alibi?"

"The cast!" someone yelled.

"Bingo!" Tricia said. "And ex-cast, some of who may turn up like bad pennies, and even have permanent drive-on passes, which can happen when you sleep your way up the ladder. Show of hands: who here re- members Joey Rafferty, who played Persimmon Paget?"

"What's your alibi, Tricia?" I asked. "Given that you had a good rea- son to kill David, since he was about to write you out of the show, de- spite the fact that you'd once slept with him?"

Tricia froze. She went so still that for a moment I pictured her dead, with the same thick makeup layering her skin, applied by an undertaker. Then she smiled. "Why, aren't we unexpectedly vicious? But fair enough. I was at Barneys, far, far from the crime scene. Shoe shopping, nine A.M., when the doors opened. Day-after-Christmas hours. I had a party to throw that night. Who here just has to wear something new to her own party?"

Enough people to applaud vigorously.

"So back to Joey Rafferty. Persimmon Paget, you'll remember, if you're that *old,* was a stripper–turned–oil magnate. *And* a killer. On the show, she shot her first husband, Ferro Grotto, and his lover, Platinum, after Ferro dumped her. In *real* life, guess who dumped Joey? That's right. David Zetrakis. *And* her own husband, Elliot Horowitz. And where are they now? Why, pushing up daisies."

I can't tell you what strange physical reflex it was that made my leg reach out and kick Tricia's bar stool just as she put the ice water to her lips again, causing the water to spill out onto her chin and also onto her lovely sundress, drenching the bodice and making her nipples visible.

For a moment I thought she'd come for me, but her professionalism kicked in. She turned her back on the audience, called, "Wardrobe!," and walked off the set. Leaving me alone with the audience. No one clapped.

"Let's break for lunch," Max said, over a public-address system. "One half hour."

⋅ ⋅ ⋅

Apollo could not contain his enthusiasm. "Fantastic! This is the best fun!"

Max, escorting us off the set, was less sanguine. "It wasn't dull, I'll give you that. Whether we get through two more episodes with you today is an open question. Tricia is not at her happiest and we've got to wrap by six, to clear the lot for Special Effects."

"I'm sorry about this," I said, "but it's okay to fire me. Maybe where I'm supposed to be right now is the police station, bugging them to find Joey."

"I am also okay with that," Apollo said. "A police station would be fantastic."

Max opened Sound Stage D's heavy door and waited for us to precede him out into the daylight. "I doubt Jen will fire you. They can edit out the . . . awkward moments. I'll have C.G. bring you lunch in your trailer. There's a dining tent, but—"

"Trailer's better," I said. "Thanks, Max, you're very considerate."

"For what it's worth," he said, "the Tricias are few and far between. Most actors are human beings. Don't let this sour you on show business."

We stopped to let a pickup truck loaded with painting supplies pass. The weather had turned beautiful, and I looked at the California blue sky and the buildings of the back lot that rose up to meet it, big charm-less sound stages where magic was made.

The truck honked at a golf cart in its way, and drew my attention.

To its license plate.

SUDSTUD.

Fifty-two

Apollo saw it too. "Wollie, look."

"What?" Max said.

"That white pickup," I said. "Who owns that?"

Max squinted. "One of the carpenters. From the Art Department."

"What's his name?"

"I think that's Polin's truck. Michael Polin. Why?"

The truck turned a corner and disappeared. "Is Michael—is he a nice guy?" I wasn't sure how to put it—*Is he a murderous type?* seemed a little graceless.

"Nice?" Max said. "He shows up for work on time. That's a nice quality."

"Was he at the production meeting last Friday morning?"

"Probably," Max said. "Normally it's just department heads, but we had a full house, due to the special effects. Why?"

"Just curious," I said. Max, because of his large size, reminded me of Simon. They both had that capable "Step aside, little lady, I'll handle this" attitude, and I didn't intend to step aside.

In my trailer, I covered my puce angora with a man-sized blue chambray work shirt, left by a thoughtful wardrobe person in case I was a sloppy eater.

"Apollo, stay here, okay?" I said. "If C.G. brings lunch, say I just stepped out for a minute. And if I'm gone an hour, send help. But I won't be. And you've got the cell phone number." I had Joey's phone practically velcroed to me at this point.

I walked in the direction the truck had gone. Unless I'd drastically miscalculated, I was in no danger from this Michael. I'd talk to him, then see what I could do about getting fired. Or I'd quit. I'd rather spend the afternoon with Ike Born than with Tricia.

I also wanted to make Elliot's funeral, for Joey's sake and for my own, because I'd liked Elliot, even with all his marital sins. Of course, both Tricia and Camille could denounce me for showing up uninvited. I try to let years elapse between publicly embarrassing moments, and this morning's had been particularly grim, but oh, well.

A man in coveralls passed me. I asked him where to find the Art Department, and he pointed to a building straight ahead.

The white pickup was parked near an open loading dock. I peeked in the back, but there were no bloodstains visible, just paint cans and drop cloths.

I walked up a ramp into the Art Department and was greeted by the smell of freshly cut lumber and the whine of power tools accompanying a radio playing "Bad Moon Rising." A man who looked like he hadn't shaved or slept for a week walked past, and I asked him where I might find Michael Polin.

"POLIN!" he screamed, without breaking stride.

"WHAT!" someone screamed back. I followed the sound into an adjoining room.

He was loading plywood doors onto a cart. I knew even before I saw the tattoos on his arms—"Stud" and "Hot Guy"—that he was the man who'd complained about his truck to Sophie, Jen Kim's assistant, the first day I'd come to the lot. Suspicion confirmed: this was not the killer.

"Michael? My name's Wollie." I held out my hand.

"Mike." He shook my hand and frowned at my orange beehive hair.

"Someone went joyriding with your truck last Friday morning, didn't they?" I said. "When you were at the production meeting."

He stared.

"The keys were in it," I said. "So they hopped in and drove to Toluca Lake and back. How long would that take?"

He was still staring. "Fifteen, twenty minutes."

I thought of David, proud of his fast cars and short commute. "Okay, but with no traffic, shortcuts, going fast enough to collect dings—how long then?"

"Ten minutes. If they hauled ass."

"The length of a cigarette break," I said. "Or a phone call. Could've been anyone in the meeting."

"Friday's when our producer died. You saying someone used my truck to do it?"

"Don't you think?" I said.

"Who was it?"

"No idea. But it wasn't Joey Rafferty. Thanks."

"No problem," he said.

There would be a problem, I knew, as soon as I called the cops and they impounded his precious truck, after seeing it on the guard gate's surveillance-camera footage.

But it wasn't my problem. I smiled and headed out.

Fifty-three

Max sat in my trailer watching Apollo work his way through a tray holding mashed potatoes, steamed vegetables, barbecued chicken, Parker House rolls, fruit salad, green salad, three-bean salad, potato salad, Jell-O salad, and a carton of milk.

"Not only are you not fired," Max said, "Jen wants you to do promos."

"What's a promo?" Apollo asked.

"Promotional announcement—a kind of commercial for the show," Max said. "Come watch. Wollie will read copy from a tele-prompter."

"Okay," I said. "But I need to talk to Jen. I have to—" The word *quit* wouldn't come out of me, so I settled for "run a quick errand. And go to Elliot's funeral." The errand was Ike Born. I'd left a message for him, giving him Joey's cell number.

"That shouldn't be a problem. We're shooting three segments at Mount Sinai that don't involve you, after the funeral. You can take a break then." He looked at his watch. "We'll wrap here and move there in an hour or so. Jen's on Stage Nine, where we're set up for the promos. We'll okay it with her."

Max led us out of the trailer, away from the Art Department, pointing out items of interest to Apollo, who'd brought along a cookie the size of a Frisbee to fortify himself. I trailed them, distracted by my own thoughts, which had turned to wigs.

The killer must've worn a wig in case he or she was spotted near David's, or seen hopping into the SUDSTUD truck. It wouldn't fool the guard-gate camera, with its close-up lens, but maybe it wasn't meant to. If Clay hadn't noticed the missing gun, no one would be paying particular attention to *At the End of the Day* personnel. And they weren't even now, thanks to the production-meeting alibi, and the cops being fixated on Joey.

I would change that. It wasn't that I was smarter than the cops, only that they were probably operating on—what was that thing Max had mentioned?—Occam's razor. That the best explanation is based on what's already known. Joey was walking like a duck and quacking like a duck. I just happened to know what they didn't, which was that Joey could never be a duck.

"There's Building Twelve," Max said, pointing. "Our 'nuclear plant.'" I'd expected a deserted structure, roped off, with DANGER signs everywhere, but it was humming with activity and crew members. One man on a ladder was painting the underside of a second-story balcony, and two more were installing windows.

"They're breakaway windows," Max explained. "Fake. We took out the real ones so we won't have exploding glass. We'll put in fake doors too."

"Why are they painting?" Apollo asked through a mouthful of cookie.

"To disguise the mortars and the detonating cord—see those orange lines threaded through the structure? We need it to look like a power plant, not like a special effect waiting to happen."

"Very cool!" Apollo said. "I wish I could watch this tonight!"

I didn't share this wish, finding nothing appealing about pyrotechnics.

"That's a possibility," Max said, slowing as we approached the condemned building. "It's a closed set, of course, but since I'm the one in charge—" He stopped as a guy in camouflage gear shuffled over to him.

"Freund," the guy wheezed. His shuffling could be arthritis, I decided as he drew closer. He was easily Uncle Theo's age, wearing a baseball cap that said PYRO GUY on it. "I think we might got a leaky turkey bag on one of the trap mortars."

"How can you tell?" Max said.

The guy tapped his nose with his index finger. It was the only finger remaining on his right hand, although his thumb was mostly intact.

"Well, find it," Max said, pulling out his cell phone. Pyro Guy hobbled off.

"What is the problem?" Apollo asked.

Max frowned at his phone, pressing buttons. "Either of you have a cell phone?"

Apollo didn't. I handed him Joey's. He dialed. "Thanks. I can't get a signal on mine, but different carriers sometimes can—" His voice changed. "Jen? Max. Can you meet us at the FX site? . . . Really? Where's the FSO? . . . Okay, we're coming in."

He pressed END, then dialed a second number. "Jen, always trying to be four places at once. She's inside already with the fire safety officer." He started walking, phone to his ear. "C'mon. Let's see if she'll let you go off-lot. At this rate, we won't get to the promos today. Realistically, she should release you. Let you go to the funeral, then home. Come back tomorrow to finish."

"Is it safe in the building?" I asked. Beside me, Apollo was practically skipping.

"Very. We're hours away from ready. Haven't put the detonators in the prima cord . . ." Max led us around to the back of the building. "Although we may have set the turkey bags too early. Using nonunion operators has its drawbacks. Something Jen doesn't seem to understand."

He unclipped from his belt a carabiner that held a heavy set of keys and rifled through them, phone still to his ear. I was puzzling over the fact that the front of the building had no doors while here in the back was one made of steel, requiring a key.

"How will you do the explosion?" Apollo asked.

"There are two aspects to it. We do the flash and bang for the camera, but the actual building has to implode, collapse into itself." Max found the key he needed. He had dozens of them, which was why he always jingled a little as he moved. "We've already weakened the structure, cut through the beams and so forth, and cleaned out the place so nothing will feed the fire."

"What fire?" I asked.

"From the detonation." Max opened the door and let us through. "It's our job to put it out afterward, so we want to minimize it."

"Won't the fire department be here?" I asked.

"They're already here. The fire safety officer. He oversees things, but he'll stay on the sidelines, dressed in a nice white shirt. We're the whole operation, except for the demolition crew that comes tomorrow morning to shovel out debris."

We stood waiting for our eyes to adjust, even after Max flicked a wall switch that produced a dim overhead light.

"There is still electricity?" Apollo asked.

"The power company has to come disconnect us from the grid," Max said. "But that'll be last-minute, after the safety inspections." The building was empty and echoing and the walls were dirty, the way walls are that have been stripped bare, dirty in a way you don't notice when you live with them, don't notice until you're moving out. And there was the faint scent of gasoline.

Max led us down a stairwell, moving slowly now, keys nearly quiet on his tool belt. I tried to imagine Jen negotiating these stairs in her incredibly high heels. Of course, she'd have a fireman with her. You'd always feel safe with a fireman.

I didn't feel safe.

Max was like a fireman, I thought, looking down on his tousled hair, flecked with gray. Max, who couldn't even sleep in when his show was behind schedule. Sleep-deprived. Like me. That's what was making me so anxious. That and the fact that what little sleep I'd gotten had taken place on hard furniture. In an all-but-haunted house.

Now, that was a funny thing. How had Max known I was staying in Pasadena yesterday? How had he known to leave a message at Joey's house for me?

I hadn't mentioned it to him, had I?

We reached the bottom of the stairs and Max switched on another light.

Joey must've told him.

When would she have done that? She'd been missing for nearly two days.

My steps faltered. *Go back,* the voice inside said. *Turn back.*

Max was moving ahead, down a hallway. I turned to Apollo, next to me, stopping him with a hand on his arm. "Apollo," I whispered, "let's go back."

"Coming?" Max, up ahead, turned.

I looked at Max for the briefest moment, saw his features transform in the dim light, showing angles and caverns that hadn't been there before. Hollows around his eyes. They looked almost bruised. I was right. He wasn't getting enough sleep.

"Yes, I just—" I grabbed my foot as though there were a rock in my shoe, holding on to Apollo for support, feeling a biceps so skinny I could wrap my hand around it. I pulled him closer. "We gotta go, right now, we have to run—now—"

And in the split second it took for the whisper to leave my mouth and reach his ear and travel to his brain and activate his muscles, Max moved in on us.

I pushed Apollo at the same moment Apollo began to pull me up the stairwell. But by then Max's hand was on my shoulder like a bear paw, throwing me aside so that I was falling back and tripping over him just as he reached past me and got Apollo by the ankle.

By the time I was on my feet again, adrenaline screaming, blood pumping, Max was holding Apollo in front of him, easily, as if the teenage boy were a cardboard cutout. Max's big, hairy arm was tight against Apollo's throat, the inside of his elbow forming a wedge pressing into the boy's larynx or carotid artery, one of those important body parts, and Apollo was silent, except for his breathing.

"Look," Max said. "I can make him black out with just a little squeeze, and kill him outright if I squeeze harder. Like this."

Apollo's body jerked, then went limp. A second later Max must've relaxed his grip, because Apollo began coughing, clawing ineffectually at Max's forearm.

I stood perfectly still.

"You see how little it takes?" Max said.

I nodded.

"Good. Now walk. Straight ahead, to the end of the hall."

I did. I moved ahead, as though my body were attached to someone else's legs. I turned around once, but Max told me to just keep going, so I walked, listening to two pairs of running shoes behind me, shuffling and squeaking.

I tried to think, but there was a lot of shouting going on inside my head. I turned again, unable to help myself, but I couldn't see if Apollo was freaking out or not, because his face was upturned, forced into an unnatural position by Max's hold.

"Left turn ahead," Max said.

The corridor came to an end, but it was L-shaped, allowing me to turn. At the end of a short hallway was a door marked PROJECTION BOOTH—DUBBING ROOM A. I looked at Max, who'd stopped ten feet away from me. With the hand not holding Apollo, Max unhooked his key ring. He brought the keys to eye level and maneuvered them until he found the one he wanted. "Here," he said, tossing them to me. "Silver key, says 'Ilco.' Open the door."

I took the keys and squinted, trying to find the right one, then struggled with the door. The key was a tough fit. And my hands were shaking badly—my whole body was. It seemed that there would be a moment, and maybe this was it, where I had the advantage and should do something daring, but for the life of me, what was it? What would Achilles do? I thought. Or Hector? Odysseus? I prayed, then remembered that they were not gods, just heroes, and all dead now. I worked the key, sweat gathering on my face even though I'd been cold only minutes before. If I ran, Max would chase me, but first he'd get rid of Apollo, and while I couldn't see how you could kill someone just by pressing against his throat, this was not the time to further my education. When I got the door unlocked, I'd turn and throw the whole mass of keys at Max's eyes, hard, and then—

The lock clicked. This was it.

"Leave the key in the door," Max said behind me. "And walk in."

I hesitated.

"Now."

Shaking, I pushed open the heavy door and walked into the darkness. Something hit me from behind and I went down.

The door slammed.

Silence.

Fifty-four

The room was so warm.

"Wollie?"

Relief pulsed through me. "Apollo? You're okay?" I moved toward his voice.

"I am okay." He coughed repeatedly, then said, "Ouch. That is my face."

I removed my hand from his nose. "Sorry. I'll try to get to the door. See if there's a light switch."

But the room was completely black, and I'd lost my bearings once I'd gone down. I picked a direction and crawled, stretching my hands in front of me. We were on carpeting. I went slowly, expecting to encounter a wall, but there wasn't one.

"Wollie?"

"I think I got turned around," I said. "I'll try the other way."

"I'll go this way," Apollo said. Whatever that meant.

I heard him shuffle, probably on his knees, like me, and I heard him bump into something across the room and say something that might have been a curse in Greek. And then my hand encountered something soft. Something pliant.

Skin.

A body.

Fifty-five

shrieked. Not a bloodcurdling scream, just a short burst of hysteria that nevertheless must have aged Apollo several years.

"What is it?" he shrieked back.

"A—a—an arm." Attached to a torso, and the whole thing was alive, because it was warm. And there was hair everywhere, wavy hair, and I knew without seeing that it was red. "Joey. It's Joey," I said. But I couldn't tell if this was good news or bad because Joey was not moving or talking. Still, the warmth of her skin was something.

The lights came on. Apollo, his hand on a switch plate, stared down at us.

Joey lay on her back. She was dressed in gray sweatpants and a matching sweatshirt that were several sizes too large, as if she'd borrowed them from a football player. She looked vulnerable and deathly pale. Her face was bruised. Her breathing seemed normal. I reached for her wrist.

"She has a pulse," I said.

I looked around. The light switch Apollo had found was near steps that led to a platform dominated by a large console. It sat beneath windows that looked out onto another room, but the other room was dark. The console must have been state-of-the-art at one time, with endless buttons and levers, as complicated as a cockpit. Now it was reduced to a couple of wires leading nowhere; the guts of the operation had been removed, and probably the heart and soul. The room was bleak.

I left Joey and walked up onto the platform and picked up a telephone on the wall, then saw that the wires from the handset were dangling, disconnected from the base.

I looked around for a fire alarm, but there wasn't one.

Apollo was on his feet now too, checking the door, which was, of course, locked. I imagined editors bolting it after a day's work, keeping cleaning crews away from costly equipment and irreplaceable film. It was solid, made of steel. Not the sort of door that people are always kicking through in the movies. I knocked on the glass window that looked into the second room, but it was thick, like a car windshield. I thought about the workmen above us, putting fake glass where the real stuff had been removed. Maybe no one cared about the basement, since everything here would be covered by rubble. The room's walls were carpeted, for insulation purposes. Soundproofing. It worked. The quiet was unearthly.

I started screaming.

Apollo joined in, yelling "Help!" and "Hey, we're in here!," but we knew it was pointless, and after a minute we gave up. Max was no idiot. If there'd been a chance anyone could hear us, he'd have thrown us in here dead.

For that matter, why hadn't he?

Apollo was now in the corner, trying to peel back the carpet. I went back to Joey and stroked her hair, which produced an audible inhalation and a slight movement of the head. This thrilled me. I noticed something near her neck, obscured by her long hair. A syringe.

"Look, Apollo." I held it up.

"Is it drugs?" he asked. "Did she take an overdose?"

"No. She's phobic about needles. It's not something she'd do to herself." I looked around for signs of a struggle. There was a water bottle with a quarter inch of liquid, and a few wet spots on the floor, but no blood. A wastebasket was overturned but empty. Apollo picked up something from the corner of the room, a small glass bottle. "Morphine sulfate," he said, reading the label. "For D. Zetrakis."

"There's another one. Near the steps," I said, and then we found six more. "It looks like Max was using David's medication to drug her."

"This is good," Apollo said. "Perhaps he thought, If she is conscious, she will find a way out. That means there is a way out."

"Or maybe he was trying to kill her. This must be a lot of morphine."

We looked at each other, real eye contact. His eyes were brown and velvety, his skin olive, his features finely drawn. The whites of his eyes were pure, his face unlined, his hair cut short but trying to curl anyway, and damp with sweat. He might be the last person I'd talk to in this life. I might be the same for him.

"What time do they blow up the building?" Apollo asked.

"Nine P.M."

He looked at his watch. "Then we have more than six hours to rescue ourselves."

* * *

While Apollo searched the room again, now standing on the overturned wastebasket, mumbling, "Ceiling ducts," I checked out Joey for anything that might turn into a useful tool. There was no gun under her armpit. She wore a silver-and-gold Ebel watch, a pair of diamond stud earrings, an ankle bracelet, and a wedding ring. I paused at the ring, holding on to her hand, which gave a little jerk. I squeezed it. Her husband would soon be lowered into the ground at Mount Sinai, not far away. I felt the edges of panic close in on me, wondering where the three of us might be buried. Here?

"Elliot," I whispered, "if you loved her at all, help us out of this." I wasn't sure Jews believed in the afterlife, and Elliot had been a secular Jew in any case, but it was my belief in spirits, not his, that counted. Did I believe in spirits?

I searched myself, but I had even less in the way of useful items. No pockets. Hoop earrings and a chunky carnelian necklace, compliments of Laurie, the costumer, and several dozen bobby pins holding my beehive hairdo in place. Ugly loafers with rubber heels. I took one off and banged it on the window leading to the other room, which only made me feel stupid. I was working up a sweat doing practically nothing. "Why's it so hot in here?" I asked Apollo.

"Insulation."

I found a light switch for the adjoining room and peered through the window. I imagined actors standing there, recording dialogue. Every-thing looked worn out: carpeted walls and floors, some empty theater seats, a utilitarian table, and a broken music stand.

"No subfloor space," Apollo said, "but the good news is, we have elec-tricity."

"That is good news," I said. "Except that we're locked in a room that's going to explode, with no phones, fire alarms, or windows to the outside. It's like one of those brain teasers, with the answers at the bottom of the page, upside down."

"It is like a test in my electrical engineering class."

"It's like the underworld."

Apollo reached into the pocket of his utility pants and pulled out a black gadget the size of a woman's wallet.

"What's that?" I asked.

"A PSP," he said. "PlayStation Portable."

My heart raced. "Can you send messages on it?"

"No."

"Why not?" I yelled. "What the hell do they teach you in engineer-ing school?"

Apollo's face fell and his shoulders sagged.

"I didn't mean it," I said. "You're great, Apollo. There's no one I'd rather be stuck with in a hot, soundproof room. Honestly. You're it. You and Joey." I turned to Joey. "WAKE UP, JOEY!"

I was losing it.

"What if there is no way out?" Apollo said, sounding punctured now. Deflated.

"Look," I said, reeling in my panic. "Someone will notice we're gone. They will. My boyfriend's in the FBI. He'll—"

"The one you were fighting with yesterday?"

"Oh, you heard that? Okay, that—that's just the nature of relation-ships. Peaks and valleys. That doesn't mean he won't come looking—or Fredreeq will come—or your—" I stopped myself.

"My mother," he said, his eyes wide. "If I die, my mother—"

"Nobody's dying. We're just gonna put on our thinking caps," I said. "Can we drill a hole in the wall somehow? Mental telepathy of some sort? Can I hurl myself through the window and into the next room? Because maybe that door's not locked, or maybe there's a phone in there, or—smoke signals. Heating vents. Where's Simon with all his doohickeys? Morse code! Ham radios! Why wasn't I a Girl Scout? *Joey, wake up, you were in 4-H!*"

"Ham radio!" Apollo screamed.

"What? What about it?"

"My grandfather loved ham radios. He used to say—" He jumped to his feet and bounded over to the editing bay, then fell to his knees to examine the wires coming out of the wall.

"What? What did your grandfather say?"

"It is easier to make a ham radio than to make a good moussaka."

"Is that true?" My heart was beating rapidly.

"My grandmother did not let him in the kitchen. I believe he spoke figuratively. But . . . receiver, transmitter, antenna, power supply—" He looked around the room. "How hard can it be?"

It was at this point that Joey started to wake up.

Fifty-six

t was a moan so soft she had to moan again before it registered.

I went to her and put my hands on her face. "Joey?"

Her eyes opened. They didn't focus. They closed again.

"Joey, it's Wollie and Apollo. Not the god Apollo, the Caltech student. Wake up, okay? We need you." I wasn't sure what use she'd be, but I needed her anyhow. For emotional support. Selfish of me, because maybe she'd prefer to sleep through impending doom. But that's me. Selfish.

Apollo was the type who thinks out loud, and he kept up a steady mumble, using words like *megahertz* and *propagation*. I too kept talking, telling Joey that once we got out of Dubbing Room A her troubles were over—not entirely accurate, maybe, but relative to certain death, what's a lawsuit or two, or bankruptcy? I told her that Max had killed David, which I assumed she knew, and that too many other people knew it now for her to worry about ratting him out, and that Charles Zetrakis would be telling the police all about his own . . . history. I said I'd talked to her brother, that her whole family was about to descend upon her, hoping that would shock her into full consciousness.

She made little snuffling noises and even licked her lips, but that was it.

Apollo's mumbling was now reduced to grumbling—*inductors* and *ca-*

pacitors—and when I asked how it was going and he told me not to ask, I grew less sanguine. "Joey," I said, "snap out of it. We have to leave the building or get someone to come rescue us. Help me out here. Joey Rafferty. Mary Josephine Rafferty Horowitz."

She opened her eyes then, focused, and said, "What's going on with your hair?"

.   .   .

There was something wrong with her voice, which was little more than a croak. I told her to save it, and she said, "For what?" and drifted off again. She kept doing that. Maybe it was the heat. It bugged even me, I who spent October to April shivering. Apollo was dripping with sweat, and Joey was clammy, but that might've been the morphine.

It was nearly five P.M.

Joey cleared her throat. "FYI, Max killed David."

"Yes. Good. Keep talking."

"David gave Max money to hire a professional to kill him," she said in her laryngitis rasp, "but Max had gambling debts to pay off, so he just hired himself and kept the money. He was scared of the loan sharks. They said they'd break his other knee."

"Wouldn't David have lent him the money to pay them off?"

"He had, a bunch of times. Then he cut him off. Told Max to go to Gamblers Anonymous. David liked to tell people how to run their lives."

"But David changed his mind about being killed."

"Yeah. He told Max to cancel the hit and bring back the money, but Max didn't have it anymore. The loan sharks did. So David told him that was his inheritance, to forget the stamp collection. Which is worth a lot, believe me. He was going to change his will and cut out Max. So Max shot him."

"Max told you this?"

"I figured out most of it. I hitchhiked to the set yesterday. Laurie was here working. Max caught me talking to her, asking her if he'd left the production meeting last week, even for a few minutes. She couldn't remember, but Max knew what I was getting at. He knew then that I knew, and I knew he knew I knew."

She started crying. "I totally messed up. I thought I'd talked him into coming with me to the cops. He let me think he would. Then he got my gun. Oh, God, how dumb of me. I'm not usually that dumb." She wiped her eyes and stopped crying.

"Why didn't he shoot you?"

"Couldn't. Said shooting David put him off guns and blood. He had all David's morphine and said he'd give me enough to knock me into the afterlife."

"How'd you get beat up?"

She tried to sit up. "I didn't like the morphine plan. Needles, you know." She pushed up her sweatshirt sleeves and saw half a dozen little dots along her veins. She shuddered.

I shuddered too. So Max had an issue with guns, but no problem putting his fist in Joey's face and needles in her arm. "So why aren't you dead?"

Joey lay back down. "I would be, but I've got a problem with narcotics. A really high tolerance." She yawned. "Although I am awfully sleepy."

"This is a problem too," Apollo said. "The radio."

Joey sat up. We looked across the room.

It was less like a radio than something you'd see in a sixth-grade science fair. There was a piece of cardboard from somewhere, loose pieces of the wire that had been sticking out of the wall, the nonworking rotary phone, and Apollo's PlayStation.

"The problem is this," Apollo said. "With no data interface—"

"Never mind explaining, I won't get it," I said, but he kept on, very upset.

"—and also, the signal is too weak, and the walls are too thick, so yes, perhaps we create interference, perhaps the gate guard sees it, but what will he do? And also, I have antenna problems and a better receiver would be nice also."

"Like a radio?" Joey said. "Would that help?"

"You have a *radio*?" Apollo said.

Joey reached under her sweatshirt to the All-Caliber Camisole and pulled out something not much bigger than a cigarette lighter. "My husband's MP3. I wanted to hear the songs he listened to. It has AM/FM too, so he could hear the weather report from the beach." She disentangled the device from its earphone wires. "Pointless to carry around. Ran out of battery power yesterday."

"That is okay." Apollo took it like it was the Holy Grail. "You are wonderful. I love the United States."

"So that's it?" I said. "Problem solved?"

"There is still the antenna. I once made one from a can of Pringles potato chips, and another from a wok, for fun, but here I have no wire. Those wires which are in the wall I cannot pull out. There is nothing else."

But there was. I'd felt them all day long, digging into my skull and my rib cage. I pulled thirty-two bobby pins from my basketball beehive hairdo and the underwire from my bra, and forty-six minutes later, Apollo had us listening to static and hum.

It was music to our ears.

Fifty-seven

There were just a few glitches.

The human voices were garbled and the reception so poor I could barely identify it as English. They came through the rotary phone that Apollo had hooked up to the rest of the apparatus, the MP3 with AM/FM, his PSP, and some odds and ends scrounged from the editing bay. I listened, then handed the phone to Joey, who listened, shook her head, and handed it back to Apollo.

He tried to interject himself into the conversation, finally resorting to a loud "We are exploding in a soap opera!"

This did not have the desired effect. Nor did my subsequent attempts to clarify our situation or even generic screams of "Emergency!" I was met with patchy exclamations and static, indicating that they heard me about as well as I heard them. One sentence came across clearly: "No lids, no kids, no space cadets." I could guess its meaning.

"Another problem," Apollo said, covering the mouthpiece, "is, there is protocol we do not know. Also, we have no license. No call sign. This can upset them."

"What's a call sign?" I asked.

"Like a passport number but short, with letters."

"W8DX?" I asked. "Like that?"

"What's W8DX?" Joey asked.

But Apollo was already repeating it into the phone. "W8DX! W8DX! Over." He paused, frowned, and said, "Yes, that is me. W8DX. Truly."

I took the phone from him. Someone was saying, "—and I *know* W8DX. I'm *friends* with W8DX. And, mister, let me tell you, you are no W8DX."

"You know W8DX?" I said into the phone. What was that man's name? Elmer! "Elmer! You know Elmer Whistler? Can you get him on the line—airwaves—whatever?"

"—Elmer," the voice squawked back. "And—FCC and ARRL while— at it."

"Yes! Great!" I said. "But get Elmer first, would you? Whistler. Electra Drive."

The three of us stared at one another. We were all sweating. I kept the phone to my ear, but sound degenerated into static and jargon. "Do we have a Plan B?" I asked.

Apollo said, "For my school project I made a global positioning system. There is an apparatus over here I do not recognize, but . . ."

We followed him to the editing bay. "That's an old sound reader," Joey said.

"It is possible," Apollo said, "that I can turn it into a GPS, then send out SOS by Morse code, then—let me think."

He thought for a long time, thought and mumbled and took things apart and tinkered with them. It seemed like a long time, at least, but it might have been only a half hour. Then the radio's squawking got my attention, repeating something I understood. W8DX.

"Guys," I said. "That's us."

We raced over to it, with Apollo yelling, "This is W8DX. Over," then holding the receiver out so we could all hear.

"W8DX? Whiskey Eight Delta X-ray?! No, by gum, it is not. *This* is W8DX. QRZed? QRZed?! Over!" It was Elmer.

"Elmer!" I called. "This is a life-threatening emergency—"

"QRZed? Over."

"Elmer, please, please." I was dripping sweat everywhere. "Please, just call nine-one-one for us, would you? We're trapped in a building and we haven't got much time."

"QTH? Over."

"A sound studio. Burbank. West Olive Avenue. On a movie set. Well, TV."

"Is this . . . *Candid Camera*? Some kinda reality show?"

"Elmer, listen, okay? If you go next door to your neighbor's, ask Sheffo and Navarre and they'll know what I'm talking about. Tell them—"

"Those degenerates put you up to this?"

"Myrtle!" I shrieked. "Tell your wife—Myrt—that—that—" What the heck was her name, the person Myrtle had mistaken me for? "Betty Buckley!"

"You're Betty Buckley? *Betty Buckley?*"

"No, but—"

"Yes!" Joey and Apollo yelled in unison.

"*CATS?*" Elmer asked.

"Broadway," Joey croaked out. "Original cast!"

"She is!" Apollo said to the radio. "She is—"

"—Betty Buckley—" Joey said.

"—and now she is in television and we are about to die," Apollo said. "Over."

"Elmer, listen carefully," I said. "Tell Sheffo to call nine-one-one and stop the Moon Lake nuclear explosion. Got that? The Moon Lake nuclear plant. Elmer? Elmer?"

"Keep talking," Apollo said. "He may hear us, even if we do not hear him."

"Elmer?" I said. "I know about the rat poison. Myrtle told me. And what happened to Muffler. You're thinking, How can I go into the enemy camp? But Elmer, W8DX, buddy, I don't know if you ever read *The Iliad*, but toward the end, and I only know this because I read ahead—" I stopped for breath, just as Joey put her hand on my arm. There was no more static coming from the rotary phone.

Our radio was dead.

Fifty-eight

looked at my watch. Forty-two minutes had elapsed since the radio had died. Fifty-six minutes left. How was that possible? "Apollo," I said. "Not to bug you, but how's that GPS thing going?"

"I cannot tell. I am sending, but who can say? Perhaps it is too ambitious. Perhaps I now try a simple spark-gap transmitter—"

"Yes," Joey and I said, in unison.

"Since there are antennae on the building, which are connected by wire or coaxial cable to our wall outlets . . ." Apollo went back to work, mumbling about pentodes, fly-back transformers, and high-tension leads, and the danger of undischarged capacitors. I paced the room. Joey, usually the live wire at any gathering, closed her eyes and leaned against a wall.

"At best," Apollo said, making a sizzle in the editing bay, "we may cause the radios and televisions in the neighborhood to grow a little crazy."

"And how will that help us?" I asked.

"They will trace the problem to this location and know something is alive in this building."

Especially, I thought, if there was a really important football or basketball game on. That would energize the populace to find the source of the problem. Would they find us in the next forty-one minutes, though? "What can I do?" I said.

"Hold this in place," he said, handing me some sort of monitor doohickey while he worked on getting some long tubular thing out of its insides. I noticed DANGER: HIGH VOLTAGE signs and consoled myself with the thought that warnings like that were for ignorant people like me. Not for insiders like Apollo, who were smart enough to—

The lights went out.

BOOM.

Fifty-nine

awoke to sound. Like someone mowing the lawn in my head. And darkness. And smell. Heat. Heavy air. Burning. I could taste it.

I couldn't tell if my eyes were open or closed. As a matter of fact, I wasn't sure if I was alive or dead. But death dulled the senses—didn't it?—and I had all of them except sight. Then I noticed that the air was gray, not black, and that there were shapes, shifting, and particles floating.

My vision cleared. A lump to my left turned into Apollo. Joey was farther off, against a wall. I crawled toward Apollo. I knew their names, and I knew I was in a dubbing room, but what else? What had happened? The last thing I remembered was . . . lunch. From what day, though? Pita chips. In my head a song played. The one from *Cats*. The famous one. *Midnight, not a sound from the pavement, has the moon lost her memory* . . .

I didn't need to find Apollo's pulse, because I could hear his breathing and feel his chest moving under my hand. He erupted into a cough. "Wake up. You're okay," I said, not knowing if it was true, then left him to drag myself through the grayness to Joey.

The fact that I could see at all meant there was a light source somewhere. I realized this just as something else registered.

I could hear voices.

At first it was undistinguished yelling, distant. Or maybe not so distant, but competing with the ringing in my head. I tried to yell back, but my voice came out hoarse and weak. I found Joey's neck and felt for a pulse, but as with Apollo, I didn't need it; her thin body heaved with breath. I began to cry.

I left her and crawled toward the light and sound. I crawled because my legs weren't working well; they had a wobbliness. I tried standing, but crawling was faster.

The door was wide open. I remembered that this room wasn't on the main hallway but at the end of an L-shaped wing. I kept crawling and calling.

The gray was everywhere, cloudy, like looking out the window of an airplane in the midst of a storm. It floated through the air like snow-flakes. Ash. It seemed I was heading toward heat and the smell of burning. Nevertheless, I kept moving. My only experience of disasters was earthquakes, and earthquakes had aftershocks. Things collapsed. Joey and Apollo had to be rescued, and I couldn't do it alone.

"Hey!" I called out. "Hey!"

I was through the doorway now, onto linoleum. "Hey! We're here," I called again, wondering why no answering cry came. Was I yelling only in my head?

I was halfway down the short hallway when I heard it.

It was an innocuous sound, and it terrified me.

Go back. The voice in my head was clearer than anything outside me, so I listened to it. My body scrambled backward, back into the room, over the threshold, back onto the carpet. I waited to the right of the doorway.

The sound came close. A jangling, like keys on a carabiner.

When the foot came through the doorway, I reached for it.

I missed.

But I got the other one, just at the ankle. And Max went down.

Sixty

He dropped with a grunt onto the floor, like big game felled by a hunter.

I had no further plans. I'd reacted on instinct, not strategy. I am not a person you'd back in a fight.

Max had fallen face forward. He turned and reached for me. I scrambled away, out of the room, still on hands and knees.

He caught my foot. I kicked with all the strength I had and succeeded in freeing it, leaving Max holding on to my shoe. I crawled down the hallway and again tried to stand, screaming all the time, but then he was behind me and wrapping his big arms around me in a parody of an embrace and I thought of that southern expression "Let me hug your neck" and I knew that if he got my neck, it was curtains for me.

I whipped myself back and forth in his arms, fast, like a fish freaking out, so that he couldn't get a grip and also kicked at him with the foot that still had a shoe on it, only I couldn't connect with any of his body parts. Finally I just grabbed the shoe right off my foot and began beating on him with the ugly rubber heel, but he knocked it easily out of my hands, and then I had nothing.

He hit me on the side of my head, which felt like running into a wall ear-first.

And that was it. Even great warriors meet their match one day, and I was no warrior at all. I felt myself sliding once more to the floor, amazed that I'd lasted so long.

But I held on to him on the way down and his knee, in my hands, gave way. His bad knee. And suddenly he was on top of me, which was painful and a little strange, but even stranger was being hit with white foam. I think it was aimed at Max, because he yelled that he'd thrown down the gun, that he wasn't armed. The foam stopped.

I looked up, pushing against Max's shoulder, and saw a guy in a fireman costume. He held a hose, quiet now, but still aimed at Max. The source of the white foam. Behind him, the thick air of the hallway filled up with others, yelling that they'd found them. Us.

The guy in the fireman costume came closer as others arrived to lift Max off me. He wore a nice yellow coat and a big red helmet and clown gloves, really the best costume ever invented, fireproof armor, and he put one arm around me and another under me and lifted me as easily as if I weighed nothing at all. *How gracious,* I thought. *How delightful you are.*

"Don't worry, Betty," he said. "We got you. We're gonna get you all outta here."

Sixty-one

The night air was cold on my face, even though patches of fire
sprouted up in the ruins of Building 12. I was carried by my
fireman, still calling me Betty, whoever Betty was, toward a crowd of
people, their faces illuminated by enormous lights, the kind used for
night baseball games. I felt shy and kept my focus on my fireman. I
wasn't burned, which seemed like a miracle—to move through fire and
come out unburned. But not untouched: I felt raw and naked, even covered in smoke and dirt and a couple of bruises and a little blood. And
with the white foam, like marshmallow cream, dotting me here and
there.

"Blew the door right off the hinges," I heard someone say, "but the
room's still there. Like one of those fireproof wall safes."

Like one of those old editing rooms, I thought. History.

A man approached as the fireman set me on my feet. The man was
filthy, the whites of his eyes standing out in a face flecked with gray ash,
and the irises were ice blue and he looked scared, the one expression I'd
never seen on Simon before. He held a flashlight and his gun was visible, in a holster, because for once he wasn't wearing a suit. "I'm fine," I
said, although he hadn't asked. And I was. A phoenix rising out of the
ashes.

He seemed unwilling to touch me, as if he might hurt me. I took his hands and put them around my waist, pulling him close. After a minute he freed them, to touch my face and brush aside my bangs so he could kiss my forehead, repeatedly.

"Watch the hair," I said.

Sixty-two

The thing I've noticed about Greek mythology, even in the Cliffs
Notes, is how easy it is to piss off the gods in the midst of trying
to do the right thing or avoiding some dreadful prophecy—which never
works, by the way. I thought about it all weekend, lying around Solomonhaus, recovering. David had tried to direct and produce from beyond
the grave, mostly—although not entirely—to help out people he thought
he'd failed in life. Joey had tried to facilitate that. I'd tried to keep Joey
from danger. I'd also tried to show Apollo a good time on a television set.
None of us had been totally successful, and all of us had suffered conse-
quences that seemed excessive.

On the other hand, gods, like people, rarely reach consensus, which
meant that one or two of them had been on our side. Not only had Elmer
broken through the walls that separated him from Sheffo, but a sound
man at *SoapDirt* had been picking up our SOS on his headset at the
same time a guard at the gate was seeing it on his TV monitor. This led
to calls to the FBI, the FCC, and the Department of Homeland Security. There were also calls among ham radios in the San Fernando Valley.
Twelve people notified the fire department.

Meanwhile, Fredreeq had grown agitated when I didn't answer my
phone, since I'd promised to keep her updated on the *SoapDirt* shoot.

When she saw Tricia and Angel Ramirez attending Elliot's funeral on Channel 9, she called Simon. "There is no way Wollie would neglect to tell me about that funeral unless she's facing death herself," she said, "because she knows I would kill her. You go rescue her."

Finally, Apollo's mother was in a panic because Apollo never missed dinner, so Uncle Theo called my cell phone. This was answered by Rupert, who'd wandered into my trailer to borrow the macadamia nuts from my guest star gift basket, having come to the set to ride with Jen to Elliot's funeral. When he was told by Max that I'd left hours earlier, he grew suspicious, especially when he saw my car was still on the lot. He missed Elliot's funeral, trying to figure out where I was, and was still there when Sheffo and Navarre arrived. Which was just in time to watch Apollo blow up the whole operation forty-one minutes earlier than scheduled, helped by the power company throwing a switch on rather than off at the moment our spark-gap transmitter got working. Or maybe the spark-gap transmitter hit the same frequency as the remote control for the explosives. Or maybe it was the leaky turkey bag and not us at all. They were still sorting this out, three days later.

What Max had hoped to achieve after the explosion was also getting sorted out. Killing us and hiding us in the rubble, presumably, but Max wasn't talking. A normal person might've cut his losses and headed for the border when he saw his plan unraveling, but as Rupert pointed out, Max was a gambler, and not a very good one. His luck was always just about to turn and he never knew when to fold.

Fredreeq and I rehashed all this at Solomonhaus as I dressed for "Elliot's Funeral, the Sequel," as she called it. She zipped up my little black dress and told me to brace myself for photos. The media was now following Joey's Rags-to-Riches-to-Rags story, since a homicidal stage manager, after the first twenty-four hours, was considered to have limited entertainment value. The media would tire of even Joey's story soon, which was moving to probate court and law offices and promised to be long and tedious, but at the moment Joey was hot.

"I'll be giving a small press conference," Fredreeq said, "but they'll want shots of everyone." She'd become Joey's official spokesperson and had agreed to talk to Monica Pulliam, the reporter, as A Source Close to the Former Star. "I like this dress on you," she added. "Too much cleavage for a state funeral, but perfect for this town."

A man's head came through the guest-room window, which remained stuck in the open position. Ziggy. "Showtime, ladies," he said. "Joey and I want to make two meetings later today." He'd taken it upon himself to get Joey's court card filled, albeit late; she, unexpectedly, was finding AA meetings tolerable with Ziggy beside her, providing a running commentary.

I looked past Ziggy to see if the Bentley might be hiding among the news vans cluttering Joey's street, but it seemed Simon's current operation did not allow for funeral attendance. I had no more knowledge now about that operation than I had a week earlier, and no prospects of satisfying my curiosity for six months. That's how long it would go on, he'd estimated. And even when it was over, he'd never tell me the details. I was still debating whether or not I could live with that.

We walked to the front lawn, filled to capacity with white folding chairs. Joey climbed onto a podium and took the microphone. She wore a severe Armani dress with matching coat, no makeup, and her hair was loose. Her bruises were fading, the colors changing, and her voice was back to its normal gravelly quality.

"Thanks for coming," she said. "Some of you went to Elliot's earlier funeral. Some of you went to his earlier weddings. I only got here for Elliot's last act, and I've loved hearing from so many of you about his life before me." She coughed, then went on. "As you may have heard, Elliot died from an interaction between Hytrin, a vasodilator he took for his blood pressure, and some borrowed Viagra. It was otherwise a normal day for him, one that included stress, sex, surfing, and a bottle of Cristal. Some pleasures, his doctor tells me, should not be combined, or done within three hours of one another, but my husband"—here she paused—"was a man of great appetites. And great heart. He thought he would live forever. I'd like to believe he does."

Joey walked away from the podium, escorted by Van Beek, who then spoke a few words, followed by one of Joey's sisters, then one of her brothers, then a lot of other people, until a woman in a blue suit stood and unfolded a paper. "My name's Debbie," she said into the microphone. "I first met Elliot on a 747 to Paris, twenty-three years ago. I want to share a letter that I got yesterday, having been out of town most of last week. 'Dear Debbie,' it starts." She stopped to put on reading glasses. "Okay, then he goes on to break up with me. I'll just skip to the end."

She turned the letter over. "He says, 'I've never been able to hang on to good fortune very long, as you know, but I'm going to give it my best shot with Joey. Even if it's a long shot . . . because I said I would. And because I love her.' "

The crowd was silent. At least, it seemed that way to me, although my ears were still ringing, so I couldn't be sure. Debbie folded the paper back up, removed her glasses, wiped her eyes, and said, "Thanks for letting me come today, Joey. You're a good sport."

As Debbie walked away, speakers set up on the lawn blared out "Surfin' USA" and people got up and moved toward the food. Fredreeq went to oversee things in the kitchen and I stayed seated, thinking about Elliot and Joey and how it would've turned out for them. Which got me wondering about Charles and Agnes and how it would turn out for them. Which got me to wondering about me. And Simon.

I stood, finally, found a plate, and made my way around tuxedoed waiters, taking one of everything offered until my plate was full. Then I headed to the roof. I was alone. Maybe no one wanted to brave the Santa Ana winds just for a stunning view of Pasadena, antennae, satellite dishes, and all.

Joey and I had liberated her chaise from my storage cubicle the day before, and here it lounged, gathering leaves and sun damage, like my copy of *The Iliad* alongside it. I picked up the book. Two hundred and thirty-six pages to go.

"I'd propose to you—" a voice whispered in my ear.

"Speak up," I said.

"I said, I'd propose to you if I didn't think it's in poor taste, doing it at a memorial service."

"And if you thought I'd say yes," I said, turning to face him.

Simon smiled. "You wouldn't?"

"No," I said. "I'm interested in a man in the textile industry."

"Textiles? Sounds to me like a tailor or a dry cleaner trying to sound important."

"Maybe," I said, closing *The Iliad*. "But imagine free dry cleaning for life."

Simon let his eyes drift down my black dress. He traced the neckline with his finger. Fredreeq was right: it was a little low cut for a funeral. "You don't look," he said, "like a woman with dry-cleaning problems."

I took his hand from my breast and led him to the chaise longue. It had a layer of dust on it, like everything else on the roof, and it didn't really go with Solomonhaus, which was why it had been banished in the first place. But it had character. "Looks can be deceiving," I said, lying back on it and pulling him toward me. "You'd be surprised how dirty I can get."

"Would I really?" he said, smiling.

"Yes," I said.

And then I surprised him.

Acknowledgments

I'm fortunate in having friends whose knowledge and expertise are exceeded only by their generosity. Among them: the Oxnardians: Jonathan Beggs, Linda Burrows, John Shepphird, Sharon Sharth and Bob Shayne; the folks: Ruggero and Agatha Aldisert; Lisa Aldisert and Jenny Aldisert; JoBeth Gutgsell, Aaron Raz Link, Delinah Blake, Lisa Bjornstad, Sherry Halperin, Joy Johannessen, Ann Kozak, Joanie Kozak, Mary Coen, Dory Goodman, AVK, Chuck and Elizabeth Lascheid, Nanci Christopher, and Patty Flournoy. Thanks to Marcus Wynne for couture advice and other help, to James O. Born, Malibu Dan, Ed Lawrence, Jeret Do Iron, Detective Gordon Hagge of the North Hollywood Division of the LAPD, L.A., T.A., and J.A., Bill "Mr. Warrant" Kelsey, Leland Tang of the West Valley California Highway Patrol, and Captain M., my favorite firefighter. More thanks to Nancie Hays, Larry Iser, Dean Petrakis, Michael and Jennifer Miller, Dawnmarie Moe, Pete Kozak, Candace Poole, Dr. Robert Kayland, Terry Sanger, Barney's New York, Bob Bennett, Jim Weiss, Brenda Johnson of Gelson's Calabasas Pharmacy, Jud from Earth-2, John Schliesser, Tippy Schulte, Rachelle at RadioShack, Paul Stewart from Martin-Lawrence Galleries, Marlene R. Vitanza of Peregrine Galleries, Zach and Jose at Best Buy, Ryan at District Skate & Surfboard, Greg Korn and Greg "Jedi" Gabriel of Kinsella, Weitzman, Iser, Kump & Aldisert, Michael Zola, Nelly Valladares, Jenni Kuhlmann, Lorie Salamati, Joy Vella, Hedy Song, Lorie Callaway, and Scott Martelle. Thanks to my fabulous blog sisters, Nancy Martin, Susan McBride, Sarah Strohmeyer, Kathy Sweeney, Elaine Viets, and

Michele Martinez, and The Lipstick Chronicle readers who hacked away at my To Do list: Alphabeter, Josh, Ramona, Toni McGee Causey, Joyce, Karen Olson, wndrgrl, Cinema Dave, Kiaduran, laurenjharwood, Margaret, Jeanne Ketterer, Carstairs38, Andi, jaunita, abbya, Jeff, Louise Ure, Densie, biscuit, Sue, and Sue's Dad. Thanks to the jurors and alternates of Elizabeth Indig v. Tadeusz M. Bugaj, et al. Particular thanks to the long-suffering Steve Shelley, Joe Kozak, Harvey Laidman, and D.P. Lyle, who read and reread, explained and re-explained, as if they had nothing better to do. Thanks to Heather Graham, Alex Sokoloff, Gavin Polone, Jonathan Levin, Hawk Koch, Larz Anderson, Lisa Rinna, and Dennis Dione, proof that there are no people like show people; and to the underrated players of daytime: Dan Proett, Crystal Kraft, John Linscott, Rob Markham, Nancy Grahn, Jill Farren-Phelps, *General Hospital* in general, and *Texas, Guiding Light,* and *Santa Barbara* for giving me five years of gainful employment and more fun than I could handle. Eternal gratitude to the friends of Bill and Dr. Bob, who showed me how to redefine fun. My remarkable agent, Renee Zuckerbrot; my editor, Stacy Creamer; and Laura Swerdloff, Andrea O'Brien, Rachel Pace, Meredith McGinnis, and Bonnie Thompson all make work a pleasure. Finally, thanks to Jinn and Fez. And to Greg, Audrey, Louie, and Gia, the best part of my life. By far.